ROSANNE BITTNER

LAWMAN *in the* HIGH LONESOME

Men of the Outlaw Trail: The Revenge

Digital: ISBN: 978-1-948835-13-8

POD: ISBN: 978-1-948835-14-5

Cover Design and Interior Format by Lisa Messegee, www.thewritedesigner.com

FROM THE AUTHOR...

There is a place in the American West where you will find some of the most beautiful and spectacular landscape in the world. It's called the Outlaw Trail. I'm not sure "a place" is the proper term, because the Outlaw Trail runs through the Rocky Mountains nearly all the way from Canada to Mexico. Its name stems from this high, lonesome country being an excellent area for known outlaws to hide, men like Butch Cassidy and Mexican Joe, and even untamed women like the Basset sisters. Some of the more famous settlements along the trail are Hole-in-the-Wall and South Pass City in Wyoming, and Brown's Park on the border of Utah and Colorado. Many of those who went there were men, and even their families, who'd lost everything or had become outlaws during America's civil war. Eventually, whole towns sprang up, settlements that had everything most American towns have ... except for LAWMEN! Those who lived on the Outlaw Trail tended to set their own rules, and true lawmen dared not venture into outlaw country.

CHAPTER ONE

APRIL, 1877...

*M*att removed his hat and knelt beside his wife's grave, still struggling with the reality that the love of his life was gone from this earth.

"Too fast, Lora, honey," he said softly. "It all happened too fast." He set his hat aside on thick, green grass, thinking how much Lora Stover had loved spring and the first flowers that opened. She'd planted daffodil bulbs all around their little house just last fall, but she'd lived only long enough to see them bloom for the first time a couple of weeks before. He laid a handful of the white and yellow bell-shaped flowers at the base of her headstone, and through vision blurred by tears, read the wording carved there.

HERE LIES LORRAINE ANNE (SMITH) STOVER
JUNE 12, 1850 – APRIL 9, 1877
AND HER BELOVED UNBORN CHILD, MELODY
CONCEIVED NOVEMBER, 1876 – DIED APRIL 9, 1877

He shall wipe away all tears from their eyes.
There shall be no more death... nor sorrow.

Matt had argued with his father over showing a date of conception on the grave marker. The Reverend Allen Stover felt it was sinful to mention conception, but since little Melody never survived to have a birth date, Matt had decided an approximate date for the beginning of her life was appropriate. Last November was the closest he and Doc Benjamin could determine. Lora had already lost two babies before, but this time she'd made it through six whole months.

"I walk around the house singing to my baby," Lora told him once. *"If this is a girl, I want to name her Melody."*

And so he had, even though the lives of both mother and baby had been snuffed out two weeks ago. The reality of it haunted him now and would haunt him forever.

If only I'd been there. I'm so sorry, Lora. So sorry!

He couldn't remember the last time he'd slept, and he didn't care. He lived in a dark place now, dark and full of vengeance. He wouldn't know any peace until he'd found and killed those who'd robbed him of his wife and child. Unlike his father, he didn't care about the right or wrong of it. He only cared about making someone pay for the senseless killing and for the fact that his own heart had been ripped out of his chest and stomped into the ground.

"Vengeance is mine, sayeth the Lord," the Reverend Allen Stover had reminded him.

"Then I will be the tool God uses to <u>seek</u> that vengeance!" Matt had answered his father. "I don't care how long it takes. I'll find them and <u>kill</u> them!"

"May God be with you, Son. And may He forgive you."

Twenty years ago, his father had founded the town of River's Bend, Nebraska by starting a church in the middle of unsettled territory. He'd decided to settle here and build a church when their covered wagon broke down and he saw a tiny trading post near a lovely lake. The Reverend

Allen Stover believed God had stranded them there for a reason.

"This is where I will build my church," he'd declared.

Matt was six then. By the time he was ten, River's Bend had grown to a full-fledged town, school and all. A good water source from a short tributary of the Platte River ending in a decent-sized lake had led to big farms that grew up around it and around his father's little church, which now sat in the center of town.

Matt thought how he'd disagreed with his father over practically everything when Matt was growing up. And the disagreements hadn't stopped when he'd reached adulthood. Especially after he decided to run for Sheriff of River's Bend two years back.

Reverend Stover didn't believe in guns or violence, but out here where everything was still new and still lawless, Matt reasoned that men with guns were needed to set things right. What had happened to Lora and his baby girl was proof of that. What haunted him most was that, while his wife was being shot to death in a bank robbery, he'd been three miles out of town investigating a problem with cattle rustling. The bank robbers had known he was gone that day and had taken advantage of his absence.

He'd run for sheriff to keep River's Bend and its innocents safe, but he'd failed the two most important, most innocent and most beloved people in his life.

A tear fell on the still-fresh dirt over the grave. Matt quickly and angrily wiped at others that tried to follow. He had to stay strong and alert for what lay ahead. With his fingers he dug a little hole on top of the grave and stuck the flower stems into it so they would stand up straight, then filled the hole and pressed the dirt to keep them upright.

God, how Lora had loved flowers. He could only hope and believe that where she'd gone, she could walk through a sea of wildflowers, carrying their baby girl with her. He could see flowers stuck into her straw-colored hair, bringing out the color in her green eyes and rosy cheeks. His little girl's cheeks would be even rosier, her little lips puckered in a kiss for her daddy... the daddy she wouldn't meet until he was himself a member of that other world where there was no evil.

And evil was the only word to describe those who'd done this. He knew who they were, just as sure as he was breathing. The Liberty brothers had been trouble in River's Bend since they were all boys and went to school together...

When Matt was ten, Joe and Tex Liberty moved into town with their drunken father and philandering mother. Joe was Matt's age. Tex was two years older and a bully. He enjoyed beating up on younger boys, including Matt. Until Matt suddenly sprouted to six-feet-three-inches, got mad, and walloped Tex until his face bled in every possible place it could bleed. Tex had never forgiven him for that. While Matt's father tried his best to "save" the Liberty boys' mother and father and bring them into his church, the troublemaking boys had been a burr in Matt's butt. This included mercilessly picking on Lora Smith, the prettiest girl in town, and one who would never give boys like Tex and Joe the time of day. They knew Matt loved her. From what he could remember he'd loved Lora since he was twelve years old and she was only nine.

Preacher Stover was always after Matt to make peace with the Liberty boys, reasoning that their lives were miserable at home because of how their parents lived. But Matt felt that was no excuse for the boys' behavior. Joe Liberty was Tex's puppet and did his big brother's bidding. Together they became the bane of River's Bend, bullying, threatening, stealing in ways no one could prove, sometimes shooting off guns and firecrackers just to startle people, and being a nuisance in all ways possible, always staying just enough above the law to keep from getting arrested... until Matt Stover pinned on a badge.

That's when the arrests started for creating disturbances and disrupting the peace. And that's when the Liberty boys left town. It's also when local cattle rustling started. And when a young farm girl was abducted and raped. And, finally, when the local Farmer's Bank was robbed in broad daylight and the bank manager shot. Along with a pregnant Lora Stover and their unborn child.

"Tell Matt Stover he's lost the fight!" Tex Liberty had shouted to on-lookers. *"Tell him he can find us out west on the outlaw trail! Any lawman who goes there dies by a hundred guns! One of them will be mine!"*

The brothers rode out of town with three men they'd picked up to ride with them, all five shooting their guns and screaming war whoops. No one knew who the other men were, and that was Matt's only problem. When he followed the Liberty brothers to Outlaw Country, and he was determined to do so, three other men he didn't know would be watching and waiting for him.

"Matt."

A woman's voice interrupted his thoughts. Matt wiped at more tears and rose to turn and face his mother. She stood there blinking back her own tears. "I knew I'd find you here."

He felt sorry for the look in her eyes. Such deep sorrow for her son's broken heart. His mother was a kind, patient, loving, Christian woman, and he hated hurting her, but his mind was made up. "Don't try to talk me out of it, Mother."

The graying woman whose plump arms and shoulders were a soft comfort whenever she hugged him shook her head and gave him a sad smile. "I didn't come out here for that. I just… I went to your house to see you and noticed you'd already packed some things. I was afraid you'd leave without saying good-bye or letting me pray over you."

Matt heaved a heavy sigh. "I wouldn't do that to you, Mother. But you don't need to pray because right now there is nothing Christian about my thoughts. I've never been much like Pa. You know that. Davie is the Christian one," he reminded her, referring to his older brother, who'd already gone to Colorado with a wife and two sons to start his own church.

Arlysse Stover nodded. "I know that, but your heart is just as good as your brother's. God simply chose you to be one of His avenging angels rather than a preacher."

Her remark surprised Matt. "You mean you understand why I'm going, and you approve?"

Arlysse's lips quivered as she struggled not to break down. "I'm afraid so, much to your father's chagrin. But that doesn't mean it doesn't break my heart. I just want you to come back, Matt, alive, and a whole man again. You're only twenty-nine, strong and handsome and able, eyes as blue as an October sky and a smile that melts women's hearts. You'll find love again, Son. Most widowed men and women do. Time and prayer heal a lot of things, so promise me you will pray. Promise me you haven't lost your faith."

Matt looked away. "I'm not sure I can. Right now, I'm just kind of numb to such things. Hate and revenge are my only feelings."

Arlysse walked closer and reached up to touch his shoulder. "It's one thing to lose someone you love, Matt. A man can live through that. But if you turn away from God —" She shook her head. "That's a terrible, terrible loss, Son. Just know that He has other plans for you. Those Liberty boys need to be dealt with, not just for what they did to your Lora and your baby, but what they did to that farm girl, and for nearly bankrupting Paul Sidney when they stole his cattle. The whole town knows it was them that did it, and the whole town is behind you." She moved to rest her head against his chest. "That's where I get my hope that you'll come back. So many people are praying for you."

Matt put his arms around her. "That's good."

He didn't know what else to say. He didn't want her to know that right then he took no hope in prayer, or in his faith. God had failed him. If he needed to turn to someone for help, he'd be better off turning to Satan, the source of hatred and revenge, the force behind his gun.

"I'm leaving at dawn," he said, "and I'd rather no one saw me off. I just want to leave quietly."

His mother sniffed and hugged him tighter. "I'll tell your father, and he'll tell the congregation tonight."

"Promise me you'll keep flowers on Lora's grave all summer."

"Of course, I will. I'll plant live ones around it."

"Thank you. And write to Davie so he knows what's going on."

"Maybe you could stop and see him and your nephews, since you're heading west anyway."

"I can't. I'd lose too much time. The Liberty boys are already two weeks ahead of me, but I'll catch up to them."

Arlysse straightened and kept her arm around him. "Come to the house and have supper with us. Will you at least give us that much before you go?"

Matt squeezed her close. "As long as Pa doesn't give me one of his sermons about how wrong it is that I'm going."

"He won't. We had a long talk. I told him to remember that God has different plans for different people, and you were never meant to be docile and forgiving. You're a good person, Matt, but the way you go about it is different from your father. Sometimes it's hard for fathers to understand that."

"Sure."

Arlysse stopped walking and turned, touching his shirt again. She moved his leather vest aside. "I just realized you aren't wearing your badge."

"I took it off and put it in my pocket." He grasped his mother's arms. "Where I'm going, and the way I feel, I won't be acting much like a sheriff, Mother. I'll be just as much an outlaw as the men I'm after. And a man can't wear a badge in country like that. It's like inviting death."

Arlysse shook her head. "And what if they find out you *are* a lawman?"

Matt put an arm back around her and began walking again. "That's a chance I'll just have to take."

They headed down the hill toward the little town where Matt Stover was sheriff, where he'd lived joyfully with his wife, looked forward to the birth of their baby. That was all changed now… maybe for good. Maybe he'd go into Outlaw Country and never return. Maybe he'd become just like them.

CHAPTER TWO

*E*lly tucked a quilt around the china she'd packed into a crate of straw, hoping all the cushioning would protect the precious dishes on her journey to California. If she and those traveling with her had been rich, they could ship themselves, their horses, livestock and belongings by train. She thought how much easier that would be. But nothing in life had ever been easy for her or her family.

Her mother was gone, which was why the quilts and china she was taking meant so much to her. Her mother had made the quilts, and the china had belonged to Elly's maternal grandmother. Her brother Mark and his wife Betty were also packing quilts made by their mother, who'd died from heart failure at only forty years of age.

Elly was only seventeen then. Her grief-stricken father, fifty-five then, had never fully recovered. John Grace had gone from happy and hardy to a deep depression that prevailed, even after all these years. Elly helped care for him through it all, cleaning the house, doing his laundry, cooking for him, all on top of caring for her own home and husband, whom she'd married at eighteen.

Now, even her husband was gone. William had died an ugly death from cancer only three years after her mother died. Twenty-five. William had been twenty-five when he was buried. Thank God they'd had no children, so she wasn't left to raise a child with no father. That had been four years ago now, and she still felt empty and lonely.

Maybe California would bring better luck and bring all of them hope and some kind of happiness. Last fall, a Kansas prairie fire started by lightning had wiped out the family farm, some of the animals, all their crops and their barns and supplies and homes. These couple of quilts and some of the china, along with a family Bible, were all Elly was able to save.

The whole family had run the farm together, and now it was gone. Thank God Mark and Betty and their two sons had survived. None of them had been injured, but they were left destitute. There just wasn't enough money left to start over, but more than that, their spirits were broken after a long winter of living hand-to-mouth, all together in one small house a kind neighbor had let them use while they tried to sell the farm.

Spring had brought that sale and the sorely-needed money from it. Betty had a brother in California who'd been after the whole family to come there, where *the sun always shines, and the valleys are perfect for farming*. He'd promised no more long, Nebraska winters, and he'd promised that the soil in the California valleys was easy to plow. He'd just built a big new barn and promised they could live in it until they could build new homes for themselves.

And so, they were leaving. The farm sale had provided just enough money to buy more supplies and three covered wagons for the trip. Their journey would be helped along by Glen Baker, a neighboring farmer who'd also lost everything in last fall's fire. Glen was a widower with one grown son who'd gone off to college in Ohio. Glen was lonely, and that loneliness had turned his attention to Elly, which meant she had some decisions to make. Was she lonely enough to marry a man she liked but didn't truly love?

Elly's thoughts were interrupted when someone called out, "Hello, there!"

She turned to see Glen driving his wagon up the road toward their little rented house. Anxiety filled Elly at seeing him, knowing he'd likely bring up the subject of marriage yet again. She shaded her eyes to watch him, reminding herself Glen Baker was a nice-looking, kind and able man. But she was twenty-four now, and Glen was forty-two. A lot of men didn't live beyond fifty, and after watching her beloved William die such a terrible death, she wasn't ready to go through that agony with another husband. Besides, she wanted love again. *Real* love. She wanted that same spark she'd felt with William that wasn't there when she was close to Glen.

Still… a woman needed a man in too many ways to count, and a man needed a woman in a hundred other ways. She wasn't old yet, but neither was she getting any younger. And Glen wanted more children. He wanted young ones around him again, a full family again. That meant mating with a man she didn't want in that way, and it also could mean being left with a brood of children with no father if Glen died before they were grown.

Glen's wagon came closer, and Elly's father walked past her to greet him. "Pour us some coffee, Eleanor, will you?" he asked, always calling her by her full name.

"Sure, pa." Elly walked over to where her sister-in-law, Betty, was removing a fry pan from an open fire. The house they'd rented was now being used by their neighbor's son and his new wife, so they'd camped out the last five days while preparing to leave.

"I'll be so glad when we get to California and can build our own homes, Betty told Elly. "I'm already tired of living outside like this, and we have that whole trip ahead of us."

Elly still watched Glen, noticing there were two horses and three oxen tied to the back of his wagon, which was pulled by four big, strong draft horses he intended to use to pull a plow once they reached California. The plow was tied to the side of the wagon. Glen planned to alternate travel between the oxen and the draft horses so that neither became over-worked on their journey.

Elly found two tin cups and poured coffee into them. "I'm tired of it, too, but such is life," she told Betty. She straightened when her father and Glen approached the fire. "We already ate, Glen," she said, "but I have a couple of biscuits left if you're hungry."

Glen waved her off. "I'm fine. I ate on my own." He took the cup of coffee from her, and Elly read his brown eyes as his gaze lingered on her face, trailed down her body and back to her face. "Thank you, dear."

"You're welcome." Elly handed the other cup to her father. "You look tired, Pa, and we haven't even left yet."

"I'm okay." His reassuring smile only accented the deep lines of age on his face, and strands of his thinning white hair danced from under his black hat. "I'm more tired of getting ready for this journey than tired physically," he added. "I'm glad we're getting started. It's early spring and we should reach California by July or August. It should be real pretty there in summer."

Elly noted a little sparkle in his blue eyes that she'd not seen there in a long time. This trip would be good for him.

"Betty's brother claims it's real pretty there year-round," Glen added.

"He also says they have earthquakes," Betty spoke up. "The whole ground shakes and sometimes splits apart in places. That scares me."

"Oh, heck, I've heard too many good things to be worried about that," Glen answered. "From the letters you let us read, it sounds like the beautiful weather and good soil more than make up for the earth shaking a little once in a while." He smiled a handsome smile, and Elly took note that he still had nice teeth. She told herself she really should consider marrying the man.

"Are you sure we don't need a guide?" she asked her father aloud.

"No reason. Your brother and Glen and I know horses and wagons, and the trail there is pretty easy to follow. Maybe when we reach the mountains, we'll look for someone to get us through, especially the Sierras. We're used to wide-open land that's easy to travel. The mountains will be a whole different matter, but we'll worry about that when we get closer."

"All three of us should be able to do some hunting along the way," Glen added, "so we should have plenty to eat. And there are homes and towns and forts where we can stop and rest—not much real danger until maybe we get to the foothills and the higher mountains. But the danger will be more from the elements than from hostiles or outlaws. Most hostiles in that area have been rounded up onto reservations, and what trouble is left is more right here and north of us than to the west. And if we find the right guide, getting through the mountains won't be a problem, not in summer anyway."

Elly shivered with doubt. This farm was all she'd ever known. There was a safe feeling in living with what was familiar. And she wasn't fond of leaving behind her mother's and husband's graves, probably never to see them again. But there was no staying even if she wanted to. The farm was sold, and that was that. If this move would help bring her father out of his mourning and give him new energy, it would be worth it.

Her father and Glen finished their coffee just as her
brother came riding toward them, whistling and
whooping at about fifteen head of cattle he managed to
herd ahead of him. Glen hurried to a saddled horse tied to
his wagon, a black gelding with a white face. He mounted
up and rode out to meet Mark.

Yes, he's a fine and able man, Elly thought. The dark hair
that showed from under his wide-brimmed hat was
already showing some gray, but he sat a horse fine. He
wasn't a tall man, but he was solidly built and seemed to
be healthy.

"Are you going to marry him?" Betty asked, as though
reading her mind.

Elly turned to see her sister-in-law watching her and
smiling. "I don't know," she answered, feeling a flush
come to her face.

"Well, you're too pretty to waste your years as a
widow," Betty told her. "You have the greenest eyes I've
ever seen, and that dark hair has such a shine to it, and a
beautiful deep red glow in the sun. And any man would
take a second look at a woman shaped like you."

"Honestly, Betty, you're embarrassing me." Elly poured
left-over coffee onto the fire to put it out and stepped
closer to her sister-in-law. "Glen is kind of old to be
starting over," she said quietly. "I don't want to go through
the death of a husband again, and maybe be left on my
own with kids to raise." She stepped even closer and
lowered her voice even more. "Besides, I don't feel that
spark when I'm near him. I want to marry for love, not just
because it's convenient or necessary. Can you understand
what I mean?"

Betty smiled with a hint of sadness. "Of course, I can.
I'm a woman, too, and I'm crazy about your brother. Any
woman wants that special feeling, especially if she's going
to let a man bed her."

Elly's eyes widened. "Betty Grace! Such talk!"

Betty laughed. "Well, that's how I got two sons, and another one on the way!"

Elly watched her sister-in-law's cheeks glow pink under her freckles. "Betty! Does Mark know?"

"Not yet. I want to be well on our way before I tell him, so he can't use it as an excuse to wait. I want to get going and get this trip over with. Don't you feel the same way?"

"Yes, I do!" Elly quickly embraced her. "I'm happy for you. Do you feel all right?"

"I'm fine. We've been trying so long. Tommy is six already. So, I'm very happy about it, Elly. Mark will be, too."

Both women got busy cleaning up around the fire and re-packing things. Betty called her two sons, Mark Jr., ten; and Tommy, six, to come to the wagon and grab their little willow switches, taken from a tree that had miraculously survived the fire. They would use the switches to help goad the oxen pulling Elly and Mark's wagon, while the boys' father kept herding the cattle and horses behind them. Glen would drive his own wagon but keep a horse saddled at all times in case Mark needed help with the cattle.

The boys came running, their red hair blowing wildly in every direction. Getting them to sit still for haircuts was next to impossible. Their father's hair was as red as the setting sun, like Mark and Elly's mother's hair had been. The thought again brought back the feelings of loss Elly wondered if she would ever get over.

John Grace would lead the way, driving the six husky mules that pulled his and Elly's wagon. Elly would ride with Betty on her and Mark's wagon, keeping Betty company. But she would also be ready to help out any way she was needed, including helping Betty manage the four oxen that pulled the wagon. They would guide the animals from the wagon seat with a long switch, alternating from riding to walking beside the big, lumbering beasts. They'd learned that a person didn't drive them with reins, but with switches and coded orders that only oxen seemed to understand.

"You boys be careful now," Betty warned her sons. "Stay far enough away from these big brutes so you don't get stepped on."

Elly's nephews giggled and tickled the oxen behind the ears with their switches.

The sun was fully up and warming them as they prepared to leave. They all wore jackets and gloves for now, but it was obvious the day would grow warm and bright and be perfect for traveling. Thank God the spring rains had let up and the ground wasn't too muddy. Already, shoots of green prairie grass were growing through the blackened ground, new life after the horrible fire.

Now they were headed for the green valleys of California. Elly couldn't help wondering what fate held for them there, or if they would even make it all the way. She tied on a slat bonnet to protect her face from the sun and ran up to Betty's wagon.

"I'll ride beside you for a bit while the oxen are fresh," she yelled up to her sister-in-law. She used the wagon wheel to climb aboard.

"Git up there!" Betty shouted to the oxen, snapping a slender whip near their ears. "Hah! Hah!" Elly's nephews also shouted "Hah!" and snapped their whips against the oxen's rumps. The great, plodding beasts got underway, following Elly's father's wagon with its six mules. A milk cow and her calf were tied to the back of it, along with a saddle horse.

Elly looked back to see Glen ride up to his own wagon and re-tie his horse. He climbed aboard and gave Elly a nod and a wave before snapping the reins to his four big draft horses.

Elly turned back around. "I've decided I will wait until this trip is over before I make up my mind about Glen," she told Betty. "How he behaves on this trip will mean a lot, and by the time we reach California, I'll know much more about him."

"What is there to know?" Betty answered. "He's nice looking and he's an able, responsible man. You've already known him for three years as a dependable neighbor, and there isn't a mean bone in his body."

"But I told you—I don't love him the way a woman should love a husband."

"Well, my mother used to say that in an unsettled land like this, you can't always marry for love." Betty smiled. "Of course, I got lucky when I met your brother. I sure do love him."

Elly watched the western horizon, thinking how far away California was. "I want that same feeling, Betty. When the right man comes along, I'll know it."

"I hope you're right, and I hope you find him," Betty told her. "Maybe the right man is waiting for you in California."

Elly smiled. "Maybe."

CHAPTER THREE

*M*att lit a cigarette as he rode at a steady gait across the vast, endless grasslands of Nebraska. His roan gelding, Rusty, was a strong and dependable mustang he'd caught three years before and raised himself. He guessed the horse's age now at about ten. His pack horse, a Pinto named Sadie, came from a neighbor who raised both wild and home-bred horses. As a teenager, Matt had worked hard for the breeder—evenings after school and after helping with chores at home—in order to have his choice of one of the man's foals. Sadie was fourteen now, a very healthy, dependable animal.

It seemed strange to be traveling alone. All his life he'd known only family—his own, plus Lora, the church congregation, and the citizens of River's Bend. There were always people around him, and they liked him. He'd left those friends behind as he headed for very *un*friendly country.

He'd often hunted alone, but of course that was only for a few hours a day in the right season. Being alone now was different. It was a rather devastating aloneness because now he had no wife to go home to. Gone was their small house, the empty baby bed, clothes Lora would never wear again, baby clothes that would never be used. He wasn't sure he could ever go back to any of it, even if he found and killed the men who'd stolen so much from him.

River's Bend would never be the same, and to deliberately kill those he hunted would change all that was once Matt Stover, the stern but amiable sheriff. The son of a preacher. The doting husband. The good friend. The father he thought he'd be. Yes, he'd killed two brutes back in Omaha when he was a sheriff's deputy there. They'd beaten and killed a woman just for the money in her handbag. In their attempt to flee, they'd shot at him, so he'd shot back. He'd wounded two others in shootouts and had put a good many others in jail. He told himself it was all just part of the job that needed doing, and he was able to live with that.

Now, deliberately going after men to kill them, no matter what the situation, was a different matter. This trip would probably change him. Whether it would be for the better or for worse was yet to be seen. He was in no huge hurry, simply because he didn't want to wear out the horses and be caught on foot in country that became more wild and wide-open the farther west he traveled. And because Joe and Tex Liberty had announced where they were going, he wanted to give them time to worry and fret over whether he would come after them.

Let them sweat it out, wondering when I'll show up. Let them constantly look over their shoulders and lose sleep over it. They damn well had to know he'd come. They might even make themselves easy to find.

He slowed Rusty when he saw three riders in the distance, coming in his direction. As they drew closer, he realized there were actually four of them. Two were riding double on one horse.

A bad sign.

"Looks like they need a horse, Rusty," he said softly. "I expect they think they're going to get mine." He dismounted and pulled his Winchester repeating rifle from its boot, then led Rusty to a young pine tree struggling to stay alive and tied the horse, leaving Sadie tied to his saddle horn. He casually finished an already-lit cigarette while he waited, keeping the horses between the men and him. He cocked his rifle and rested it on his saddle as he carefully watched them.

He knew how the Liberty boys sat a horse, and this wasn't them. Besides, they should still be far ahead of him. Even so, two years as sheriff of River's Bend and three years before that as a deputy in Omaha had helped hone an instinct for who could and could not be trusted. A sneaking chill up his spine told him these men were the "could not" type.

It was one thing to be faced with a couple of men with guns in a city, where there were a lot of people around and usually at least one other deputy. But in the wilds of the open, lonely country outside of even the smallest town, one man alone was a prime target. A man could get killed out here and go for weeks without being found. These men damn well knew that.

The riders reined their horses to a halt, close enough to talk. For a few seconds they just sat there watching Matt, who threw down his cigarette butt and pressed it out with his boot.

"You alone?" the apparent spokesman asked. He was a stout, big-chested man with a beard, wearing a buffalo-skin coat with a collar made from the long, shaggy hair of the animal's shoulder hump.

"Not your business," Matt answered. "You buffalo hunters?"

"As long as it keeps paying good," one of the others answered. He was as overly skinny as the first man was overly stout. He wore the same kind of coat, but it looked too big on him.

Matt reminded himself there could be all kinds of weapons under those coats. "Don't you have a camp and supplies somewhere?"

"Damn Injuns stole it all," the skinny one answered. "We're lucky we got away with our horses."

"Well, you can just ride on," Matt told them.

"No need to get all hot under the collar, Mister. We were just makin' a friendly stop," the stout man told him. "Out here we always check up on others we come across. Make sure there ain't somethin' they need or they aren't wounded or in trouble or anything like that. Sometimes a body needs help, just like we do now."

Matt steadied his repeater. "I'm thinking most men only need help *after* you've stopped to check on them. Now get going. There's an army fort just south of here."

The stout man chuckled, his belly jiggling under his open coat. "You don't give a man much of a chance, do you, Mister?"

"Not when I'm alone and the other man needs a horse."

"Well, now, you're pretty savvy," the skinny one told him.

"I *have* to be. I'm a lawman."

The big man's eyebrows shot up in surprise. "That so?"

"It is."

"You good with that there rifle?"

"You don't want to find out."

The big man looked back at the other three. "What do you think, boys? Is he worth the trouble?"

"He ain't," the skinny one answered. He spit tobacco juice to the side. "But them horses he's got with him *are* worth the trouble."

"I figured that's what you were after," Matt told them.

"Hell, we've got money, Mister. We can pay you. At least let us buy one of them. You can see we're burdened with four men and only three horses." It was the skinny man who talked again. "Pete back there, his horse went lame on him."

"Then go buy a horse from some farmer or rancher. I have a big trip ahead of me, and I need *both* my horses, so ride on."

The stout man sighed deeply. "Hell, Mister, are you crazy? There's four of us and only one of you. Do you know the kind of hole a buffalo gun makes in a man?"

The skinny one moved his big-barreled rifle into shooting position.

"You don't want to die that kind of awful death out here all alone," the stout one added.

"What's your name?" Matt asked him.

"What does it matter?"

"Because when I bury you, I think it's only Christian to try to make some kind of marker with your name on it."

The stout man chuckled again. "Name's Manny Tooms. That tall, lanky man to my right holding a buffalo gun on you is called Moses, and these other two, who have their hand guns ready under their coats, are Pete and Bartley. And since we'll be the ones doin' the buryin', what's *your* name?"

"Matt Stover, from River's Bend." Matt didn't miss the little twitch of Moses' fingers at the trigger of the buffalo gun. He instantly fired his rifle. Moses flew backwards off his horse, but before his body even left the saddle, Matt had cocked and fired twice more, hitting Manny Tooms in the face and the one called Pete in the side. Bartley, who sat behind Pete on the same horse, also cried out when Matt's bullet skimmed through Pete and into the much-bigger Bartley, somewhere in the groin.

"Get moving, or you're both dead!" Matt yelled. "Take the other two horses with you and you won't need mine."

"We're bleedin'!" Pete shouted in reply, the inflection in his voice that of a man about to cry.

"And if you'd got your way, *I'd* be dead," Matt answered. "I'm real tempted to finish off both of you, so *leave.* I'll bury your friends."

"Maybe they ain't dead," Bartley complained.

"They're dead, all right. When I shoot a gun, I know where the bullets go. Moses got it in the heart, and Manny in the face. Now get moving before I decide to put a bullet in both of you in a more vital place!"

"Shit!" Bartley grumbled. He grunted as he slid off of Pete's horse and, holding his belly, walked over to Moses's horse and grabbed its reins. With more grunting and groaning, he mounted the horse then grabbed the reins to Manny's horse and turned to ride up to Pete.

"Let's go," he said as he winced with pain.

"If either of you comes back, I'll dig your graves out here, too," Matt warned.

The two men rode off with all three horses. Matt waited and watched, not moving until they disappeared into the endless grassland. He heaved a sigh of relief and shoved his rifle into its boot. He patted Rusty's rump.

"You did a good job, boy, of not bolting when I fired."

The horse snorted a little and nodded its head.

Matt took a short-handled shovel from his pack horse and began digging, figuring the graves would have to be shallow. He didn't have time to dig proper ones, and he'd have to keep his eyes open for a few days to make sure the other two buffalo hunters didn't come back to kill him. He paused for a moment, looking over at the dead bodies.

So, he thought, *the killing has begun.* He already felt harder, less bothered by shooting a man. That was good. It would help his determination to kill the Liberty brothers.

May God forgive you. He could hear his father's voice.

"By the time I'm done, I'll be beyond forgiving," Matt said aloud. He jammed the shovel into thick sod and started digging. "I call to the Lord, and He saves me from my enemies," he muttered, reminding himself of a verse from *Psalms.* "Well, Lord, you saved me this time. Keep it up." He grinned at the thought of finding his *real* enemies. "Praise the Lord," he growled. He dug faster, wondering if he was starting to go mad from grief.

CHAPTER FOUR

*E*lly sat down on a barrel and took a deep breath before sipping some coffee, taking advantage of a rare moment to be off her feet and resting. A week of traveling north had brought their little wagon train into Nebraska with no real troubles other than a heavy rainstorm two days after they left. Avoiding muddy spots had not been easy because there was really not a good road going north from Kansas into Nebraska.

At one point, Glen's wagon bogged down in a mucky puddle hidden by sod. It took two hours to push and pull and shove and curse at his draft horses before they finally freed the wagon. By then they were all covered in mud, and the horses were so worn out that Glen had to switch to his oxen for the rest of the day.

Still, after the initial woe over their condition, they couldn't help getting a good laugh over how they all looked. Finding a pond swollen from rainwater afforded them an opportunity to take turns washing off the mud and changing clothes, after which the women washed the muddy clothing and hung it in various places over the wagons to dry out while they made camp.

So far, mosquitoes had not been a problem, but the warmer the weather became, the more likely the pests would come out of hiding to feast on them. The spring weather they enjoyed now brought nights that were still cool enough to be comfortable.

"Feels good to just sit for a while, doesn't it?"

Elly turned at Glen's voice. He walked into the light of the campfire and sat down on a crate on the other side of the fire.

"Yes, it does," Elly answered. "Everything hurts. I thought the hard work of farming would prepare me for this, but I've never walked every day all day long, while climbing hill after hill."

"Well, tomorrow you can ride my buckskin. She's pretty gentle."

"I wouldn't want to wear her out."

"Don't be silly. You're half the size of a man. For her it will be hardly more than hauling a kid. In fact, I should have thought of it sooner. I'm sorry about that."

"Don't be. I know how important it is to spare the animals. At any time, you might have to jump up on Jenny and ride hard after stampeding cattle or horse thieves. Your riding horse should be rested and ready."

"Doesn't matter. I should have put you first." Glen took a cup of coffee Elly poured for him. "And I promise I will, once we're married."

Elly slowly set the porcelain coffee pot back on the fire. "I don't remember saying that I *would* marry you, Glen."

"Well, I say you will. I hope saying it will make it come true."

Elly met his gaze. The guilty feeling she always got over not being able to give this man an answer returned to nudge her conscience. "I'm sorry, Glen. I promise a solid yes or no once we reach California. I figure this trip will be a test of our patience with each other and will give me time to be around you more and to give your proposal some serious thought." She looked down at her coffee cup. "I do appreciate the fact that you want to marry me, but..."

"But you don't have those kind of feelings for me," he finished for her. "I'm too old for you."

"I never said that."

"But you thought it."

Elly sighed again. "Yes, but not in a way that would make it impossible for me to marry you. Not at all. It's just that..." She looked at him pleadingly. "Glen, I've already lost one husband, and he was young besides."

"And since I'm so old, I could die after a short marriage, too, and you'd be widowed twice."

Elly blinked back tears. "Something like that. I'm sorry, Glen, for thinking that way, but—"

"I understand completely, Elly. But I'm healthy and strong for my age. I'm a good provider, a hard worker, and I know I can still give you children."

Elly felt heat come into her cheeks. His remark made it all embarrassingly clear. Marriage meant mating with a man she had no such desire for. And sometimes she wondered if he was thinking the same things about her as he'd said about himself—a good provider, a hard worker, and young enough to bear him children. She didn't want to be that kind of wife. She just wanted to be a full woman again, loved simply for who she was, faults and all. Just loved. It dawned on her then that Glen had never said those three words. *I love you.*

So, those were his words for marrying ... *hard worker, good provider, able to make babies.* "You don't need to remind me about your proposal every day, Glen, because I take it very seriously, which is why I need more time. I loved William very much, and we were so right for each other." She sipped more coffee. "I'll never forget his awful death.

What it was like to sit by his bed and literally watch him die. You know what that's like yourself, watching your wife die gasping for breath because of pneumonia. Surely you fear having to go through that again."

Glen nodded as he pulled a slim cigar from his shirt pocket. "I do." He held up a match. "Do you mind?"

"No. Go right ahead."

He lit the cigar. "Martha was the same age as me, not young like you. And we can't live our whole lives worrying about what *might* happen."

"I know that. And I pray about it. By the time we reach California, I'll know in my heart what the right thing is to do. I won't keep you waiting any longer than that. I promise."

Glen nodded. "That's all I can ask, I guess." He finished his coffee and handed back the cup. "I'm going to check my gear." He got to his feet, the slim cigar between his lips. When Elly looked up at him, he was looking her over the way a man would study a fine horse or a wagon he was going to buy. "You're some kind of woman, Elly Lowe."

Elly set her cup beside Glen's and stood up. "Thank you." *I guess,* she thought, since the remark seemed like an odd compliment. "I think this is your night to keep watch for a while. I'll leave these cups here and leave the coffee over the fire. If you need another cup later, it will be here."

Glen nodded and grinned. "Thank you. You're a right good cook, Elly, another fine point about you."

Elly just nodded, waiting for the right words. But they didn't come.

Glen stepped closer and touched her arm. "May I kiss you?"

Elly wished beyond wishing that she could honestly welcome his request, that the man would stir something deep inside, but those feelings were not there. "Of course."

She raised her head a little and turned her face to offer a cheek. Glen leaned down and kissed it.

"Thanks, Elly." He walked off into the darkness.

Still no 'I love you,' she thought. And his lips had felt cold.

CHAPTER FIVE

*M*att finished eating his supper, a young rabbit he'd shot and skinned this morning. He wished he could follow up his meal with a piece of Lora's wonderful apple pie. His mother's strawberry-rhubarb pie would do just as well but, alas, it would be a long time before he'd enjoy such desserts again. And never again would he taste Lora's great cooking. Every time it hit him that his wife really was dead, he felt the stabbing pain in his chest all over again. He wondered when the agony would end.

Dusk was fast falling into darkness, but there was just enough light left to notice another camp south of his. Nebraska was a long, east-west state. He'd been on this main road nearly two weeks, and he'd only reached the middle of it. The wagon wheel ruts were deep from the thousands of emigrants who'd used this road before him, so he rode just to the north of it to avoid one of his horses stepping into a rut and bruising or breaking a leg. Either the campers south of him were also trying to avoid those ruts, or they were coming from the south to meet this road. By what light was left he could see only three wagons, but it looked like they also had cattle with them, and more than a few horses - prime targets for men like the buffalo hunters who'd tried to steal Rusty and Sadie.

He wondered if he should warn them about such men —like Bartley and Pete. It would be a good excuse to meet up with others for a day or two, in hopes of being offered some woman-cooked food. A small wagon train usually meant married couples, and his aching loneliness told him it would be nice to have a little company, although a wagon train would travel far too slowly for his liking. Meeting them would simply be a nice break until they reached Fort McPherson, where he could rest the horses and re-stock a few supplies. After that, he could go his own way again.

He intended to stop at the fort anyway, just to ask about a couple of wounded buffalo hunters and find out if they'd shown up at the fort to find a doctor. After Pete and Bartley had ridden off with his bullets in them, he'd been on the lookout, wondering if they would keep their promise about coming back to even the score. And it was only fair to at least warn those with that small wagon train about the danger of men out to steal cattle and horses.

He poured himself some coffee and leaned back against his saddle to light a cigarette, then noticed someone riding from the camp south of him toward his own camp. He got back up and held his cigarette between his lips while he strapped on his .44 and watched man and horse approach. The horse was a black gelding with a white face and looked like a good, strong animal. Likely home-raised and not a mustang.

Matt walked out to where he'd hobbled Rusty, putting a hand on the horse's neck while he waited for the rider to come closer. By the time the stranger reached him Matt had finished his cigarette. He dropped the stub at his feet and stepped it out. Each man nodded at the other, and the stranger pushed his hat back a little, revealing dark brown hair. Matt thought him a nice-looking man, maybe forty years old, with soft brown eyes and a stubble of a beard, common for most men on the trail.

"Something I can do for you?" he asked, his hand on his gun. Out here he didn't trust any person he didn't know, although this man appeared pleasant enough.

"Care if I get down off my horse?" the rider asked.

"Fine with me."

The man dismounted and kept hold of his reins. "Name's Glen Baker," he said, reaching out his hand.

Matt shook it. "That's a fine horse you have there."

Glen turned and stroked his horse's nose. "Yeah, this here is Midnight. Raised him myself. My wife named him, but she's dead now—pneumonia—couple of years ago."

"Sorry to hear it. I lost my own wife about a month ago."

Glen frowned. "That's too bad. You look too young to be a widower already."

Matt felt the familiar ache in his heart. "Long story." He nodded his head toward the camp south of them. "I take it you're with that camp. I saw your fire." They let go of hands. "And you obviously saw mine."

Glen nodded. "Yes, sir. We have a small problem back there and thought we'd inquire if you could help."

"Depends what you need."

"Well, some laudanum, if you have any. It's one of those things we should have thought to bring along and didn't. I can't believe we were foolish enough not to. 'Course we have some whiskey along—for medicinal purposes. None of us drinks much. But we have somebody down there that needs something a little stronger."

Matt frowned. "What's the problem?"

"Well, sir, a couple of men came upon us—both of

them wounded by gunshots that were several days old. They said some man shot and killed two of their friends for no good reason and then wounded them as they rode off. They tried to doctor themselves, but things just got worse for one of them, and he's in a lot of pain. One of the women along—her name is Betty—she took a bullet out of his belly, but it's infected. We keep draining it, but it's awful painful for him every time we cut into him. We thought laudanum would help."

Matt closed his eyes and sighed. "Let me guess. Their names are Pete and Bartley."

Glen looked at him warily, backing up a little. "How do you know?"

"Because I'm the one who *shot* them," Matt answered flatly. "And they deserved it. They're buffalo hunters, and they tried to steal my horses. If I hadn't shot them when I did, I'd be lying out there on the prairie somewhere with a nice big hole in my chest from one of their Sharps rifles. Those men are dangerous, and you shouldn't be harboring them."

Glen shuffled nervously and looked Matt over. "Look, Mister, we don't turn away somebody who's in bad need of help. How do I know you're telling the truth? Maybe it was the other way around. Maybe you're—"

"My name is Matt Stover, and I'm sheriff at River's Bend, about a hundred and fifty miles east of here, not all that far from Omaha. I'm headed for Outlaw Country farther west, looking for some men who robbed a bank in my town and shot and killed my wife and our unborn baby. I know men pretty damn good, and those two can't be trusted, wounded or not. You need to move on and leave them behind."

Glen looked toward their camp, then back at Matt. "There's two women back there, one married and one a widow I hope to marry myself when we reach California."

He shuffled nervously again. "You know how women are. They won't take kindly to leaving wounded or dying men behind."

"And I'm telling you that neither of those women would be safe if those two were in good health and had caught them out here alone. They aren't safe even now, unless you keep a close eye on them. Those two likely have friends camped out here somewhere. They were probably looking for them when they came across your camp."

Glen rubbed at the back of his neck. "Well, I'm in kind of a fix." He looked Matt over again. "You really a sheriff?"

"I am." He reached into his pocket and pulled out his badge, holding it out for Glen to see. "I don't wear my badge because where I'm going, no man wants the rest to know he's a lawman. He could get shot or hanged for it."

Glen studied his horses, looked Matt over again. "Well, if it's true, I'm real sorry about your wife. Real sorry."

"It's true. You'd best go back and tell the others I didn't have any laudanum. I do have some, but I'll be damned if I'll waste it on those two. You need to keep watch tonight and be on your way tomorrow. Tell them you've done all you can for them, and that you have to get going. Then get the hell out of here come morning. Were you heading up here to meet up with the main road west?"

Glen nodded. "We can't afford to travel by train. We're going to California to join the brother of one of the women. He's got a farm there and wrote us several times about how pretty California is and how good the valleys are for farming. We lost everything to a prairie fire down in Kansas, north of Topeka." He shoved his hands into his pockets and looked around again. "Looks like fate kind of made us cross paths. It must have taken you about as long to reach this spot from River's Bend as it took us to come up from the south."

"Looks like." Matt sighed. "What do you want to do about those two men?"

Glen looked back at his camp. "Well, if it's true what you said... I don't know. I mean, the women, they'll think it's cruel to leave them behind."

"Not cruel at all. You helped them the best you could, but believe me, if they get better and you turn your backs, they'll put a knife right in your spine and take everything you have, including the women. I noticed you had cattle and horses along. Sounds to me like you have quite a bit of stock and supplies those men could sell, and believe me, they know people who will buy it all and buy the women, too. You'd best go back and just say I didn't have any laudanum. Set your foot down that you need to leave in the morning and those two will have to try to make it on their own. You need to get rid of them and be on your way. Only trouble is, now they know about you and know what you have along. They could go find some of their friends and come after all of it. The farther west we go, the less law there is, and the easier it is for men like that to have their way."

Glen rubbed at his hips. "Well, you can see I don't carry a gun on me. Neither do the other two men with me, but we do have rifles and know how to use them. We're farmers by nature, good, Christian folks who don't want any trouble."

"I'm sure you don't. I didn't want trouble either when those two and their two friends came across me. They were four men with three horses and they meant to take mine free of charge. I wasn't about to let that happen."

Glen looked back at his camp again. "Well, I'm wondering... would you be willing to come to our camp with me? It would come out better if you did the explaining and, well, maybe set your foot down to those two and let them know they'll be left on their own come morning. They already know you mean business. Maybe if you're the one who gives them what-for, they won't think to come after us later and take what's ours. I'm thinking we'd all feel safer if you traveled with us for a bit... maybe just three or four days, 'til we reach Fort McPherson."

Matt wrestled with the idea. Traveling with a wagon train would slow him down, but having company and woman-cooked food for a few days sounded good. And he didn't trust the buffalo hunters not to cause trouble for people who weren't used to men like them. He'd had run-ins with such men back at River's Bend, when they came into town to drink and raise hell, bother the women and steal what they could get away with. And still haunted by what happened to Lora, he hated the thought of the two innocent women with the wagon train possibly being abused.

He ran a hand through his hair, thinking how he wished he could wash and shave before being around the women. "Look, I need to get myself to the Rockies and the place where I think the men I'm after are headed. But I don't like the idea of those buffalo hunters being with your party. Besides, I'd like to keep an eye on them for my own health. I've been wondering when they might show up again or come after me. But I can't guarantee there won't be some kind of violence once they realize it's me that's coming. Are there kids down there?"

"Two boys. Six and ten."

"You go down there first. Get those boys and the women into a wagon. Make up some excuse. Tell them you aren't sure you can trust me and want them to stay inside until I can come down there and introduce myself. How many other men do you have?"

"Two. One kind of old. He's the widow's father. The other is maybe your age. He's the father of the two boys."

Glen shifted his stance and looked back at their camp yet again. "I hope I'm not trusting the wrong man."

"You aren't. Hold on a minute." Matt walked over to his gear and fished a piece of paper out of his supplies. He brought it back to Glen and handed him the papers. "In case you think my badge was a fake, here's a certificate, signed by the mayor of River's Bend. It's my official papers that I'm sheriff there and that I served as a deputy in Omaha for two years. And my own father is a preacher at River's Bend. I'm a law-abiding man, Mister Baker, at least until I find the men who killed my wife. I might not be so law-abiding then, but you and yours won't be anywhere around by then."

Glen looked the paper over and handed it back. "Like I said, I'm real sorry about your wife. Must have been an awful thing."

Matt re-folded the paper and put it into his jacket pocket. "I'm wrangling with a lot of hate and a need for revenge right now, Baker, but only for the men who killed my wife. Other than that, I believe in law and order, but I assure you, those two men down there *don't*."

Glen mounted his horse. "I thank you for what you're doing. I'll make sure the others go along with whatever you think needs doing."

Matt nodded. "Go on down there, and I'll saddle up and come down in a few minutes. In the morning we can stop here first, and I'll pick up my pack horse and the rest of my supplies. I think they'll be safe here for the rest of the night. My pack horse is hobbled, and I can stash my supplies in a hollow about ten yards from here. Nobody will see any of it since it's almost full dark."

"Whatever you say."

"Just don't mention my name in front of the two wounded men. If they know it's me coming, they just might lay in wait and shoot me right off my horse before I get too close. They want my blood, Baker, so gather your family and talk to them out of hearing distance. Just tell those two men that someone you found camped nearby has some laudanum and is bringing it on his own because he'd enjoy some woman-cooked food."

Glen nodded. "Sure." He turned his horse and headed for the wagons. Matt watched after him a moment, then walked over to pick up his blanket and saddle. He carried them to Rusty and threw the blanket over the horse's back.

"I hope I'm not making a big mistake, boy," he told the horse before heaving the saddle onto the blanket. "I sure didn't plan on something like this." He reached under the horse to strap the saddle tight. He yanked on the cinch until it was buckled where he wanted it, then threw his saddle bags over Rusty's back and strapped them to the saddle. "I expect this is all I'll need for tonight," he muttered, realizing then that he'd already grown used to only his horses for company.

He untied the hobbling strap from Rusty's front legs, then picked up his rifle from where he'd laid it near him earlier. He shoved it into its boot, then mounted up, patting the horse's neck and settling against the cantle. He turned Rusty in the direction of the wagons.

"I expect it's time I spent a couple of days talking to humans again," he said. He trotted Rusty toward Baker's wagons, not at all eager to face the two men he'd shot.

CHAPTER SIX

*E*lly and Betty ordered young Tommy and Mark to stay inside Betty's wagon, but the boys peeked through the rolled-up canvas at the side as the stranger rode toward their camp. Elly stood out of sight at the back of her father's wagon and glanced at Betty to see her sister-in-law watching from the inside front of her wagon. Both women and Betty's boys were excited and curious about the stranger approaching.

"He's a lawman," Glen had told them quietly in a family gathering away from where the buffalo hunters lay with their wounds. "His name is Matt Stover, but he doesn't want the buffalo hunters to know who's coming in. There could be trouble, so stay back."

Betty asked why there might be trouble.

"Because he's the one who shot them!" Glen answered. "And for good reason. And he killed two others."

"What the hell are we getting ourselves into?" Mark asked. "We never should have gone for help."

"It's a good thing we did. Stover says these men are dangerous," Glen answered.

"But they're wounded!" Betty argued.

By then the hunter called Pete called out to them. "What's goin' on over there? Did you find help?"

Pete was the one who seemed to be healing. The bullet had gone through his side and into Bartley, who had the infection and seemed to be dying. Glen shouted back to them that someone was coming, but that he was a stranger and he was telling the family to stay out of the way until they knew the stranger could be trusted. "He has laudanum for your friend!" he yelled.

Glen turned to the rest of them then and quietly told them Matt Stover seemed like a man who could be trusted, but they had to keep his name to themselves until he got here. "I was just making an excuse as to why I'm talking to the family first. I'll explain more later," he told them, "or at least Stover will."

What on earth kind of man was riding in? Elly wondered. He rode closer on a roan-colored gelding, and she could tell from how he sat his horse that he was fairly tall, certainly taller than her brother or Glen. He wore a tan, sheepskin jacket, and the right side was pushed back to expose a six-gun on his hip. Apparently, he wanted to be ready to use it. As he came closer, from what Elly could tell, he was a handsome man, broad in the shoulders. But that mattered little, since he was not against guns and killing. The buffalo hunter named Pete slowly rose as he approached, and that's when, to Elly's surprise, Glen stepped closer to the hunters, rifle ready.

"Take it easy," Glen told Pete.

Matt rode right up to the hunters and pulled his six-gun from its holster. "Evening, boys," he said, cocking the gun. "I'll bet you wish you'd not asked these good people here to see if they could find laudanum."

Bartley, who lay flat on his back nearby, groaned, "What's... goin' on?"

"It's that goddamn sheriff who shot and killed Manny and Moses!" Pete told him.

Bartley grunted as he seemed to be reaching out, most likely for his rifle, but he had no strength.

"Take their guns, Glen," Matt ordered. "Make sure they aren't hiding pistols on their persons. The one standing near you will shoot me down like a rabbit if he gets the chance."

"You bet I will!" Pete shouted.

Elly and Betty watched wide-eyed.

"That's why I came here," Matt answered. "These people had no idea what kind of men they've been good enough to try to help, and now I know where you are. I don't want to have to worry about you crawling up on me in the night like snakes."

"We just wanted help! We needed a horse!" Pete argued.

"And you were going to kill me and take *both* of mine, plus my weapons and supplies," Matt answered. "You must have friends out here somewhere. Where are they? And why didn't you go to *them* for help with your wounds?"

"Our friends already moved on, and we can't find them," Pete snarled. "We came across these people and we seen women along. Women are better caretakers than men."

Matt dismounted.

Yes, he's tall, and so well built, Elly thought, wondering why on earth she cared. She supposed it was because this man could either be good protection, or trouble. Out here, any man experienced with guns could turn on them.

"You had more ideas about the women than their just being good caretakers," Matt told Pete. As Glen picked up the men's rifles, Matt spoke to Mark.

"Help Glen check them for personal weapons," Matt told Mark.

Elly's brother walked up to Pete and felt inside his jacket, then pulled a six-gun from an inside pocket on the garment. He showed it to Matt.

"Go put it in one of your wagons," Matt told him. He glanced at Glen. "Check the wounded one. He's alive and kicking enough to shoot me dead if he has a gun on him."

Glen knelt beside Bartley and rummaged through his blankets and the coat that lay beside him. "No gun," he told Matt. "In fact, he's only half dressed because we took a bullet out of him and had to bandage him up."

"Then there's probably a gun in his gear. Check it out."

With a sigh of resignation, Glen rose and walked over to where the hunters had stashed their gear and began looking through it.

"What are you going to do now?" Pete asked Matt. "Kill us in cold blood, like you did Moses and Manny?"

"You mean like Moses and Manny were going to do to me?" Matt slowly put his own .44 back in its holster. "I shot them in self-defense, and you know it. I was hoping never to see you two again, but here we are."

"Did you really bring some laudanum?" Pete asked. "Bartley there is hurtin' pretty bad."

"Dying?"

Pete shrugged. "Could be. He's all infected. Looks bad."

"Then I won't waste my laudanum on him," Matt answered.

Elly sucked in her breath in shock. She marched out from behind her wagon and up to Matt to boldly confront him. "You can't do that! The man is in awful pain!"

The startled look in his eyes confused her. He seemed surprised, and for a moment she thought he was going to speak her name, as though he knew her. And there was something more in his eyes—sorrow, admiration. Something about seeing her had caused him to step back a little.

"Ma'am, if the tables were turned, that man wouldn't dream of helping me," he told her. "The only way he'd consider putting me out of my misery would be to put a bullet in my head. Believe me, I know men like these."

"And is that what *you* intend to do to the poor man lying over there in pain? Put a bullet in his head?"

"No, ma'am. I intend to just let him die. From the looks of him, and that infection being in his gut, I expect he'll be gone by morning. Then we'll send Pete on his way… *without* his weapons."

Elly glanced over at Bartley. "But…" She looked back at Matt. "That's just cruel when you have something that will relieve his pain."

There it was again, a rather startled look in his eyes.

"Lady, I'm only looking out for *you*. Mister Baker said there were women along, and a couple of young boys. Believe me, you don't want men like these two anywhere around decent women. You can't trust them any farther than you could throw them, and they might do things you wouldn't want those boys to see. Let alone they could leave all of you out here dead and leave those boys to die from starvation and exposure."

"Don't believe him, lady," Pete argued.

Elly glanced over at him. Pete's hair looked as though it hadn't been washed in weeks. His beard spoke of just as many weeks without shaving. Both men had reeked from needing a bath when they first met up, and it was difficult to look at their brown teeth, stained from chewing tobacco. Their condition told her Matt Stover could be right, but it just didn't seem right to let a man lie in pain. She looked back at Matt, whom she could see by the firelight had a sure look in his amazingly blue eyes. Their color sparked up by the firelight, which also showed a tanned face and very dark hair. Still, how could a man be so unfeeling as to let another man grovel in pain?

"Right or not, Mister Stover, I wish you would allow that man something to kill the pain, even if he's dying."

Matt sighed deeply and turned to his horse. He reached inside his saddle bags and took out a brown bottle. Looking disgruntled and a little angry, he held it out. "Just a couple of swallows," he told her. "I'm on a long journey, and I could end up needing this stuff myself. I'll tell you once more that Bartley over there doesn't deserve to be put out of his misery, but if it makes you feel better, go ahead and let him have some of this."

Their gazes held. Elly felt a surprising and unwanted attraction, yet also felt a bit repulsed by his seemingly cruel, uncaring attitude. "Thank you." She took the bottle from him, feeling ridiculous things she should not feel when his fingers touched hers. She left Matt and walked over to where Bartley lay, kneeling down beside him and putting the bottle to his lips.

"Not too much," she told him.

"You're a… kind woman," Bartley told her.

"You lying bastard," Matt called to him. "If you were well, you'd shoot the men here and do what you want with the women."

"Please don't say those things in front of my wife and sister," Mark said.

Matt sighed and shook his head. "I apologize, but I know the nature of men like those two, and they want me dead. It's a little hard to be civil around them."

Betty climbed down from her wagon. Her boys jumped out behind her and ran up to Matt.

"Are you really a sheriff?" the older one asked.

"Well, temporarily I've given up my badge, but yes, back in my home town I'm a sheriff."

"Why'd you give up your badge?" the boy asked.

"Tommy! Stop asking questions," Betty ordered as she walked closer. She nodded to Matt. "My name is Betty, and these are my sons, Mark Jr. and Tommy. I'm sorry for all the questions."

"Maybe Mister Stover can answer a few questions over by the fire," Mark spoke up, still frowning in disapproval of the things Matt had said.

By then the whole family had surrounded Matt.

"Come and have some coffee," Mark told Matt.

Elly walked up and handed the laudanum back to Matt. "Thank you for the medicine."

Matt took the laudanum, and again Elly felt drawn to him.

"My name is Elly," she told him. "Please understand that this whole situation is quite out of the ordinary for people like us."

Matt glanced at Pete. "You stay put there by your friend. Tomorrow morning these people are leaving after we give Bartley there one more dose of laudanum, if he isn't dead by then. Either way, you're on your own after that. And we'll damn well take your buffalo gun before you go. You can keep your pistol, but I know how far a buffalo gun can shoot, and I'd be the buffalo."

"You aren't the law out here, Stover."

"Around good people like this, I am. And I'll still set the rules for men like you, like it or not."

Elly couldn't help admiring Stover's concern, even though he seemed too uncaring over the wounded man. He met her gaze just then.

"I'll have that coffee," he told her, "but tonight I'll bed down over there by those two no-goods. You're better off if I keep an eye on them. After breakfast you folks need to be on your way. Don't be wasting supplies and travel time on men like these. You'll live to regret it."

Elly shook her head. "I think you're wrong, Mister Stover. The one who's worst wounded can't possibly do us any harm."

"Maybe not, but once he's gone, that one called Pete wouldn't leave here without holding a gun on the rest of you and taking some of your horses and supplies, at the least."

Glen walked up and took hold of Elly's arm. "Elly is the woman I intend to marry when we get to California," he told Matt a bit defensively. "Go fix that coffee, Elly, and maybe see if we have some of those home-made biscuits left. Matt mentioned he'd enjoy some woman-cooked food."

Elly looked at him and forced a smile. "Sure, Glen." She left, a bit irritated at how he seemed to take it for granted she belonged to him and would be his wife. She thought how strange it was that one look into Matt Stover's intensely blue eyes had stirred more in her than any feelings she'd felt around Glen after knowing him for years. It didn't make sense. She couldn't understand why she felt so nervous and self-conscious as the whole family gathered around the campfire, insisting Matt sit down for coffee and biscuits.

CHAPTER SEVEN

"So, you say you're headed for Outlaw Country," Glen stated to Matt. "Sounds like dangerous territory."

"I'll be all right," Matt answered. "I have something that needs doing, and I aim to get it done." He rubbed his stomach, full of warmed and buttered biscuits. He watched the dancing flames of the campfire, wishing he'd not told Glen Baker his story earlier. Glen had spilled it to everyone, and Matt hated for his feelings to be so exposed. He also didn't like too many people knowing where he was going and why. He blamed this interruption to his plans on the buffalo hunters.

Worse than all of that was the disturbing feelings Elly Lowe had stirred in his soul. He'd been temporarily taken back by the beautiful young woman with dark hair and lovely curves who'd so boldly confronted him. He'd just met her, yet something about Elly made him feel comfortable, almost the way he'd felt around Lora. It didn't make sense. Her eyes were unusually green - like Lora's. Damned if it wasn't as if Lora herself was looking right at him through Elly Lowe's gaze. It had actually startled him when he first laid eyes on her.

"Finding and killing those men won't bring back your wife and baby," Elly said. "You should give more thought to what you are doing, Mister Stover."

A piece of wood popped, and embers exploded upward, lighting up everyone's faces. Matt noticed a sadness in Elly's eyes. Why did she care that it might be wrong to hunt down Lora's killers? He was a total stranger to her.

"It doesn't matter what the after-effects turn out to be for killing the men I'm after," he answered. "It still needs doing."

He sipped some coffee, thinking that the biscuits he just ate were the best he'd ever tasted, except for Lora's.

"My father tried to talk me out of it, too," he told all of them. "He's a preacher back in River's Bend and doesn't believe in violence. Actually, he more or less founded the town when I was a kid. He came west from Omaha and built a church for the farmers who'd settled there." He decided not to talk about being the rebel of the family, or about the Liberty boys and their history in River's Bend. No sense in going into details with people who'd be here today and gone tomorrow. "I have a brother. Davie. He went to Colorado to start his own church. Has a wife and two little girls."

"Well, we're very sorry about what happened to your wife," Betty told him.

"Thank you, Ma'am." Matt drank more coffee, deciding to leave out the fact that the Liberty boys had also raped a young farm girl. Women didn't like to hear things like that.

"The men I'm hunting are also cattle thieves," he added. "And that money they stole the day of the bank robbery belongs to all the local farmers. It's hard-earned money that will leave those farmers unable to buy needed supplies for their spring crops. I don't know if I can recover it, but I'm going to try."

"Well, we wish you luck there," Mark told him. "And we thank you for warning us about the men we decided to help. Of course, the worst-wounded one can't be any harm."

Matt drew on a cigarette. "You might be surprised," he answered as he exhaled. "Out here you have to be careful, no matter what the other man's situation is. I'll ride with you to Fort McPherson. It's only a couple more days' ride. I suggest you find a guide there for the rest of the way. A good guide can steer you away from the worst of Outlaw Country so you won't need to worry about being attacked and having your supplies and horses and cattle stolen. In fact, if you can find a guide and another wagon train to hook up with, you'd be a lot safer."

"Well, you've helped us learn what to watch for," old John Grace told him. "And me and my son, and Glen there, we're all good with rifles and not afraid to stand up to anybody."

Matt glanced at Elly—young and pretty, as was her sister-in-law Betty. He hated alarming them, but he feared these men didn't understand how dark a man's nature could be, especially in country where women were scarce. "Just keep in mind you have some pretty valuable things along—women, horses, cattle—and some men figure people moving on to other parts of the country probably also have money on them. You only have three wagons, so if you could travel with a bigger train, you'd be better off. I'm sorry about the fire and all your losses where you came from, but you don't want to add to those losses on your way to California."

"Have you shot a lot of bad men, mister?" young Mark asked.

His little brother sat wide-eyed beside him.

Matt scowled at them both. "That's not something a man talks about, son. It's not something to brag about either. You'd be best to hope you never have to shoot *anybody*." He rose. "I'd better get on over to those two no-goods you took in and keep an eye on them for the rest of the night." He handed his empty coffee cup to Betty. "Thank you, ladies, for the fine biscuits and good coffee. You'd better all get some rest."

"And so should you," Elly told him. "You don't plan on staying awake all night, do you?"

"If I have to, but a man can't help but doze off a time or two. I think I'll handcuff Pete to a wagon wheel, at least by one hand. He can still sit by his friend, but he won't be able to sneak up and shoot or clobber me while I sleep."

"Oh, that's just mean!" Elly protested. "I'm sure he won't—"

"He *will*, ma'am. Please trust my judgment." He tipped his hat and walked out of the firelight to where Pete sat next to Bartley. "He still alive?"

"Barely—no thanks to you, you sonofabitch!"

Matt reached into his back pocket and pulled out handcuffs. Before Pete realized what he meant to do because it was too dark to see the movement, Matt slapped one cuff on Pete's wrist and yanked his arm to snap the other cuff to a wheel on Glen's wagon.

"Hey, you can't do this! I ain't done nothin' to these people!"

"And I'm making sure you don't, although it's not them I'm worried about so much as me getting my head bashed in while I sleep tonight."

"Take these damn things off of me!"

"Go to sleep," Matt told him. He unsaddled Rusty and carried his saddle and supplies to plop them down just far enough away that Pete couldn't reach him with hand or foot.

"You *bastard*," Pete growled.

Bartley merely groaned.

"Just pay attention to your friend there," Matt told him. "I'll let you go in the morning." He left for a few minutes to walk Rusty out to higher grass, where he hobbled the horse to graze.

"Mister Stover."

Matt turned at the sound of a woman's soft voice in the darkness. He walked closer to see Elly standing there in the moonlight.

"Do you really need to handcuff that man?" she asked.

Matt thought what a pretty, gentle voice she had. Lora'd had a voice like that. His wife had been in her grave only a month or so, and he still ached for her, yet something about Elly Lowe nagged at his senses. It made him feel guilty. "Yes, I really do. Go on to your wagon now and get some sleep. I'm doing this more for you and your sister-in-law than for any other reason."

"Not every woman needs protection from bank robbers, Mister Stover," Elly told him. "And Pete there has so far been respectful, in spite of his filthy condition. He only wanted us to help his friend."

"And he and his friend and two more with him meant to murder me and take my horses and supplies just a few days ago. Remember that. Out here you can't trust *anyone*. Remember that, too. Now go tend to your business and I'll tend to mine."

Their gazes held in the moonlight. "I'm sorry for you, Mister Stover, and I don't believe it's really your nature to be so rude. You're full of hate and revenge and remorse and sorrow. I'm so sorry about your wife and child. I want you to know that I will pray for you."

Matt sighed and stepped away a little, disturbed by her

gentle presence in the warm, dark night. "Thank you, ma'am."

"Don't be prayin' for that hard-hearted, uncaring, cruel man," Pete called from the darkness. "He's lying, lady. We wasn't gonna' kill him. We would have paid him for one of his horses. He's so full of hate that he just doesn't trust anybody. He had no reason to kill my friends and put Bartley through all this pain."

"Shut up!" Matt told him. He turned to Elly, wondering why it bothered him that she might believe the man. "Study us both and think about why I'm out here," he told her. "I think you're wise enough to know who's telling the truth. Now please go to your wagon. Things will be better come morning."

"Yeah. We'll be buryin' my friend!" Pete growled. "And it's Matt Stover's bullet that killed him!"

Elly reached out and touched Matt's arm. "It's all right."

She turned and left, and Matt watched after her, still disturbed by feelings of a strange connection to her. He walked to his bedroll and settled in, while Pete yanked at the handcuffs. "You'll pay for this, Stover! I might ride off in the morning, but I won't forget this. I have *friends!* And I know where you're going."

"You come after me and you'll regret it," Matt told him. "I've already killed four men since putting on a badge. A couple more won't make much difference now. It'll just help me practice for the men I'm *really* after."

"Well, I hope they shoot you then skin you alive," Pete told him.

Matt forced himself to ignore the remark. He turned his thoughts to Elly Grace Lowe and her voice... and how she reminded him of Lora.

CHAPTER EIGHT

"What do you think? Will he really come after us?" Joe Liberty tossed the bone of a rabbit's hind leg aside and licked grease from his fingers.

Tex finished chewing on meat from the rabbit's breast. "You kidding? Matt Stover's hated us since grade school." He bit into the breast again while Joe stood up, his towering frame looking bigger than usual when it was set against a bright moon.

"True," Joe answered with a sigh. He looked around. "How close do you think he is?"

Tex shrugged broad shoulders and stood up to face his brother. He was a barrel of a man, bigger in girth than Joe and always hard for Joe to put down when they wrestled just for fun.

"Not close at all," he answered Joe, "so quit worryin', little brother. The man wouldn't leave before his wife was buried. He's too Christian. Burials always take two or three days—preparation, services, all that shit."

"Jesus, Tex, ain't you got any feelings at all?"

Tex wiped his fingers on his denim pants. "Do *you?*"

"Well, no," Joe told him. "Not for Matt Stover anyway.

All those fights we got into. And him thinkin' he's almighty perfect just because his pa is a preacher. I don't know. I don't care about gettin' the best of the man, but we did go to school with him and Lora both, and I kind of liked Lora."

"Hell, she was just as uppity as the rest of the girls who snubbed us."

"Yeah, but I'm not real crazy about us killin' a woman," Joe grumbled. "It's botherin' me."

"You'll gladly force them into your bed, but you won't *kill* them?" Tex snickered.

"You know what I mean. Killin' Lora Stover in that bank robbery wasn't part of the deal."

"Well, it wasn't your bullet that got her, so relax," Tex answered. "It was *my* bullet. And maybe even one of the other men's. She got hit twice."

"Could have been *my* bullet." The words came from Bill Howard, called "Fats" by most because he weighed a good three hundred pounds. He rode a horse as big as a plow horse just to carry the weight. "I fired a lot of bullets —mostly just to scare those inside the bank—broke some lights and such."

"Well, I was actually aiming at a bank teller, but damn Randy there bumped my arm," Tex explained for the tenth time. "That's the only reason Lora got it instead."

The man called Randy scratched at the stubble of a beard and took a drink of whiskey from a flask he'd just opened. "Hell, a lot of shoving and shouting went on in that bank. Only reason I bumped your arm, Tex, is because that young boy ran out right past me. I was tempted to shoot him for yellin' outside that the bank was bein' robbed, but I ain't yet stooped so low as to shoot a kid."

"But shooting a woman is okay?" Joe asked Randy.

Randy grinned. "Havin' at one whether she wants it or not is okay. I haven't really given much thought to shootin' one. But I guess if she was aimin' a gun at me, I'd have no choice. Either way, the last shot I fired killed that bank teller, so we're wanted for more than the woman's death."

Joe looked at the fifth man, Tim Blankenship, who had a deep scar on his left cheek. He'd never explained where he got it and refused to talk about it. "What about you, Tim? You ever shoot a woman?"

Randy handed his whiskey over to Tim, who took a swallow before answering. "One," he said, handing back the whiskey. "It's been a while back. I strangled her to death for mouthin' off. I'd been beddin' her for a while. We got along okay at first, but she started givin' me orders. Know what I mean? Then one day she lit into me about what an ugly, worthless bastard I am. She was mad at me for takin' some savings she had in a tin can. Yelled about how she'd worked hard doin' other people's laundry in order to make that money. I told her to shut up, but she wouldn't. So, I shut her up on my own. I took the money and a couple of her horses and lit out. That was way back in Illinois or Indiana. I can't remember any more. I've stayed out here ever since to avoid the law. Now, thanks to that bank robbery I agreed to with the rest of you, I've got a lawman on my ass again."

"Stover won't dare wear a badge into Outlaw Country," Tex told them. "That's why we're goin' there. And once we tell others he's actually a lawman, he won't last long."

Joe grunted as he sat down on his bedroll. "Let's hope so. You have to admit he's pretty good with a gun, and he's bound to be full of a hatred few men carry. He's loved Lora since they were kids."

"And there's five of us," Fats reminded him. "I'm not the least bit worried."

"You don't know how stubborn and determined Matt Stover can be,". Joe told him. "And to him everything is black and white. Won't matter to him that killin' his wife was an accident. We were robbin' the bank, and his wife and unborn kid got shot. That's all he needs to know to come after us with guns blazin'."

"And you and I used to beat the shit out of him back in River's Bend," Tex reminded his brother.

"He was younger and smaller then. He grew up to be bigger than anybody thought he would. Used to be a good hunter, too. He'll track us for sure."

"Let him come," Tim spoke up. He took another drink of whiskey from Randy's flask.

"Maybe we'll get the chance to take our time killin' him," Fats suggested.

"I'll just be glad to know when he's good and dead." Joe lit a cigar. "I know there's five of us, but he ain't gonna' just walk straight up and take all of us on at once. He ain't that stupid. It's what might be lurking in the shadows that makes me nervous."

"And we've been takin' turns keepin' watch at night," Tex reminded him. "There's only one direction he can come from and that's east, so that's all we need to worry about."

"I just think it was wrong to announce to everybody where we were headed when we rode out of town," Joe answered. "'Tell Matt Stover he can find us out west on the Outlaw Trail!' you had to go and shout it to everybody."

"Fuck you, little brother. I had fun yellin' that out. Matt put us in jail too many times to count, and it's time we had a final show-down with him. Killin' his wife might be the best thing that happened. If he's crazy enough to come lookin' for us in Outlaw Country, it will be the end of him, and he'll finally be off our backs for good. Besides, do you have any idea how big that country is? We'll be like needles in a haystack. Stover will be hard-pressed to ever find us in the first place. He'll end up goin' back home to his preacher daddy and kind mama. Half the women in River's Bend would be glad to marry him and keep him warm in their beds."

"How do you know the man's wife even died?" Fats asked him.

"Oh, she died, all right. I saw where she got hit," Tex answered. "Once in the chest, and once right through that baby and into her belly. I know bullet wounds, and there's no way that woman lived. Even if she didn't die, she would have suffered real bad, and the kid in her belly wouldn't have lived. Matt wouldn't let somethin' like that go. He'd still come after us just for what she would have gone through."

"Well, we have plenty of money," Tim spoke up. "We can live high wherever we go. We can buy the best whiskey and the best women. Maybe even start up a ranch. We could steal some cattle on the way there. I hear there are other ranches out there, men who'll be lookin' to buy some stock. There's real towns and real businesses, and I hear there are still wagon trains headed west— people who can't afford to go by train. They'd be easy pickin's. And speakin' of trains, I ain't never robbed one, but I'm willin' to try. They say there are such good places to hide from the law on the Outlaw Trail that a man can get away with pretty much anything and never get caught."

Joe sighed. "I hope you're right. I'm just glad to be out of River's Bend and away from those stale, righteous people. We never should have stayed as long as we did and worked Pa's worthless farm." He looked at Tim. "Best thing we ever did was leave there and go to Omaha and find you three and set up that bank robbery. It was a great way to bid farewell to the fine citizens of River's Bend."

They all chuckled.

"And we're all still young," Tex reminded them.

"Ain't one of us over thirty. We ought to have a lot of fun ahead of us, havin' at the women, drinkin' good whiskey, playin' cards and enjoyin' life the way it ought to be lived."

They all nodded.

"I'll still feel better once I know Matt Stover is no longer a part of this world," Joe reminded them. "Don't forget you raped that farm girl, Tex, right before the first time we left town. Goin' back to rob the bank and then killin' Lora Stover and that bank teller just added to Stover's determination to come after us."

"Stop your worryin'," Fats told him. "We're all young and able and good with guns. The man ain't got a chance."

"Yeah, Joe, you're embarrassing me," Tex told him. "Quit talkin' like a damn coward."

"*Coward!*" Joe tossed his cigar aside and jumped up. He walked to where his brother still stood by the fire. "You callin' me a *coward*?"

Tex laughed. "If the boots fit, little brother."

Joe lit into him, and the wrestling match was on. He barely missed shoving Tex into the fire. For the next few minutes, the two big men tossed each other around like five-year-olds while the three they'd picked up in Omaha looked on and laughed. Fats shouted for Tex to win and the other two rooted for Joe. Finally, the stout, brawny Tex landed a hard fist into the taller Joe's belly, sending him sprawling.

"Okay! Okay!" Joe said, putting out his hand. He rolled to his side and threw up the rabbit he'd just eaten. "I give up, you bastard."

Tex laughed hard, reaching down to grasp his brother's hand and help him up. "Might be me that loses next time, boy."

"I hope it is," Joe answered. "And don't call me boy or little brother." He wiped at his mouth with his shirtsleeve, then made a face. "Jesus, we all need to find a good bath house, don't we?"

"I'm sure we'll come across one in the next town. I think it's Sidney. Most of those railroad towns have good places to eat, good saloons, and bath houses. Won't be long after that we'll be in Wyoming and closer to Outlaw Country."

"We should have taken the train," Randy suggested, his words beginning to slur from too much whiskey.

"Nah, too expensive," Joe answered, rubbing at his stomach as he walked back to his bedroll. "Let's save our new-found cash for after we get where we're goin'." He brushed himself off before sitting down. "Besides, lawmen sometimes ride those trains, and sometimes it's those Pinkerton men the railroad's hired to keep a lookout for train robbers."

"I thought we already talked about robbing a train ourselves," Tex reminded him.

"I think we'd best lay low 'til we reach the mountains," Joe advised.

"'Cuz you're scared of Matt Stover?" Tex asked with a snicker.

"Shut up," Joe warned. "I'm just bein' smart, that's all."

"Whatever you say." Tex sat down and rested against his own saddle. "All I know is that I'm lookin' for a bath house in the next town and for the prettiest whore there."

"Get in line, boss man," Fats told him. "Get in line."

They all finally settled in for the night, except for Fats, who groaned and grunted as he got to his feet. "My turn to keep watch. Tim, I'll give you a nudge later and you can take over."

"Okay." Tim rubbed at his scar, then pulled a blanket over his shoulders, thinking how it was finally getting a little warmer at night. At least it was too early to be eaten up by mosquitoes. Soon as they reached the mountains, they wouldn't have to worry about such things. At least that's what he'd always heard.

"Don't be worryin' about Matt Stover," he heard Tex tell Joe. "Let him come, big brother. We'll be ready for him."

CHAPTER NINE

$\mathcal{M}$att struggled with grief and memories of seeing Lora buried, as now he watched Glen and Mark lower Bartley Kincade's blanket-wrapped body into the hole they'd dug for it. How strange that one burial could be so deeply grieved, and another meant nothing to him. He was a little surprised at his lack of feelings for Kincade. Worse, over the fact that he'd killed the man himself.

Sometimes he feared that in going after men like the Liberty brothers, he would become just like them, yet there was a little part of him that didn't care.

Losing Lora had affected his ability to care about *anything.* He'd loved her since he was a kid. And after losing two babies, they'd both been so excited about finally bringing a child into the world, a baby made in joy and love. Already he ached to be with a woman that way again, but he couldn't yet imagine even *wanting* another woman the way he'd wanted Lora, her nakedness against him in the night, wanting him inside her with as much passion as he felt *being* inside her.

I missed you, Matthew. He could hear her whispering to

him after he'd been gone a few days hunting someone. He felt so sorry that she could no longer enjoy the birds and the flowers she so loved, no longer dream about being a mother. It wasn't fair that she'd died so young. Someone had to pay. If Lora had to be dead, then so did the men who'd caused her senseless death...

..."Ashes to ashes, dust to dust," old John Grace said. He went on to read the Lord's Prayer from the Bible.

Matt thought how he'd heard that prayer too many times, preached over other people's graves. *Yea, though I walk through the valley of the shadow of death...* Lora had walked through that valley and had never come out. He took no hope in that prayer any longer.

Surely goodness and mercy shall follow me all the days of my life... Goodness and mercy had shown him no favors, and both were something he no longer carried in his own heart and soul. Hatred and revenge were more fitting.

He glanced at the woman called Elly, who seemed to be praying diligently. Why did she or any of these people care about the murdering horse-thief they were burying? Still, he couldn't help sensing a kindness and sincere goodness about Elly that reminded him of Lora. And she was herself a widow. What had her husband been like? Was he good to her? He'd been gone three years, he'd learned, died a slow death from cancer. Was watching a loved one take time to die different from or any worse than losing one in a shocking instant, the way he'd lost Lora? Was she grieving any differently? Had they loved each other the way he and Lora had? Did Elly Lowe miss being with a man? Miss feeling a man inside her in the fulfillment of love?

Elly raised her eyes and met his gaze. It seemed she was trying to tell him she was sorry for him—that life goes on and he'd be okay. He looked away, feeling guilty for thinking how pretty she was and wondering if she wanted a man to hold her again. Guilty for wanting to feel a woman in his arms, if for nothing more than to pretend it was Lora. He wanted to smell Lora's hair, feel her breasts against his chest, hear her gentle voice, taste her lips again.

But that could never be, and he had to get used to the idea. And he couldn't expect to find Lora again through some other woman. That was impossible. Lora was Lora, and she was gone. Dead. Lifeless. Buried. And so was their little girl.

Mark pounded a cross made from two pieces of scrap wood into the ground to mark the grave.

"Why mark it?" Matt wanted to ask. *"The man had no friends or family. He won't be missed, and no one will look for his grave."* He glanced at Pete, whose last name he'd learned was Garner. He'd uncuffed him this morning and let him eat breakfast. Betty and Elly had insisted he be allowed to sit and eat with the rest of them. Matt objected, but the women won out.

Now at the burial, he saw no true grief or regret in Pete's eyes, and he was sure Bartley had meant nothing to the man. He was just another hunter, someone to ride with, someone to help him kill men and steal horses. He figured the only reason Pete hadn't caught up to other fellow buffalo hunters was because Bartley had slowed him down. He was probably glad the man was dead.

"Well, I guess we'd best be on our way," Glen Baker spoke up. He put a hand on Elly's arm and walked her to the wagon she shared with her father. The quick burial had been the last event before leaving. Everyone and everything was packed up and ready to go.

Matt glanced at Pete again and caught him eyeing Elly like she was a fresh slice of pie. He moved into Pete's line of vision. "Time for you to leave."

"Who put *you* in charge?" Pete asked, scowling.

"*I* did, so get moving. You have two horses now, and you seem to be recovering just fine from your wound, so be on your way. And head southeast for a while. If I see you anywhere on the horizon and think you're following these good people, I'll put an end to it, understand?"

"Maybe they don't care."

"I think Mister Stover is probably right," Mark spoke up. He stood nearby, holding the reins to Pete's horse. "Glen and I talked last night and decided the sheriff here probably knows best. We're sorry you lost your friend, Pete, but my wife caught you looking at her last night in a way that made her uncomfortable. We've all been good to you and tried to help your friend, so I hope you'll afford us the same courtesy and just be on your way with no trouble." He handed a small gunny sack to Pete. "My wife packed you some biscuits and a couple of potatoes. You're lucky she was kind enough to do so."

"Thanks." After taking the bag of food, Pete turned to Matt and put his hand out to him. "No hard feelings?"

Matt looked him over scathingly. "*Plenty* of hard feelings." He refused to shake his hand. "Mount up, Pete, and quit trying to look like the good guy here. Take Bartley's horse and ride out. I intend to follow you for a few miles before re-joining these people and heading for Fort McPherson."

"You sonofabitch," Pete grumbled. "You have an eye on the widow over there, don't you?"

He hardly got the words out before Matt landed a fist into Pete's jaw, sending him flying. Both women cried out in surprise when they heard the blow and saw Pete hit the ground. Pete's horses skittered sideways and Mark had to jerk on the reins to steady them.

"Get going!" Matt ordered.

Pete slowly got to his knees and wiped at a bleeding mouth with the sleeve of his ratty-looking buffalo coat. Without another word, he tied the bag of food onto his saddle horn and mounted up, taking the reins to Bartley's horse and glaring with hatred at Matt. "We'll meet again," he promised.

"You'd be wise to make sure that doesn't happen," Matt told him.

Pete rode off and Matt met Mark's gaze. "I'm sorry for that remark he made. Apologize to your sister if she heard it. And to Glen. I know they're to be married." He put out his hand and Mark took it, shaking Matt's hand firmly.

"I don't think they even heard, and I know that man was just trying to make trouble."

"He was. I'm fresh widowed, Mark, and I have no interest in *any* woman. Not for a good long time. I appreciate the hospitality all of you showed me, and I'm sorry things had to be this way, but I know men like that. I'm sorry if I upset the women by my behavior."

Mark nodded. "I understand. I wanted to hit him, too." He pushed his hat back a little and picked up another gunny sack from where it sat beside him on the ground. "Betty packed you some food, too."

"I'm grateful." Matt told him, taking the bag of food. He nodded to Mark and headed for his horse.

"You really going to follow that man for a while?" Mark asked.

"You bet, even though it means heading backward for a day or so. But I'll catch up at Fort McPherson, and we'll say our final good-byes there. I'll have some time to make up for in finding the men I'm after, so I won't stay long at the fort."

"Well, we all wish you good luck," Mark told him.

Matt mounted Rusty and waved to the others. "Thank you, folks, for your kindness and for the food. Sorry about what just happened. Mark can explain."

The others waved, and Betty's two boys shouted enthusiastic good-byes.

"Come back and see us!" Tommy yelled.

"I plan on it." Being around the Grace family had stirred an ache inside Matt to have his own family again, but when he was finished with what he had to do, he wondered if he could ever live that way. It could never be like with Lora, and he was beginning to feel harder, beginning to lose those types of feelings.

He turned Rusty and headed to his camp to pick up his pack horse and the rest of his supplies. He wondered if he should just shoot Pete Garner so he wouldn't have to worry about what the man might do next. He decided not to look back at the Grace family and their wagons. It wasn't good for him to think about that kind of life... not when he was on a mission of revenge.

CHAPTER TEN

"*Y*ou're thinking about him, aren't you?"

The question came from Betty. Elly sat with her in Betty and Mark's wagon, helping rearrange some things so there would be more sleeping room for the boys.

"Thinking about who?" Elly asked coyly.

"You know exactly who I'm talking about. That sheriff who ran off that buffalo hunter and probably saved us some big troubles." Betty shoved a crate into an area at the edge of the wagon where it hardly fit. "I think he's handsome, and I saw how he looked at you... and, I might say, how *you* looked at *him*."

"Betty! You're such a romantic. Why would I be interested in a man I only *might* see one more time before we part ways forever?" She finished folding a pair of little Tommy's pants. "Besides that, he's freshly widowed and has no interest in another woman, especially considering he's headed for Outlaw Country, where no decent woman would dare go, and he's on a mission to kill men. He hardly sounds like a man any woman should even consider with any kind of interest at all."

"But you *are* interested, aren't you?" Betty hung a pan on a hook above. She then grasped Elly's hands. "Stop folding and answer me, Elly. And look at me when you do."

Elly met the discerning gaze in her sister-in-law's brown eyes. "You can be such a little devil sometimes, Betty Grace."

Betty smiled. "I'm *right*, aren't I?"

"Yes," Elly answered with a sigh. "It's ridiculous, I know, but I can't get him off my mind." She let go of Betty's hands and toyed with a loose thread in Tommy's pants. "I can't get over how sad and lonely he must be. I think he's even lonelier because he's going against his deepest beliefs by wanting to murder those men. I can understand he might need to shoot a man in self-defense, and in keeping the law. But to just decide to kill men out of vengeance is a whole different matter. I just don't think it's truly in his blood to do something like that."

"Maybe when the time comes, he'll find another way. Or maybe once it's out of his blood, he'll go back to the man he was. And that man will eventually want a woman again, and a family to make up for the one he lost."

Elly frowned and shook her head. "Honestly, Betty, you're talking nonsense! We're on our way to California, and Matt Stover's on his way to a place of lawlessness. He might never even get out of there alive. And if he does, we'll be settled in California by then, and he won't know where we are."

"Unless when we get to Fort McPherson you tell him the general area in California where my brother lives," Betty suggested. "Who knows? Matt Stover might go there first once he's done with what he intends to do, before he goes back home."

"And by then I'll probably be married to Glen."

"You don't love Glen that way. You told me so yourself. But you could love Matt Stover, couldn't you?"

"Pish-tish!" Elly waved her off and reached for another pair of pants to fold. "It's no wonder you're always happy. You have a difficult time facing reality. I wish I could be more like you that way, but reality says that what you're thinking is absolutely ridiculous and impossible. I wish you would change the subject."

"Well, I won't, because I don't think you'd be happy with Glen Baker even if another man *wasn't* in the picture. You need to start telling Glen that now, so he doesn't get his hopes up for California. All he talks about is marrying you when we get there. The poor man is lonely, Elly, but he needs to understand he should look elsewhere once we settle."

Elly set the second pair of pants in a pile. "I know." She blinked back tears. "I'm so torn, Betty. I like Glen, but I don't love him. I know I should consider another husband, but I think I should wait until we get to California and meet new people." She met Betty's gaze again. "Didn't Lester mention in one of his letters that he had a neighbor about my age who wasn't married and was interested in meeting me?"

"Yes. I never told Mark because I was afraid he'd tell Glen. And I was afraid Glen wouldn't come along at all if he knew what my brother said in that letter. I feel sorry for the man, and Mark and I both wanted him to come along and start a new life in California. And when I answered Lester's letter, I didn't mention that you might be interested in meeting his neighbor. I just hope he really did get the letter and knows we're coming."

"I'm sure he'll be happy to see you whether he knows or not." Elly put a hand to Betty's cheek. "How are you feeling? Have you told Mark yet that you're carrying?"

"No. I want to wait until we get into Wyoming and it's

too late to turn back." Betty smiled, taking Elly's hand again. "Don't be worrying about me. I've had two very healthy pregnancies. This one should be no different. And it's time you found a good man and had children of your own."

Elly reached for a shirt. "I heard the unspoken words in that statement, dear sister-in-law. I'm not getting any younger. I know that."

"Well you *are* still young and you're beautiful. And don't think Mister Matt Stover didn't notice. That first time you marched up to him and scolded him for not giving that buffalo hunter any laudanum, I saw the look in his eyes. You surprised him, and not just by your demands. He was taken back by your looks. Maybe you look a little like his dead wife. I don't know. But he darn well noticed, and he liked what he saw."

"Maybe so, but it's all useless, Betty. He might not even show up at Fort McPherson before we get there and leave again, so I might never see the man again."

"Then we have to think positive."

"That he'll be there?" Elly sighed and shook her head. "I almost hope he *doesn't* show, because if he does and we talk more and get better acquainted, it'll just be harder for me to see him ride off, never to be seen again."

Betty snickered. "So, you *do* have a strong interest." She set the folded pants into a trunk. "You listen to me, Elly Grace Lowe. If that man shows up at the fort, you *talk* to him, and you tell him where we'll be settling in California. I'm willing to bet he'll come looking for you, so you set things straight with Glen and you give yourself a few weeks or months after we settle before you make any big decisions. You don't love Glen anyway, so it won't bother you to wait."

"Yes, well Mark would be angry with you for talking like this. He and Glen are good friends."

"Phooey! Men don't understand a woman's heart. And it's your life. If you decide against marrying Glen, he'll just have to live with it. You leave Mark to me. I can handle your brother just fine."

Elly smiled. "Considering you're carrying again, it sounds to me like *he's* the one who handles *you* just fine."

Both women laughed, and someone knocked on the side of the wagon.

"What are you two doing in there?" came Mark's voice.

"Just sharing a good time," Betty answered.

"You done rearranging things?" Mark asked, walking around to the back of the wagon.

"I did the best I could."

"Yeah, well, the boys are going to have to sleep with Elly some night soon, woman, so I can have you to myself."

"Mark Grace!" Betty chided, her cheeks quickly turning beet red.

"Just speaking the truth, honey." Mark laughed and turned away.

"We'd better fix some lunch," Elly told Betty. "Fill a man's belly and he's not so frisky. I remember that much from being married."

Betty smiled but quickly looked sorry. "Oh, Elly, you must be so lonely. Mark shouldn't talk that way in front of you, and neither should I."

"It's okay. I'm happy that *you* are both happy. That's all that matters. And if makes you even happier if Matt Stover shows up at Fort McPherson, I'll talk to him again, but only if he asks. I'm not going to be so forward as to approach him first. And I have to be careful of Glen's feelings."

"I understand." Betty closed the trunk. "It's just that I have kind of a premonition about that man running into us, or us running into him, whichever way you look at it. I figure everything happens for a reason, and there's some reason Matt Stover ended up in our camp that night. I'll bet any money he's thinking about you right now, just like you're thinking about him."

"And you need to write romantic poetry or something," Elly told her. "I prefer to see things as they really are. It saves disappointment later." She crawled to the back of the wagon. "I'm going to start lunch." She started to climb down, but someone grasped her about the waist and lifted her down.

"Did I hear the word lunch?" Glen asked, setting Elly on her feet.

Elly struggled to act pleased at his help. "Yes, you did. I'll fix something now."

"Thanks. Mark and John and I are hungry." Without asking, he leaned down and kissed her cheek, then walked away.

Elly realized her heart had gone from hopeful and fluttery over the thought of possibly seeing Matt Stover again, to being a bit dashed to the ground by realizing what Glen expected of her. And that she needed to set him straight.

So, she thought, *again you see me as someone who can cook for you.* She suspected a man like Matt Stover would see her as much more than that, then scolded herself for giving Matt any thought at all.

CHAPTER ELEVEN

LATE MAY...

*M*att kept Rusty at a slow amble as he rode into Fort McPherson. It had taken four days to get there—the first full day spent making sure Pete Garner kept heading southeast, another spent going back, and two more reaching the fort. He'd be surprised if the Grace party was still there, and he told himself he shouldn't care. He was irritated that he'd lost so much time chasing after Pete.

He told himself it was ridiculous to even stop at the fort, but then he did need a few supplies, and Rusty and Sadie needed a good rest.

That was his legitimate excuse, but he couldn't deny his other reason for coming. Her name was Elly. He wanted to see her again, and he damn well couldn't deny it.

What he couldn't understand was *why*. She was headed for California, and he was on a mission to find men somewhere along the Outlaw Trail. What he was doing could take weeks and weeks, while the Grace family went on to California and settled and, likely, Elly would marry Glen Baker and that would be it.

So why in God's name did he care about seeing her again? There was just something about her... those green eyes, her build, her gentle voice. It was probably nothing more than missing Lora. And it could be that part of his reason was because he hated the fact Elly Lowe probably thought him a cold-hearted killer. She'd said she didn't believe he was, but for some reason he wanted to be sure she truly understood that he wasn't.

He headed for the supply store, the other side of his inner argument reminding him that Lora's horrible death and the loss of his baby girl were still so fresh in his heart that he wasn't even interested in finding another woman. To be thinking about Elly Lowe made him feel like he was committing some kind of sin against Lora. Yet a little part of him felt he'd been led to that wagon party, and Lora's belief that "everything happens for a reason" nagged at him.

Was Lora's spirit leading him? Was this her way of trying to make him change his mind about going after the Liberty boys? If she were alive, she'd beg him not to go. She would tell him he was doing this for all the wrong reasons. He was behaving not as a lawman but as a determined killer led by hate. And that is what Elly Lowe had told him in so many words.

So be it. That's exactly what he was, and that's what he'd remain until he found his revenge. He'd never rest or be able to live with himself if he didn't do what he'd set out to do.

He halted Rusty and looked around the sprawling and very busy fort. The officer's quarters, mess hall, commissary, barns and the buildings and cabins for regular soldiers were all made of what looked like cedar logs. Soldiers marched in drills far to his left, and a huge corral nearby held a herd of horses. People of various walks of life milled about. Some appeared to be trappers or hunters, a couple of natives he figured scouted for the Army, and quite a few emigrants, most likely heading for places farther west.

He shaded his eyes to study a cluster of covered wagons sitting just beyond the corral of horses, straining to see if the wagons belonging to the Grace party might be among them. He couldn't help a little jolt of joy when he recognized them by the plow tied to the side of Glen's wagon, and an American flag sewn to the side of the canvas top of Mark and Betty's. He figured Glen or Mark must be guarding their horses and cattle somewhere on the sprawling grassland beyond the fort.

So, they're still here. With a sigh of actual anger at himself for caring, he dismounted and tied Rusty to a hitching post, figuring he might as well get his supplies now and find out if the fort had a bath house for travelers. If he decided to look for Elly, he'd like to be clean and shaved this time. He'd certainly been neither one when he stayed with them the night he took laudanum to them, and after four more days of hard riding, he figured maybe Rusty smelled better than he did. And lately when he scratched at his chin, he'd noticed the stiff stubble there had turned softer, which meant it was turning into an all-out beard.

He walked up a couple of steps and into a supply store he could tell wasn't part of the fort. Civilians often ran their own businesses and farms in and around army forts, and sometimes they stocked more supplies than the Army did, often at cheaper prices.

A hefty, bearded man who wore no uniform stood behind a glass counter that boasted an array of tobacco products, guns and ammunition.

"The price stands, mister," the big man was telling a

customer wearing buckskins whose body odor filled the small store with the stench of old blood.

Matt knew the customer had to be another buffalo hunter. Too many such men did their skinning without washing afterward, let alone the buffalo blood getting on their clothes. Matt noticed a woman shopper put a handkerchief to her nose and hurry out.

"I ain't payin' that kind of money for ammo for my buff'lo gun," the man in buckskins told the bearded man.

"Then you ain't *gettin'* any ammo," the bearded man answered.

The man in buckskins grabbed the store keeper's vest and jerked him half-way across the counter. "Maybe I'll just *take* what I need without *payin'* for it!" he roared.

Matt quickly pulled out his .44 and, pressing the barrel Iagainst the buffalo hunter's left temple, cocked the gun. "Maybe you should just let go of that man," he suggested.

The hunter glanced sideways with mostly just his eyes, turning his head only a little. "Who the hell are you?"

"Just a traveler who doesn't like thieves and bullies."

With Matt's gun still to his head, the bullish hunter let go of the clerk, giving him a little shove as he did so. "This ain't your business," he warned Matt.

"I'm *making* it my business. I've been on a hard ride for days, and I'm tired and dirty and sick of running into vermin like you." Matt stepped back a little and aimed his gun steadily. The hunter's body odor made Matt's upper lip curl a little. "You wouldn't happen to know a man by the name of Pete Garner, would you?" he asked.

The hunter squinted as he studied Matt closer. "Hell yes, I know him. Been lookin' for him and three other men that took off from our party to hunt on their own."

Matt looked around the store and it was then that he noticed Betty Grace standing in a corner by some bolts of material. She looked terrified but nodded to him. He looked back at the hunter. "Mister, you won't find any of your friends, except maybe for Pete, but he's a good four or five days from here and headed in the wrong direction... southeast."

"How would you know that?" the hunter asked with a frown.

"Because they all tried to kill me and take my horses, and let's just say they made a big mistake."

"What the—? Did you *kill* them?"

"I had no choice." Matt backed a little farther away but kept his gun pointed at the hunter. "Now, either pay the man behind the counter, or get out of here. You're stinking up the place."

The short but very burly man put a hand on the handle of a big knife he wore at his waist.

"A bullet is a lot faster than a knife," Matt warned.

"Depends on how experienced a man is with one of these toothpicks," the hunter answered.

"And your friends died because one of them went for his weapon. Two went down right away and two more were wounded. One of them died later. Which way do you want to go, mister? Quick? Or slow? Where I put a bullet can make all the difference."

The hunter relaxed a little, stepped back a little more, then started to turn to the man behind the counter. He was met with a big club that landed across the side of his head. Betty let out a little scream when the stranger fell to the floor with a thud. Another man inside the store gasped and hurried out. The bearded man behind the counter grinned, revealing that one tooth was missing in front.

"You didn't need to help out, mister, but thanks," the bearded man told Matt. He held up the wooden club. "This is how I generally deal with anybody who threatens to steal from me or threatens to kill me because he doesn't like my prices." He put the club down and held out his hand. "Darryl Mason."

Matt holstered his gun and shook Mason's hand. "Matt Stover."

Darryl nodded, still grinning. "Would you mind dragging him out of here? I have a bad back and can't do it, and you look big and strong, Stover. I'll give you some free tobacco for your trouble. Just throw him outside. He'll wake up in time."

Getting that close to the buffalo hunter was the last thing Matt wanted to do, but he also wouldn't mind some free tobacco. "I'll get rid of him for you," he answered. He glanced at Betty and nodded. "Hello, Mrs. Grace," he told her. "Sorry you had to see all this."

Betty just stared at him, looking a bit bewildered. She finally found her voice. "Hello, Matt. I didn't recognize you at first." She looked down at the unconscious buffalo hunter. "You just did what you had to do," she added, meeting Matt's gaze again.

Matt smiled. "You'll recognize me better after I find a place to take a bath and shave. I'm glad to find your family still here."

Betty nodded. "We're leaving in the morning. I'm sure Mark and Elly and the rest would like it if you visited this evening."

"I'll do that."

"Mister, are you going to drag that sonofabitch out of here or not?"

Matt directed his attention back to store owner. "For free tobacco? Sure, I'll get rid of him." He glanced at Betty again. "I'll see you later."

"Everyone will be glad to know you're all right and you made it here before we left," Betty told him.

Matt reached down to grasp the buffalo hunter under the arms.

"Oh, by the way, I hear there's a dance tonight," Betty told him. "Elly and I definitely want to go. I'm sure Elly wouldn't mind one or two dances with you." Her cheeks reddened, and Matt had a feeling she wished she hadn't said that. He picked up the hint that Elly had been thinking about him.

"If I can clean up properly by then, I'll be there," he told Betty. "Thank you." With a grunt he got a good hold of the buffalo hunter and dragged him to the door, held open by the man who'd run out earlier but came back to peek inside and see what was happening. Matt pulled the unconscious man along the boardwalk and off into an alley between the supply store and a livery, then let go of his heavy, limp body. He looked down at blood on his shirt from the man's head wound, and it hit him then that things like this were going to grow more common the farther west he went. Law meant nothing out here. Men had to deal with issues like this as best they could, and life would become more and more a matter of survival of the fittest. He didn't even know this man's name.

He straightened and headed back to the boardwalk, then stopped in surprise when he saw a woman standing at the corner watching him.

"Elly!"

Her eyes were wide with a mixture of shock, joy, confusion and apprehension. "What on earth are you doing?"

Matt realized how awful this situation must look to her. And he was embarrassed at his filthy, bearded condition. All he could think of was to get the hell away. "I—uh—Betty's inside the supply store. She can explain." He hurried past her and walked over to Rusty, untying the horse and mounting up. He rode to what looked like a laundry station. Maybe he could get a bath there.

He figured he'd have to go back later for his free

tobacco, and now he wasn't sure he should bother looking up the Grace family at all. Betty had seen him hold a gun to man's head, and Elly saw him dump that man in an alley like so much garbage.

"Damn! What a way to run into Elly Lowe again," he grumbled.

CHAPTER TWELVE

*I*t seemed to Elly that every time she saw Matt Stover, he was involved in some kind of violence. She wanted to believe he wasn't really the hard, uncaring man he'd become since his wife's death, but he'd dropped that hunter's body beside the supply store as though the man were no more than a sack of flour. He did seem embarrassed when he caught her watching, and now she felt embarrassed herself that she'd watched at all, especially because she'd actually cared about Matt's well-being. What he did was not her business.

"It's a nice night," Glen told her, bringing her thoughts back to him as they danced together.

"Oh, it is. Cool and clear. Just perfect," Elly answered.

Small talk, she thought. She couldn't help glancing at others, a little part of her hoping Matt would show up after all. She and Glen moved in circles at arm's length as they waltzed to a lovely tune played by a fairly decent army orchestra comprised of three fiddles, a guitar, a coronet and drums. She smiled at Glen, feeling guilty at the fact that her thoughts had been on someone else. Here she was dancing with a man she'd known for years and who wanted to marry her, but she was thinking about a man she'd met just a few days ago and who'd come and gone like the wind.

Running into him again in that awkward encounter at the supply store could hardly be counted as another meeting. There had been no conversation. Just the embarrassment.

Still, she couldn't help being impressed by what Mark had told her was the reason Matt hit Pete Garner the morning he chased the man away from their wagon train. He'd defended her and Betty against Pete's rude remarks. Of course, her sister-in-law explained both encounters like a giddy school girl would tell a secret, again insisting she felt the handsome, brave and able Matt Stover was meant to be a part of their lives.

"Have you thought any more about getting married?" Glen asked her. "I think the commander of a fort can perform marriages, or they might even have a preacher here. Most forts have chapels or some way to worship on Sundays."

Elly watched his eyes, where she saw practicality and a tiny bit of sternness that said *Isn't it about time you made up your mind?* But she didn't see adoration or passion, and he still had not said those three magic words—*I love you.* The music ended, and she led Glen aside while an Army private began calling a square dance. Others whooped and whistled and began stepping to the music and the calls while Elly and Glen stood away from it all.

"I'm going to wait, Glen. It's like I told you. I don't want to act on mixed feelings or need while we're traveling like this. I want to be settled and relaxed, but even then, I—" She took a deep breath before saying the words. "I just don't know if I love you that way. You've been a good friend and a big help to my whole family through losing loved ones and that awful fire. You suffered, too, and I'm sorry for that. But I just feel you want a wife only to cook and clean for you and to give you more children. Most men want those things, but I don't want to marry for that only. I've waited all this time and you've never once said you love me."

Glen frowned. "*Love* you?" He leaned down and kissed her lightly, but again, his lips felt cool. "Of *course,* I love you. I figured you knew that."

Elly shook her head. "A woman needs to *hear* it, Glen. And willingly, not just because she asks a man to tell her if it's so."

"Well I *do* love you. I'm sorry I haven't said it before. I guess I'm just not the gushy, passionate type."

Maybe I want gushy and passionate, she thought. "I understand. But even if you do love me, a woman needs that special feeling in order to fully be a wife. I thought traveling together all the way to California would help, and it just might. We'll be sharing a lot of time together, and we'll have more time to talk than we did back home where there were so many chores to do and tending to the farm and all. This trip forces us to be together more."

Glen nodded. "Elly, sometimes you just have to be practical about these things. Heck, there are mail-order brides who come out here to marry total strangers because men and women need each other for a lot of different reasons."

There it was again—that word practical. "I am well aware of that, but I'm not the kind of woman who thinks she can't survive without a man. I don't want to marry just for that or for money and property. I'm so sorry I can't give you a better answer or just hurriedly get married because it's the practical thing to do. You're a good, kind, hard-working man, Glen. I appreciate that. And after a few more weeks together, maybe I will feel completely different. I just don't want to make any decisions until we get to California."

"I guess I can understand that." Glen grasped her arms. "Just know that I won't change my mind about this. We'll keep talking on this trip, and I'll help you any way you need it, and I'll protect you and hunt game for you and at least be your friend. You keep in mind that I want to be *more* than a friend, but I'll try not to press you on the subject anymore."

Elly smiled for him, while couples whirled past them, laughing, the women sometimes letting out little screams of joy and humor as the private called out all kinds of silly moves for the square dance. "I appreciate your understanding. Just your patience makes me care about you more." She leaned forward and kissed his cheek. "Thank you for the dances and the fun, but don't you have to go relieve Mark in watching over the cattle and horses?"

Glen pulled out a pocket watch and studied it by the light of an oil lamp. "Yeah, it's my turn for watch. I'm sure Betty would like a few dances with Mark." He squeezed her arms. "You stay close to the others. This country out here isn't the safest for women, so don't go beyond the light of this area."

"Yes, sir," Elly answered with a smile. "And you be careful out there."

"Sure."

Glen left, and Elly stood there alone for a moment, watching the dancers, wondering if she was a complete fool for constantly pushing away a man who was solid and steady and a good provider, as well as a good friend. She watched Betty dance with a soldier and her father with an older Army wife who'd recently been widowed. She realized Glen was right. Out here marriage sometimes did have to be for practical reasons.

"Elly?"

She turned at a man's voice. He stood just enough in the light that she recognized him. She'd never seen him so cleanly-dressed and shaved, his dark hair lying in soft waves and pushed behind his ears, his eyes a glittering blue by the light of a lantern.

"Matt!" Why did she feel like running into his arms?

CHAPTER THIRTEEN

*M*att stepped closer, thinking that Elly looked prettier than ever. Her dark hair was pulled up at the sides with spring wildflowers pinned into it at the crown. She wore a green gingham dress that perfectly fit her slender curves. He noticed an auburn glint to her hair by the light of the lantern, and her green eyes seemed to have flecks of gold in them. Right now, they glittered with what he could only interpret as joy at seeing him.

He immediately warned himself he should ignore any interest he saw in those lovely eyes. Maybe he shouldn't have come here at all. It wasn't good for his determination that this would be the last time he saw this woman. But he'd seen her with Glen, saw him kiss her and her kiss him, though only on the cheek. Why in God's name did that bother him?

"I just... I wanted to apologize for what you saw earlier today."

Now it was Elly who stepped closer. "It's all right. Betty explained what happened, and that the supply store owner actually hit that man over the head. In fact, Mark told us why you punched Pete Garner the morning he left us. That was quite chivalrous of you."

Matt shook his head. "There was nothing chivalrous about it. The man's remark made me angry, so I hit him. I seem to be controlled more by anger lately than anything else, and you seem to keep seeing the worst of me."

Elly folded her arms and looked at him confidently. "Well, I sense a very *good* side to you, too. I've had time to think about why you are headed for Outlaw Country, and how much you must be hurting deep inside. A man has his pride, and you seem to be the type who believes in righting a wrong. You couldn't do a good job as sheriff if you weren't that type of man, and I had no right judging you over your treatment of Pete. In fact, since we hardly know each other and have met only once, I had no right judging *anything* about you."

Matt shrugged, trying not to be bothered by the light scent of some soap or perfume when he stepped even closer. It made him want to nuzzle her neck or sniff her hair. *Damn!* What was it about this woman he hardly knew and who should mean nothing to him?

"First impressions," he told her. "And I sure didn't make a very good one when I first met up with you and your family. Heck, I didn't make a very good *second* impression this morning, either! That's why I didn't wear my gun tonight. See?" He held out his arms. "No weapons."

They both laughed lightly. Nervously. Shyly. It was so obvious she wanted to say more, and he *definitely* wanted to say more. "Is, uh, is Glen coming back to dance with you?"

Elly looked off into the darkness. "No. He went out to relieve Mark watching our stock so Mark could come and dance with Betty."

Matt told himself not to let his relief show in his eyes.

"Would you be willing to allow me one dance? I promise not to hit anybody."

They both laughed again. "Yes, we can dance."

The band started another waltz. "Thank goodness it's a slow one," Matt told her, taking her arm and leading her out to where the others were dancing. "I'm no good at square dancing. I never get all the calls right."

Elly smiled. "Well, if I knew you better and we saw each other more often, I'd teach you. You'd enjoy it." She took his left hand with her right one and put her left to his right shoulder. Matt put a hand to her waist. He wanted to pull her close, but he kept her at a proper arm's length. "I'm not even real good at *slow* dancing," he told her.

"Didn't your wife teach you? Surely, she liked to dance. *All* women like to dance."

There it was again. That awful stab to the chest. His smile faded as he turned her to the music.

"Oh, I'm so sorry," Elly exclaimed. "I shouldn't have said that! She died so recently." They turned more. "Please forgive me."

"It's okay. It's a natural remark. And you're right. Lora did try to teach me. I pretty much got the hang of waltzing, but for some reason I'm just no good at the other. Back in River's Bend, I always let her square dance with a friend of mine who loved the crazy calls and even entered contests."

They turned to the music again and again, experiencing a sudden awkward silence. Matt realized Elly was still embarrassed at her remark. He squeezed her hand. She looked ready to cry.

"It's okay. Really."

"But it's still so fresh for you." She stopped dancing. "Would you like to just get some punch and go someplace and talk for a bit? I mean, we're leaving in the morning, and we'll likely never see each other again. Maybe it would help you to talk about your wife."

"What about you? Aren't you a widow?"

"Yes. And that's why I understand, although the way I lost my husband wasn't nearly as shocking and tragic as what happened to your wife. I mean, I'd known he was dying for weeks before it happened."

Matt frowned. "That's too bad. I'm sorry." He kept a hand to her waist and led her to a table of food and punch. Betty was helping serve while she waited for Mark, and her face lit up when she saw Elly and Matt.

"Well, hello. My goodness, Mister Stover, you look much better than when I saw you earlier today."

"Yes, well, I was pretty filthy from too many days of hard riding. And I had a pretty good beard started."

Betty dipped a ladle into a punch bowl and poured each of them a glass. "I'm so glad you decided to come to the dance."

"Thank you." Matt took his punch, thinking how a good, stiff drink right now would be more to his liking. Maybe then he could relax more around Elly. "And I apologize for what you saw in the store this morning."

"No need," Betty answered. "That man got what he deserved. He had horrible manners, threatened that store owner, and he was the worst-smelling human being I've ever encountered." She laughed and glanced at Elly. "Have you two been dancing?"

Elly took her punch. "Just for a few minutes. We've decided to go talk instead, since we'll probably never see each other again."

Betty's eyebrows raised, and Matt didn't miss the way Elly looked at her—one of those "let's talk later" kind of looks.

"I think that's a very good idea," Betty told them. "And you, Mister Stover, be sure to look up me and Mark before tomorrow morning. Mark will want to see you once more before we all part ways."

Matt nodded. "I'll do that." He looked at Elly. "Let's go over there to the mess hall, where those kerosene lamps are lit. It isn't safe for you to be in the dark, and there's a bench over there we can sit on." He headed past the dancers and the make-shift orchestra, past the crowd of travelers and soldiers and traders and up a couple of steps to a wooden walkway in front of the mess hall. He let Elly sit down first, then sat beside her. He drank the whole cup of punch quickly and set the glass on the boardwalk. He put an arm across the back of the bench behind Elly, wanting to put it around her shoulders instead. "You warm enough?"

"Yes, I'm fine. It really warmed up today, didn't it?" She drank some of her punch.

"Pretty soon it will be all-out hot, but by then you'll be in the mountains, so you don't have to worry about the heat or the mosquitoes. You won't find either one in the mountains, or so I'm told. I'm a man of the prairie myself."

"So are we. Kansas is all I've ever known."

"Nebraska isn't much different."

Their gazes held. Small talk again. Why on earth was he even sitting here with this woman?

"No, it isn't," she answered. "I'm a little nervous about the mountains, but you might like to know we've found a guide and four other wagons to travel with."

Matt put his left foot up on his right knee and relaxed a little more at the news. "Good. I'm glad your father took my advice on that. I won't worry so much about you now."

Again, they shared a look that said more than words. "May I ask you something, Matt?"

"Sure."

"*Why* would you worry about people you hardly know?"

Why did he want to grasp the long hair that brushed against his hand? He took his arm from the back of the bench and put his foot down so he could lean forward and rest his elbows on his knees and not look at her. "I guess because I can see what nice people you and your family are, that's all. When I run into people like those buffalo hunters, it angers me to know how badly they would treat you if they had the chance. After what happened to my wife, I know just how evil some people can be. I don't like to see that." He finally met her gaze again. "I want you to be careful. Don't trust strangers out here, Elly."

She smiled softly. "But I trusted *you* almost from the minute I met you."

"That's because you already knew I was a lawman and that Glen had already met and befriended me."

She finished her punch and set the glass on the boardwalk near her feet. "I suppose. But most people have a natural instinct about others. You think I trusted Pete, but I didn't. I just thought that helping him and his friend was the Christian thing to do, and the best way to keep him friendly. Glen and Mark and my father were wary and were ready to defend us if necessary, although they weren't as defensive and judgmental as you were."

"That's because Pete and Bartley had already tried to kill me and take my horses."

Elly nodded. "True." She sighed. "It's a different world out here. It's always a little frightening and lonely to be away from all things familiar."

"More for a woman than a man, I suppose. I've had to go after lawbreakers far from home before, and I was a deputy sheriff in Omaha for a couple of years, so being away from River's Bend isn't so bad for me. It's not the town or even my folks I miss." He sobered more. "It's

Lora. I could live anywhere or go back home to our house there, and the pain wouldn't be any better or any worse." He studied her beautiful eyes. "You know the pain I'm talking about."

She held his gaze. "Yes, I do. But it's a tiny bit easier for me because it's been three years now. Time does help ease the pain, Matt, and life does go on. You'll find that out. In the meantime, I'll pray for you—for your safety in what you're determined to do—and that you'll find love again. I hope you satisfy whatever it is you need to satisfy when you find those men, and that you'll go back home where there are people who still love you and you'll find happiness again."

Matt nodded. "I hope the same for you, except, of course, that you find those things in California. Will you marry Glen?"

Elly closed her eyes and looked away. "I don't know. It feels more like a marriage of convenience, and I don't want that. I want true love again." She suddenly sucked in her breath and put her hands to her cheeks. "I can't believe I just admitted something so intimate to a complete stranger, let alone a *man!*"

Matt smiled. "There's nothing wrong with that. I'm hoping for the same thing myself, but like you said, it's all too fresh for me. Right now, I can't even consider loving another woman like I loved Lora." *We have so much in common, don't we?* He wanted to say the words, but it would embarrass her, and what did it matter? He rose. "I'd better get you back to the others. It wouldn't look too good, us going off alone like this for too long. I don't want to cause problems with you and your family, or you and Glen."

"It's all right." Elly picked up her glass and also stood up. "Glen Baker doesn't own me, although sometimes he behaves as though he does." She smiled softly. "He's a good man, Matt, a hard worker, a good provider, and kind. I have no doubt he would never abuse me or anything like that. But I can't say that I love him the way a wife should love her husband. He's more just a good friend, so I have a lot to think about."

Matt felt lost in her eyes. "For all you know, once you settle in California, you'll meet some other man who suits you better." Why did he care? That was a ridiculous thing to say.

"And the same could happen to you, once you go back to River's Bend."

"*If* I go back."

"What do you mean?"

Matt shrugged. "I'm not even sure. What happens in Outlaw Country might change me completely. Maybe I'll never leave there." He stepped closer, studying her gaze again, smelling that lovely scent, noticing the deep red sheen to her hair. "Or I might even go on to California and look up you and your family and make sure you got there okay."

Surprise lit up Elly's eyes. "You would do that? *Why*?"

He held her gaze again, not sure how to answer. Instead, he pulled her away from the light. "Elly—" He found her mouth then, tasted it, parted her lips, relished the feel of kissing a woman again. To his surprise she kissed him back—deeply.

Elly threw her arms around his neck, and the kiss lingered, and lingered. She let out a little whimper, and he groaned with the feel of a woman against him again. He pressed her close, enjoying the taste of her mouth, the feel of her warm breath, the smell of her skin and hair. He ran one hand into the thick tresses that hung down her back.

Wake up! A voice screamed at him then from somewhere deep inside.

He quickly let go of her and pulled away. "My God,"

he uttered. "I'm so sorry, Elly. I'm so sorry. I don't know why I did that!"

She seemed speechless. She put her fingers to her lips. Were those tears he saw in her eyes?

"Please forgive me. I was missing my wife, and you're so sweet and you remind me of her... I mean... your eyes. They're just like hers. But I had no right!" He turned away. "Sweet Jesus," he muttered softly. The taste of her mouth still lingered on his lips. The smell of her was still in his nose, probably on his shirt.

"I... I shouldn't have let you," she said in a tiny voice then. "I mean, we're leaving in the morning and I'll likely never see you again. And I hardly know you! What... what must you think of me."

"I don't think anything bad, Elly." He reached out for her, but she stepped away. "It's all right. *I'm* the one who was in the wrong."

She stepped farther away. "Did you... did you mean what you said? About coming to California?"

Matt looked her over. So beautiful. So devastated. "I don't even know. It all depends on what happens when I find those men—how I feel by then. I mean, I'm just confused and lonely right now and I—" He didn't know what else to say.

"You were missing Lora. That's what you said. That's all it was." She let out a little whimper. "I'm sorry, too, Matt. You go do what you need to do. I still intend to pray for you." She stepped even farther away, heading toward the dancers. "I'll go back on my own. It might be better if we don't walk back together." She watched him a moment longer. "Good-bye, Matt Stover. God bless you." She turned and half ran back to the dancers.

Matt watched after her, feeling like the biggest fool and worst cad who ever lived. What in God's name had gotten into him? "You *idiot!*" He cursed himself every which way and looked around for his punch glass. He couldn't find it in the dark. "The hell with it," he muttered. Someone would find it. He hurried off to where he was camped for the night. It was senseless now to go back to the dance and see Betty or Mark. And God knew he didn't want to face Glen Baker. Seeing them off in the morning was going to be so awkward.

Would Elly tell Glen what he'd done? He wouldn't blame the man if he socked him right in the mouth. If he did, he'd not hit the man back. He *deserved* a sock in the mouth, and a slap from Elly.

This was the result of his intense grief for Lora—a grief he didn't know how to handle. He could only hope Elly understood that. The taste of her mouth, the feel of her body against his—it all just heightened his devastation over losing Lora. He walked off into the darkness.

"My God, Lora, help me with this," he muttered, feeling like he needed to cry. He leaned against a pine tree and let the tears come, realizing that through all this grief over losing Lora, he still had not truly cried. Men weren't supposed to cry, were they? Yet somehow, he felt that if he finally released this pent-up, desperate sorrow, he'd feel stronger afterward, more ready to go after the men who'd caused all of this, and more able to put Elly Lowe out of his thoughts. He sank to the ground, groaning Lora's name.

CHAPTER FOURTEEN

*E*lly forced back tears as she folded her sleeping
quilt and stuffed it away along with her pillow
and feather mattress. She hadn't had a chance to talk to
Betty about walking off with Matt Stover last night. When
she got back, Betty was dancing with Mark, and they'd all
soon retired to their wagons to prepare to leave early this
morning. With Mark and the boys around Betty constantly
until they all went to sleep, she'd not had one moment
alone with her.

She wore a simple gray dress with only a couple of
slips, which was more practical for travel. Her hair was
pulled back and pinned into a plain bun at the back of her
head, and because the morning had turned chilly, she wore
a light woolen shawl mantle, a bit dressy for traveling in a
covered wagon, but a secret part of her wanted to look
nice in case Matt showed up.

She had to admit that last night she'd wanted to look
pretty, too—for Matt Stover. Now she could kick herself
for caring. Her guilt over his kiss burdened her, and she
felt like a traitor to Glen, even though she was in no way
committed to him.

If only Matt's kiss hadn't been so wonderfully warm and soft and delicious and gentle and genuine... a kiss that said everything. He'd wanted her. The worst part was that *she'd* wanted *him*! She felt like a harlot, a cheater, a lonely, desperate woman who'd turned to a complete stranger like some saloon woman.

Was that how Matt was thinking about her this morning? Loose and wanton? She felt humiliated, and she wanted to cry - not because of all these mixed emotions, but because she could hardly stand the thought of parting ways and very likely never seeing Matt Stover again.

Had he meant it—about coming to California to find her? Surely not now—not after the way she'd returned his kiss with such blatant desire. She grabbed the coffee pot and a little cloth bag of ground coffee beans, then headed for the campfire her father had already started.

"Just coffee and biscuits this morning, honey," John Grace told her. "We need to get underway. It's going to be a clear day, and our new guide wants to get in plenty of miles today."

"Sure, Father."

John frowned and put a hand on her arm. "You aren't ill, are you? You look a bit pale, my girl."

"I'm fine." Elly put on a smile for him. "I didn't sleep very well, but it was because my mind was racing with thoughts of what we need. I worry we didn't pick up enough supplies."

"Oh, I think we're fine, dear."

Four more wagons clattered their way, all emigrants ready for the next course of their journey toward the Rockies, the Sierras, and finally, California. Elly carried the coffee pot to a barrel of water at the side of Mark's wagon and turned a spigot on, filling the porcelain pot. She carried it to a grate over the fire, set the pot on the grate and dropped the gauze bag of ground coffee beans into it.

By then she noticed Betty coming toward her with a gunny sack of biscuits. As usual, Betty was smiling. She wore pink today, her favorite color. Even her shawl was pink.

Betty's cheeks seemed rosier than normal as she knelt beside Elly near the fire.

"Tell me!" she said in an excited whisper. "What happened last night when you walked off with Matt Stover?"

Elly looked past her to see Glen walking their way. "I can't talk about it right now," she answered, also in a near whisper. "Glen is coming."

"Then it's something you don't want him to know," Betty answered, laughing softly. "We have got to talk, Elly Lowe!"

"I'll ride with you in the wagon when we first leave."

"What are you two twittering about?" Glen asked with a smile.

Betty rose. "We're just excited about finally getting underway and having new people to travel with." She handed the biscuits to Elly. "I'm going to see if the boys are up and properly dressed."

Elly stood up and faced Glen. "Just biscuits today, according to my father. He doesn't want us to take the time to cook and clean up because our guide wants to get an early start."

Glen nodded. "I'm not fond of our grizzly old guide, but the man's supposedly very knowledgeable about where we're going and about the land, but a couple of the others said he's a bit overly stern at times and is adamant about his word being the last word. But then I guess it has to be that way to keep proper order."

"I suppose." The water in the coffee pot began to steam. "The coffee will be ready in about ten minutes. There might be enough to share with some of the other travelers if necessary."

Glen frowned. "You okay? You look a little pale."

Elly put her hands to her waist and cast him a look of confidence. "You're the second one who's told me that. I assure you I'm just fine, Glen. I just didn't sleep well. There was too much to think about." She thought how Glen looked especially nice this morning. He wore a clean blue shirt and a brown leather vest. He was clean-shaven, and it looked like he'd changed his dusty pair of denim pants for a pair of clean ones. Even his boots looked polished.

He stepped closer, studying her intently. "Mark says you took a little stroll last night with that Matt Stover."

Elly hoped he wasn't seeing more color go out of her face. "He was only there for a few minutes, and it was so noisy that we walked a little bit away from the crowd. That's all. Matt wanted to know how all of us were doing, and he was glad to find out we'd found a guide and others to travel with. He said to wish our family good luck."

Glen nodded. "That's it?"

"Yes. Why?"

Glen sighed. "Well, anybody could see when we all first met up that the man had an eye for you. And to walk off alone means something, that's all. I hope you understand he's just a lonely man we'll never see again once we leave today, Elly."

Elly waved him off. "Of course, I understand that. I was just being nice. That's all. He will probably stop by this morning to say good-bye to you and father and Mark and the boys. He likes the family and wanted all of us to know that he made sure Pete Garner was well on his way in the opposite direction by the time he made it here to Fort McPherson."

Glen looked her over. "And you're a pretty woman, Elly Lowe. Music and moonlight can do things to a lonely man. Just remember what he's setting out to do, and that there's a good chance he won't come back from it." He put a hand to the side of her face. "I hope you'll keep giving thought to marrying me in California, Elly."

Elly grasped his wrist. "Glen, all I did was say good-bye to the man and wish him luck. It was no more than any of us would have done." She felt irritated at his almost-fatherly attitude, as though he thought she needed guidance when it came to men.

They both turned then when they heard Elly's father yell out, "Matt! Good to see you!"

Elly felt her heart skip a beat at the sight of Matt riding into their camp, pack horse in tow.

"Well, now I guess the rest of us can wish him luck and have a final good-bye," Glen told Elly with a note of chagrin.

Betty's two boys joined their grandfather in welcoming Matt, saying their excited hello's as Mark and Betty walked up to join them. Glen left Elly, who stood there with mixed emotions as she watched him walk up to Matt and add his own greetings. He shook Matt's hand solidly. Elly remained near the fire, trying to ignore Matt's big, strong build, his handsome smile as he greeted everyone, telling them all that he was glad to see they'd joined up with more travelers.

"…safety in numbers."

"Yes, and we have a good guide, too," old John told him.

Elly hardly heard the the entire conversation. All she saw was the man who'd kissed her last night like no other man had kissed her—the man she wanted but hardly knew—the lonely widower who was likely riding to his death, never to be seen again. She saw only what might have been but could never be.

Matt said his good-bye's, leaned down and squeezed

Betty's hand when she offered it, thanked all of them for their wishes for success and safety.

"I hope we can find a way to know if you made it through okay," Elly's father told him. "We'll always wonder, you know. Look us up in California when you've satisfied your mission. But I have to say I hope you'll change your mind, Matt, and go home to your family back in River's Bend, where I'm sure there are a lot of people who care about you."

"Thanks for your concern, but I'm on my way," Matt answered him. "I just felt I couldn't ride off without seeing all of you once more and making sure you were traveling under safer circumstances." He glanced over at Elly and tipped his hat. She caught the apologetic look in his eyes, and the wish that they could talk more.

So, maybe he doesn't think of me as too forward. He had, after all, apologized profusely, but that only meant he'd acted out of pure manly need and out of a yearning for his wife, not out of a true desire for her as her own woman. He was leaving, and he was likely trying to tell her he wouldn't come to California after all.

"I'm sure all of you have plenty to do to get ready this morning," he told Mark. "I'll be on my way."

"Don't you want some coffee first?" John asked him.

Matt glanced at Elly again. "No, thank you." He looked back at John. "I already had some, and it's a beautiful morning. I can get quite a few miles in by noon." He turned his rust-colored gelding, a beautiful horse she knew he called Rusty. "I just wanted to tell all of you God bless and good luck."

"The same to you," Glen told him. "Watch your back, Sheriff Stover."

"I will." Matt smiled. "You take good care of that lovely lady over there by the fire."

"I intend to," Glen told him with a smile.

Rusty skittered sideways, as though anxious to get moving. Matt patted the horse's neck. "I was going to give these horses a couple days' rest, but Rusty seems just fine, and after losing time chasing after Pete, I figured I'd better get going."

"Bye, Mister Stover!" the boys said, almost in unison. They waved and jumped up and down as Matt waved back and headed toward Elly, who stood there feeling plain and awkward and nervous and ready to cry.

"I can't apologize enough for last night, Elly," he said softly. "I'll never forget you, in spite of knowing you such a short time. And if I get down from this horse to talk, then I'll never leave, so this is good-bye. I only came here this morning to make things look good. I hope you're all right."

"I'm… fine," she answered. *And I think I love you, Matt Stover. Please don't go!* She tried to tell him with her eyes.

"People sometimes make bad decisions when they're lonely and full of grief," he told her. "Don't you do the same. Take care of yourself, and do whatever makes you truly happy. Don't look for me to come to California. It wouldn't be right." He backed Rusty away. "And it won't look good if I linger here by you. God bless you and keep you safe."

He turned and rode past the others again, yelling his good-byes as he rode out.

"And God bless *you*, Matt Stover," Elly said softly. She turned away, and her whole body jerked in a terrible need to cry her eyes out. The next thing she knew, Betty was beside her.

"What was that about, Elly?"

Elly couldn't help a quick sob as she rapidly wiped at her eyes. "I'll tell you later. Just pretend everything is normal, Betty. Please don't ask any more questions right now."

Betty frowned, touching her arm. "Sure."

Elly knelt by the fire and opened a gunny sack of biscuits to set them into a fry pan for warming on the hot coals. She thought how much Matt had liked her biscuits that first night he came to their camp to warn them about the buffalo hunters.

Such a brave and able man. Such a lonely man. She was sure she'd never see him again, and hiding her disappointment would not be easy. *Last night he kissed me, Betty,* she wanted to tell her sister-in-law. *He kissed me, and it was more wonderful than anything I've ever experienced.*

She already knew she couldn't marry Glen now, even if Matt Stover never walked into her life again.

CHAPTER FIFTEEN

*L*onely couldn't begin to describe how Matt was feeling as he headed through wide-open prairie, feeling like the only man on earth. The only thing that broke the horizon was the endless line of cottonwood trees far on his left that followed the Platte River to the south. Even though the horizon ahead looked flat, when he looked behind him he could see the path behind him went downhill. He was climbing, gradually, almost unknowingly, but climbing nonetheless.

The trail was forcing him ever higher as he headed for the Rockies. He'd learned from a guide back at Fort McPherson that looks could be very deceiving out here. *"You're headed for the mountains, so you'll be goin' up-hill from here on,"* the old man had told him, *"even though it doesn't seem that way. Hell, Denver, Colorado is a whole mile high, and when you reach that same level, you ain't even up in the mountains yet."*

To the northwest he could see huge hills that one might take for the beginning of the mountains. "Them's only the Nebraska sand hills," the guide had explained. "They ain't nothin' compared to the Rockies. Don't be mistakin' that's

as high as you'll go, mister. You ain't seen nothin' till you
reach them Rockies. That's why outlaws go there to hide.
Hell, there's all kinds of caves and rocky hills and places
hard to get to once you reach Outlaw Country. You'll have
a hell of a time findin' them men you're after, but then
again there's kind of a network of communication out
there that only the outlaws understand. You're bound to
run into somebody who's heard of them Liberty boys you
told me about—maybe knows where they are."

Matt hoped the man was right. He still had a long way
to go before he reached his destination, and right now he
felt like the only man headed that way. The only signs of
life he'd come across were a small herd of buffalo, now
almost depleted because of the hunters who killed them
for their hides and bones and left the meat to rot. And
endless sightings of birds, mostly cranes and ducks,
seemed to be everywhere in Nebraska.

This morning he'd seen a deer and shot it. Its gutted
carcass hung over Sadie's rump now. When he made
camp, he'd cut up some of the meat and salted it down
good, then packed it into a small wooden barrel of lard
that hung at Sadie's side. The lard would preserve it so he
could eat a little at a time. He'd saved the rest of the
carcass by salting it, too, figuring he could eat from it for a
few more days before what was left would spoil. He
regretted that he wouldn't be able to save all of it, hating
to waste half the meat by leaving it somewhere along the
trail, but, no doubt, some wild animal would come along
and make a feast of it.

His only other company was the wind, which became
almost constant the farther west he went, mainly because
the cold air from mountain snows fell to the valleys and
forced more air eastward, so through Wyoming and into
western Nebraska the wind was almost constant.

"Some people go crazy from it," the old guide had told

him. *"It's so endless that sometimes you want to scream at God to please shut it off for a while, just for the peace and quiet."*

Right now, Matt enjoyed the breeze. It was, in a way, like company, whispering to him to keep going, bringing with it the scent of spring wildflowers, sometimes making a kind of singing sound. He could see Lora standing out on the prairie, her blond hair blowing away from her beautiful face, her hands resting on her swollen belly that held their precious daughter.

I love you, Matt. He thought he heard her voice on the wind. He felt her with him today, then wondered if all this loneliness was caused by the kiss he'd shared with Elly Lowe. Was she missing him, too? Was she remembering that kiss the same way he was... something beautiful and passionate and needed by both of them? He couldn't help wondering what the kiss might have led to if they'd had the opportunity to be alone together those next few hours.

He had to stop thinking about Elly, about the taste of her mouth. He could still smell her, and he knew instinctively the juices had been flowing in all the right places when she kissed him back.

Life could be so damn cruel. If things were different, a woman like Elly would have been the perfect answer to his loneliness. He knew instinctively he could fall in love with a woman like that. He knew that she could have helped him cope with missing Lora, missing a woman in his bed, missing woman-cooked food and the scent and softness of a female around.

Some people were just naturally drawn to each other, and that's how it had felt with Elly. Out here a man lost track of time, but he sensed Lora wouldn't mind if he fell in love with another woman and took pleasure and companionship in her. She would want that, and he would have wanted the same for Lora if the tables had been turned.

He heard a kind of cry then, a bit like a bird. He was almost grateful that the sound took his mind off the want of a woman, off the one woman who might have changed his path and relieved his loneliness. He halted Rusty and looked around. It was then he saw them, a small band of hostiles on the western horizon.

"Shit," he muttered.

He'd always lived in settled places and had no experience with natives, although he figured the ones he saw now couldn't be much more dangerous than some of the criminals he'd encountered as a lawman. Most natives were on reservations now, or had been chased north and south, where they'd joined up with other tribes to continue their fight for what they considered their land and their hunting grounds. He couldn't really blame them.

What made him most nervous was that it was only about a year ago that George Armstrong Custer and over two hundred of his men had been killed at the Little Big Horn up in Montana, which started a new round of government searches for renegades they would force into reservation life. He'd read about Custer, and a little part of him figured maybe the man had asked for what he got.

At the moment, it didn't matter much what he did or didn't know about Custer or about the natives themselves. The ones he'd spotted, and who'd spotted him, were riding his way. He waited, deciding not to pull out his rifle or his six-gun. There were seven of them. Maybe looking like a man of peace was the best way to keep from being killed, or from being stranded out here without horses or supplies. If he tried to out-run them, it would only encourage them to chase after him and probably overly excite them. It looked like they carried only bows and arrows, but from what he'd heard about the Plains Indians, they could be just as accurate with an arrow as a man could be with a gun, and sometimes just as fast.

Besides, that, he might run poor Rusty and Sadie to death for no good reason.

Well, Lord, if it's my time, it's my time, he thought. He sat still and tried to show no fear as seven painted men surrounded him. He nodded to one who rode closer as though their leader, figuring that in these parts they were most likely Cheyenne, possibly Sioux but not as likely.

"Matt Stover," he said aloud, touching his chest.

The Indian nodded. "Fast Wolf." He touched his own chest.

Matt noted the proud look in the man's dark eyes and felt the power and danger of seven warriors against one white man. "You understand English?"

"Some."

"I mean no harm. I'm just heading to the mountains to look for white men who killed my wife. I have nothing against any of you." Matt turned to see the others seemed to be eyeing the deer carcass he still carried. He looked back at Fast Wolf. "You want it? You can have it. I just killed it this morning and it's salted down good, so it should last a few more days."

Fast Wolf rode around to study the dead dear, then rode up next to Matt. "We head north. Join Red Cloud and the Sioux. We were hunting. Our women and children are hungry."

Matt nodded. "Like I said. You can have the deer if you need it. I'll manage with the meat I already saved off it and packed into lard." He pointed east. "About two miles back I came across a small herd of buffalo. They were headed this way, so you might be able to find them and kill one or two."

Fast Wolf nodded. "You are good to offer the deer. We will see about the buffalo." He studied Rusty and Sadie with admiration. "You have fine horses."

I was wondering when you would mention the horses, Matt

wanted to answer. "I do. And I need them to keep going after the men who killed my wife." He wished he could read Fast Wolf's eyes, as the man simply sat there staring at him for a few silent seconds. The Indian leader suddenly barked something to those with him, and one of them pulled the dead deer off Sadie and threw it over his own horse's neck.

Fast Wolf nodded to Matt then. "We take the meat that you offer. Do you have tobacco?"

"Some." Matt was glad he'd taken advantage of the supply store owner's offer of free tobacco back at Fort McPherson. With that and what he'd paid for, he had plenty. "I have to reach into my saddle bag. Just making sure you know I'm not reaching for a weapon." He turned and untied the right-hand saddle bag, pulled out a can of McRae Fine Tobacco. He hated giving it up, but if the tobacco and the deer carcass were all he had to sacrifice for his life, he didn't have much choice. He handed the small can to Fast Wolf. "Good brand."

Fast Wolf actually smiled as he took the can. "I see good in your eyes," he told Matt. "And the deer meat will fill many bellies for our journey north."

Matt nodded. "I also see goodness in *your* eyes. Looks to me like you are on the run. If I come across any army men or other white men looking for you, I will not tell them I have seen you."

Again, Fast Wolf studied him for a long time. Matt looked right back at him, figuring facing him squarely only accented he was not afraid and was a man of his word.

Finally, the Indian nodded. "This is good. We will not take your horses or your weapons. I know the feeling of wanting to kill those who have killed your woman. Since it is white men you hunt, and not Cheyenne, we will let you go." He barked something to the others.

All seven men rode off, heading north. Matt wondered how soon his heart would stop racing as he headed west. He worried he might still feel an arrow in his back—that Fast Wolf and the others might change their minds - but after a good ten minutes of riding, nothing happened. He halted Rusty and turned around to see Fast Wolf and his men were gone. He breathed a deep sigh of relief, wondering how on earth he'd managed to escape the encounter alive, then reached into his shirt pocket for a pre-rolled cigarette and a large wooden match. He struck the match and lit the cigarette, deeply inhaling the tobacco smoke to calm himself, and hoping he'd have no more encounters with Plains Indians. He left the cigarette between his lips and started riding again.

"Well, Rusty, we're learning a lot about the land out here, aren't we?" He drew deeply on the cigarette again. "I'm wondering more and more if we'll ever go back to River's Bend once we get used to this."

From what he'd heard about the Rocky Mountains, he figured they had to be beautiful. Beyond that were the Sierras, and beyond that—California. And Elly Lowe. Whether or not he decided to go there depended on what lay in store for him in Outlaw Country. So far, he'd survived buffalo hunters and Indians, and the temptation of a beautiful woman. Whether he could survive the Liberty boys was yet to be seen.

CHAPTER SIXTEEN

*E*lly studied the horizon, wondering how far ahead of them Matt was, and if he was thinking about her.

"Are you ever going to tell me what really happened the night of the dance?" Betty asked.

Elly sat with her sister-in-law on the wagon seat of Betty and Mark's wagon.

"I see you gazing into the distance with a worried look on your face," Betty added. "You're thinking about Matt Stover, aren't you?" She snapped a long switch over the oxen. "We're five days from Fort McPherson now, and I can tell by how quiet you've been that you and that man did more than dance. I saw you walk off with him, and after you went over to the mess hall, the two of you disappeared from under the light for a few minutes. "

"Did you tell Mark that?" Elly asked, wishing Betty hadn't noticed.

"No. And if something else happened that you don't want me to tell him, then I won't. You know you can trust me, Elly, but I'm dying of curiosity."

"I love you like a sister, Betty Grace, but sometimes you get as giddy as a schoolgirl who can't keep a secret."

"And the reason I never said anything about you two leaving the lamp light is because I know it's nothing to be giddy *about*. Matt made it pretty obvious that when we parted ways at Fort McPherson, we'd never see him again, so I know it's nothing that will lead to anything more. I saw the sadness in your eyes that morning, and you, my dear sister-in-law, haven't been yourself since then."

Elly pulled her slat bonnet down farther against a setting sun that was angling into her eyes, making it hard to see the trail ahead. She hesitated, finding it surprisingly difficult to talk about.

"We have to stop and make camp soon, Elly," Betty reminded her. "We won't be able to talk then because the men will be around."

"I don't want Glen to find out," Elly told her. "It might hurt his feelings, and I don't want to do that over something that can never be anyway. I don't think I'm going to marry him, but I don't want him to think it's because of another man."

Betty grinned a little. "But it *is*, isn't it?"

Elly remained quiet for several seconds. "Yes."

More silence.

"And?" Betty finally asked.

"He kissed me, Betty, and I let him. I even kissed him back."

Betty sucked in her breath.

Young Mark snapped a small whip behind one of the oxen's ears and ordered it to "Git up there!"

"You be careful, Mark," Betty yelled to him. "Thank God these oxen were bought as a pair and work well together," she told Elly. "They haven't given us any trouble. The boys decided to name them. Toby, the one on the left, seems to be the dominant one. Pepper is the one on the right."

Tommy lay asleep in the back of the wagon, worn out from running more than walking during the day.

"Elly and I will walk tomorrow," Betty shouted to Mark. "We'll guide and tend the oxen and give you and your brother a break."

"Thank you, Mama," Mark answered.

"You're doing a good job, Son." Betty turned to Elly. "What was it like?"

"The kiss?"

"Of *course*, the kiss!"

Elly wondered if the hurt would ever go away. "It was wonderful. Warm. Soft. A little bit demanding, yet gentle. He kisses like a man who knows what a woman wants. But it was kind of a hungry kiss, too. I know he was thinking about his wife—wanting *her*, not me. But I didn't care. A part of me wanted to please him, make him feel better, soothe his broken heart. I think that's partly why I returned the kiss. I was trying to tell him I understood, that it was okay. And I haven't been kissed like that in so long."

Betty frowned. "Doesn't Glen kiss you sometimes?"

The thought of Glen brought Elly back to reality. "Almost never. When he does, it's just kind of a peck, and his lips are always cool. Matt's were so warm and moist and—" She covered her face. "Good Lord, Betty, I shouldn't be telling you these things. What must you think of me? And what must *he* think of me?"

"You didn't do anything wrong, if that's what you're concerned about. I'm a woman, too, you know. And Matt Stover didn't do anything wrong either. That man wants you bad, Elly. Maybe he even loves you."

"Don't be ridiculous! We hardly know each other. He's acting on feelings for his wife, that's all. He misses her terribly. It's awful how she died, and so sudden that Matt still hardly knows what day it is or if it's morning or night. I think he's still in a bit of a shocked stupor over all of it, and I don't think he's thinking straight when it comes to going after those men." Elly felt tears sting her eyes. "I'm so scared for him, Betty, and the worst part is I'll probably never know if he survived his mission, or if he died all alone out there in the mountains."

"Well, he knows he has an invitation to come find us in California. If he still has feelings for you after everything's over, I think he'll come out there."

Elly quickly wiped at a tear that tried to escape down her cheek. "I highly doubt it. He was pretty adamant about it that morning when he said he wouldn't come to California. The night before, he said he probably would, but he changed his mind. He feels bad about what he did, and he more or less said it was out of missing his wife and that he was sorry. He seemed genuinely regretful that night, embarrassed and apologetic."

"But he enjoyed that kiss, nonetheless. And so did you," Betty stated flatly. "It's too bad the whole situation means nothing can ever come of it. I like Matt, and I know your father and Mark like him, too."

Elly took a deep breath and sat straighter. "Well, the whole thing was just so odd, two strangers passing in the night. It's kind of poetic when you think about it. We were both acting out of loneliness and pent-up need. It woke me up to the fact that I do want to marry again. But I don't want to marry Glen. I feel kind of bad about it, but I can't help realizing now what I thought all along. I don't want to marry out of necessity or practicality. Maybe God sent Matt to teach me that I wouldn't be happy with Glen."

"Maybe."

Their guide, a bearded, stocky man named Orlando,

who'd offered no last name, held up his hand as he rode down the line past the seven wagons.

"Circle the wagons!" he ordered. "We'll camp here tonight."

"I'm glad we're stopping," Betty told Elly. "I feel extra tired." Using "Gees" and "Haws" she turned the oxen with young Mark's help.

"Have you told Mark yet that you're carrying?" Elly asked her.

"No. I'll tell him soon."

"He needs to know."

"I know. But I'm fine, so don't worry."

Elly had her doubts. Betty almost never admitted she was tired. She always seemed to have the energy of a young bunny.

All parties circled their wagons, and things became too busy for Elly and Betty to talk any more about Matt Stover. Elly figured it was just as well. She had to forget about the man and think about California and a new life. She climbed into the back of Betty's wagon, carefully crawling around little Tommy to find a crate that held the coffee pot, a fry pan and some tin plates and cups. She moved them to the back of the wagon and untied the gate, then paused when she heard the wagon master talking to another man.

"Find another man to stand guard tonight," Orlando told the traveler. "And find two more men to relieve you later on. I think I seen some men followin' us to the east, and right in these parts I don't think it's In'juns. Might be buffalo hunters."

Elly frowned, remembering Matt's warning about men like Pete Garner. He thought the man in the supply store might have been Pete's friend.

Were they following the wagon train now? Maybe Pete and the man from the supply store had found each other and were hunting for Matt. They both surely had grudges against him.

Her thoughts were interrupted then when she looked over to where Betty was making a campfire while Mark unyoked the oxen. Betty suddenly dropped some logs and went to her knees.

"Betty!" Elly shouted, running to her side. She rolled Betty onto her back while Mark hurried over to join them.

"The baby," Betty muttered.

CHAPTER SEVENTEEN

*M*att saw the clouds from a distance, the
darkest, most ominous on-coming storm
he'd ever seen. Being raised in Nebraska, he wasn't
unfamiliar with tornadoes and had seen more than one in
his lifetime. Even River's Bend was hit a few years back,
destroying several buildings and killing two people. He
was only ten then, but he remembered how terrified he'd
been as a little boy hiding in the root cellar. His father's
home and church had only been slightly damaged, and he
remembered the church was used the next few weeks as a
make-shift hospital for wounded citizens.

River's Bend had two doctors now, and a new building
that had been built for sick and wounded people. He
looked at the nothingness around him, and thought how,
out here, there was no shelter, and no such help.

"Looks like that storm heading our way is not bringing
a gentle rain, boy," he told Rusty. "That dark horizon is full
of dust—dust the wind's sucking up into the air." It was so
quiet where he was riding that it almost hurt his ears.
Another bad sign.

"Calm before the storm," an old friend of his father's

used to say. "Any time there ain't one tiny blade of grass movin', but you can see dark clouds headed your way, you can bet somethin' bad is comin'."

Matt took a deep breath and studied his surroundings. He had to protect the horses. He'd passed the town of Sidney and was moving into higher, rockier country. Wyoming and Fort Laramie weren't that much farther ahead, but for the next few days he would remain in unsettled country where he'd find no help. Not far ahead he noticed a high hill that looked as though it had been built up with layers of flat rock and shale. Maybe he could find shelter there, since this side of the hill would be away from the on-coming wind and storm. It would be better than facing the wind head-on and letting it batter him and the horses with stinging dust and gravel.

He kicked Rusty's sides and headed at a gallop for the wall of earth and rock. The wind picked up rapidly, a low roaring sound coming with it and growing louder by the second. The pack horse, Sadie, balked and yanked at the lead rope, pulling hard on Matt's saddle horn and forcing Rusty to dig his hooves into the ground and rear up.

"Whoa, boy! Whoa!" Matt shouted, hanging on for dear life. He steadied Rusty, but the horse turned so that the rope leading Sadie crossed Matt's side. Rusty reared again when a sudden clap of thunder followed a huge lightning bolt. The thunder actually hurt Matt's ears. Sadie jerked again on the rope as Rusty whinnied in something more like a scream and kept turning as he reared over and over, forcing Matt out of the saddle as the rope cut into his side.

Thunder boomed all around them, and almost instantly the roaring wind was upon them. Matt felt his left boot caught in the stirrup, felt the earth cutting through his shirt and into his back as Rusty charged away, pulling Sadie with him.

"Whoa, Rusty!" Matt yelled over and over, but the howling wind carried his voice away into places unknown. He felt his head hit a rock, felt the gravel and plants and rope cutting into his back. He felt the sting of dirt and tiny rocks pelting his face as Rusty dragged him, his hooves throwing the ground against Matt with shattering force. Matt had no idea how far they'd gone before his foot finally came out of the stirrup. The rope still caught around his body yanked him when the rope came loose from Rusty's saddle and Sadie charged off. Matt tumbled and rolled as the rope came unwound. He felt a jolt then, and a heavy thud against his ribs, so painful he cried out.

His body finally stopped rolling, and he lay there on his back for a moment, his knee and ankle screaming with pain, his ribs hurting so badly he couldn't take a deep breath. Somewhere in his confused thoughts he figured the pounding jolt to his ribs could have been a confused Sadie galloping right over him in panic and terror.

Rain came down so hard he felt as though he was drowning in it. Somewhere in his thoughts he wondered how the storm could have hit so fast. He'd been sure he had time to reach the shelter of the side of that hill. He tried to get up, but his legs wouldn't work for him. Everything hurt, all his limbs, his back, his knee, his ankle, his head from hitting the rock. The rain turned amazingly cold. He rolled to his belly to avoid so much water pelting his mouth and nose and eyes.

He began coughing violently, noticing brown streams of water running under him, so heavy that if he should put his face all the way down, he would drown. It was raining so hard that the earth beneath him was becoming more like a river. Somewhere in the distance he heard Rusty scream out more whinnies. Was the horse running away? Where was Sadie? What about his weapons and supplies?

What the hell was he going to do out here if he lost the horses and everything on them?

His head ached even more, and now he saw blood mixing into the water that rushed beneath him. He got to his hands and knees, thinking to crawl to the rock wall he'd tried to reach, but it rained so hard he couldn't even raise his head and open his eyes to see where he was.

Harder. The rain came down even harder. Everything around him was black. A tornado. It had to be a tornado. The roar in the air was almost more than his ears could tolerate. Something else hit him in the head. Stones pelted his body. He folded his hands and arms around his head to protect himself, realizing that his hat had long before blown away with the wind.

What was happening to the horses? He couldn't hear them anymore. Thunder and lightning split the sky and shook the earth. The wind was so wicked he thought it might pick him up and carry him off. The coughing started again. It felt as though his lungs were full of dirt. He coughed so hard that he vomited. He got to his hands and knees again and tried to crawl, but things were going dark. The howl of the wind began to recede, but he wasn't sure if it was because the storm was moving on, or because he was losing consciousness. He put a hand to the back of his head and felt a wet warmth. He looked at his palm and it was covered with blood, which was soon washed away by the continuing downpour.

More stones pelted him. Everything hurt so badly he couldn't crawl any farther or even call out for the horses, or for help if anyone might be near. The rain continued to soak him to the bone—cold, wet, miserable.

Then, in almost an instant, the roaring wind finally stopped and everything grew dead silent again. Matt rolled to his side to look around, but everything was black. He wasn't sure if it was because the atmosphere around him was black, or if it was because he literally couldn't see. He lay down on the saturated ground, felt water everywhere, running in rivulets under his back, over his arms and legs, splashing across his face. He couldn't move. He couldn't see. He couldn't talk. And he could barely breathe for the awful pain in his ribs.

CHAPTER EIGHTEEN

*B*etty hung a shirt on a make-shift clothesline of rope strung between two wagons. "I don't know what I would do if Mark hadn't been so good about me losing the baby," she told Elly. "I thought he'd be angry that I never told him."

"My brother loves you very much," Elly told her. "He understands you didn't say anything because you knew this trip was important to him and the rest of the family. If he was going to be angry about it, he'd be angry with me, too, because I knew you were carrying."

"I suppose."

Betty draped a pair of Mark's pants over the clothesline, then glanced into the distance where the wagons were parked in a circle outside of the small town of Sidney. "I still just feel so bad now for not telling him the truth."

Elly stepped closer, putting a hand on Betty's arm. "Stop punishing yourself. You have two wonderful sons, and if that's all you ever have, you and Mark should both be happy about it."

Betty met her gaze, then burst into tears. Elly pulled her into her arms and patted her back.

"The doctor in town said you should be able to have more, Betty. You're still young and strong and healthy. Something must have been wrong with this one, so God chose to take back its spirit. He'll put it into another baby and give it back to you."

"I hope you're right," Betty sobbed. "I just wish... I could get over this depression."

"Your feelings are perfectly natural. I just wish you would rest more. I can handle the wash."

Betty pulled away and took a handkerchief from the pocket of her apron. She wiped at her eyes and nose and shook slightly with lingering tears. "I won't have you doing all our laundry by yourself."

"It helps keep me busy." Elly walked Betty to a bench beside the laundry shed, where three Chinese women kept water heated so travelers who stopped in Sidney could get some laundry done. "Now, sit down for a while," she told Betty.

"Is she all right?" The question came from Tilly Willett, one of the other women with the wagon train. Tilly stopped scrubbing a shirt on a washboard to look sympathetically at Betty.

"She'll be fine," Elly told her. She sat down beside Betty for a moment to rest. "Thank you for asking."

"It's so sad, her losing her baby. Life is so hard out here. Things will get better when we all get to California," Tilly assured both women.

"Thank you," Betty answered. "I'm glad we have so many others to travel with now. Everyone has been so kind, and there are children for Tommy and Mark to play with." She leaned against the side of the shed. "I don't like our ornery old guide, though. He's pushing us too hard. I think that's part of my problem."

Elly frowned. "I agree with you there. I'm also getting irritated with Glen. It's gotten so he expects me to clean up after him, as though I were already his wife."

"You're *not* his wife," Betty scowled, "and you shouldn't have to do one thing for him, Elly. You make sure he knows that."

Elly put an arm around her shoulders. "I've dropped a lot of hints, and I've made him do some things himself." She sighed and lowered her voice. "On the other hand, I don't mind keeping busy because it saves me from having too much time to worry about Matt Stover and how he's doing."

Betty wiped at more tears and straightened. "I *knew* you still think about that man." Her eyes brightened a little and she actually smiled.

Elly realized she'd found a subject that gave Betty something to think about besides losing her baby. Talk of Matt Stover, to Betty, was exciting and romantic.

"Foolish as it is, yes, I do still think about Matt," she said, glad to see Betty's familiar smile.

"I think about him, too," Betty answered. "Out there all alone like he is - if he gets hurt, who's there to help him? My goodness, there are still Indians out there, and outlaws and those awful buffalo hunters and—"

Elly shook her head. "You should write books, Betty Grace. You have a wild and romantic imagination." She rose to finish hanging clothes. There were five other women with them, and clothes hung on all the lines, as well as over barrels and posts. Elly looked at her hands, red and chafed from so much scrubbing with lye. It would be next to impossible to do much ironing out here on the trail. The men would simply have to wear wrinkled pants and shirts, and the women's dresses would be the same, but it didn't matter. In the struggle to keep going and in fighting weather, balky animals, wagons that broke down, and now mosquitoes beginning to pester them, no one cared much about how they looked, or whether they were able to bathe. She took one last shirt from the clothes basket and made ready to hang it up when Betty was suddenly at her side.

"Elly! It's *him*!" she whispered. "Pete Garner!"

Elly draped the shirt over the line and looked to see the man walking toward them. "Yes," she answered Betty softly. "And look at the kind of men who are with him."

Pete was accompanied by two more men dressed in filthy, stained pants and shirts, their faces unshaven, their hair long. Even their hats were floppy and worn and stained. They wore high boots trimmed in fur, and they all carried rifles.

Betty wiped away more tears. "How on earth did he catch up to us?"

Elly scrambled to think straight. Why had Pete come back and followed their wagon train? Maybe he hadn't done so deliberately. Maybe his being here was just a coincidence. Still, Matt had warned them he was not to be trusted. "We've stopped several times," she told Betty, "and we were held up for two days when you lost the baby because you were so sick. If he headed right back after Matt left him, he would have had time to catch up to us. One man on a horse travels much faster than a wagon train of thirty-two people, with slow oxen and a herd of horses and cattle to look after."

"But *why*?" Betty asked.

"I don't know. I'd like to think it's just to thank us for helping him."

"I have a sick feeling that's not the reason," Betty answered.

"Just relax," Elly told her. "We're traveling with a lot of people. Nothing can happen." Elly knew what Betty was thinking. After what she witnessed back at Fort

McPherson with the buffalo hunter Matt dragged outside, she no longer trusted men like those approaching.

"I'll bet he's looking for Matt Stover." Betty grasped one of Elly's hands and squeezed it.

Elly straightened, facing the men as they came closer. She was resolved to be firm with them and show no fear.

Pete nodded to some of the other women and tipped his hat. "Ladies," he said with an ugly smile that showed brown, tobacco-stained teeth. He looked them over as though he could take his pick of any of them. Only one of the women smiled back and said hello, but she quickly turned away. They all looked at each other, obviously with the same thought. Why were these big, bearded, filthy men walking among a bunch of women who were busy doing laundry?

"Oh, my gosh, Elly," Betty whispered near her ear. "One of those men is the same one Matt confronted at that supply store back at Fort McPherson!"

Elly felt true alarm at realizing Betty was right.

"Well now," Pete said as he approached, setting his gaze on Elly and Betty. "There you are! I figured I'd catch up to the kind Grace family before my trip was over. How are you two fine ladies doing?"

Betty said nothing. Elly raised her chin and boldly faced the man. "Why aren't you out on the plains somewhere hunting buffalo? Isn't that your profession?"

Pete put his hands on his hips and looked her over. "Well, a man doesn't just come across buffalo every day, you know. And he has to stock up on supplies once in a while. I came back this way to find my friends."

"And did you find them?"

"Oh, I found them, all right." He nodded toward the man who'd stayed back. "That there's Stacy Bodeen. Come to find out, Matt Stover dragged him into an alley and left him to die, back at Fort McPherson." His dark eyes narrowed. "Stacy says Stover put a gun to his head and threatened to blow his brains out. That wasn't too kind of the man, was it?" He looked Elly over like she was a fresh piece of pie. "He also says he seen you dancin' with the man later that night. I don't suppose you know where our esteemed sheriff is right now, do you?"

Elly felt a cold fear running through her veins, along with a sick dread for Matt. "How would I know that? He was on his way to Outlaw Country, the last I knew, and that was over two weeks ago."

"Mmmm-hmmm." He looked her over again, and stepped so close that Elly stepped back. Betty kept hold of her hand and stayed behind her. "Stacy also said he seen you and the law-abiding sheriff suckin' at each other's lips that night at the dance... said you two snuck off into the dark. He was watchin'—seen it all." He smiled a lecherous smile that made Elly feel ill.

So, that buffalo hunter had been watching them all along, probably giving thought to killing Matt for what happened in the supply store. Strangely, she didn't feel humiliated. She only felt furious over how Pete Garner was making it all sound ugly and sexual and filthy.

"What difference does that make?" she spat back at Pete. "We parted ways, and I have no clue where Matt might be now. We are all on our way to California, and that's the end of it. I suggest you also be on *your* way."

"Or what?"

"Or I'll warn our wagon master about you and your friends."

"Won't help much. I know the man. Besides, what are you gonna' say? That we were hurt and needed your help so you helped us? That we didn't do a thing to harm anyone? That it was your kissin' friend, Matt Stover, who did the hurtin'? You gonna' tell him in front of everybody about how you practically lifted your skirts for Stover, while the man you're supposed to marry was out tendin' horses not all that far away?"

Elly had never wanted to hit someone as badly as she wanted to hit Pete Garner right now. She let go of Betty's hand and folded her arms, refusing to buckle in front of him or in front of the women there who watched and listened. "It was nothing like that and your friend knows it! Why don't you tell all of us what it is you *really* want, Mr. Garner?"

Pete shrugged. "Nothin' special. I just was hopin' ole' Matt had changed his mind about goin' to Outlaw Country and decided to stay with your wagon train instead. I was hopin' maybe he'd decided to stick around and see if he can sneak into your wagon some night and pick up where he left off back at the fort. Stacy said he thought you two were gonna' go at it that night, but the prim and proper lady and the honorable sheriff decided to leave off sharin' spit and go back to the dance. Must have been hard on ole' Matt. I reckon' he had to do somethin' to relieve his frustration once he got off alone."

Elly drew in her breath and made ready to slap him, but he caught her arm.

"You filthy bastard!" Elly told him.

Betty moved from behind Elly and faced Pete squarely. "Let go of her!"

By then the other women had walked closer. "Get away from here!" one of them told Pete.

Pete just grinned. He let go of Elly and stepped back a little.

"Sorry, ladies." He nodded and tipped his hat again, eyeing the bunch of them. "This woman helped me out once when I was wounded. I was just thankin' her, but I reckon' I said somethin' wrong."

"This is how you *thank* someone?" Elly fumed. "You can rest assured I'll make sure my father and brother and

Glen know you threatened not just me, but *all* of us! I saw how you looked at these women when you first came over here."

Pete put up his hands as though to ward them off. "No offense, ladies. It ain't every day a lonely travelin' man gets to see so many pretty young and proper women all in one place. I mean no harm." He backed away more, addressing Elly again. "If there are any single women in your group who need a man's help when you leave, just let me know. I'll be glad to travel along and lend my expertise for survivin' in this land."

"I'm sure you would, but no, thank you," Elly answered with a sneer. "You've shown your true colors. You are a reprehensible, filthy man! What on earth makes you think there's one woman here who'd welcome your help? We'll make *sure all* the men know about you, and *they* will make sure you get nowhere near us! Now, get out of here, and take Stacy Bodeen with you!"

Bodeen raised his chin and stepped closer. "You're one to talk," he said with an ugly grin. "I seen how you came close to layin' in the tall grass with Stover back there at the fort—him and you hardly knowin' each other."

Elly noticed the other women exchange looks, some of them glancing at her with questions in their eyes.

"Get out of here!" Betty practically screamed, surprising Elly with her sudden anger and bravery. "My sister-in-law is a good, Christian woman, and my best friend! How *dare* you exaggerate and make up lies about her!"

"Hey! What's going on over here?" The words came from a husband of one of the women, a big man who was carrying a rifle. He walked closer, frowning. "Are these men bothering you women?"

"Yes!" his wife answered. "Make them leave, Herbert!"

Herbert raised his rifle. "You two get the hell away from here."

Pete gave Herbert an arrogant sneer. "We're leavin'. But not because of some hill farmer with a squirrel gun." He laughed deep in his throat. "My buffalo gun could blow you clear from here to the other side of town." He glanced at Elly once more, then turned. "Come on, Stacy."

Elly glanced at the other women as Garner and Bodeen walked away. She felt obligated to explain so she could erase their confusion. "I'm sorry about this," she told them. The one called Pete came to our wagon train a good three weeks back, maybe longer. He and a friend of his were wounded. Matt Stover, a sheriff from River's Bend, Nebraska, happened by and found out Pete and his friend were with our party. He'd shot them a few days before because they threatened his life and tried to steal his horses. Pete's friend died and Matt chased Pete off the next day. Later Matt had a run-in with that big man called Stacy Bodeen. I think Pete has been deliberately following us. He's probably looking for Matt, but Matt is headed someplace completely different from where we are going, so we have no idea where he might be now." She folded her arms and held her chin proudly. "Matt Stover became a good friend to all of us for a short time, but he's gone now. Anything else Pete and his friend said about Matt or me is lies. They're just angry bullies. Now that they know Matt has gone in another direction, I'm sure they'll leave us alone." She felt sick inside at the thought of such men being on Matt's trail.

"Well, they had no right saying those ugly things in front of you women," Herbert told them. "I'll make sure the others know about them and keep a lookout when we leave for Fort Laramie." He nodded to Elly. "You okay, Ma'am?"

"Yes," Elly answered, grateful that none of them seemed to believe the ugly things the hunters had said.

"I'll hang around a few minutes while you ladies finish your scrubbing," Herbert told them.

"Thank you," several women replied.

They went back to their washing, and Elly led Betty back to the bench to sit down. "I'll help you to the wagons after you sit here a minute," she told Betty. "I'll come back to take down the clothes once they're dry." She put a hand to her stomach, sickened by what Stacy Bodeen had said in front of the women. She forced back tears. "It wasn't ugly like that, Betty," she said softly. "And I didn't... we didn't..." She brushed at a tear. "It wasn't like that."

"Of course, it wasn't." Betty reached out and pressed her hand. "Don't you let his words make it ugly for you. You have only sweet memories, Elly, and nothing more. Right now I wish Matt Stover *was* here! He'd give those men what for. He'd protect you from that filth."

Yes, Elly thought. *Matt would protect me.* That was part of what had attracted her to him. He was so sure and able, so ready to right a wrong. "We have to pray for him—pray that those men don't catch up to him."

Betty nodded. "I agree."

"Oh, Betty, between those hunters, and the outlaws Matt is looking for, how on Earth is he going to survive?"

Betty shook her head. "I don't know. Just think positive thoughts, and like you said, we should just pray for him. He might be just fine and come to find you in California."

"It's a nice thought." Elly felt sick inside at what Matt might be in for. She wished she could warn him about Pete Garner and Stacy Bodeen. And she wished more than anything that he'd stayed with their wagon train and gone to California with them. She'd feel so much safer if Matt were with them now.

CHAPTER NINETEEN

*M*att struggled to breathe. The panic that he couldn't woke him up. He sat up in bed, then cried out in pain—pain that seemed to be everywhere from his neck down. A coughing fit engulfed him to the point he almost vomited trying to get rid of choking phlegm. He saw a small bucket beside the bed and spit into it, then wondered where on Earth he was and where the bucket had come from. Pain that racked his body caused him to collapse back down against a pillow.

A woman walked into the small room then. She looked older, more the age of his mother.

"Mister Stover!" she exclaimed. "Are you fully awake at last?"

Matt started coughing again, only then realizing he was sweating profusely. He rolled to his side and looked around, confused. "Who are you? How do you know my name?"

"We found your supplies scattered out on the plains and found some paperwork with your name on it, Mr. Stover." The woman turned toward the door. "Hank, bring that steaming kettle in here," she called out. She turned back to try covering Matt better. "You shouldn't take a chill. It's best you sweat out the fever and the awful sickness. I fear you have pneumonia. "

Matt finally managed to take some deep breaths. Confused, he disobeyed her request and threw off the covers. He turned to sit up on the edge of the bed and looked around the room. The walls were logs and the furnishings sparse—just the bed and a small table beside it, a chest of drawers, and a braided rug on the wooden plank floor.

"Please lie back down, Mister Stover. My husband and I have worked too hard to keep you alive. My name is Henrietta Volmer."

A big, bearded man walked into the room carrying a kettle that had steam coming from its spout. He set it near a kerosene lamp on the small table beside the bed. "Let me help you get back in that bed," the man told him.

"This is my husband, Hank," Henrietta explained.

Through his foggy mind Matt determined that both the Volmers had kind eyes, but Hank seemed stern and determined. Matt had a feeling that if he didn't lie back down, the man would make sure he did. At the moment he was too weak to argue, so he sank back against a stack of pillows, realizing only then that he wore only the bottoms of his long-johns. A little embarrassed by his bare torso in front of the woman, he let her help him cover up again. He tried to think straight—to remember how he might have ended up in this bed in a house that belonged to strangers.

"What... happened?" he asked. "Where am I? And where... are my horses? My things?" It seemed he had to struggle to find the breath for each word.

"Relax, Mister Stover," the woman told him. She tucked the blankets around his shoulders. "You are very sick—and wounded. My husband found you this way not so far from our farm. We can understand the pneumonia, after lying out in a cold rain for so long - and your injuries are apparently from the tornado. We saw it dancing across the plains, but it didn't damage our home, thank the Good Lord." She wet a cloth and put it to his forehead. "You have a serious head wound, and your ribs are very bruised. It seems your whole body is covered with bruises and scrapes. Hank thinks blowing debris injured you, or perhaps your horse was frightened and dragged you over the ground."

Matt watched Hank move around to the other side of the bed. He pulled up a wooden chair Matt hadn't even noticed before and sat down near the bed, nodding kindly.

"There was a bad storm and it scattered my horses," Hank told him.

Matt realized both of them had distinct German accents. "I went looking for my livestock, and that is when I found your horses mingled with mine. One was still saddled, and most of your supplies were still tied to the pack horse. I knew then that whoever owned them must be lying wounded somewhere, so I kept looking, and I finally found you near Castle Rock."

Matt closed his eyes and tried to remember it all. "I... it was so black. I think the tornado... whipped right over me... scared my horses. I remember landing on the ground and thinking I might be carried away by the tornado. I was trying to reach... a rocky hill."

"Henrietta and I call it Castle Rock because it is like a big rock wall that just sticks up out of the ground like a fortress, and in a place where there should be only sand," Hank explained. "It reminds us of the wall of a castle in our homeland of Germany, but we have not lived there since we were little, when our parents came to America."

"That does not matter to this man right now," Henrietta chided Hank. She smiled softly and touched

Matt's shoulder. "You are badly wounded, but you will be fine now. And your horses and supplies are safe."

Matt rubbed at his eyes. "I remember now... the storm spooked my horses. The rope I was using to lead the pack horse got wrapped around me and it yanked me out of the saddle. My foot... got caught in the stirrup and my horse panicked and dragged me quite a ways." He struggled to remember. "I think my pack horse might have stomped right over me when the rope broke loose. She was confused by the wind and the rain."

"Ya, that explains the purple bruises around your ribs," Hank told him. "Do not worry about your horses and supplies. Everything is safe in our barn. I found some papers in your supplies that showed your name and that you are a sheriff from a place called River's Bend."

Matt winced with pain when he tried to adjust his position. "That's right. Thank you for... taking care of my things."

"We could not leave you out there to die," Hank told him. "It was only right to try to help you, and with all our children grown and gone, my wife enjoys having someone to take care of."

Henrietta rose, putting the rag into a bowl of water beside the bed. "I will get you some coffee. Once you feel you are ready, I will bring you some chicken broth and noodles. You need to eat to get your strength back, but even as your wounds heal, it is the coughing that concerns us. You should stay in bed until your chest clears."

Matt saw dim light coming through the curtains at the one and only window in the room. He realized then that he had no idea what time of day it was. He remembered the storm had hit in the morning. "What time is it?"

Henrietta left to get the coffee.

"It is six o'clock in the evening," Hank answered. "This is your second day here."

Matt tried to sit up again, but pain seared through him.

"You had better lie still," Hank warned him. "You could get dizzy and pass out. You have been mostly unconscious up to now. It is good to see you truly awake and talking."

"But I, I have to get going. I was on my way to Wyoming. There are some men I'm after. I'm losing so much time."

Hank sat back and folded his arms. "Then you will have to lose *more* time, Mister Stover. Your injuries are too severe for you to be going anywhere, and your head wound is serious. Most of your face is purple, and you –"

Before he could finish, Matt half sat up again with another deep bout of coughing that literally wore him out so when he was through, he collapsed against his pillow, panting.

"There. You see? You cannot go anywhere for another few days—maybe even a week or two," Hank repeated. "Henrietta is good at taking care of people. Though you are a stranger, I will have to trust you with her because now that the weather is clearing, I have to start plowing and planting. And I know you are a lawman, so I will rest easy leaving you here alone with Henrietta."

Henrietta returned with a cup of coffee. "Hank will help you sit up a little. You might feel better with some hot coffee in you. Would you like some fresh bread and some chicken broth?"

Matt struggled with confusion. His whole body screamed with pain, and he felt strangely removed from the real world. Were the horses really okay? What the hell day of the week was it? How long would he have to lie here helpless, while the Liberty boys went their merry way on to Outlaw Country? And he figured he'd stayed ahead of Elly's wagon train, but if he ended up here for a week or more, their wagon train would proceed well ahead of him.

Had they already reached Sidney? Fort Laramie? Were they still safe?

What did it matter? What did *anything* matter? They were on their way to their own life in California. The Liberty boys were drinking and shooting their way into Outlaw Country. And somewhere out there Pete Garner had probably found his filthy bunch of hunters, maybe including the one Matt had left in an alley back at Fort McPherson. The Volmers would operate their farm, and life was probably going on as usual back at River's Bend. He was one man alone against outlaws and the elements. His present condition proved that *anything* could happen out here and that it was dangerous to be caught without help in this country.

Why did he feel this terrific loneliness—this awful depression over the fact that most people didn't know or care who he was or where he was or why? Only his mother and father cared, and they were probably back to living their normal lives, praying for him and waiting for him, but they were among friends back home and living a good life. Elly probably cared and still thought about him, but she was of no help now. He'd never even see her again.

Was all this vengeance worth it? He thought of Lora, lying dead, their baby dead, too. So cruel. So unnecessary. So violent and so unfair.

Yes, the thought of Lora made him realize that vengeance was worth every last thing he might have to suffer catching up to the Liberty boys.

"Drink some coffee," Henrietta told him again, holding the cup to his lips.

Matt sipped some of the hot brew. It did help settle his thoughts. "Thank you. Not just for this but for everything. I'll try to get out of here as soon as I can and not be a burden."

"I do not mind," Henrietta told him. "And I will be very upset if you leave too soon. Whatever you want to do, and wherever you are going, it is not worth dying for, young man."

Matt thought about the Liberty boys again. The sight of his pregnant wife lying dead. "It *is* worth dying for," he answered. "You have no idea."

"Well, for now you must lie back and not think about it." Henrietta leaned closer to fluff his pillows. "If it is so important, then do what you must do in order to be strong enough to leave. You will never accomplish what you want if you leave too soon and die on the way."

Maybe I SHOULD have died, Matt thought. He clutched his chest as another coughing fit engulfed him, which in turn caused excruciating pain in his ribs.

"You poor man," Henrietta fussed. "I will bring you some of that hot chicken broth. It is good for fever and bad lungs."

She left, and thunder rumbled outside. Another spring storm was coming. But no storm, or even a tornado, could match the black storm in Matt's heart, the thunder of revenge, the lightning that flashed from the end of a gun, the kind of storm he'd bring the Liberty boys, a storm they'd not survive. His current situation was not going to stop him.

He closed his eyes, wondering if the awful storm that put him here had hit Elly's wagon train.

CHAPTER TWENTY

MID-JUNE...

*F*ort Laramie sprawled before them as the travelers pulled into an assigned area.

"This is the busiest place we've seen since we left home," Elly told Betty, who walked beside her.

"It is! We should be able to find plenty of supplies here." Betty wiped at her damp forehead with the back of her hand.

Elly put an arm around her sister-in-law. "First you're going to lie down in the back of the wagon for a while. We'll roll up the sides so you can lie still and cool off. This sudden hot, muggy weather isn't good for you. You *must* stop and let yourself heal more."

"I don't want to seem weak."

"No one would think that. And there are plenty of women along to do all the chores and share the laundering and such while we're here. I'm sure Mark will agree you need to rest. You keep trying to do everything you've always done, and I keep telling you to slow down."

"Just let me get out what's needed for a fire and coffee and supper. You go unhitch the oxen, but let Mark and your father get the yokes off."

There was little time to talk while travelers unhitched teams and removed harnesses and other hitching gear before turning the animals out to an area where they were left to graze. Men shouted orders to each other and to their teams, women carried on conversations while they tended to chores and children, pots and pans clattered, children began running about, and in the distance a soldier shouted rhythmic orders of "Left—right, left—right" as he drilled his men. Cattle mooed in the distance and horses whinnied. Orlando, the wagon master they'd all grown to dislike, shouted his own orders.

"We're in Wyoming now, folks, headed for the mountains. Got to be alert once we get there. Part of the trip will be through Outlaw Country."

Outlaw Country. The words brought to mind Matt Stover. Elly wondered where he was now—how far ahead he was—if he thought about her anymore. It had been roughly two weeks since that night, that kiss. Roughly two weeks since he rode out of her life and into a danger he might not survive.

She couldn't help wondering if maybe he'd been here and gone, and she decided to ask the fort commander if he knew anything about him.

To her relief, she'd not seen hide nor hair of Pete Garner or Stacy Bodeen, and that was just fine with her. She couldn't help worrying they might be following with some kind of evil plans, or that they might have hung back and gone looking for Matt, intending to kill him.

She walked back to Betty's wagon to get some things from her, gasping with dread when she saw Betty bent over, clinging to a wagon wheel for support. She hurried up and grasped her arm.

"Tommy!" she called to the boy who sat nearby tracing something in the sand. "Go get your father! Right now!"

Tommy glanced up and saw his mother slowly wilting

to the ground. He ran off to find Mark, and Elly sat down beside Betty and let her lay her head in her lap.

"I just—couldn't stand up anymore," Betty said weakly.

"You'll be all right. You just need to lie down and do absolutely nothing for the next few days." Elly smoothed some hair back from her face.

"I think I'm bleeding again, Elly." Tears came then.

"We'll get you into the wagon, and I'll help you clean up. You'll be fine, love."

Two other women walked over to offer their help. Elly assured them they should tend to their chores, which would be the most help of all. "We'll get her into the wagon and let her rest. That's all she needs," she told them, hoping she was right.

Mark came running then. "Betty!" He bent down and picked her up.

"She's got to rest, Mark. She's got to stop driving the oxen, stop walking miles every day, and she can't do any chores for a while."

Glen hurried over and helped Mark get Betty into their wagon. Elly climbed inside and started undressing her.

"Have one of the women outside bring me a bowl of water," she told Mark. "I've got to cool her down." She reached for a canteen and helped Betty take a drink.

"I'll get her all the help she needs," Mark told Elly. "Damn it, Sis, she didn't let on she was feeling this bad."

"That's because she loves you and didn't want to appear weak or slow us down."

Mark leaned down and kissed Betty's cheek. "Don't you be lying to me, about how you feel, sweetheart. You stay right here and you rest, understand? I'll see if there's a doctor here at the fort who might be able to give you something to help you rest. Okay?"

"Yes," Betty answered softly.

Mark looked at Elly with tears in his eyes. "I had no idea."

"She's been putting up a good front. Just go get a woman to help me and bring a pan of water. And roll up the sides of the canvas. There is a nice breeze now. That should help."

Elly closed her eyes and prayed, while Mark climbed out of the wagon to get more help. She opened Betty's dress at the throat and loosened her camisole, then dripped some water from the canteen onto her chest and throat.

"Oh, that feels so good. You're such a good sister-in-law and good friend."

"You've been the same to me."

Betty breathed deeply and relaxed more. "Maybe your Matt is here."

"*My* Matt? Why on Earth did you call him that? And don't forget he's gone for good. I hardly think about him anymore."

"I don't believe you. And I know it sounds silly, but that's how I think of him—as your Matt."

"There you go again with your unrealistic look at the world, Betty Grace. And yes, it *does* sound silly."

Betty managed a smile. "Life is easier when you ignore the realities."

Elly shook her head. "Whatever helps you relax is fine with me."

"It *was* fun and interesting—the way he walked in and out of our lives, wasn't it?"

"Oh, it was interesting, all right." Again, Elly thought about Matt's kiss—so deep and gently demanding—the kiss of a man who knew what he wanted and could have easily convinced her she wanted the same thing.

The strong smell of coffee brought her back to the present. "Someone's boiling coffee already," she said, to change the subject. "When Mark comes back, I'll have him get some for you."

"Yes. Thank you."

Dear Lord, don't let anything happen to this woman, Elly prayed. *This whole trip will seem to be for nothing if You take her from us. And Mark will be devastated.*

Mark finally returned with a bucket of water and one of the women, Martha Sims, who'd tried to help earlier. He helped Mrs. Sims climb inside, then lifted the bucket to them. "I have to go help Glen and John with the livestock," he told them. "I found a doctor. He'll be a while, but he said he'd come see what he can do for her. She okay for now?"

"I think so," Elly told him. "We can handle things for now."

Mark left again, and Elly and Martha helped Betty undress and wash, relieved to realize she wasn't bleeding as badly as they'd feared.

"We don't need anything else going wrong on this trip," Martha grumbled as they helped Betty slip on a clean nightgown. "We've had broken wagon wheels and injured travelers and animals, and that awful rain we got a couple of weeks ago. I thought we'd all drown. My husband thinks he saw a funnel cloud in the distance. Thank God it didn't come our way."

"Yes. That rain was bad enough," Elly answered.

"Well, if we can get Betty settled and healed, it will be a good sign. The only trouble is those awful buffalo hunters."

Elly helped Betty drink more water. "Oh, they're gone now. We haven't seen them since we left Sidney."

"Until today."

Elly met Martha's gaze, and her chest tightened at the worry she saw there. "What do you mean?"

Martha closed her eyes. "I saw them. Just a few

minutes ago. I walked farther out to talk to my husband, and there they were, riding into the fort. They were close enough that I could tell they were those same two men who bothered us when we were doing laundry back in Sidney—the ones who said those insulting things about you. Only it wasn't just the two of them. There were three other men with them."

Pain shot through Elly's stomach. Why had those two shown up again? Had they been following them all this time?

"A lot of men, traders and such, stop here for supplies," she reminded Martha.

"I suppose, but those two that bothered us make me nervous."

If Matt was here, he'd send them running. But Matt was well on his way into the mountains by now. "We just have to stay close to the men and the wagons."

Martha nodded. "Yes." She swallowed. "I just thought you should be aware. I told my husband, so the men will be alert to them."

"Good." Elly smoothed back Betty's now-damp hair again, realizing Betty was nearly asleep and didn't seem aware of their conversation. "Don't say anything to Betty. I don't want her to worry. Losing that baby took a lot out of her, and she's still heartbroken over it."

"I understand," Martha answered. She reached out and touched Elly's arm. "You be careful, Elly. I'll always remember how those men looked at you, and some men have certain ideas about the needs of a widowed woman."

Elly thought about the kiss she'd shared with Matt. Men like Pete Garner knew nothing about how to treat a woman, but Matt had awakened long-sleeping needs she'd tried to ignore all these years. The thought of those buffalo hunters even touching her made her skin crawl, yet she longed for Matt's touch. She could only hope Pete Garner and Stacy Bodeen were only here for supplies and would soon be on their way, never to be seen again.

CHAPTER TWENTY-ONE

*H*ank Volmer drove two big draft horses that pulled the farm wagon, while Matt pitched hay into a field for the man's small herd of cattle. Three weeks of getting over what Henrietta was sure was pneumonia, and healing from his bruises and scrapes from Rusty dragging him, left Matt feeling almost normal but still sore. He was determined to get back on the trail, but he felt obligated to do something for Hank before leaving. The man was getting older, and it was harder every year for him to keep up his small farm and ranch.

"Young blood, that is what I need," he'd told Matt just the previous night at supper. Matt was getting used to the couples' strong German accent, enough to understand them when they sometimes even reverted to using German words for things.

"My sons, they did not want to farm," Hank lamented. *"Off they went back East. They are good boys, but they wanted to explore the cities. I suppose that is normal, but now I fear they will never come back."*

Matt felt sorry for the man. He'd come out here with a dream and fought Natives and the elements and sometimes outlaws to keep what he'd claimed. Now he'd likely have to give it up.

"Do not waste your young years filled with hate and revenge over the men who killed your wife," Hank had warned him. *"You are young and strong. You should find another woman, start a new family. A man has to go on, or he wastes his life over things he cannot change."*

Matt thought how Hank's words sounded very much like what his parents had warned him about, but he couldn't get over the fact that he, too, once had a dream, and the Liberty boys had destroyed it. He wished he *could* go on, but the memory of Lora lying dead made his thirst for revenge more important than going on with any kind of life without her.

He'd been a sheriff long enough to know the way of the gun, and how to read a man for what he was. He'd be fine amid towns full of outlaws. Something had gone wrong to turn such men into what they were now—and the same thing was probably happening to him.

"Don't become one of them," his father had warned.

He scraped out the last of the hay feed and sat down in the back of the wagon while Hank drove the horses to the house. Matt winced and grunted every time the wagon bounced over ruts and rocks, his ribs still hurting, his left leg still giving him problems from being stretched almost beyond endurance while his foot was caught in that stirrup. He couldn't blame poor Rusty. The damn horse had been scared out of his mind and dragging poor Sadie with him. He couldn't blame either horse, even though Sadie had charged right over him. Luckily, his ribs were only bruised but not broken. Sadie had suffered a bruised leg but was healing nicely.

Hank drove up to the front door of the cabin and both men climbed down, ready for lunch.

"Beautiful day," Matt told Hank.

"Ya, that it is."

Both men stopped to wash their hands and splash water on their faces before going inside.

"I can't thank you enough, Hank, for helping me like you did, and for putting up my horses and supplies." Matt grabbed a small towel hanging nearby and dried his face and hands.

"It is not necessary to thank me. And you have helped me a great deal the last three days, even though I know you are still in pain."

Matt wiped the towel across the back of his neck. "Pain or not, I'm leaving tomorrow. Between this and stopping to help that wagon train I told you about, I've lost a good month of travel."

Hank wiped off his own hands and face and met Matt's gaze. "I still think you are leaving too soon."

"I'll be fine."

The stout German sighed deeply, putting his hands on his hips. "Ya, well, that is easy for a strong young man to say. I can tell you that when you get older, you start to pay for abusing your body when you are young—in ways you would not even understand now."

Both men grinned.

"My own father' has told me that," Matt answered, "and he doesn't work nearly as hard physically as you do." He hung up the towel. "As far as paying for my injuries later, I think I'll just wait and find out for myself. If you tell me everything now, I'll dread getting old more than I already do."

Hank laughed heartily. "Ah, well, there are good things about it, too. One of them is that you get wiser. That is why I know it will do me no good to tell you again to give up what you want to do and just go home. Learn to accept what is and go on from there. You have a lot of good years left in you."

Matt shook his head and sobered. "Think about it, Hank. You're a proud German man, and I can see how much you love your wife. What if men came through here and shot her down? What if you had a young child and they shot him, too? You can't tell me you wouldn't want to go after them."

Hank closed his eyes and quietly nodded. "I suppose I would. But at my age I truly would have nothing left to live for." He studied Matt with obvious sympathy. "But you have many years ahead of you. You *will* love another woman, Matt Stover, because it is natural for a man to be with a woman and to produce young ones."

Matt put a hand on the man's brawny shoulder and guided him toward the front door. "But it's *not* natural for that woman and young one to be taken away from him through violence. Sickness or an accident, I could accept after a while. But needless violence that could have been avoided is different." He followed Hank through the front door and into a room that smelled of fresh-baked bread, frying chicken and warm pie.

"Come in! Come in! I have made an extra nice meal as a farewell to our guest," Henrietta declared. "Sit down, and I will put food on the table."

Matt took a chair. "You didn't have to do this, Mrs. Volmer."

"Ah, yes, I did. A young man who is still healing needs to eat well. I will pack you plenty of fresh bread and some chicken and dried meat for your journey, and I have extra potatoes. They are a little soft and shriveled from being in the fruit cellar all winter, but they are still plenty good."

Matt shook his head. "You need your food. You two have already done enough for me."

"And the money you insisted we take from you will pay for plenty of *new* supplies," Hank answered. "I still do not feel right taking it."

"I brought enough along that I'll be fine. I'm just grateful for all you did to help me heal, and for the fact that you could have stolen my horses and all my supplies and weapons and left me out there on the prairie to die. No one would have known the difference, and I never would have recovered to track you down."

"Ah, you are good at tracking men, I am thinking," Hank told him. "A lawman has to do those things."

"I've learned a lot, and I've also hunted game most of my life, so I'm not worried about having enough meat along the way."

Henrietta placed a treasure-trove of food in front of him. "Well, for now you will eat well because of my cooking," she told Matt. She set another plate in front of Hank.

"Henrietta!" Hank scolded. "I'll get too fat to do my chores."

Henrietta poured coffee. "You work too hard to build any fat."

Matt studied her as she poured the coffee. Stout, plain, yet pretty in a strong, devoted woman sort of way. Watching her brought Elly to mind. She seemed to have the same spirit and strength as Henrietta, and he realized that had attracted him to her just as much or more than her lovely shape and soft smile.

He'd avoided thoughts of Elly as much as he could the last couple of weeks, but now that he was feeling stronger, he couldn't help wondering how she was doing. How far ahead were they now? He had no doubt Elly's wagon train had passed him a good two weeks ago and had probably already arrived at Fort Laramie and gone on from there. They could end up going through Outlaw Country, but they'd be farther south of where he was headed. They would go straight through, but that same country was where his own journey would end. He would instead search for the Liberty boys.

"So, you will still leave us tomorrow?" Henrietta sat down across from Matt.

"Yes, Ma'am."

Henrietta shook her head. "Ah, I hate to see you keep going, son. You should go back to your hometown and the people there who love you."

"I won't be happy until I get this done." Matt dished some potatoes onto his plate and handed the bowl to Hank.

"I think that you will learn revenge does not taste so good in the mouth," Hank told him. "But it seems all young people have to learn things the hard way."

"I'm not new to guns or to hunting wanted men." Matt took a chicken leg from a platter and handed the platter back to Henrietta. "I can handle myself, Hank."

"We are sure you can," Henrietta told him, "but we will miss you and we will worry about you. Try to stop and see us when you go home. Let us know you are all right. If you cannot stop here, write us a letter. Send it to our attention to The Sidney waystation. It is a stagecoach station north of Sidney and they keep supplies there and take mail."

"I'll do that, Ma'am."

The meal continued, and all ate silently. Matt filled up on chicken and potatoes, planning to eat pie later. If he was headed for disaster, he might as well enjoy what could be his last, big home-cooked meal.

He would miss the Volmers. And he would miss Elly and her kind family. Traveling into the unknown was a strange, new life, and already he felt as though he was losing Sheriff Matt Stover—losing track of who that man was. He still thought occasionally about going on to

California, but it was possible that he'd arrive there such a changed man that Elly wouldn't even want him anymore.

CHAPTER TWENTY-TWO

LATE JUNE...

"*A*re you feeling better today?" Betty was up and dressed, and Elly helped her fold a blanket, then set aside two pillows.

"I feel *much* better," Betty answered. "I really needed those four days of rest at Fort Laramie, and letting me stay here in the wagon for those next many days also helped."

"This higher, cooler country also helps," Elly told her.

This was pretty country. They were in Wyoming now, a much hillier landscape with a lot of rocks, pine forest and, on the western skyline, mountains. Elly didn't relish how hard it might be to get *over* those mountains, let alone being faced with yet another wall of mountains after that... the Sierras. But others had made it over both ranges, and grumpy and grizzly as he was, their guide seemed to know what he was doing, so she preferred to think positive about reaching California.

"You look more like your old self," Elly told her sister-in-law. "And your color is good. I think you lost too much blood with that miscarriage, and it took a while for your body to build it back up." Elly laid the blanket aside. "But don't overdo it yet. Take it easy a few more days."

Betty smiled softly. "Everybody's been so kind and patient in agreeing to wait with us at the fort. And your dear brother has been good about it, too. Some men wouldn't understand, but Mark did. I think Glen was a little ornery about waiting that extra few days at Fort Laramie, but it made a big difference for me."

Elly frowned. "Yes, well, Glen showed a few true colors back there that told me I definitely will *not* marry him when we get to California. It seemed to me that all he was worried about was the fact that you couldn't do your share of the work. I don't think he understands much about women. I keep getting the feeling he only wants to marry me for cooking, cleaning, helping work a farm, and for his own—well, you know—pleasure."

Betty laughed lightly. "Well, if *you* think you wouldn't enjoy that same pleasure in return, then it's good you won't marry him."

Elly couldn't help a smile. "You just remember that enjoying that pleasure is what got you pregnant, Betty Grace, so you should refrain from that kind of pleasure for several weeks yourself."

"And it's been six years since little Tommy was born," Betty reminded her, "so it's not as though we thought it would make any difference. We thought maybe I couldn't have any more, so we weren't worried about me getting pregnant again before the trip. Besides, I had no problems with my other pregnancies."

"And you weren't traveling over fifteen hundred miles through dangerous, rugged country in a wagon that sometimes bounces so hard it nearly throws you off, let alone walking a good share of the way. Add to that all the extra work involved trying to cook and launder with no regular facilities, and no real bed to fall into at night. This trip is much too rough for a woman carrying, and I intend to talk to my brother about that, no matter how embarrassing that will be. That miscarriage was a message to slow down until we get settled."

Betty pressed her lips together in resignation as she heaved a deep sigh. "I have to agree with you, much as I don't want to. And you don't need to go through the embarrassment of talking to Mark. I'll do it. He usually does whatever I say, and I know he truly was worried over this and scared I'd die. He doesn't want to take that risk again. We'll manage."

"Promise me. I thought we'd lose you, Betty, and you're my best friend, let alone my brother's wife. I don't want to go through something like that again, either, and I don't want *you* to go through it."

"I promise." Betty moved toward the back of the wagon. "I'll start coffee while you fold those other couple of blankets." She paused. "Elly."

Elly met her gaze. "What?"

"Do you still think about him?"

Elly didn't need to ask what she meant. "Sometimes," she answered. "And stop asking. I'm trying very hard to *stop* thinking about him."

"Well, sometimes I wish Matt Stover would come riding into our camp and whisk you onto his horse and declare he wants to marry you."

Elly shook her head. "And you just promised me you and Mark would abstain for the rest of this trip. You're such a hopeless romantic, Betty Grace. I'm not so sure you'll be able to stick to your promise." She moved toward the back of the wagon and picked up a frying pan to start cooking potatoes. "Come and make that coffee, and remember that Matt is long gone, probably nearly to the mountains by now. I'm the last thing on his mind, and you need to stop talking about him. He is a man in deep grief and full of revenge, not a man looking for another woman to love." She climbed down from the wagon and reached up for Betty. "Come on. I'll help you out."

"I only talk about Matt Stover because I don't want you to be lonely," Betty told her as she climbed out of the wagon.

"I'm *not* lonely. I have you and my brother and father and my darling nephews to keep me company and keep me busy."

Betty reached for the coffee pot. "If you say so."

"I *do* say so." Elly handed Betty the frying pan. "And right now, I'm going to relieve myself behind that big rocky hillside the men told us to use. I'll be back to help you in just a few minutes." She sent Betty off with both a coffee pot and the frying pan and headed for the area designated the night before as the place for privacy. She picked up her skirt as she walked through tall grass and up the nearby hill, then around boulders and a couple of pine trees to a place hidden from camp. It was quiet here, buffered from the sounds of busy breakfast-making and haltering of oxen and shouting going on below as the men made ready for another long day of travel.

Elly thought how she missed pure quiet, but even here, away from all the camp noise, there was the constant drone of Wyoming's eternal wind. She'd noticed that the farther west they went, the windier it became, and not necessarily just in gusts. Just like the horizon in all directions, the wind was endless - caused, according to their guide, by cold air dropping down from the mountains and hitting warmer air. There was never any letup in the rustling sound of grass and trees bending and bowing to the wind.

She looked around, realizing that just behind the low, rocky hill was a thick stand of pines, and just to her left were higher piles of rock beyond which she couldn't tell if the ground dropped off again or leveled off. The men had been right in saying this was the perfect place for a person to have complete privacy, something sorely missing in the first part of their journey in wide-open prairie for days on end.

She bent down and lifted her skirts to urinate, closing her eyes for a moment to listen to birds singing, and to the wind that moaned softly through the pines. She finished her business and started to rise when she thought she heard something behind her. At the same time, she heard a rattling sound. She looked down to see a rattlesnake not far from her feet. Before she could react or even scream, a man's big hand clamped around her mouth, and a strong arm came around her middle, pinning both her arms to her sides.

It all happened lightning fast. She felt a searing pain at her ankle.

The snake!

She smelled the awful odor of someone's long-unwashed body, mingled with the smell of whiskey. She heard an odd thud, then the sound of men's voices as she was dragged away while slowly blacking out.

"...got it with the butt of my rifle. I couldn't shoot the goddamn thing or they'd know what's up."

"...didn't plan on no goddamn snake!"

"...just get her over the horse. She's passin' out."

"...got to move fast before they miss her!"

"...busy... makin' breakfast... loadin' up."

"...won't miss her for a good bit yet."

"...cut that thing open... get the venom out..."

"...if she dies, she ain't no good to us."

Elly couldn't hear the birds singing anymore. She couldn't hear the wind. She thought she opened her eyes, but she couldn't see anything. She couldn't even feel anything, except for a sudden pain in her lower right leg, a pain even more excruciating than the initial snakebite—or at least that was what her fading senses told her had just happened.

There came another horrible pain at her ankle. She tried to fight, tried to scream, but nothing worked, and blackness engulfed her, along with the horrible realization that whoever had grabbed her was not taking her back to camp.

CHAPTER TWENTY-THREE

*M*att rode into Fort Laramie, half hoping to find the Grace family's wagons there. At the same time, he was relieved they weren't. It seemed as though every time he ended up losing time, it had something to do with the Grace family or buffalo hunters. If he hadn't taken that extra couple of days to chase Pete Garner away from Elly's wagon train, and then waited around to spend time with her back at Fort McPherson, he might have missed that tornado that laid him up for over three weeks.

He'd made up his mind that from here on, it was business only, and that business involved finding the Liberty boys and making them pay for their awful crimes.

His thoughts were interrupted by a voluptuous, painted woman with orange hair who hailed him from the balcony of a saloon just outside the fort.

"Hey, cowboy! You want some female company?"

Someone back at Fort McPherson had told him that the farther west he went, the more prostitutes he'd find hanging around the forts to make money off lonely soldiers. Businesses and homesteads of all sorts were sprawled haphazardly outside the fort, and the building he passed now said only "SALOON."

He tipped his hat to the young woman who'd called to him, wanting to be respectful in spite of her obvious trade, but having no intention of taking her up on her offer. "No, thank you, Ma'am."

He did, however, want a beer. He dismounted and tied Rusty as riders and wagons of all sorts passed in and out of the fort gates. He wondered how far ahead the Grace family was now. They should be getting closer to the Rockies, and he wished he could quit worrying about Elly. He had no doubt they had a rough journey still ahead, having to conquer two mountain ranges before reaching California. He'd heard nothing but good things about that state—sunny, warm, and great for farming. If he were a farmer, he'd go there, too, just to start over someplace new to help him get over Lora.

He walked up two steps and through swinging doors into the saloon, where he was immediately met by the woman who'd hailed him from the balcony.

"Hi, honey."

Matt nodded. "Ma'am. I'm just here for a beer."

She took hold of his arm. "Then make sure the bartender thinks I talked you into one. He owns the place, and we're supposed to help him sell as much alcohol as possible."

Matt couldn't help glancing at her milky-white breasts that bounced with every move she made. She wasn't even close to how pretty Lora was, and she wasn't a woman of gentle honor and faith like Lora. He felt a little sorry for her nonetheless, and when she led him to the bar, he did as she'd asked.

"This woman here says you have the best beer around, and that it's actually cold. I'll have one."

The bartender grinned and nodded. "We get ice from

down out of the mountains. Keeps the kegs cold." He filled a beer mug and set it in front of Matt. "That there young lady can provide you with some other refreshments, if you know what I mean, mister."

Matt paid for his beer. "No, thanks. No reflection on her, but I'm a fresh widower and just not looking for that kind of refreshment."

"Oh, I'm sorry!" the woman told him, stroking his arm. "Maybe if you came upstairs, I could help you forget and relieve some of your stressful needs."

"He said no, Darcy."

The words came from a man even taller than Matt. He stood on the other side of the woman Matt now knew was called Darcy. He looked Indian, with long, black hair tied behind his neck. He wore a gun and had an intimidating air about him.

Darcy turned to the Indian and stood on her tiptoes to kiss his cheek. "Just drumming up business, Sage. I'll take *your* business any time you want to come back upstairs.

Sage grinned. "We'll see. Right now, I figure the man beside you there would like to be left alone."

Darcy turned to Matt. "You know where I am, honey, any time you need me."

Matt finished a slug of beer. "Yes, Ma'am. Thank you for your hospitality."

Darcy laughed and left, and Sage grinned and shook his head.

"Thanks for rescuing me." Matt put out his hand. "I'm Matt Stover."

"Sage Lightfoot."

Matt noted the roughness around the edges of the man and decided it was best to stay on his good side. There was a hint of wild Indian about him, but he spoke well, as though he'd had a decent education. He decided not to ask questions as they shared a firm handshake. "I can tell you're not a man to cross, Mister Lightfoot. And neither am I."

Sage kept hold of Matt's hand for a few extra seconds. "You're right about not crossing me," he answered. "And yes, I'm Indian. I know you're wondering, But I was well educated by a white family, so don't treat me like some white men treat what they consider ignorant savages. They aren't savages, and I'm not ignorant. I like to make sure a man understands that before he says something that hits me the wrong way." He frowned, studying Matt's eyes. "You a lawman?" Sage let go of his hand and leaned his left elbow on the bar so he could face him.

"How did you know?"

Sage shook his head. "Something about you. I can't put a word to it. Maybe you were too nice to Darcy, like maybe you were afraid of hurting her feelings. There's nothing wrong with being nice, and I'm not one to abuse a woman, but in these parts men aren't quite so gentlemanly with women like her. And I assure you, you can't hurt her feelings. She's being nice to you because that's how she makes her money. Darcy has a mean streak you don't often see."

"Have *you* seen it?"

Sage laughed again. "A time or two, but I don't get here often. I brought some beef cattle to sell to the Army, then I'm headed west to the foothills of the Rockies. I've claimed some land there for ranching—prettiest piece of land you'll ever find. I call it Paradise Valley."

Matt wondered how he man was able to claim land if he was Indian, but he decided not to ask probing questions. He drank down more beer. "Sounds real nice. Can we sit down a minute?"

"Sure." Sage ordered two more beers and paid for them.

"Thanks."

They found a table and sat down. Matt sensed there was an edge about Sage Lightfoot that could turn him from friendly to mean with one wrong word. "I asked you to sit down because I have a couple of questions and a favor to ask," he told Sage. "If you say no, I have no problem with it. I just might need help with where I'm going, and I have a feeling you might be a man with answers."

Sage swallowed some of his beer. "Where are you headed?"

"The Outlaw Trail. In and around that area anyway."

Sage studied him again for several quiet seconds. "Pretty dangerous country."

"You been there?"

"Sure have. Plenty long enough to know you need to rough yourself up a bit and not be so friendly. You don't want any man there to know you're a lawman. That's a piss-poor place for a lawman to go. Why in hell are you putting yourself in that kind of danger?"

Matt studied the frost on his beer mug and ran a finger over it. "I'm out to kill two men—brothers—Joe and Tex Liberty." He met Sage's dark gaze. "They're from River's Bend Nebraska, where I'm the sheriff. They robbed and shot up a bank there, killed my pregnant wife in the process. They also killed the baby girl in her belly. I'll never rest easy until they're both dead by my hand."

Sage nodded. "I can understand that."

Both men drank down more beer.

"I need to know more about the Outlaw Trail. How to handle the men there. It's not that I'm ignorant of the outlaw-type, and I happen to be damn good with a gun. But I've never been someplace where practically every man I meet is wanted or a law-breaker of some sort— where every man is a bit desperate in some way or another. Surely not every man there is bad at heart."

Sage shifted in his chair and leaned his elbows on the table. "No, not every man. I've spent a lot of time there myself, for my own reasons. And yes, I've gone against the law, but sometimes a man is forced into that life." He leaned back again. "What you have to know is there's a kind of code in that country—their own form of law—the law of the gun mostly. Survival of the fittest, or maybe I should say the fastest. But men are there for a host of reasons. Some actually have families there—businesses, farms and ranches. They're wanted someplace back East and are afraid to go home. A whole lot of them lost everything in the War Between the States. They robbed and killed out of revenge, got their mugs on wanted posters." He studied Matt intensely. "But then you aren't fleeing revenge killings, are you? You said you were headed west to *get* your revenge."

Matt nodded. "I need to fit in, so tell me what to do."

Sage looked him over. "Well, I'd stop shaving so close, in case by chance you run into some man who might recognize you too easily. And grow your hair a little longer. Water your horses with that hat and get some stains on it. Find ways to stain your saddle if it's too new. Sounds strange, but dirty yourself up a little so you fit in better. And don't take any shit off any man. If some man insults you or calls you out, deck him. If he threatens something worse, go ahead and draw first. Show him how fast you are and that you won't hesitate to put a hole in him if he doesn't leave you alone. I guarantee he *will* leave you alone after that, and so will those around who see your behavior and how fast you are with that .44 you're carrying."

Matt raised his eyebrows and grinned. "I'm not used to *starting* trouble."

"That's because you're a lawman. In Outlaw Country, *you* shoot first and ask questions later. *Forget* about law, because there isn't any out there, except the law of men who will respect how good you are with gun and fist. Men who understand they have to have *some* kind of order to survive. When I get my own ranch going in Paradise Valley, I intend to live the right way and raise my own cattle and try to stay on the right side of the law - mainly because I see the law coming here, too, eventually. Life won't always be like it is right now in Outlaw Country, but for now you need to understand how to survive it, and you won't do that by being nice. Just like with wild animals, it's survival of the smartest, the boldest and the fittest."

Matt finished his beer and set down the mug. "You said some have families. What's it like for their wives?"

Sage yelled out to Darcy, "Bring us two more beers, honey."

Darcy sauntered to the bar to order the drinks, and Sage leaned closer again. "To begin with, there are a whole lot more women like Darcy out there than not, and those who abuse them are dealt some pretty bad punishment because the prostitutes are needed and protected. I've seen men shot or hanged for beating on a saloon woman. Some men *marry* them, so they have them all to themselves. For the most part, a man's wife is someone you don't touch. They're seen practically as angels. The single ones are held in even higher respect. I've seen a lot of fist fights over single women."

Matt glanced at Darcy as she set beers in front of them. This time he paid for the beers.

"Enjoy," Darcy told him, leaning extra low. "I hear they taste real good."

Matt raised his beer and touched her breasts with the cold mug, making her let out a little scream and jump back. She laughed and walked away.

Matt shook his head. "This life will take some getting

used to." He swallowed some beer. "You said 'single.' Why would there be any single women in places like that?"

Sage shrugged. "Lots of reasons. Daughters of some of the family men—young girls who are growing up out there. They even hire female schoolteachers. There are three or four that I know of, but one of them also sells herself for extra money. Overall, life in Outlaw Country isn't all that different—just more dangerous. But most men have a sense of decency down inside and don't want to live a life of lawlessness any more than most common men do. Still, you're better off if they don't know you're a lawman, so you need a good excuse as to why you're there."

"I'll be asking around about the Liberty boys."

"Then let them know that those two murdered your wife and baby. You're just a man from Nebraska out for revenge. They aren't fond of any man who'd shoot down a young, married woman carrying a baby, so you might even get some help going after them."

"I might *need* that help. I already know the Liberty brothers have at least three others with them."

"Then you know what I mean."

Matt nodded. "I do."

Sage finished his beer. "You said you had a favor to ask."

"I do." Matt swallowed most of his own beer. "If you're headed into the foothills of the Rockies, I'm wondering if I could ride along. I need someone to show me the way into Outlaw Trail country, and to explain a few things about mountain living. I'm from wide-open prairie land, so I need to be prepared for life in the mountains, and I need to learn more about the Outlaw Trail—the towns, the trails—the cabins and caves where men hide out—the weather. All of it. Have you been there enough to know all that?"

Sage shoved his beer mug aside. "I have. And you can ride with me if you want, but I have other men with me, most of them outlaws like I once was. They're good men, loyal. But you'd be wise not to ask too many questions. They're the kind of men who'll befriend you and let you get closer if that's what *they* want. I shook your hand over at the bar there because I could read you pretty good, but I'd advise you *not* to offer your hand too readily from here on. The minute they sense you're a decent, friendly man, they might try to take advantage of that, thinking you're the trusting type."

Matt nodded. "It's not like I haven't dealt with that type before."

Sage grinned. "Don't ask for last names tomorrow when I introduce you. My men don't care much for giving out last names. Some don't use their real names at all."

Matt finished his beer. "All right. When do you leave?"

"Sun-up, day after tomorrow."

"Good. That gives me time to rest my horses and stock up on a few supplies."

"From here on, keep a good watch on your horses *and* your gear. There are plenty out here who'd have no qualms about riding off with both, but most get hanged for it if they're caught. No trial. Just outlaw justice." Sage rose. "We'll be gathered north of the fort by five a.m. Be there, or we'll leave without you."

"I'll be there." Matt also rose. "I'd thank you for all of this, but I guess that's too friendly."

Sage laughed lightly. "It is. No thanks are needed out here. A man just does what he wants or needs to do and doesn't expect anything for it."

Sage Lightfoot turned and left.

Darcy walked up to Matt and ran a hand over his rear-end. "You sure you don't want some female company, honey?"

Matt smiled at her, thinking she looked a little more tempting now that he'd had a few beers. But she wasn't Lora... or Elly. "No, thanks," he answered.

He walked out, upset with himself for thinking about Elly again, and realizing that yes, he *did* want some female company, but that it would likely be a long time before he came across another woman like Elly. He told himself to remember to treat the prostitutes out here like ladies, which most of them probably were at some time in their lives. Who knew what had led them to sleeping with men for money? He had too many other things on his mind to care.

He walked outside to Rusty and mounted up. "Well, boy, I guess I don't need to shave for a while." He patted the horse's neck. "Or get a haircut."

He headed for a supply store, relieved that he was finally getting closer now—closer to the Liberty boys— closer to avenging Lora's death.

CHAPTER TWENTY-FOUR

*E*lly smelled cigarette smoke, body odor, and whiskey. She opened her eyes to the light of a dimly-lit lantern, and a room with red roses in the wallpaper. She heard the laughter of both men and women, piano music, and loud voices—mostly men using cuss words she'd never heard come out of the mouth of any man she'd ever known.

She fought panic, telling herself to stay calm and think things through. She struggled to remember how she might have gotten here, wherever "here" was. Some man let out a wild war whoop somewhere. More laughter. A woman screamed, but not a terrified scream. It was more a scream someone would make when having a good time.

She stirred, yelling out when pain shot through her right ankle. She realized then that the bed and blankets she lay in smelled of body odor, unwashed bedclothes that made her shudder with disgust. She felt her body, relieved to discover she still wore her dress. But she felt hot. Too hot. She threw off her covers and looked at her dress. The blue checkered cotton garment helped her remember where she had been when she wore it—behind the rocks at the top of the small hill where she'd gone to urinate this morning, if, indeed, this was the same day. Maybe it wasn't just this morning. Maybe it had been longer than that since he memory of someone grabbing her.

From what she could tell, it was night now. Dread and horror shot through her then when she remembered someone putting a hand over her mouth... someone dragging her away... a terrible pain in her leg, and someone talking about a snake... someone strong and smelly hanging on to her. She'd been on a horse. Men's voices.

"Why'd you pick morning to do this?"

"Because at night they sit around and talk. Then she'd sleep in one of the wagons. It'd be impossible to get her out of one of the wagons without the rest of 'em knowin'."

"I guess you're right."

"'Course I'm right. In the mornin' they're all busy as hell makin' ready to leave. They wouldn't miss her near soon enough to realize we rode off with her. And Orlando ain't gonna' take the time to let them go lookin' for her. He'll insist they keep goin'."

Orlando? Their *guide*? Did he know whoever had taken her? Was he a part of the plan?

"My God," Elly groaned. She managed to sit up a little. She pulled her dress up enough to look at her leg, then gasped and cried out at the sight of her ankle swollen at least three times its normal size. Worse than that, her dress was horribly soiled. She'd apparently been left here alone to drift in and out of consciousness, and to urinate right where she was! A dirty rag was tied around her ankle.

Pain forced her to lie back down, and she couldn't help the deep sobs that came then. Where in God's name was she? Who'd taken her? Would she just lie here and die? "

Help!" she called out, then realized she'd not yelled the word loudly enough. "Help!"

Footsteps outside the door. The door opened, and a

heavy-set woman walked inside. She wore a dress that left no doubt about the size of her breasts, and a gaudy, red-stone necklace hung around her neck, the end of the baubles lost in her cleavage. Her dark hair was twisted into glittery combs and her lips were painted a dark red. She smiled as she walked closer.

"Well, now, you finally woke up." She looked Elly over. "You did a good job of soiling my bed, I'll say that. I'll have a time cleaning up the mess. Maybe now that you're awake you can get yourself up and take care of things yourself. I expect one of my girls can find some clean underwear and a clean dress for you."

Elly wiped at tears. "Who... are you?"

"I'm Sally Dean, and I own this saloon and brothel."

"*Brothel?*"

Sally smiled through puffy lips. "Yes, dear. You're in a brothel, and I'm getting paid to let you lie here and heal so you can keep going."

"Keep going?"

"Yeah." Sally reached over to a small table beside the bed and picked up a pitcher and glass. She poured some water into the glass. "Pete and Stacy meant to take you with them to Brown's Park or maybe Robber's Roost. Someplace on the Outlaw Trail."

Pete and Stacy. The buffalo hunters? "Dear God," Elly muttered.

Matt Stover had been right about Pete, and here she'd defended Pete back when she and Betty nursed him! Oh, dear God, if only he knew about this. He'd help her.

"I don't understand any of this," she told Sally. "How did I get here? And how *long* have I been here?"

"Three days, honey." Sally handed her the glass of water. "You'd better drink this. It's good for a fever, and you've sweat enough that you've probably lost a few pounds."

Elly sat up more and drank the water, realizing she truly was horribly thirsty. She handed it back. "Thank you." She looked around the room. Sally reeked of cheap perfume, and Elly struggled not to show her aversion to where she was and what went on here. She shivered at realizing what the bed she was lying in was likely used for under different circumstances.

"Let's get you cleaned up, dear," Sally told her.

"Wait." Elly met the portly woman's gaze. Would Sally have any sympathy for her current situation? "Please be honest with me. Where am I and what's going on? And can you help me find the people I was traveling with?" She suddenly felt weak and dizzy, and pain shot through her ankle again.

Sally, much bigger and stronger, grasped her arms and scooted her to the head of the bed so she could sit up by leaning against pillows. She folded her arms and looked down at Elly. "As far as where you are, you're north of Rawlins and south of nothingness. My place isn't in what you could call a town. This is just kind of a way station for lonely men, if you know what I mean. We serve food, beer, liquor and women, and of course the men do plenty of gambling downstairs."

Elly put a hand to her stomach, feeling ill.

"As far as what's going on, all I know' is that Pete Garner and Stacy Bodeen brought you here snake-bit. They'd managed to get out most of the venom over the two days it took to get you here, and they paid me to put you up until you either died or came around. I'm no nursemaid, mind you, and I'm glad you're awake and can start taking care of yourself. Another couple days of food and water and rest, and you'll be good to go."

Elly shivered with dread. "Go where?"

"I told you. Someplace along the Outlaw Trail. I think those two mean to sell you there, probably to other men or to a brothel. There's lots of lonely men out there, and not enough women to keep them satisfied."

Elly ran a hand through her hair, which had long ago fallen out of the bun she'd pinned it into. If it had taken Pete and Stacy two days to get here, and she'd been here for three... She'd been gone from the wagon train for five days! Was anyone looking for her? She blinked in a continued struggle to understand what was happening. "But I'm no... I mean... I'm a war widow, Sally. And I was traveling with family, headed for California. I don't do... what you do. I don't belong here!"

"Oh, I know that." Sally patted her arm. "Honey, you wouldn't believe how women out here end up like me eventually. It's not so bad. In Outlaw Country, a pretty, skinny thing like you could make a fortune. And the men there are mostly pretty respectful of women like us."

Elly wanted to blurt out that she could *never* be like Sally, but she didn't want to offend the woman. She might need her. Still, she couldn't help the tears that welled in her eyes. "Why are they doing this?"

Sally shrugged. "I'm not sure. Something about Pete getting back at you for snubbing him somewhere along the trail. And he said he hoped some man named Matt Stover would find out and come after you. He wants to kill the man for some reason. He's bragging to everybody that if a man by that name comes looking for you, we're to tell him Pete Garner and Stacy Bodeen have you and are taking you to Outlaw Country. Who is Matt Stover, anyway?"

Matt. Where are you? Elly felt she needed to warn him. When he went looking for the men he wanted to kill, Pete and Stacy would also be looking for him. He'd be walking into a den of murderers, all wanting him dead.

"He's a—" Elly hesitated. Matt had warned that no one should know he was a lawman. "He got into a fight with Pete and some other men who tried to steal his horses and supplies. He killed two of them, but Pete and his friend got away, and now Pete's after him." She wondered if Pete was telling everyone Matt was a sheriff. Of course, he was! That would make things much more dangerous for Matt once he reached Outlaw Country.

"How do you know all this?" Sally asked.

Elly rubbed at her aching head. "Pete and the other wounded man found our camp and asked for help. Then Matt came along and we asked if he had any Laudanum. When he found out who it was for, we learned the whole story. The other man died, and Matt chased Pete off because he didn't trust him. They've been after each other ever since."

"Well, apparently Pete figured out a way to lure Matt Stover to him. So, I take it that means there's something between you and Matt Stover." Sally grinned. "Am I right?"

Elly felt helpless and doomed. God only knew where Matt was. He didn't know she'd been taken by those horrid buffalo hunters. He'd think she was well on her way to California. He'd likely never find her.

"No. We were… just friends. I have no idea where Matt is now, and he has no idea I've been taken. He probably thinks I'm half-way through the mountains by now. We—well—we just both happened to meet and talk back on the trail here—when we asked him for the laudanum. That's all there was to it. Matt's headed for Outlaw Country, searching for men who killed his wife. He could be anywhere in this big country. I don't know how Pete expects him to find me. He knows nothing about this."

"Well, they know he's headed this way, or might already be somewhere on the Outlaw Trail. If they spread the word that they have you, he'll find out one way or another. You'd be surprised how fast word spreads among outlaws. Pete seems to think Stover will come looking for you, so I'd say you two must have been more than friends. Bodeen had a pretty interesting story to tell about you two at Fort McPherson."

Elly shook her head. "Bodeen is a filthy liar." The room swirled around her, and she closed her eyes to stop the dizziness. "This is all so senseless. I just want to get back to my family. My poor sister-in-law must be out of her mind wondering what's happened to me."

And what about her poor father? Mark? Had the wagon train moved on without her? Had anyone bothered to come after her? Would Glen even care? Mark shouldn't come at all. He should stay with Betty and the boys. And her father was too old to venture into country like this looking for men like those who'd taken her. If by some miracle Matt did find out about this, he would be her only hope. She remembered Pete and Stacy talking about the wagon guide, Orlando. Betty and Mark and the others should know what kind of man he was.

Tears began streaking down her cheeks. "Please help me, Sally. Isn't there *someone* around here who could help? Maybe some man you trust could buy me. He'd be paid back and then-some if he could take me back to my wagon train. And my family would give him extra money to give to you when he returned. Please don't let those two filthy buffalo hunters take me to Outlaw Country!"

Sally shook her head. "We're out here in the middle of nowhere. And there isn't a man around right now who'd go up against Pete and Stacy. They'd end up dead. And most of them know those two and have hunted with them. They're all friends. They had three others with them when they got you here, but they left. Said they didn't want to go on to Outlaw Country."

Elly broke into sobs, her body shaking. "I don't understand any of this. It's like a horrible nightmare. I want to go back to my father and my brother."

"I can't help you there," Sally said matter-of-factly. "About all I can do is if somebody asks about you, I can let them know who has you and where they took you. Maybe Matt Stover will hear about this after all and look for you. But he'll have a time going up against Pete and his friends. Pete might still pick up extra men before he gets where he's going."

"It's more likely my brother would come, and he'd bring a friend of his." Would they end up dead? Dependable and able as they were, her brother and Glen weren't the best at tracking, especially in this new country of rocks and hard ground. And they'd be no match for the kind of men who lived out here—seasoned men, hunters, outlaws, renegades, wanted men, buffalo hunters and mountain men who knew the land, knew how to track in places like this, men who were handy with rifle and handgun. And this was big, big country. She might never be found. Even if she was, God only knew what kind of horrible predicament she would be in.

"I'll get one of my girls to find you some clothes and help you clean up," Sally told her, rising. "And we'll clean that snake bite—douse it with whiskey—and put a clean wrap on it. I have a little laudanum, if you need something for the pain."

"Thank you." Elly wanted to remain on Sally's good side. She suspected the woman could be as mean as a snake if she wanted to be. Any woman who'd survived this country and could deal with men like those downstairs didn't do so by being a wilting flower.

"I'll bring you some food once you're cleaned up. I'm actually a pretty good cook." Sally chuckled. "I expect you can tell that by my size."

She started to turn, but Elly quickly sat up straighter and reached out for her. "Sally, tell me something. The *truth*."

"The truth about what?"

"Pete and Stacy. Do you know if they... did they do anything to me?"

"Did they have their way with you while you were out?"

Elly felt her cheeks burning as she nodded.

"No. You've been way too sick and too soiled. They were actually afraid you'd die before they got you to Outlaw Country."

"Are there were other men with them?"

Sally nodded. "Pete said some of his friends didn't want anything to do with taking you because a lot of men on the Outlaw Trail don't take kindly to a woman being mistreated, so they left to do more hunting. It's Pete and Stacy who intend to keep going."

Elly felt a tiny bit of relief. At least Matt would face only two men if he came after her. And Sally seemed to have a tiny thread of caring in her veins. The woman sighed and sat down on the edge of the bed, looking at least somewhat concerned.

"Look, lady, you have to use your head. Be smart. Most men out here respect women who don't ply their trade the way I do. Fact is, they even respect women like *me*, as long as we don't steal from their pants pockets while they sleep. I think those two downstairs want to get you to Outlaw Country looking all clean and fresh, so they might keep their hands off of you. Stand right up to them. Don't show any weakness or cry and cringe and carry on. Be strong. Most men like those two talk big around women, but when it comes down to it, they won't follow through on that big talk. They're just lonely and hungry to get some satisfaction, so they mostly turn to women like me. Being an outlaw and breaking other laws doesn't make a man abuse women. That's inborn, and not as common as you think. Some men are just plain mean that way, but where you're going, most men actually hang another man for forcing a woman against her will, even if she's a whore. Keep all that in mind."

Elly took a deep breath and wiped at more tears. "I will."

"That's the only help I can give you. Some madams will buy women like you and drug them into selling themselves. I'm not one of them, and they're pretty rare. Once you get where you're going, you might even find a man who'll take you back to your people—for money, of course. Then again, maybe the one called Matt Stover will hear about this and come looking for you."

Elly sat up even straighter, wishing she could take hope in those words. But finding her in such big country, or the likelihood of Matt even hearing about this, was not likely, and in the meantime, she had to survive whatever Pete and Stacy had in mind.

"I appreciate the advice."

Sally stood up again and walked to the door, her many slips rustling as she did so. "I'll get Betsy. She likes to take care of people. She'll help you get cleaned up. And I'll tell those two no-goods downstairs that you aren't ready to travel yet. That'll buy you a little more time. Maybe somebody will find you here before you have to go any farther." She nodded toward a curtained room. "There's a chamber pot in there if you need it, but you'd better wait 'til Betsy can help you. You might not be able to walk on that ankle."

Sally walked out, and Elly sat there feeling ill, her ankle throbbing. She supposed she should be glad she was still alive, but what would life bring her now? Would she ever get away from all of this and find her family again? Would *they* find *her*? Was there any hope at all that Matt would find her?

She told herself to pay attention to Sally's advice. A

woman like her would know about survival, and now she had nothing left but her own strength and courage, her own fierce determination that men like Pete and Stacy would never touch her. And she had her faith. She must not forget her faith. Surely God would find a way to help her out of this.

CHAPTER TWENTY-FIVE

EARLY JULY...

*B*etty wiped at more tears before addressing her father-in-law. "What should we do, John? I feel so torn, and I'm so worried about Mark!" She sniffed back an urge to break into all-out sobbing, hating to seem so weak. Her poor father-in-law was also suffering with grief over Elly, and worry over his son. Both his children were missing and in danger. "We're headed through the South Pass, and Mark and Glen have been gone for nearly three weeks. If they're alive, maybe they won't even find us."

They sat together by a small campfire while Mark and Tommy chased each other in and out between wagons, their playful, little-boy minds oblivious to the danger their father and Glen could be in.

"They *have* to find us," John Grace answered.

Betty didn't know what to weep for the most—the possibility Elly could be dead, the worry over what might have happened to Glen and Mark, poor old John's deep grief, or her own devastation over her sister-in-law and best friend's disappearance. She studied the awesome but intimidating mountains that surrounded them now. Their guide had insisted they keep going after Mark and Glen left to try to find Elly. Other men helped with herding the Grace family's few cattle and with driving Mark's and Glen's wagons.

"It's the not knowing that's worse even than if Mark came back with bad news," she told John. "At least then we'd have some answers."

John nodded. He glanced at their guide as the grizzly, bearded, buckskin-clad man barked some orders to one of the travelers about greasing a wagon wheel.

"You'll burn that thing up if you don't take care of it," Orlando griped.

"I was getting ready to grease it up tonight before we turn in," the traveler answered. His name was Weston Price, a middle-aged man with kids ranging from eighteen to three. The oldest, Billy, was the one who'd been driving Glen's wagon for him.

"I don't like that man," Betty told John.

"You mean the guide?"

"Yes. There's just something about him that bothers me." Betty took a deep breath and wiped away her tears. "He certainly wasn't very upset about Elly's disappearance. And back at fort Laramie, I saw him talking to those buffalo hunters."

John shook his head and rubbed at his ageing face, which now showed a good deal of white stubble from his not having shaved the last few days. Betty suspected he simply didn't care about his appearance, or about anything else, ever since Elly disappeared and Mark left with Glen to find her. She could swear John's hair had grown even whiter over the last three weeks, and the farther they traveled away from where they'd last seen Elly, the more despondent he became. Part of this trip had been to boost John's spirits and give him something new to work on since his wife's death, but this new disaster could kill him. Betty wondered if she'd arrive in California a widow with two sons and no one else left in her family.

"I don't know what to think about our guide," John spoke up. He's—"

"Someone's coming!" A traveler named Brady Mullens yelled, interrupting John's words.

"Might be them two that left to look for that woman," someone else shouted.

"Dear God," Betty gasped. She helped John to his feet. Both of them walked over between two wagons to see someone approaching by the soft light of a setting sun. There were two riders, one of them bent over his horse's neck. "Dear God, I think it's them, John. But there are only two of them. That means they didn't find Elly!"

John put an arm around her. "Let's just hope they're both okay. And maybe they know something. I just pray they didn't find her dead."

"Coulda' been anybody," Orlando had told them. "Buff'lo hunters, Indians, renegades, outlaws. Could even be a bear dragged her off."

What angered Betty was the *way* he'd spoken the words, as though it didn't much matter what had happened to Elly. And Orlando had insisted on continuing the journey after Mark and Glen left. "*Gotta' get through the mountains in the dead of summer,*" he'd explained. "*Can't take no chances. We have two mountain ranges to get over, and in this high country, winter can set in right fast. You can get snowstorms in September, so we can't waste no time lookin' for one woman who got careless.*"

The riders drew closer.

"Mark!" Betty cried out when she realized one of them was, indeed, her husband. She ran out to greet him, followed by young Mark and Tommy, both boys shouting, "Daddy!"

Mark dismounted and embraced his wife. Glen kept riding, leaning over as though in pain. The entire scene was instant commotion, people gathering around to take hold of Mark's horse, helping Glen down from his, surrounding and helping both men into camp. Questions abounded. Betty glanced at Orlando, who stood off to the side with his arms folded and a cigar between his lips. He showed no particular interest as people helped Glen sit down on a barrel. Betty, John and Mark all sat down near him, and Betty noticed Glen's upper left arm was wrapped in bloody bandages. Blood also stained his checkered shirt around his left ribs.

"What happened!"

The question came from practically everyone's lips.

"Glen needs some attention," Mark spoke up. "He was attacked a few days ago by a bear. I managed to shoot it before too much damage was done, but those wounds need to be cleaned and dressed and doused with more whiskey. I ran out. If we can keep infection away, he'll be okay."

"What about Elly?" Betty asked.

Glen closed his eyes and shook his head. "We couldn't find her." He removed his hat and ran a hand through his hair. "I failed her. We couldn't even find any tracks. The ground is too hard, and it rained the second day and washed away what little there was to follow."

"It's big country out there," Mark added. "Bigger than anything I've ever seen. There are a hundred places she could be. Elly is just... just *gone*. We did everything we could—asked every traveler we came across—stopped at a couple trading posts. We came across other travelers, but none of them knew anything about a captive woman, or even a woman stranded alone."

"Oh, my God," Betty said softly. "Poor Elly!"

John choked back a broken sob. "All we can do is pray for my Elly."

Betty glanced at Orlando again. He'd not asked one question.

"I have a feeling she isn't even alive," Glen told them.

"Don't say that," Mark barked at him. "Elly's a *survivor*! She's alive, and, somehow, she's going to find us again. I just know it!"

"Come let us dress those wounds," Brady Mullens's wife told Glen.

Glen glanced at Betty, deep sorrow in his eyes. "I'm sorry, Betty." He turned his gaze to John. "John, we had to call it off. We just aren't cut out for tracking in this country, and we don't know all the nooks and crannies where men live and hide out here, or where renegade Indians might take a woman."

He looked pale and ready to pass out. Mrs. Mullens and another woman took his arms and walked off with him.

John shook his head and wiped at tears. "If I'd known something like this would happen, I'd have insisted we all stay in Kansas and start over. Why did God let this happen?" He broke into sobs.

Betty struggled not to cry. Poor old John needed her now. "God will help her," she tried to assure her father-in-law.

Mark moved to kneel in front of his father. "Yeah, Pa. Elly's strong and brave, and she has a lot of faith. Maybe we'll run across Matt Stover again. If he knew about this, he'd go after her, I'll bet."

John shook his head. "We can't count on something like that. Stover's on his way to Outlaw Country. He doesn't know about this, and he never will. He thinks we're all into the mountains by now, headed for California."

"But he's going in the same direction," Mark reminded his father.

"Even if he was going where we are, he'd be way ahead of us by now," John answered. "One man on a horse travels a lot faster than a wagon train. He was just a passing stranger we befriended for a short time, but he has his life, and we have ours."

Mark looked at Betty. "I did all I could, Betts." Deep agony and regret showed in his gaze. "But then Glen got attacked by that bear and needed my help, and we just... We took a good look at the country around us—" He shook his head. "It's so damn big, Betts. It just kind of overwhelms a man. We might have ridden for days—weeks—in the wrong direction. I had you and the boys to think about."

"I know, Mark." She reached out and put a hand to his face. "No one doubts how hard you tried to find her. And I don't know how I could have gone on if you hadn't come back. Your first duty is to me and Tommy and young Mark." She felt sick inside, confused, devastated, broken-hearted. "We just have to pray and pray and hope Elly's strong enough to endure whatever has happened to her. We have to pray she's not being horribly abused, or that she's not in great pain. She's in God's hands now. And she has deep faith."

Mark closed his eyes and shook his head. "That snake we found. Somebody killed it. Smashed its head—probably so we wouldn't hear a gunshot. I can't help wondering if it bit Elly and whoever took her is the one who killed the snake. Either way, if Elly was bit, what must she be suffering? Maybe she died from the snakebite." He stubbornly wiped at tears. "She might be buried way out there somewhere all alone, Betts. Glen and I feel so helpless. I failed her, and I'm scared I could fail you the same way."

"You didn't fail her," Brady Mullens spoke up. "Everybody knows you tried your best. If *you* failed her, then we *all* failed her. No one person is to blame." He looked around the crowd. "But we all have to be vigilant from here on," he announced. "Everybody wants their privacy, but out here it can't be had. Nobody goes off alone for any reason—not *any* reason. The women should tend to private matters in groups, and one of them should always carry a gun."

Others agreed, nodding heads and voicing their approval.

"We have the hardest part of this journey ahead of us," Orlando finally spoke up in his gruff voice. He'd moved closer to the others. "It's too bad what happened with Mrs. Lowe, but that's how it is out here. Out here people travel at their own risk. We have no choice but to keep goin'. We can leave messages about Mrs. Lowe everyplace we go. That's all we can do. I can't emphasize enough that we get through the two mountain ranges ahead of us in this good weather so with any luck we'll be in California by September. You'll all feel better when you get there."

"I'll never get over the loss of my daughter," John told Orlando angrily.

"Maybe not. I can't do anything about your loss, Mister Grace. I can only do my job and get you and the rest of these people safely to California. How you handle your grief is your business, not mine." Orlando scanned the crowd. "You'd all best be gettin' things ready to rest the night and leave here at sunup."

The guide turned and walked off. People expressed their condolences and returned to their own camps. Betty grasped one of John's hands, then took hold of one of Mark's hands. She called Tommy and little Mark to come to them, and the three adults circled around the boys to pray for Elly. The boys clung to their mother's skirt and cried, confused and scared for their aunt.

"We need a miracle, Lord," Betty prayed. "Please bring our Elly back to us. And until that happens, give her strength, and protect her from harm."

Wolves howled in the distant mountains. All Betty heard was Elly crying out for them.

CHAPTER TWENTY-SIX

"This is where we part ways." Sage Lightfoot pointed to the northwest. "If you go north here, along the foothills, you'll find the Oregon Trail. You'll know it because you'll likely see travelers. Maybe you'll even run into those people you told me about, and that woman named Elly." He grinned at Matt. "You told me they're well gone by now, but I have a feeling you'll go looking for them once you've finished what you came here for."

Matt shrugged and shook his head. "It's best left alone."

"Well, I know from experience that a woman can get under a man's skin and create an itch that drives him crazy." Lightfoot pointed to the south. "Out there's the valley I told you about. That's where I'm headed." His horse tossed its head and turned in a restless circle. Lightfoot tightened the reins. "Calm down, boy." He nodded toward the north again. "Once you find the trail, it'll take you through to South Pass City. Just west of that is Atlantic City. Both towns are a gateway into Outlaw Country and good places to start asking questions. If those

Liberty boys did come out here, they'll very likely go through the South Pass. Travelers do the same, but not all of them. Some head straight south from there along the Mormon Trail down almost to Rock Springs, where they pick up the Oregon Trail again and stay north of Utah. They can avoid the worst of Outlaw Country that way."

Matt took off his hat and ran a hand through his hair, which had grown nearly to his shoulders. "I can't thank you enough for all the information and for being able to travel this far with you."

Lightfoot paused to light a cigarette. "Well, you made my boys a little nervous at first, being a lawman and all, but once they knew your reason for coming out here, they were fine with it." He took a drag on the cigarette as Matt fished in his shirt pocket for his own pre-rolled smoke. "You sure you don't want one of my men to go along and help out?"

Matt shook his head. "You need every man you have, and this is something I have to do on my own. I don't want to get some other innocent person involved."

Lightfoot scanned the horizon. "Just be extra alert from here on. It's big country, Matt, and there are a thousand places to hide out. A man with a long rifle can do a lot of damage, especially one with a buffalo gun. You said there could be a couple buffalo hunters after you besides the men you're hunting, so you're riding into some serious danger, my friend."

Matt lit his cigarette. "And if I die, I'll at least have died trying to avenge my wife and my little girl. That's all I'm out here for."

Lightfoot put out his hand. "I wish you luck, Matt. If things work out and you want to see Paradise Valley, just head south from here. You're bound to find me one way or another."

"Thanks. I hope you have success in building that

ranch you're planning." Matt shook Lightfoot's hand firmly.

"Thank you. Just remember to watch your back. Once you're in the South pass, men there can tell you the best trail to follow south to Brown's Park, or north to Lander and Hole-In-The-Wall. Men use caves to camp out of the weather when they're traveling, so keep an eye on anything that looks like a cave. I'd tell you to stick to the pine forest, but you'll run into country where there *aren't* any trees. There's a lot of canyon country out here, so big you'll feel like an ant. Back East you run into a town every few miles, but not out here. And watch for snakes and grizzlies and wolves."

Matt exhaled as he took his cigarette from his mouth. "You don't paint a very good picture."

Lightfoot, hatless, tossed his long, black hair behind his back. Matt noticed how dark his skin was, a combination of his heritage and the Western sun. He wondered how dark his own face was getting from so much out-door exposure. He hadn't looked into a mirror in weeks.

"It's an incredibly *beautiful* picture if you consider the landscape," Lightfoot answered, "but a real ugly picture sometimes when it comes to the kind of men who live out here. But overall, they're fairly law-abiding because that's how they were raised. Some live fairly normal lives. That's what I intend to do." He turned his horse. "You just remember that your best protection is yourself—your attitude. Make sure men understand you won't put up with their bullshit and you'll do okay."

Matt nodded. "I'll remember that." He decided there were a few men he wouldn't want to *have* to challenge, and Sage Lightfoot was one of them.

"Ride tall, Matt Stover!" Lightfoot yelled as he rode off to catch up with his men, who were already herding his cattle south.

Stolen cattle, Matt thought with a grin. He shook his head at how different life was out here. Men were such a mixture of good and bad that reading a man was a lot harder. He put his cigarette between his lips again and scratched at his roughly two-inch beard as he scanned the surrounding country. Right now, he saw mostly yellow grassland broken up by rocky crags, and here and there a cluster of cottonwood trees and flat plateaus stretching for miles. To his left rose the intimidating Rocky Mountains.

"Let's go, Rusty." He headed north, pulling Sadie along with him. He wondered where Elly was by now.

CHAPTER TWENTY-SEVEN

"I say we have at her." Stacy Bodeen swallowed more whiskey from the flask he kept filled from a stash of liquor they carried in their supplies. He laid back on his saddle eyeing Elly, who sat across the fire cleaning a pan after using it to heat beans.

"And I say no. The only madam willin' to buy decent, healthy women is Frieda at South Pass City. And she won't give us a dime if we abuse the woman first."

Elly eyed them both warily, sick of living in constant terror of one of them forcing himself on her some night—or day—it wouldn't matter to such men. Both were drunk again. Drunk men hungry for a woman were the worst. Her head and every muscle in her body ached from the constant tension of wondering when she would have to fight one of them off.

She could hardly believe they'd left her alone so far and wished they'd get to a town sooner than later. Her only chance of escape was to find someone to help her once they reached some kind of civilization, if civility was even possible out here.

"Since when did you start carin' about what you do to a woman?" Stacy growled at Pete.

"Because this one helped me and a friend once. It ain't so much her as it's the man who'll come *after* her that I want. I aim to lure Matt Stover right into my gun sights. Besides, I'm just bein' practical."

"*Practical?* How do you figure that?"

"We need *money,* you stupid sonofabitch! The hunting so far has been for shit! Us and others have killed off so many damn buffalo there ain't hardly any left. Frieda pays good, especially for somebody clean and proper! There ain't that many women come along out here that's as pretty as this one."

Stacy rubbed at his privates. "How do you figure to get Stover? God knows where he is, and wherever *that* is, he don't know a damn thing about this."

"We'll spread the word once we're to South Pass City. I know for a fact the man's gonna' end up there cuz' he's lookin' for a couple of men who killed his wife." Pete got up and paced. "He's *bound* to end up askin' around in the first place he lands, and that'll be South Pass City."

"He's probably already been there and left. You called me *stupid,* you bastard. I think *you're* the stupid one. This whole thing's a bad idea. The woman's slowin' us down and keepin' us from huntin' buff'lo. I say we strip her and have us a good time. Keep her with us 'til she's all used up then get rid of her. Sell her to Indians or outlaws willin' to have their turn with her, or kill the uppity bitch."

Pete glanced at Elly, his gaze moving over her hungrily. "I wouldn't mind doin' just that, but she helped me and Bartley. Ain't her fault Bartley died." He looked at Stacy. "It's Sheriff Matt Stover that treated us like shit. It's *him* that killed Manny and Moses and it's *him* that caused Bartley to suffer like he did. And I didn't do nothin' to the woman and her family, but that bastard chased me off and ordered me around like I was *nothin'*. He's got a bullet comin' to him, and I'm the one who's gonna' pull the trigger."

Stacy waved him off. "You're crazy."

Pete kicked the flask of whiskey out of Stacy's hands. "I know what I'm doin', so shut the fuck up!"

Stacy jumped up. "And I know what *I'm* doin! I'm gonna' fuck that woman over there. It won't make any difference to Frieda if I do. I'm tired of lookin' at her day and night and achin' to get inside her."

"You ain't touchin' her!"

"I *am* touchin' her, and *you* ain't stoppin' me!" Stacy went for his gun. Pete pulled his own pistol and Elly let out a little scream when both guns went off. She dropped the pan and stepped back, watching both men standing there, frozen, staring at each other before Stacy dropped his gun and stumbled backward, blood beginning to stain the front of his filthy shirt. Finally, he collapsed.

"You... rotten... sonofabitch!" he gasped.

Pete stood there, smoke still drifting from the end of his gun. Finally, he holstered it and walked over to grasp Stacy's wrists and drag him into the darkness away from the fire.

Elly watched in terror, astounded at Pete's cold reaction. He walked back into the light of the fire.

"Sorry about that," he said matter-of-factly. "You gotta' admit, it'll be easier travelin' without the stink. I ain't never been around anybody who stinks as bad as Stacy Bodeen." He picked up Stacy's flask and drank some whiskey down. "I know I don't smell a whole lot better, and I've traveled with some bad-smellin' men, but that one out-did them all. His name should have been Stinky, not Stacy." He chuckled and capped the flask, then sat down on his bedroll. "You can sleep now without that sonofabitch attackin' you."

Elly was at a loss for words. How was she supposed to understand men out here? They could kill someone, even a supposed friend, in the blink of an eye and not regret it. Yet for some reason, Pete hadn't touched her sexually, even though he'd admitted he'd like to do exactly that. Somehow, somewhere deep inside, he apparently had a hint of decency to him, a sense of right and wrong. He apparently hadn't forced himself on her because she'd helped him and Bartley. It was *Matt* he wanted to hurt… to kill. Still, he was apparently willing to sell her to some Madam who forced good women into prostitution.

Was she supposed to be grateful that? So far, he'd not touched her, even though he intended to sell her? What kind of feelings did men like Pete Garner have? She'd not said much to either him or Stacy because she wasn't sure what words might turn them into monsters and what words would keep them calm.

Since they'd left Sally's place roughly ten days before, she'd said little to either man, figuring it was best to keep quiet. They'd brought along an extra horse for her to ride, and she was grateful for that. She'd not had to sit in front of or behind either man and put up with their odor, but she'd suffered continued pain in her still-swollen ankle, and she'd been forced to fetch wood and build fires and cook. They'd even laughingly referred to her as their "squaw," and bragged in front of her about what they liked to do to native women and whores whenever they got the chance.

Apparently they thought she'd be worth more untouched. She suspected one other reason they'd left her alone was also because she'd taken Sally's advice and had stood right up to them, no crying or begging. It was a real struggle not to show her true terror, but it seemed to help keep them at bay. All she could do was pray beyond all faith that someone would help her once they reached the

town called South Pass City. It was all Pete had talked
about.

The clean gingham dress one of Sally's girls had given
her after helping her bathe was now getting stained and
worn. She had one extra dress, but Pete had refused to let
her wear it. He wanted her to bathe and put on the clean
dress just before he took her to the woman named Frieda.
The thought of it turned her stomach, but at least she'd be
reasonably safe until then... unless Pete ran into a bunch
of no-good outlaws who might kill him so they could have
their way with her, or men who would be willing to pay
for her services.

Pete lay back against his saddle. Elly returned to the
fire and finished wiping out the cast-iron fry pan. She felt
Pete watching her. No matter how often he promised not
to touch her, she couldn't help worrying when he'd change
his mind. He could attack her just as suddenly as he'd shot
Stacy Bodeen, and for no truly good reason.

"Are you going to bury Stacy?" she asked.

"Hell no. He ain't worth the trouble. The wolves will
have his bones cleaned off before his body has time to rot."

My God, Elly thought. "How far are we from the South
Pass?" she asked.

"Couple of days."

Elly moved to her bedroll. She'd often given thought to
running, but never in her life had she seen such desolate
country. Where in God's name would she go? A person
could die in a matter of days in a place like this—
intimidating, snow-capped mountains to the west, and
nothing but endless horizons in the other three directions.
No sign of water, nothing but mile after mile of yellow
grass and boulders and high plateaus. She had no idea
which direction might take her to a town or a wagon train.

Besides that, Pete or Stacy would have caught up with
her and probably beaten her for trying to run, or maybe

raped her in the excitement of the chase. Both had hit her more than once when ordering her around, but not hard enough to leave lasting bruises because they wanted her in good shape when they reached the South Pass.

That was her best hope for escape—civilization—but right now it was difficult to believe there were other people around *anywhere*.

"I guess maybe I should thank you for keeping that horrid man away from me," she spoke up, hoping to play on Pete's sense of protection, if it could be called that. Compliments might keep her on his good side.

"I guess you should, but I was more sick of his threats and his smell than anything else. It wasn't all just for you. I've given plenty of thought to rippin' those clothes off of you and doin' what women are meant for, but I know the kind of people you come from, and you did tend to me and Bartley back there on the trail."

"Will I at least be allowed to give a letter to someone in South Pass City that they could take to my family? They must be out of their minds with worry. My father is too old for this kind of worry and grief."

"That'll be up to Frieda."

Elly swallowed back an urge to vomit. "What is she like?"

"Frieda?" Pete laughed. "She's rotten to the core. Drugs good women and lets men have at 'em 'til they just give up and are too ashamed to go back to their own people. By then, if they had a husband, the husband doesn't want 'em anymore."

Elly remained sitting up, always afraid to lie down and fall asleep before the men did. She might be awakened in a most humiliating and filthy way, but at least now she was down to one man instead of two. "Why would you let her do that to me when you yourself won't touch me?"

"Because I'll *sell* you to her. After that, it's up to Frieda what happens to you. I won't be able to do anything about it. Now go to sleep and stop asking questions before I change my mind about leavin' you alone."

Elly wondered how someone so reprehensible could have gotten that way. "You won't change your mind," she answered, sneering. "You're too drunk to do *anything*."

With no warning, Pete sat up and grabbed a fistful of dirt and threw it in her face. "Shut the hell up!"

Elly let out a little scream and brushed at her face and hair. She couldn't see for the moment because of dirt in her eyes, and the next thing she knew someone grabbed her wrists and started tying them together. Pete pushed her down onto her bedroll and jerked the rope down to tie the other end around her ankles.

"You're gettin' might uppity," he told her. "Now that Stacy's dead, I'm realizin' you just might decide to get up later when I'm passed out and take my gun and shoot me."

"I wouldn't—"

"The *hell* you wouldn't!" Pete threw some blankets over her. "Now, get some sleep. And watch your mouth, or I'll run out of patience with you and make you wish you never opened it!"

Elly lay there in a near fetal position because of her wrists being tied to her ankles. "I have dirt in my eyes. Please give me enough rope that I can bring my arms up to clean my eyes."

Pete picked up a canteen and poured it over her face and hair. She spit and coughed and rubbed her face on a blanket that lay over the saddle that would be her pillow for the night.

"That's all you get. Maybe by mornin' you'll have learned not to smart off to me." He returned to his bedroll, pulling his hand gun and rifle in under his covers. "Damn bitch," he muttered, then yelled, "I'm bein' too nice to you!"

Nice? Elly needed to cry and cry and cry. But Pete would enjoy hearing it, and she reminded herself to be strong. *Thank you, God, for keeping me safe and alive so far.* She could easily have died from the snake bite, or worse, been the object of both men's "affection." She told herself to be grateful for what so far had *not* happened to her, rather than to give in to the horror she'd seen so far. Surely, she'd find some kind of help once they reached a town. Not all men there could be filthy creatures who abused women and killed each other off like mad dogs.

It was hard to imagine there even *were* towns in this god-forsaken country. Why would *anyone* want to live out here in this nothingness? Yes, glorious nothingness. That was the only way to describe it. Deceivingly beautiful. Awesome evil. Stunning landscapes that lured people into its unforgiving expanse of... nothingness.

God, help me, she prayed. *It will take a miracle only You can bring to get me out of this. And take care of poor Betty and my father and brother. They probably had no choice but to keep going, thinking me dead. And so, I pray for the biggest miracle of all—that somehow, we'll all be reunited.*

What a strange turn her life had taken. She wondered sometimes if she'd died and been sent to hell. She wondered if Glen had bothered taking part in looking for her. She reasoned that if she made it to Frieda's place and the worst happened, a man like Glen wouldn't want her anymore. *No* man would want her. She'd be branded no matter what happened.

Her only hope was in the fact that Pete was trying to lure Matt Stover into a trap. If he was successful and Matt survived, he would surely help her, but it was more likely she'd watch Matt Stover get shot to pieces.

CHAPTER TWENTY-EIGHT

MID-JULY...

*M*att had seen a lot in his career as a lawman, but nothing compared to the sprawling, disorderly place called South Pass City. He kept a close eye on everyone as he rode among homes and businesses scattered over the hillsides with no true "street" to speak of. The place was an unorganized mix of wooden buildings, stone buildings, and mere tents, with nothing but churned mud from a recent rain in between them all.

He'd learned that in high country like this the weather was "as changeable as a woman's mind," as one of Sage Lightfoot's men had put it. Smoke wafted from stovepipes that stuck up through tent roofs and through the sides of some of the buildings. Horses were tied to hitching posts in front of just about every building and tent, most of which appeared to be saloons and bawdy houses. He'd seen quite a few covered wagons just outside town, but as expected, the Grace wagons were nowhere in sight. They'd likely taken the southern route and were well on their way into the Rockies by now.

"Hey, cowboy, you in need of a woman's company?"

Matt looked up to see three women hanging over a

railing above a saloon, advertising their wares. One who was more heavy-set wore a glittery green, ruffled dress so low there was little left to wonder about. Another wore a pink, gauzy, see-through robe, and the third woman was a young, skinny blond who wore only ruffled pantaloons and a very revealing camisole with mere see-through netting for cups. He nodded and tipped his hat to all three women and rode on, deciding to get a feel of the town and those in it before he started asking questions.

By now he should fit right in with most men here, as a good share of them needed baths and clean clothes, shaves and haircuts. A few lay passed out on the boardwalks, and from the way others were dressed, Matt guessed the town was comprised of everything from miners and buffalo hunters to cattlemen, gamblers and businessmen. Whether any of them was honest or had any sense of justice or respect for others was doubtful.

He rode past more saloons, a barbershop, a livery, supply stores, liquor stores, a place where hides were sold, a lawyer's office, a doctor's office. Every place he went, men in the street stared, weighing their own thoughts on the new arrival. He wondered what would happen if they knew he carried a sheriff's badge in his pants pocket.

He cringed a little when he heard a man screaming inside a dentist's office and wondered just how legitimate any of the supposed professionals really were. Another store sold saddles and other tack, as well as boots. A trip up and down the hillsides presented a women's clothing store, where a sign read "Seamstress Wanted," and a millinery, a store that sold only tobacco and one that sold weapons of all sorts, including not just rifles and hand guns, but knives, spears and arrows.

He decided to go back to the saloon where the women on the balcony advertised themselves. He figured that of all the places the Liberty boys would show up and be remembered, it would be the saloons, or with the women upstairs who had other things to sell besides whiskey.

Halfway down the hill he passed a log building with a sign across the front that read FRIEDA'S PLACE. A painting on the side of the structure showed a naked woman lying down with a blanket wrapped between her legs and over her breasts. He shook his head. A man out here sure didn't hurt for the pleasure of a woman's company.

He continued downhill, nodding to a few men who in turn studied the new man in town with great suspicion. He couldn't help wondering when he'd feel a bullet in his back. He was new, which meant men would ask questions but be ready to shoot first if they had to. One thing was certain. The Liberty boys were the type who'd leave an impression. They'd make trouble and challenge others every place they went. They'd gamble and likely get into drunken fights and visit the ladies of the night, so if they'd been here, everyone would remember them.

"He's back, Nettie!" the heavy-set woman in the green dress told the skinny blond when he returned to the first saloon. A sign in front read WHISKEY GOLD SALOON. Matt reminded himself he must fit in at places like this or end up dead for no good reason, so he'd have little choice but to be friendly to the whores. "Sorry, Lora," he muttered as he dismounted and tied Rusty. He untied Sadie from Rusty's saddle and re-tied her to the hitching post so she'd be closer to the building.

The women on the balcony were calling out all kinds of tempting offerings as they watched him. They let out light screams and laughter when Matt re-mounted Rusty, then stood up on the saddle so he could reach up and grab the support bars of the balcony railing. He hoisted himself up and climbed over, figuring he might as well show an interest.

All three women cheered and hugged him, and the part of man in him that had been neglected for too long wanted to give in to their offerings. But the smell of cheap perfume and the sight of faces too heavily painted only made him miss Lora even more. She'd been so naturally beautiful, and she always smelled good without any help from strong perfumes.

"My God, mister, for looking like you've been on the trail too long, you don't smell so bad." The woman who wore the pink see-through robe gave him what he figured must be a compliment.

"I can't believe you can stand me," he answered with a fetching smile, hoping his friendly attitude would help him get information.

"Heck, Mister, most of the animals who come to see us when they're fresh off the trail smell worse than their own horse," the woman wearing the revealing camisole told him. She moved in on the one in the see-through robe and put her arms around Matt's neck and kissed his throat.

Matt grasped her arms and pulled them away, then stepped back a little. "Ladies, I'm sorry. You're all lovely, but I didn't climb up here to enjoy what you have to offer." Still, he couldn't help drinking in the sight of those nearly-naked breasts and their inviting pink nipples.

"Well, then, what *do* you want?" Pouting, another reached out and ran a hand over his left arm. "To let you walk away seems like such a waste of a strong, handsome, hard man. And you look like you could use a hot bath and a shave. We do those things, too. You'd enjoy the feel of a hand slippery with soap, wouldn't you?"

Matt's baser needs nagged at him. "There's a lot I want and need, Ma'am, but not just yet. And not this way. You're all beautiful," he lied, "but I have a wife back East whose grave is hardly cold yet. Our baby girl is buried with her, and I'm still grieving. I came out here looking for the men who killed them, and I'd love all three of you very much if you can help me find them. You probably know every man in town and those who are new or maybe have already passed through recently."

The words caused all three of the women to pout their lips and voice various forms of, "Awww."

"That's terrible, mister," the skinny one told him. She folded her arms over herself as if in a sign of respect for his situation. "We'll help any way we can."

She appeared to be the youngest of the three, but in spite of her age, she had the look of a much older woman about her. He wondered how and why she'd ended up standing half-naked on the balcony of a saloon full of outlaws and no-goods in the middle of country so big a man wondered if he'd ever find his way back out of it.

"Thanks for the offer," Matt told her. "I'll pay any of you who might know something about the men I'm after." He glanced at the other two. The heavier one had dark hair that showed streaks of gray, and heavy makeup only accented the lines about her eyes and mouth. The other woman was perhaps twenty or so, with dishwater-brown hair decorated with a pink plume that matched her sheer pink robe.

"You have the most beautiful blue eyes I've ever seen on a man," that one told him.

"Let's hear what he has to say," the young blond told the other two. She put her hands on her hips authoritatively. "And by the way, Mister, my name's Nettie. Green Dress there's called Bertie, and the gal in pink is Sonya."

Matt removed his hat and nodded. "Ladies, I thank you for offering to help."

All three smiled and swayed a little in a demonstration of their wares. Matt couldn't deny he was sorely tempted. "It's like I said, I'm looking for someone, but I'm not saying who until all of you damn well promise me you won't tell another soul about it. No other women you know, not the Madam or the man who owns you, not the bartender or any other man downstairs."

Nettie shrugged. "Nobody owns us. We're fee spirits, but we do pay Robbie, he's the owner downstairs, to let us live here and do business." She gave him a provocative once-over. "If you know what I mean."

"And lots of men ask us to keep secrets, so we do," Sonya told Matt.

"Most of the time it's married men who don't want their wives to know they came to see us," Bertie added.

All three women snickered at the remark.

Nettie sobered. "But in your case—your wife recently taken from you in a violent way—we understand why you're not ready for our favors. And I guess you don't want the men you're looking for to be somehow warned, so we won't tell anybody you were asking around."

"What's your name, cowboy?" Sonya asked, looking him over as though he were something delectable.

"It's best you don't know."

Bertie shrugged. "Okay. Names don't matter that much to us."

Matt looked around to make sure he wasn't being watched. He glanced down at his horses and supplies, which appeared to be untouched. He figured that in spite of the kind of men who hung out here, the inborn knowledge that a man didn't mess with another man's horses, supplies, weapons or wife, if he had one, was shared by all. He guessed it was likely a law that was simply understood, even by lawless men in a lawless land. He suspected that even out here, or maybe *especially* out here, a man was still strung up for stealing another's personal possessions, especially his horse. He turned back to the women and reached out to herd them closer to the bedroom windows they'd climbed out of.

"I'm looking for two men," he told them. "They're brothers—Joe and Tex Liberty. Tex is tall and dark, big and strong. Joe is shorter, more wide than tall, but he's strong as a bear, too. They're both close to my age, just a couple of years older. They might have bragged about robbing a bank back in Nebraska. They're troublemakers and are always getting into fights. They came here after killing my wife, and—"

Before he could finish, Nettie gasped and stepped back. "You're Sheriff Matt Stover!"

Matt was momentarily at a loss for words. *What the hell?* He glanced at the other two women, and they, too, stood there with their mouths open. They seemed to know exactly what he was talking about. He couldn't believe his luck... or maybe it *wasn't* luck. They knew he was a lawman. "You know who I'm talking about?"

"Nobody forgets the Liberty boys," Sonya told him. "*We* sure won't! They were here, all right, and they beat on me and Nettie. And you're right about them being braggarts and troublemakers. By the time they left town they'd shot three men and got in a couple of fist fights. They did business with us, but it was more like being forced than just regular business. Some men like to beat on a woman some, but they don't get away with it here at the Whiskey Gold. They even tried not paying us."

"The owner of this place got after them," Bertie added. "Him and a bunch of others ran them out of town. They left fast, with bullets flying after them. They're damn lucky they got out of South Pass City alive."

Matt turned away, his thoughts racing. Tex and Joe Liberty had actually come here, just like they'd said they would. He hadn't been positive they'd follow through. All this time he had only hoped he'd find them in this wild country. He took one of his pre-rolled cigarettes from his shirt pocket and lit it. "Which way did they go?"

"West," Nettie answered, "but they said something about Brown's Park. That's south of here. Either way, I can guarantee, the men out here don't put up with their kind of behavior. It's a bad bunch that hangs out in Outlaw Country, but believe it or not, there's a kind of a code here. You don't mess with another man's personals, and you don't cheat at cards. You pay for your drinks and your meals and your supplies. And you pay the whores for their services."

"And you damn well don't *beat* on them," Sonya added. "The men out here don't put up with that."

"Those men could end up dead before you ever reach them," Bertie added.

"The only other law out here is that there *is* no law," Nettie declared. "And you *are* the law. That's pretty dangerous business out here, Mister. Any man that finds out you wore a badge back home had better know why you're here. They won't mind that you're after those Liberty boys on account of what they did to your pregnant wife. You might be safe, them knowing that. You just have to be sure they understand you didn't come out here for any other reason."

Matt faced them. "I can take care of myself."

Nettie shook her head. "Maybe you can, but you'd better know those two had three other no-goods with them. Bad to the core, all of them. You go after them, and you'll be up against five men, not just two. That's the only reason they managed to get out of town in one piece. They're good at intimidating people and good with their guns."

"Do you really plan to go after them all alone?" Sonya asked.

"I don't have any choice. I *have* to do this. I have to

avenge what they did to my wife and baby girl. I'll never rest until I do."

Nettie sighed deeply, looking truly concerned. "Then God be with you, Matt Stover, because those Liberty boys aren't the only thing you need to worry about."

Matt frowned and watched all three women look at each other knowingly. "What the hell are you talking about?"

Bertie shook her head. "You're more popular out here than you realize."

Matt took another drag on his cigarette. "This is the first time I've even stepped foot in this country."

"Well, those Liberty boys blabbed your name to everybody they could. Said you'd be coming for them," Sonya told him. "And this past week *another* man came riding into town looking for you. A buffalo hunter named Pete Garner."

"*What?*" Matt threw down his cigarette and stepped it out. "We had a run-in weeks ago, clear back in Nebraska. I never even saw him after that. I killed three of his friends —found another one back at Fort McPherson and had a run-in with him, too, but he's still alive as far as I know."

"Well, we don't know about the other one." Nettie walked to the railing and looked around the street below, then turned and gave Matt a gentle push. "You'd better get inside. The one called Pete is watching for you—said you're bound to come through here, and that he'd blow your guts out with his buffalo gun when you did. He roams around watching for you all the time, but mostly he hangs out at Frieda's place, up the hill. Maybe he was drunk or sleeping when you rode past there. It's still early for men like that. He said if anybody meets up with you, they should tell you he took your woman, whatever that means. You said your wife is dead, so why did he refer to someone else as your woman?"

Matt felt as though the blood was draining from his veins. "My *woman?*" He turned away again. "Jesus," he muttered. What in God's name had Pete Garner done? There was only one person he could mean.

Elly? Had Pete somehow gotten his hands on her? Maybe he didn't have her at all. Maybe this was just his way of luring Matt into his gun sights. He faced the three women again. "Did anybody see him come here with a woman, or is he just trying—"

"I saw him ride in with a lady," Bertie told him. "Just him and her."

Matt glanced up the hill. From the top of the saloon balcony he could see the sign for FRIEDA'S PLACE. "My God," he said softly. "Can you describe her?" he asked Bertie.

Bertie shrugged. "It was hard to tell. She looked kind of sick, and sad, worn out. She had dark hair, long and thick, and she was kind of skinny."

Elly! Matt thought. Betty had blond hair, so it must be Elly that Pete had taken. Who else would Pete refer to as "Matt Stover's woman?"

"Pete rode in with her sitting in front of him, and it looked like he had to hang on to her to keep her from falling off his horse," Bertie added. "He half carried her inside."

Matt felt sick. Had his own troubles brought even worse troubles to the Grace family?

"You really need to get inside, mister," Nettie insisted. "You shouldn't let yourself be seen out here 'til you figure out how to handle this. We might be able to help you."

Matt studied all three of them. "Why would you help me?"

Sonya touched his chest, tossing her long hair behind her shoulders. "Are you kidding? *Look* at you. And you're a *lawman.* You're going to bring some real excitement to

South Pass City. And you're handsome and sad and everything that makes a woman want to give you anything you need."

"You'll need us to smooth things over for you with the men downstairs," Bertie explained. "A lawman in places like this can expect a pretty short life if he doesn't handle things right."

"Please, Matt," Nettie urged again. "Come inside, and we'll help you make some plans. If you're thinking about marching over to Frieda's Place all alone, think again. You'll need some help. The men around here won't understand, and you could get yourself killed."

All three women climbed through a window, then beckoned him inside. Matt ducked through the same window, his thoughts spinning and his heart pounding with dread over what Elly might be going through this very moment—if it was indeed Elly who Pete had stolen away.

CHAPTER TWENTY-NINE

*M*att stepped into a small room, its walls covered with red paper splattered with white roses and white birds. A red velvet loveseat sat against a wall opposite a dark wood chest of drawers, and a gold satin bedspread lay in disarray among crumpled sheets on a brass bed. Beside the bed was a night stand with a bowl and pitcher of water on it.

"Who's the woman that man has over at Frieda's place?" Bertie asked.

"Yes. This is getting interesting," Sonya added.

"Give me a minute to get my thoughts together," Matt told them.

He removed his hat and tossed it over to the bed, horrified that perhaps coming west to avenge Lora could have led to ugliness and sorrow for Elly because of his initial run-in with Pete and his friends.

The women led him to the loveseat, and Nettie moved behind him to massage his neck and shoulders. "You're tight as a drum, Matt."

Sonya sat down beside him and Bertie knelt in front of him. Matt began to wonder if he'd have to protect himself against what all three women really wanted, but they did look truly concerned.

"Tell us who this other woman is," Nettie asked. "We might be able to help you."

Matt rubbed at his eyes. He had to admit to himself that Nettie knew how to relax a person with her hands. He allowed himself to enjoy the way her fingers plied deeply into his shoulder muscles. "Let me ask you something first," he answered her. "Do you women pay any attention to wagon trains that come through here?"

"Not much," Bertie answered. "Travelers usually stay camped outside of town. Some of the men come in for supplies, but usually those that come through South Pass City only stay a night or so and move on, and usually they are married men who don't want anything to do with the saloons or women like us."

"Oh, sure," Sonya added, rubbing a hand over Matt's arm. "That's only because their wives are waiting for them at the wagons."

All three women laughed. "A lot of them stay to the south down by Rock Springs and don't even pass through here," Bertie told Matt. "They take the Mormon Trail a ways 'til it breaks to where the Oregon Trail veers northwest again."

Matt sighed and closed his eyes. Now he had Elly to worry about on top of finding the Liberty brothers—at least that's how it seemed. Everything hurt from his long ride and from constant tension. He reasoned that even if the Grace family had come through here, it would have been two to four weeks ago, yet Pete had arrived only two or three days ago.

"Pete Garner must have kidnapped Elly somewhere farther back on the trail," he said aloud. "I don't know how he managed it, but it's his way of getting back at me for killing his friends and chasing him away from Elly's wagon train."

"And who is Elly?" Nettie asked.

"Yeah," Bertie added.

"I hope you know that you're damn lucky you climbed up here," Sonya told him, squeezing his arm, "or you could be dead before the day is out, not knowing that rotten buffalo hunter is looking for you. Meeting us is the best thing that could have happened to you."

Matt rested his elbows on his knees and hoped he wasn't being foolish in trusting these women. "I thank all of you for telling me what you know. You didn't have to do that." He met Sonya's eyes, their lids heavily painted. "You three won't get in trouble for warning me, will you?"

"No," she answered. She leaned in and kissed his cheek before continuing. "We're fine, as long as we don't somehow betray one of the regulars. And what you're up to has nothing to do with any of them."

"Look, Matt, the worst saloon owner and most awful Madam in town is Frieda Nester," Nettie told him, "and that's where Pete Garner took the woman you call Elly. He claimed she's a whore he picked up back on the trail. Said you owned her and you'd be coming after her. None of the men in town cared because they believed Pete, but if he lied about Elly, and she's really an innocent woman who doesn't belong over there at Frieda's, and especially if she's being forced into something, the men in this town won't put up with it."

"He was lying about her, wasn't he?" Bertie asked. "If he was, that woman is in a lot of trouble. Word is Frieda sometimes buys good women and drugs them into working for her. Nobody can prove it, and there's no law out here to bring her up on it, but you'd better get that woman out of there. Who is she, really?"

Matt felt ill. His anger and devastation ran so deep he

thought his head might explode. "Her name is Elly Lowe. She's just a nice widow woman I met on my trip out here. She and her family had helped Pete Garner and a friend of his. I'd wounded both of them when they tried to steal my horses, and I killed two others with them. While they were in Elly's family camp, Pete's friend died, and when I came along to help, I chased Pete off. By then I'd made friends with Elly and her family. There wasn't anything special between us—just an easiness in talking to each other. She —" *My God, Elly! What's happened to you because of me?* "She was just—nice, gentle-spoken, and both of us were lonely. We went our separate ways, and I figured I'd never see her again. She was on her way to California. I thought I'd seen the last of Pete Garner, but apparently not."

He pulled away from Sonya and got up to pace, part of him wishing he could have stayed and enjoyed the massage and sleeping in a real bed. He didn't want any of the women. He just wanted to sleep for about three days. His wounds still weren't completely healed, and he realized he should probably have waited a few more days to leave the Velmers.

Now he realized it was a good thing he *hadn't* stayed any longer. "Pete must've caught up with the wagon train, looking for me, most likely. He must've decided taking Elly and advertising it all over Outlaw Country would lure me to him." He faced them. "And it damn well worked! I have to help her." He grabbed his hat and headed for the door.

Nettie ran around from behind the loveseat and grasped his arm, then moved between Matt and the doorway. "Calm down, Matt! If you go storming over to Frieda's place now, you'll cause a commotion and alert Pete. And you might draw the wrong kind of attention from the rest of the men in this town."

"I can't let her stay over there one minute longer!"

"And you won't be able to help her at all if you get yourself killed," Bertie reminded him. She and Sonya joined Nettie in blocking Matt's exit.

"Let the men downstairs help you," Nettie told him. "I promise they will once they learn the truth. It's just that a stranger can't just come barreling into this town and go storming to a whore house with guns blazing. And if Pete Garner sees you coming alone, he'll greet you with that buffalo gun and blow a hole in you big enough for a kid to walk through. If he *doesn't* kill you, one of the men downstairs might do it *for* him out of a misunderstanding, especially if they find out you're a lawman."

"Yeah, use your head," Sonya advised. "We can help."

Matt turned away. "How?"

"We'll go downstairs and spread the word that Pete Garner lied," Sonya answered. "We'll tell Robbie first. He'll know what to do. Most men around here don't put up with what Pete did. They'll probably string him up. And now we have proof of what that awful Frieda is up to. She flaunts herself and her women, takes business away from us. She needs to be run out of town."

"You stay here a bit, Matt," Nettie told him. "I'll go talk to Robbie and gather up some help downstairs. I'll make sure the others understand why you're really here. It's best to be up front about it. You can even admit you're a lawman, but tell them you intended to marry the woman you're after. That'll make those men believe that's the only reason you came here—to rescue your beloved. You'd be surprised how sentimental some of them can be when it comes to women. As long as they know that's your only intention, they won't bring you any harm, even though you're a lawman."

"I still think I should do this alone."

"No!" Nettie frowned and shook her head. "You can't do everything on your own, Matt Stover, especially not out here. Something tells me you're way too good a man to be here at all, but a man needs his vengeance. We understand that. But if you want to live to go after those Liberty boys, you'd better let us help you with Pete, because a lot of us want to get rid of Frieda Nester anyway."

Matt thought how wrong Nettie was about him being too good of a man to be out here. He wasn't good at all anymore. Knowing what Pete had done only enhanced his need to kill—first Pete—and then the men who'd destroyed his life. He turned away and lit another cigarette, realizing he never used to smoke this much, but lately it seemed like tobacco helped calm his nerves and soothe his grief.

"All right." He met Nettie's soft blue eyes. "You sure those men downstairs won't string *me* up instead of Pete Garner?"

Nettie raised her chin. "Not once *I'm* done with them."

She walked out, and Matt struggled not to explode from pure rage. He kept the cigarette between his lips. "Can you get me a shot of whiskey?" he asked Bertie.

"Sure, honey." Bertie left, and Sonya sauntered closer, patting his chest. "I hope you know that when this is over, you're going to need your rest before you go after those Liberty boys. That woman you call Elly will also need to recuperate. God knows what she's been through. Do you want me to go get your horses and put them up so you and that woman can stay here tonight?"

"Leave them for now," Matt told her. "Let's see what happens. And if I get Elly out of there, I'd rather take her to a rooming house or something. God knows what kind of shape she'll be in, and bringing her here, above a saloon... I mean... "He took the cigarette from his lips. "I don't want to make it sound like an insult, but—"

"After being at Bertie's, the last thing she'll need is to be in a whore's room above a saloon," Sonya finished for him. "I know what you mean. And I'm not insulted. It's okay."

"I'm sorry, Sonya."

"Don't be. She's obviously a good woman who will need to be someplace quieter. Don't forget that I'm a woman, too, and I know how a woman thinks and feels— even ones like this Elly Lowe, believe it or not." Sonya smiled and sauntered closer, leaning up and kissing his chin. "There's a decent rooming house over north of the main town. We'll get word to the woman who runs it to have a room ready. You wait here. *Promise* me. Don't make a move until one of us comes back."

Matt sighed "I promise, but I can't let Elly spend one more minute in that place."

"Of course, you can't. Don't you worry."

Sonya turned to leave.

"Sonya," Matt spoke up.

She turned.

"You're a good woman, too."

Sonya gave him a sultry smile and left. The room suddenly seemed too quiet. Matt walked to a front window, pulling the curtains aside to study the totally unorganized layout of the town. He smoked quietly, hoping his tired, aching condition wouldn't hinder his abilities and alertness. He'd need both in going after Pete Garner.

He felt so damn responsible for the mess Elly was in. Only God knew what she'd been through, and right now he wondered if there was a God at all. No God would have allowed Lora and his baby girl to die, and no God would have allowed the horror Elly must have been through. He'd probably go to Hell himself one day for causing all of this, and for what he intended to do about it.

CHAPTER THIRTY

*M*att cautiously walked down the steps inside the Whiskey Gold Saloon, his gun strapped on, his hand resting on the handle. A sea of faces stared at him—two saloon girls he hadn't met earlier, and the rest of them men - hard men—men of all shapes and sizes and dress, some clean-shaven and decently clean, most with beards and long hair and stained shirts and hats. All wearing guns. All looking at him warily, as though trying to decide if he should live or die.

Nettie stood behind Matt. "Boys, this is Matt Stover, and he can testify that the woman that buffalo hunter named Pete came to town with a couple days ago is no whore, or even a loose woman in any other way. She's a widow from Kansas who was on her way to California, and Matt here intended to marry her. We have proof now that Frieda Nester deals with kidnapping and probably drugging good women at her place. She needs to be dealt with."

The men all sat quiet for a moment, some slowly nodding. The room was so full of smoke it was difficult to clearly see the faces of those sitting farthest away. Besides all the smoke, the air reeked of whiskey and body odor. Cards, money, whiskey bottles and beer mugs were strewn about on every table.

"Nettie says you're a lawman," one man drawled. He sat sprawled in a chair fairly close to the stairway, a gun on each hip, ammunition belts criss-crossed over his chest. His dusty boots came to his knees, and his brown, curly hair hung nearly to his waist, as did his beard.

"I am," Matt answered with forthright honesty. "And I'm not looking for any of you. I'm not so stupid as to come here for that. I don't give a shit about any man here, or *why* he's here, if he's honest or dishonest. I originally came to Outlaw Country to find two men—last name of Liberty. They killed my wife and the little baby girl in her belly, and I intend to see that they die for it. On my way here, I met the woman Pete Garner recently kidnapped. He took her to Frieda's brothel, but I didn't know that until now. Nettie, Tonya and Bertie told me about her, and I'm grateful."

"If you just lost your wife, how can you say you were gonna' marry this other woman so soon?" another man asked.

Matt figured the women were right to advise him to say he was going to marry Elly. The news would win a few more of these men to his side. "After I met Elly, I had to leave her to come here. She and her family were headed for California, so we went our separate ways. But I thought about her a lot, and I figured once I was done here, I'd go find her and ask her to marry me. She's a widow, so she understands the need. I miss my wife, but I want a woman in my life. A family. I figured to start over with Elly, and I think it's her that's over there at Frieda's place. The man who took her there has a bone to pick with me, and me with him. He took Elly to get me to come after him so he can shoot me down, only I don't intend for him to get the chance."

The long-haired man nodded. "What you say makes sense. You have to understand that the only kind of order out here is for us men to have a meeting like this one and make a decision on things like this. There're those here who don't trust Frieda, and we sure as *hell* don't trust *lawmen,* so we kind of need to decide which one to go with. We all know Frieda, but we don't know *you.*"

Matt kept his hand on the butt of his gun. "All I can tell you is I'm not here to go up against one man in this room. I just want to help Mrs. Lowe, and I want the chance to deal with the man who took her. After that I'll be on my way, and you can all go back about your business."

"I like the girls at Frieda's place," a heavy-set man in buckskins called out. "But some of 'em sometimes seemed like they was way off. Like they hardly knew I was there. I figured they was just drunk."

Matt bristled. "Have you been there recently?"

He shook his head. "No, sir, I ain't. Bertie there is *my* favorite."

The men broke into whistles and a few nasty comments as Bertie waved to them from a balcony above the room. Matt simply breathed a sigh of relief that the man who'd spoken up hadn't forced his slovenly self on Elly. He could only hope *no* one had so far. She'd only been at Frieda's place for two or three days.

"Like Bo there told you, we ain't real fond of lawmen out here," another man spoke up. "Fact is, anybody who wears a badge generally doesn't live long in this country."

"I'm not *wearing* a badge," Matt reminded him. "I didn't come out here for legal reasons. I wouldn't care if every one of you was on a wanted poster. Makes no difference to me. Besides that, I have no authority out here anyway. I'm just after the two no-goods who shot down my wife, and when I find them, I won't *care* about authority. I intend to kill them so they can't do to another good woman what they did to my Lora. Women don't come any better than she was. I expect if any one of you had a woman like her and a man came along and killed her, you'd be after blood, just like I am."

"There are all kinds of men out here, Stover." The words came from a nice-looking man in a suit. He stood up as he continued talking, and Matt noted he was clean-shaven, and his clothes were clean and neat. He spotted a gold watch chain dangling from the man's vest pocket. "We have gold miners, businessmen, buffalo hunters, whiskey dealers—all sorts. I personally run a telegraph office and a supply store here in South Pass. I'm also a lawyer, and my reasons for being out here are mine and mine alone. That's the way it is with pretty much every man here. Nobody asks questions, and most don't offer any answers even if they did. As far as the Liberty boys, if you want to know where to find them, they mentioned Brown's Park. That's all we know. They might have gone to Atlantic City first. It's not that far away, but it's west, not south."

"While they were here, they were rough with Nettie and the other girls," Bo told him, "so they were warned to get out of town or wish they had. It's mostly men out here, Stover, and we need these lovely women who provide for us. We take care of our own. Some men out here actually have families, but even those with wives respect the whores." He looked around the room. "Hell, they never know when something might happen that they need one!"

The room broke into guffaws and war whoops and knee-slapping. Several men raised whiskey glasses and beer mugs to Nettie. Matt glanced at her as she smiled and sauntered down the stairs to stand in front of him.

"Thanks, boys!" she shouted. She waited for things to

settle down before continuing. "And since you like pleasing me and Bertie and the others, we're asking you to help Matt Stover get his woman back from Frieda. We've been talking to him, and I think we're a pretty good judge of men. I'm saying he can be trusted. It's a terrible thing the Liberty boys did to his wife, and it's a terrible thing that buffalo hunter called Pete Garner did to the woman Matt wants to marry. Help him get her back, and he'll be on his way and leave every one of you alone."

The room filled with men's voices then, while Gertie and Sonya came downstairs to serve them more drinks. Matt stood watching, ready to defend himself against any one of them who might decide to test his speed at drawing a gun. No one made a move.

"Let's take a vote!" Nettie yelled. "Everybody willing to go to Frieda's and give Pete Garner what for and kick Frieda out, raise your hands!"

All hands went up, and the room was a din of shouted "Let's get him!" and "Close the place up!"

All Matt could think about was Elly. What shape would she be in? Had she been abused in the worst way? How would she react when she saw him? Would they manage to get out of South Pass City with no trouble? These men seemed to agree to help him, but he knew any one of them could turn on him or maybe even decide to put up a fight on Frieda's behalf.

Riled up and ready for action—and always looking for excitement in a place so remote that there was little of it— the men stood in unison to charge out the door. Money, cards and drinks were left behind, apparently with the understanding that no man dared touch another's cards or cash. Matt rushed the rest of the way down the stairs and charged through the swinging doors and outside. He realized it wasn't even five o'clock yet, but half of the men heading up the hill to Frieda's Place were already drunk.

He hurried through the muddy street to catch up, Sonya, Bertie and Nettie all running after him. He thought what a stark contrast life out here was compared to the peaceful, law-abiding town of River's Bend. He dodged around horse dung as best he could, caught up with the others then pushed his way through twenty-or-so men to the front as the crowd reached the two-story log building called FRIEDA'S PLACE.

"You and the girls get yourselves off to the side there and out of the line of fire," he told Nettie. He stepped forward as the men behind him quieted, some standing there with guns drawn.

"Pete Garner," Matt yelled. "You in there? You've been looking for me, so here I am, you sonofabitch! Come on out and face me like a man!"

The front door opened. Not sure what to expect, Matt pulled and cocked his .44, aiming it at the doorway.

CHAPTER THIRTY-ONE

A stout woman wearing black taffeta stepped through the door to Frieda's Place and closed it behind her, then sauntered to the front porch steps. Her huge breasts billowed behind black netting that covered the bodice of her dress and was gathered at the neckline. If she was Frieda Nester, Matt was surprised at her plain appearance and the fact she covered her generous bosom. There was no color to her at all, not on her dress, and not on her unpainted face. She was big-hipped and thick-waisted, and she wore her dark hair in a plain bun at the nape of her neck. She folded fleshy arms defiantly and glared at Matt with a look so dark she was as intimidating as any man there.

"What do you boys want?" Her piercing eyes showed a combination of angry reprimand and stubborn pride, her stance defensive. "You have no business coming here and interrupting my business! Hell, half of you've been here for things more pleasurable." She dropped her gaze to Matt. "Who the hell are you?"

"You know damn well who I am because Pete Garner's already told you. I'm Matt Stover, and I've come here for a woman named Elly Lowe. Pete stole her from a wagon train headed for California. She's a good woman and not the kind to be forced into working in this den of drugs and filth."

"Bring the woman out, or we'll burn your place down!" a man from the crowd shouted.

Frieda raised her chin in stubborn resistance. "I don't know what you're talking about."

"Like hell you don't," Matt answered. "Pete made a big mistake bringing Elly here. I know she damn well wouldn't be here of her own free will, so bring her out! Elly Lowe is proof you deal with innocent women and drug them."

"This is *my* place," Frieda sneered. "And my girls are here *willingly*. Most of those men standing behind you have *been* with my girls." She looked at the others. "You men have no business here. Johnny! Dennis! Shorty! Bo! Get the hell away from here unless you're here for a good time."

"We don't put up with forcin' innocent women!" the one called Johnny shouted in reply.

"We figured them girls liked drinkin', and we thought they was always mostly drunk," Dennis added.

"Send out every girl who don't belong in there, includin' Elly Lowe," Bo demanded. "We'll *hang* you if we have to."

"Send Elly out or let me come in and get her," Matt demanded, stepping closer.

"Elly Lowe ain't goin' nowhere!" Pete Garner yelled from an upstairs window, pointing his buffalo gun at Matt. "And you're a *dead* man, Sheriff Matt Stover!"

Men scattered and Matt ducked to his right just as Pete's big gun boomed, sending the deadly bullet across the side of Matt's left arm and into the dirt behind him. Matt rolled to his knees and fired at the window, but by then Pete had ducked inside. In spite of the searing pain from his heavily-bleeding arm, Matt got to his feet and ran to the front door. Big Frieda stepped in front of him, blocking the doorway with her size.

"Get the hell out of my way!" Contrary to anything he'd ever done, Matt shoved the still-hot end of his gun against Frieda's neck, pinning her against the door.

Frieda's eyes grew wide with fear and fury. "You're burning me!"

"And I'll pull this trigger if you don't get out of my way!"

"You wouldn't!"

"*Wouldn't I?*"

Frieda's dark eyes turned even blacker as she stepped aside. Matt charged through the door and headed up the stairs. Behind him the crowd became a din of cussing and shouting. "Get her!" became the common cry among angry men who were worked up for more excitement.

"Wait a minute! Wait a minute!" he heard Frieda screaming.

"Make her pay!"

"You're leavin' town, Frieda Nester!"

"No! *Hang* her!" another man yelled.

"Burn the place down!"

"Get the women out first!"

Matt headed up a narrow stairway, then ducked around a corner when he saw movement at a doorway. Pete's buffalo gun boomed again, and a lantern on the wall exploded into flames. Matt charged toward the door where Pete had appeared and fired three times from his .44. He barged into the room to see Pete Garner still reloading his Sharps. Matt fired his last two bullets into Pete's chest, then kicked Pete's rifle to the side of the room.

Blood oozed from wounds in Pete's chest as Matt

holstered his six-gun and dragged him to a front window, too angry to think about the pain in his arm.

"Let go of me, you righteous sonofabitch," Pete growled.

"You should've stayed away when I chased you off back in Nebraska. And you sure as *hell* shouldn't have kidnapped Elly Lowe!" He managed to lift Pete to the window.

"I'm already dyin', you bastard," Pete groaned. "Leave me be!"

"Go to hell." He gave Pete a hard shove. "Here he is, boys!" He watched Pete slide down the overhang to the street below. Some of the men picked him up and dragged him away.

Matt enjoyed the sound of Pete's screams. He looked down then at women running out of the building through the downstairs doorway. He heard a couple more still upstairs scream about fire. He turned to see them run past the doorway and only then realized the upstairs was on fire from the lantern broken by Pete's gunfire.

"Elly!" He could hear the crackle of fire and the sound of things breaking and falling as the room where he stood filled with smoke. "Elly!" he yelled again. He turned to the bed and realized it was empty. "Elly, where are you?"

Feeling weaker by the minute from loss of blood, he ducked through smoke and flames into another room. The smoke made it hard to see, and he had to wave it away as best his could to get to the bed there. He leaned close, felt of the covers. Someone was in the bed! He leaned closer, managing then to see who it was. She had dark hair. That's all he could tell. "Elly? Is it you?"

Something big fell outside the door and he looked to see a large beam lying across the door, flames leaping from it. The building was burning harder and faster. Choking on smoke, and forcing himself into action through fire and pain, he picked up the woman in desperation. She pushed at him.

"Don't... *touch* me!"

Cooler air rushed through an open window, momentarily blowing smoke in another direction. He could see her better now. "Elly! My God, Elly! It's okay. It's me—Matt! I'm taking you out of here." He looked her over to see she wore a thin cotton robe and nothing under it.

He threw one of the blankets around her as best he could and lifted her, but when he turned to the doorway, he saw nothing but fire. There was no escape in that direction.

The room quickly filled with black smoke, confusing him until another waft of air blew through the window again. He carried Elly to the window and shoved her through it.

"I need help here!" he yelled at those who still waited below, along with some of the prostitutes from Frieda's Place.

"There he is!" someone yelled. "Come on out, Stover! Send the woman down. We'll catch her."

Matt had no choice but to trust them. He hung on to Elly as best he could and climbed out. He kept hold of her as her body slipped over the edge and the blanket fell away. Men reached up and caught her, lowering her to the ground. Bo quickly wrapped the blanket back around her then and lifted her in his arms while the others reached up for Matt.

"Climb on down!" one of the others shouted. "The place is going to collapse into the first floor any minute!"

"You're bleedin' pretty bad, Matt!" Dennis yelled.

Matt realized only then that the left sleeve of his shirt was soaked with blood. He made his way to the edge of the overhang and gripped the wood there, crying out from pain as he lowered himself. Men caught him about the waist and helped him down. He rushed over to Bo.

"Thank you for covering her," Matt told him. "I can take her now."

"You're bad wounded," Bo told him. "I can carry her for you."

Matt leaned close and smoothed some of Elly's hair off her face. "Elly. It's me—Matt. Matt Stover. You're okay now."

She only groaned, then opened her eyes. Matt knew by how badly dilated they were that she'd been given some kind of drug. He looked up at Bo. "There's your proof," he told him. "See her eyes? That's not from drinking. Besides, Elly probably never drank a drop of liquor in her life. She's been *drugged*."

Bo turned to the few men left watching the fire. "That does it!" he shouted. "You know what you need to do!"

The remaining men stormed off, and Matt looked down at Elly again. She was watching him with tears in her eyes. "*Matt*? My God," she said weakly. "*Matt*."

Nettie walked up beside them. "Carry her up to Margie's rooming house," she told Bo. "She and Matt can have more privacy there. I'll have the doc go over there and tend to both of them."

Matt grabbed his left arm, pressing on the wound with his hand. "Get my horses, would you?" he asked Nettie.

"Sure, honey."

In the distance Matt heard all kinds of shouting, a woman screaming. He looked back to see a man's body hanging from a post above the livery farther down the street. He wondered if Pete had died from his bullet wounds before he was hanged. Before he looked away again, a stout woman's body was also being strung up.

So, they do hang women out here, he thought. The same men who'd helped him in all of this just hung two people with no trial and no more questions asked. He realized he'd behaved just like them, putting a gun to a woman's neck, shooting a man with no feeling and shoving him out a window to be hung. For a brief moment he remembered his father warning him not to allow his hatred and grief to turn him into a man no better than those he was after.

The blackened sign that read FRIEDA'S PLACE fell to the street, and his heart grew heavy at the sight of Elly's limp body in Bo's arms. He'd failed Lora, and now it seemed he'd failed Elly, too. He didn't care right now what kind of man he'd become. All he cared about was helping Elly.

"Follow me," Bo told him. "I hope you can make it without passin' out."

With his last bit of strength, Matt followed Bo uphill to the rooming house. He wondered—if this was what his first day in Outlaw Country was like, what the hell was he in for when he went after the Liberty brothers?

CHAPTER THIRTY-TWO

*E*lly saw them... faces... a stern, black-eyed woman... a filthy, bearded man whose body odor made her feel ill. They were bending over her. The man squeezed her jaw painfully, forcing her mouth open while the woman poured something bitter into it. Then she thought she was lying on the hard ground. A man tied her wrists to her ankles. Her eyes were full of sand. She struggled to get free of the ropes, to get away from the cruel woman. She fought hard, but the man grabbed her wrists. He was pushing her back down, saying her name over and over.

"*Elly, it's okay!*"

He leaned on her. She feared the worst, but she felt so helpless. She pushed and fought, but he was too strong for her.

"*Elly. It's me. Matt Stover. You're okay.*"

Matt Stover? Who was Matt Stover? It suddenly dawned on her that the man holding her down didn't have that awful body odor she'd had to endure for so long. She smelled soap, and something else, something like the lotion her brother sometimes used after shaving. He'd found it in town and liked to wear it for Betty. Maybe this was Mark. Maybe he'd found her.

But no... Pete had taken her... the snakebite... the horrid, bitter liquid Pete had forced her to drink... This couldn't be her brother! Betty! Mark! Father! Where were they? How awful they must feel not knowing where she was. But that smell. That nice smell. Maybe it *was* Mark after all.

"Elly, you're okay," a man told her again. "It's me— Matt. I found you, and you're safe now."

She raked her memory. Matt Stover was a sheriff, wasn't he? She'd met him... somewhere. They'd danced. He was so handsome, with blue eyes that mesmerized a woman's heart.

She opened her eyes, focused on the face of the man who sat on the edge of the bed where she lay—the man who held her fast, but not in a painful way.

"You're okay," he repeated.

Elly lay still—staring, remembering...

"Come on. I'll help you sit up more so you can wake up and focus a little better."

He reached out, but Elly pulled away. She studied him a little longer. Those blue eyes. So familiar. "Matt?" She looked him over—checkered shirt, leather vest, wavy dark-brown hair that was longer than she remembered, but looked soft and clean. Handsome face. Those blue eyes that sort of glittered. Square jaw. Full lips... lips that, if she remembered right, had kissed hers. Clean! He was so clean and smelled so good as he grasped her in a strong grip and scooted her to a sitting position as though she weighed nothing.

What had happened? How on Earth had he found her? Where was she now? She looked around the room—also clean. It didn't smell of smoke and whiskey and body odor and a filthy bed. She touched clean blankets, then held out her arms to see she wore a clean flannel gown. The room had lovely wallpaper with green leaves in it. A chest of drawers sat against a wall, and near the bed, a small table with bowl and pitcher and a stack of clean towels alongside a bar of soap. Curtains hung at the window. They were a soft green color, not red.

Why did it mean so much to her that everything was clean? Why did it matter that Matt Stover smelled so good? Why did it feel so wonderful to feel clean herself? She put a hand to her hair, her face. The dirt was gone. That awful dirt. That awful smell! *Pete!* She sucked in her breath and looked at Matt again, looked past him.

"Pete!" she said, terror in her voice.

Matt took hold of her hand. "Pete's dead."

She frowned. "Dead?"

Matt nodded.

"You?"

"I'm not even sure," Matt told her. "They hanged him, but he could've already been dead by then from my bullets. It's a long story. For now, just know that you're okay, Elly, and no one will ever hurt you again. I'll make sure of it."

She studied his eyes—such sureness, promises kept, bravery and honesty. That's what she saw there. "But—" She looked around again. "That awful woman!"

"She's dead, too."

His answer surprised her. "You shot a *woman*?"

"No, but it was tempting. She's the kind who can hardly be considered a woman—certainly not any kind of woman *I've* ever known. Don't worry about it now, Elly. I'll explain more later. I'm glad to see you awake and alert, but that doesn't mean you don't need a lot more rest."

Elly felt a strange relief at knowing it wasn't Matt who'd killed Frieda, horrible as she was. She thought how quiet it was here. No piano music. No women shrieking and laughing. No one forcing her to drink vile things. She searched Matt's gaze. "Where am I?"

"You're in a boarding house in South Pass City. It's run by a very sweet old woman by the name of Margaret Hale. It's surprisingly quiet here, away from the main part of town."

"Oh, my God, *Matt!* You really found me! *How?*" Without thinking, Elly reached out. Matt's arms came around her. She didn't care that they were sitting on a bed, and that she still hardly knew this man. She knew him well enough to realize he'd somehow found her, and he must have risked his life to get her out of the horror she'd been in. "Just hold me."

He moved into a position that he could hold her closer. She closed her eyes and breathed in his manly scent—leather—some kind of man's cologne or after-shave.

"You smell wonderful," she told him before realizing what a silly comment that was.

Matt laughed lightly. "You wouldn't have said that when I first rode into town. I've taken a bath and shaved since then, had a little Clubman after-shave with me. I've no idea why I brought the stuff along, but I knew I'd better clean up. I was afraid if you saw me in the condition I arrived in, you'd scream and think I was one of the bad guys."

"I could never think that."

"You didn't see me at my worst. Either way, I didn't want you to wake up to a beard, and dirty clothes."

"Oh, Matt, how on Earth did you find me? How did you know?"

"I'll explain everything after you've eaten a little and slept some more. Whatever they gave you at Frieda's Place isn't out of your system yet. You'll think more clearly after a few more hours' rest." He started to let go of her.

"No, don't! Not yet. I'm scared if you let go of me, I'll

find out I'm hallucinating from that awful drink they gave me. Or maybe I'm dead, and this is Heaven."

He rocked her slightly. "It's okay, Elly. I'm so damned sorry about all of this. It's partly my fault for making enemies who took their revenge out on you."

"You couldn't help it."

He kissed her hair, and she didn't mind.

"The lady who runs the boarding house and a couple other women cleaned you up and put this clean gown on you. My God, Elly, I had no idea. I came here looking for the Liberty boys. I asked a couple of women if they'd seen them, and they told me it wasn't just the Liberty boys I needed to look out for. They said a buffalo hunter named Pete Garner also wanted my hide. Said he'd taken my woman. I knew it must be you and that I had to find you." He gently rubbed her back. "A lot of people helped me, Elly, people we need to thank. A bunch of pretty rough men at the Whiskey Gold Saloon and three of the women who work there. They aren't the kind you'd normally make friends with, but they have good hearts. We both owe them."

Pete had called her Matt's woman. *Was* she? Did Matt think of her that way? The thought reminded her of how she'd gotten there.

"Pete!" she gasped, clinging as tightly as she could to Matt. "I'm not sure what he did to me in that awful place. I'm not sure if there were other men."

"Don't be worried," Matt told her. "One of the women from Frieda's Place said nobody touched you because you were too sick. When Pete got you there you had a fever from a snake bite."

Elly felt like crying. "God gave me the snake bite, Matt. A snake bit me just as they grabbed me. It's what kept Pete and the awful man with him from touching me after they dragged me away from camp. The other man was that horrid, stinking buffalo hunter you ran into at that supply store back at Fort McPherson. He and Pete got into an argument, and Pete shot him. He just left his body out on the plains somewhere without burying him." She squeezed even tighter. "Oh, God, Matt, it was all so horrible! I was in so much pain. And once Pete tied me and threw dirt in my face. And my ankle—"

"Elly, a doctor has been to see you. He cut out some infection in your ankle and cleaned it up and put clean bandages on it. We were going to give you Laudanum, but were afraid it could kill you because of whatever drug Frieda Nester gave you. I think that put you out enough that you didn't feel anything anyway."

"Laudanum," Elly said, feeling weaker again. "Laudanum is what started all of this. Remember?"

Matt gradually let go of her. He put a hand to the side of her face, smoothed back some of her hair. "I damn well do remember. Just like I remembered you after we parted. I couldn't get you off my mind, but I thought I'd never see you again."

Elly searched his eyes. "And I thought about you and prayed for you every day. But like you, I thought we'd never see each other again. It has to mean something, Matt. God keeps finding ways to make us find each other."

Matt smiled softly. "Seems so."

She grasped his hands. "Promise me you'll take me to Betty and my brother and father. They must be completely out of their minds by now. This could kill my father. He needs to know I'm all right. It's been a good two or three weeks I've been missing, maybe longer. I've lost all track of time. We need to try to at least send someone ahead to get a message to my family."

"I'll make sure they know, one way or another. We have a lot to think about... things to talk about, Elly."

She nodded, feeling light-headed and sleepy again. Her

eyelids drooped shut, and she felt Matt helping her lie back again. She felt him arranging her pillows, tucking blankets around her.

"Don't go away, Matt."

"I've no intention of leaving you, certainly not before you're completely well. But there's another reason I can't leave you, Elly."

She again struggled to think straight. "Because you love me?" *Dear God! Did I really say that? Why can't I control my words?*

"Love is a big step for me, Elly, but I care about you more than you know. Maybe it *is* love. Sometimes I think Lora led us together because she knew how easily I could love you. It's a good thing, because the people in this town enjoy a big celebration, and they aim to celebrate our wedding."

Why couldn't she separate dream world from reality? Did he say wedding?

"I—uh—I told them I intended to marry you," she thought she heard him say. "I thought it'd help win their sympathy and support in rescuing you. And it worked. But now they expect us to get married right here in South Pass City before we leave. I don't have a real good excuse for objecting, and I sure don't want that bunch of mostly wild outlaws to think I lied to them, so I think it's best we satisfy them. I just need you to agree, once you're in your right mind."

My right mind? But in my right mind, I'd never marry a near stranger! Had she heard any of it right? Did Matt Stover intend to *marry* her? Did she *want* him to marry her? It was a ridiculous expectation. Absolutely ridiculous. Besides, he was still grieving his wife, wasn't he? That's why he'd come out here—to avenge her murder.

"I don't know," she said aloud. "I can't... I... I hardly know you." She touched her hair. "I've thought about you so often—thought about how easy it would be to... to love you, but—"

She felt it then. The kiss! That gentle, soft, sweet kiss she remembered so well. He spoke to her then near her ear, as he gently caressed her hair. "Don't think about it right now, Elly. Just sleep. We have time to talk about it after you've rested more."

Matt! This was Matt—the man she'd missed so much—the man she thought would be so easy to love—the man who'd stirred old needs that had kept her awake nights after they parted. She moved her arms around his neck again. "Hold me longer," she found herself saying.

Matt kissed her neck, her face. He laid her back on the bed, and she was already half asleep. She felt movement on the bed, felt a strong arm come around her. Someone pressed her close, her back against him.

"Matt, don't leave yet."

"I'm not going anywhere."

Yes, that was Matt Stover's voice. She felt him caressing her hair and breathing against the back of her neck.

Safe. So safe and protected. He'd promised not to leave this time. Had he really told her they had to marry?

That was her last thought before falling back to sleep in Matt's arms.

CHAPTER THIRTY-THREE

*E*lly opened her eyes and lay still to think. What time was it? What day was this? Had she dreamed everything she thought happened the first time she woke up? Maybe she hadn't awakened at all. Surely the memory of Matt Stover saying they had to get married wasn't real.

She realized she felt more normal than she had in days —weeks. She heard voices. A man. A woman.

"It looks a lot better, honey," the woman said.

Elly turned her head to see Matt sitting in a chair near the bed. He had no shirt on, and a woman, one of those painted kind, was wrapping clean bandages around his upper left arm.

"I think it's going to heal just fine. I don't see any sign of infection, but it sure is an ugly wound. You must be in a lot of pain."

"It's not as painful as it looks," Matt answered. "Thanks for re-wrapping it, Nettie."

"I sure don't mind," the woman called Nettie told him. "Any time I can help out a handsome man like you, it's fine with me. You sure do have a nice build, Matt Stover. You're a beautiful man."

Matt laughed lightly. "Men can't be beautiful."

"Sure, they can. And so is Elly. You two will have handsome children. I'm glad you've found a woman who can help you with your grief and help you not be so lonely."

Elly felt a sudden, ridiculous jealousy. Matt seemed friendly with the woman wrapping his arm. Maybe *too* friendly. Had he been in her bed? What was going on?

"Matt!" She sat up, pushing some of her hair behind her ears. "You're hurt! Did that happen because of me?"

"It sure did," the woman told her as she tied off the gauze. "You should have seen him. Matt went charging into Frieda's Place and routed out that awful man who took you—and he did it while the whole whore house was on fire! Pete shot Matt with that horrible big buffalo gun, but Matt shot Pete, too, and shoved him right out a window! It was something to see. Pete and Frieda got dragged off to be hanged, and Matt risked his life in that fire to find and save you. He managed to get you out a window and down to safety. The whole town is talking about it, and they can't wait to go to your wedding."

Astounded, Elly tried to take in everything Nettie had just told her. Pete and Frieda were *hanged*? Frieda's Place had burned down? Matt was wounded? He'd risked his life to save her, and now they were to be *married*? Apparently, what she remembered from the first time she woke up, in spite of still being so foggy-minded, was all true.

"Nettie, slow down," Matt told her as he stood up. "Let me get my shirt on. Elly probably needs to eat by now. Fix some soup or something, would you? I'd really appreciate it. I know Elly will appreciate all you've done, too, once she hears the whole story."

"Sure, love." Nettie stood on her tip-toes and kissed his cheek, then turned to smile at Elly. "I'm glad you're awake. You look so much better. I can see by your eyes you're more yourself again. There are a couple of dresses lying over the chair over there when you're ready to get up and around. Some under clothes, too." She turned and left, her hips swaying beneath a blue taffeta dress that fit a little too snugly.

Elly watched Matt pull on his shirt, a little embarrassed at seeing him with it off, even more embarrassed at thinking what a fine build he had. She remembered the checkered shirt he'd been wearing the first time she woke up. This one was blue. How long had it been since she first awoke? Was it morning or evening now?

Matt turned, and she noticed a blood stain on the left sleeve of his shirt. Apparently, his wound had broken open and bled more. His left arm was the one he'd put around her earlier, and she didn't remember seeing blood on his shirt then. His arm must have bled so much that he had to change shirts, but already, this one was also stained.

"Oh, Matt, I'm so sorry you were wounded. Pete could have killed you!"

"I didn't have much choice. I had to get you out of that place."

"But now you could lose your arm if it gets infected!"

"Believe me, Nettie has doused enough whiskey on it that it's a surprise I'm not drunk from too much of it in my blood. I'll be okay."

Elly pulled a blanket over herself, just then realizing she was still in night clothes. Her gown had scooched up so that her legs from the knees down were bare where they hung over the edge of the bed. She quickly covered them. "Matt, how did you happen to be here when I was? I would have thought you'd be far ahead of our wagon train at the time I was taken."

"I probably was, but I got caught in a tornado and the horses went crazy and threw me. I was dragged for a ways and knocked unconscious. Cracked a couple of ribs and almost drowned from a rain so heavy it flooded the ground where I landed. A nice couple found me and nursed me back from pneumonia. The whole thing held me up for about three weeks. By God's miracle I ended up here in South Pass just a day or two after Pete brought you here."

Elly shook her head in wonder. "South Pass? Is that where I am?"

"South Pass City. It's kind of an entranceway to Outlaw Country."

Elly looked him over. "I can't believe you're really here. That you really found me. If not for you, I would have been living in horror right now."

Matt left his belt buckled as he tucked in his shirt. "How much do remember of what I told you the first time you came around?"

Elly looked down at a tie on the quilt she'd covered herself with. "I think—did you lie in this bed with me earlier?"

Matt moved the chair right to the edge of the bed and sat down again. "You asked me to. I didn't do anything inappropriate, if that's what you think. You were scared and confused, and I don't blame you."

Elly rubbed at her eyes. "Start at the beginning, Matt. Is that awful Pete really dead?"

"He's really dead." Matt proceeded to tell her everything that had happened after he rode into South Pass City.

"That all happened yesterday. And once you're well and out and about, you need to thank some of those who helped me. There are some pretty lawless men out there, but they respect most women, including Nettie and the others like her. Some of those women were a big help. And some of the men could have done me in because I'm a lawman, but they didn't." He looked around the room. "You're in a boarding house now. After I got you here, you slept the rest of the day and most of the night. Until around two a.m. That's when you woke up still pretty groggy. And that's when you asked me to hold you, so I did. It's past noon now."

He reached out and took hold of her hands. Why did she let him? "I'm damn sorry, Elly. This all happened because of the rift between me and Pete. Thank God you were so sick from that snake bite that Frieda Nester never had a chance to let some man abuse you."

Elly shook her head. "But I remember being forced to put on a gauzy robe that didn't hide a thing. And I remember —" She shuddered. "I remember Pete squeezing my jaw so I had to open my mouth while that horrible woman poured something into it."

"It was some kind of drug. Maybe just to put you out of your pain, but more likely for other reasons. But the women who worked there assured me things never went that far." He squeezed her hands. "You're okay, Elly. I intend to make sure you're safe from here on."

She shook her head. "That's not your job. You came out here for other reasons." Elly couldn't help the tears then.

Matt put a hand to the side of her face and wiped at a tear with his thumb. "All that matters is you're okay now. I'm going to take you out of here, and we'll go find your father and brother and Betty. But first I'll pay someone to ride hard ahead and find them so he can let them know you're okay and that you're with me. I know that's what you want."

Elly cried harder. "Oh, Matt, that's all I want! My poor father must be out of his mind, and Betty is my best friend, and—"

"I know all that." Matt moved onto the bed and pulled her into his arms again. "I feel so responsible, Elly. Back when we parted at Fort McPherson, part of me wanted to stay with you and your family so I could be sure you were safe, but I gave in to the part of me that still wants to avenge Lora's death. This is the result."

Elly pulled away. "You can't blame yourself. You have no connection and no responsibility to me or my family."

"Don't I?" Matt reached over and grabbed a small towel near the wash bowl. He used it to wipe at her tears, then let Elly take it to wipe at her nose. She met his gaze.

"What do you mean?"

Matt pulled a blanket back around her shoulders. "Elly, there has to be a reason for the way we met. A reason for the things that keep pulling us back together. You said that yourself earlier." He rose, walking to look out a window. "I still love and miss Lora. And I still grieve for the tiny little girl who died with her. I'll always blame myself for all of it." He faced her again. "Elly, there is something about you." He walked closer and sat down in the chair again. "I feel like we're supposed to be together. I think I love you, but it's hard for me to say that when my heart is still so full of Lora. If it's possible for a man to love two women, then that's how it is for me right now. I meant to come and find you after taking care of the Liberty boys, and I was going to ask you to marry me."

Elly sucked in her breath and put a hand to her chest. "But we hardly know each other."

"No, we don't, but we know enough that we don't like the thought of parting ways forever." He took her hand. "Am I right?"

It seemed so forward to say that he was. "All I know is that I missed you terribly after that kiss at Fort McPherson."

"There. See?" He leaned closer. "It was the same for

me." He kissed her cheek. "Elly, to keep from getting shot for being a lawman out here, I told everybody in town I was looking for you because we were supposed to get married. I *had* to come up with something to win their sympathy. And now they all expect us to marry before we leave here. We have to please them because you never know when men like those here will turn on you because they think you lied to them."

Elly studied his eyes—honest eyes—eyes that showed he truly had feelings for her. "It scares me a little. I mean we've met only three times, and all three times it was only briefly. Yet I feel like I've always known you. You're a brave and honest man, and I trust you. If getting married is our only way to get out of this town and find my family, then we have to do it. But I don't want it to be for that reason, Matt. I want it to be for love. You said you think you love me. I think I love you, too." She put a hand to her cheek, which was red and warm from embarrassment over saying something that back home would sound forward and presumptuous.

"I understand it's a little soon, but you don't have to be afraid I'd force you into anything you aren't ready for yet. Surely you know by now that you can trust me."

Elly studied his eyes—those incredibly blue eyes. Honest eyes. "Yes."

"Some of the men here have told me it's pretty common for strangers to marry in places like this, with hardly knowing each other. Some of the women here actually answered ads placed back east by men looking for wives. And somehow those marriages between perfect strangers worked out. And you and I *aren't* perfect strangers. We already know each other, and I already know I don't *want* to be alone." He grasped Elly's hands firmly. "I just feel like, if I let you go, I won't find another woman like you, Elly. I felt it the first time I saw you way back there in Nebraska."

Elly relished the reassurance in the way he held her hands, as though his promises flowed from him into her blood—her heart. "I felt the same way, but I was embarrassed to admit it. And now... Matt, that woman and Pete made it all so ugly."

Matt pulled one of her hands closer and kissed the back of it. "And you know damn well it can also be beautiful with the right man. I can't let you go again, Elly, not after that kiss back at Fort McPherson. You wanted me. Don't try to tell me you didn't. I felt it in the way you kissed me back. I could have tried to take advantage then, if I didn't respect and admire you."

Elly studied the sincerity in his eyes and nodded. She knew enough about him to know he'd been brought up to be truthful. "I do trust you." Elly smiled through tears. "Can we live near my brother and Betty? I don't want to have to move to Nebraska and be so far away from my family—not after all of this."

"Then we'll live in California, close to your brother. And I promise that if it doesn't work out, or if I do one thing to offend you, I'll let you dissolve the marriage... after we get the hell out of South Pass City."

Elly couldn't help a smile at her bizarre situation. She couldn't find a man more trustworthy and dependable than Matt Stover. She watched his eyes again, sure he couldn't lie about her next question. "Please tell me you didn't sleep with Nettie when you first got into town. Or with some other lady like that. I mean—at first you didn't know I was here or that you'd ever see me again."

Matt grinned. "Hell, no. If I'd turned to paying women for those things, Lora would rise out of her grave and kill me."

They both laughed.

Why was he so easy to talk to? So easy to be with? "Then what about *me*? Won't Lora rise out of her grave and kill you if you marry me?"

Matt shook his head. "No. She'd want me to be happy again, with the right woman. And I'm religious enough to believe she led me to you."

Elly sobered. "But you're not religious enough to give up on going after the Liberty boys?"

Matt's smile disappeared. He leaned back in the chair. "No. I haven't changed my mind about that, Elly."

"And if I marry you and you're killed, I'll be a widow again."

Matt brightened a little again. "I don't know just how I'll handle finding the Liberty boys, but are you saying you'll marry me?"

Elly nodded. "But I won't give up on nagging you to *not* go after those Liberty boys. So, if you don't mind a nagging wife, then we can get married. But I'm holding you to your promise not to—" She looked down at her lap. "Not to consummate our marriage until I'm ready—and your promise we can end the marriage amicably if this doesn't work out."

He leaned closer again. "I promise. But I'll expect a kiss once in a while. And I'm not going to sleep on the floor."

"All right." Elly gave him a nervous smile. "Just know that *I* might sleep on the floor, or in a chair." She touched his arm. "No matter what, I'll always love you for what you did for me, Matt. Mark and my father and Betty— they'll be so grateful. Betty's very infatuated with you, you know. She'll be incredibly happy to learn you found me and that we got married. You'll have no problem being accepted by my family."

"I like them, too, but Glen won't be real happy about the marriage."

Elly smiled softly. "I'd already decided I wasn't going

to marry him when we got to California. All Glen wants is someone to cook and clean for him and give him babies. He'll find someone else once he gets settled out there."

Matt flashed a wide smile. "Well, Ma'am, I want you for those things, too, but not all at once. The babies can come later." He sobered. "Lora lost two before this last pregnancy took hold. That's what made losing our daughter even more tragic."

Elly shook her head. "Matt, I want you to keep in mind that I'm not Lora. And I don't intend to be her replacement. I intend to be Elly Grace Lowe Stover. I won't marry you if you're going to see Lora's ghost every time you look at me. Every woman wants to be loved for who *she* is, not for someone she reminds her husband of."

Matt shook his head. "It won't be like that. Every time I thought about you after we parted at Fort McPherson, I thought about *only* you, and how beautiful you are, and how much I missed you. We'll learn to love each other a whole different way, but I think everybody has room in their hearts for more than one love, Elly. It's how life goes on. At least that's what my mother tells me."

"Was she married before she married your father?"

"Yes. Her first marriage only lasted two months. He was killed in a riding accident—broke his neck. Life can be pretty damn cruel sometimes."

Elly thought about what life had been like back in Kansas and how everything had completely changed since then. This certainly wasn't what she'd expected could happen back when they'd been so happy and excited to leave for California. "Yes, it can. We've both seen just *how* cruel life can be."

Someone knocked on the door then. Matt stood up and helped Elly back into bed. He pulled the blankets over her, then went to the door to find Nettie standing there with a tray that held a bowl of soup.

"Coffee, toast, and chicken soup," she told Matt.

Matt took the tray from her and had Nettie come inside. "Thank you. And you and Elly were never formally introduced." He set the tray on top of the dresser.

"Elly, this is Nettie, and if not for her and two ladies who work with her, I might have come here and left without ever knowing you were over at Frieda's. We owe her a big thanks."

Elly looked at Nettie, realizing how dramatically her opinion of the kind of men and women who lived out here was beginning to change. What was considered wrong back home was accepted here as just fine. And here she was, about to marry a man she'd met only three times, but who'd saved her reputation and her life. She wondered if life back East was even real, and if she'd ever see that kind of civilization again.

"I can't thank you enough," she told Nettie.

"Glad to be of help. There aren't a lot of men out here as nice as this one here," Nettie added, putting a hand on Matt's shoulder. "We're all looking forward to the wedding." She pointed to the food tray. "Eat up, honey. You'll want to be good and strong for your wedding night."

She laughed and sauntered out the door, and Elly felt her cheeks tingle at the woman's last remark.

"Don't pay any attention to what she said," Matt told her. He took the tray from the dresser and brought it over to set on Elly's lap. "You eat up for your health and nothing more. If I'm going to take you all the way to California, you'll need to be strong and healthy for traveling by horseback for at least a few days. It's a long trip to Rock Springs, where we'll catch the train." He leaned down and kissed her forehead. "I have some things to do to get ready for the trip, so I'll leave you for a while so you can eat and sleep. And you should know that we can stay here for a while longer after we're married. - however long it takes for you to be healed. I won't drag you out into that unforgiving country again until I feel you're truly ready." He took his hat from where he'd hung it on the chair and put it on. "I'll be back. You rest."

"Don't take too long. Let me know when you're back so I won't worry about you."

Matt gave her a wink. "I promise."

Elly watched him leave. *Dear Lord, I'm actually going to marry the man.* Out here in this unreal part of the country, love and marriage seemed to have a slightly different meaning than back home, but she didn't want it to be that way. She wanted it to mean the same thing it had always meant to her.

But *strangers* marrying... it was an odd feeling, and in a place like this, it was no more out of the ordinary than to expect the sun to rise every morning. In this wild, lawless land, *everything* was out of the ordinary.

CHAPTER THIRTY-FOUR

*S*outh Pass City was a nest for cowboys, hunters, freighters, businessmen, saloon women and everything in between. The street was alive with onlookers from all walks of life, and the air was filled with laughter and yelling and whistling and the din of hundreds of voices all talking at once.

Elly was surprised to learn there was a real preacher in town. He'd introduced himself as John Pritchert, and Elly couldn't help wondering if he'd come here running from the law for some reason, or as an honest man wanting to bring God's word to this den of iniquity. He stood before her and Matt now, a tall, thin man wearing a stovepipe hat and a black suit that had seen its day.

She gripped Matt's hand, realizing her entire future now lay in this man who'd been a complete stranger not all that long ago.

"Do you, Eleanor—uh—" The preacher leaned closer. "Full name?"

Elly had trouble finding her voice. "Eleanor Louise Grace Lowe."

The preacher nodded. "Eleanor Louise Grace Lowe,

take this man—uh —" Again he leaned forward. "Full name?"

Elly realized she didn't know Matt's full name, either, and here she was marrying him!

"Matthew John Stover."

Matthew John. Of course! His father is a preacher.

"Matthew John Stover," the preacher continued, "to be your wedded husband?"

My God, what am I doing? "I do," Elly answered.

"And do you, Matthew John Stover, take this woman, Eleanor—" The preacher frowned. "What was that again?"

"Eleanor Louise Grace Lowe," Elly repeated.

"Oh, yes! Uh—Eleanor Louise Grace Lowe—to be your wedded wife?"

Matt looked at Elly. "Look at me," he said softly.

Elly obeyed, relaxing when she met his gaze.

"It'll be okay," he assured her. He turned to the preacher. "I do."

Elly hardly heard the rest of the ceremony. She wore a light blue cotton dress with white lace at the high neckline and a wide, white sash with a large bow at the back that fell over a shower of ruffles. Nettie had brought her the dress, and Elly hadn't asked her where it came from. She had a feeling she didn't want to know. Matt wore a white shirt, black pants and a black string tie —*Church-going clothes I brought along but never thought I'd actually wear out here—* he'd told her.

He looked wonderful. So handsome. The left sleeve of his shirt fit a little too tight because of the extra bandages on his arm. A wound, Elly reminded herself, that he'd suffered rescuing her from the horror she'd suffered only four days before. He filled out the shirt in other ways because of his broad chest and muscled arms—a man sure and able. He wore no gun today. He had the protection of the whole town, which would break into all-out war if anyone threatened to harm Sheriff Matt Stover. She almost wished the Liberty boys would come along now, because at least Matt wouldn't have to fight them alone.

Both of them finished their vows. Then came the kiss, and everyone in the crowd of a good hundred people broke into whoops and whistles. The ceremony had taken place in front of the Whiskey Gold Saloon, and the minute it was over, someone began banging out a wild tune on the piano inside, and the bartender yelled from the front porch that the first round of drinks was on the house.

More yelling and celebrating, as most of the crowd charged inside. Nettie, Bertie and Sonya each grabbed Matt and gave him long kisses. Elly didn't argue the issue. They'd been too good to her. Still, a pang of jealousy and possessiveness moved through her, awakening her own desire to be the man's wife in the fullest sense, even though she still fought the ugliness of what she'd been through, as well as wondering if it was simply too soon after not even having time to court each other.

Matt took her inside the saloon at the request of the man called Bo, who told them they'd cleared aside some tables and wanted the newlyweds to hold their first dance. "I would never normally expect you to go inside a saloon, but I want to please these men," he told Elly.

"I'll survive." Elly moved an arm around her husband, and he held her close as they walked through the swinging doors. Men spilled out the windows and loaded the stairs and balcony above to watch.

The piano player drummed out what was apparently his version of a waltz, and Matt took her hand and put a hand to her waist. Elly remembered their dance at Fort McPherson and the unexplainable attraction she'd felt for him then. She remembered the kiss—that long, deep, delicious, suggestive kiss. Now here she was—Mrs. Matt Stover.

They turned to the music, and the next thing Elly knew, the men in the saloon were cutting in, giving Matt money as a wedding present for a turn to dance with his woman. She found herself dancing with gold miners, a livery owner, the blacksmith, two different lawyers, other saloon owners, complete strangers just passing through, even a couple of men who were with a wagon train camped outside of town.

How she wished her own family was among those travelers, but they were well on their way into the mountains by now. She ached to hug her father and Mark and Betty and her nephews and to just be Elly again, traveling west with her family. What had happened to that life? It seemed all this change started with that first night she'd set eyes on Matt Stover. When she found her family again, she'd be the wife of a lawman. For all she knew, Matt would come across the Liberty brothers and be killed, and she'd reach her family twice widowed.

The thought tore at her heart. She wasn't sure she was truly in love with Matt until she thought about him being dead. She realized if that happened, she'd grieve even more deeply than she had for her first husband.

She realized she shouldn't put off allowing him his husbandly rights. In places like this, life was precious and sometimes short. What if she waited and Matt was killed before they ever shared that passionate pleasure? She wouldn't forgive herself for that.

By the time the wedding dance was over, Matt had enough money for them to take the train to California. They'd go to Cisco, near where Betty's brother owned a farm. Since it was summer, there shouldn't be any problem getting through the mountains. All they had to do first was head south to Rock Springs, where they would catch the next train to California. But now she wasn't sure she wanted to find her family first. Matt might return to the

Outlaw Trail to look for the Liberty brothers and never make it back. If he was going to have it out with them and maybe get hurt or die, she should be with him.

They danced until Elly told her new husband she was tired. Her ankle was starting to swell again, and she knew Matt's arm was hurting him. He'd injured that arm in his quest to save her from pure hell. This brave, able, caring man was her husband. From what she knew about him, she couldn't ask for better. They'd shared more than one kiss since the wedding, and with every kiss she felt a growing need to be a wife in every way. It had been a long time since she'd enjoyed a man's arms around her at night... enjoyed those moments deep in the darkness when their bodies touched... when she felt that erotic need for a man.

"We'd better get going," Matt told her as he whirled her around once more. "It's getting pretty wild here, and some of the men are getting a little too drunk. Drunk men often end up making trouble. I've seen it often enough in my work. Besides, you need to rest that ankle."

He'd mentioned his work. She hadn't even asked if he intended to continue the job of lawman. Or, maybe deep inside he really wanted to go back to River's Bend. She felt selfish for thinking only of her own situation and her own family. "Matt, if you want to go back home to Nebraska, we can."

He held her closer. "I told you I'd take you to California, and I will. We can always go back to River's Bend and visit. Meet my family. We can go by train, whether just for a while, or to stay. Either way, we can talk about it after I find the Liberty brothers."

After I find the Liberty brothers. She wanted to beg him to give up that quest, but he was a man who couldn't let something like that go. The thought of what still lay ahead terrified her.

For now, there was no time to think about it. Matt announced they were going back to the boarding house, and right away they were herded out the door and to a buggy decorated with wild flowers and ribbons. The whole crowd followed as Matt and Elly climbed into the buggy.

Elly felt her face flushing at some of the remarks the men called out to Matt. She avoided looking at any of them as he snapped the reins and headed the horse pulling the buggy up the hill to the boarding house, the crowd whistling and shouting their well wishes.

They finally left the crowd behind as they reached the boarding house, and Matt helped Elly down. He put a hand to her back and walked her inside and down the hallway to what was now their room together.

He led her inside and closed the door, and suddenly things seemed incredibly quiet.

It was done. She was Mrs. Matthew Stover.

CHAPTER THIRTY-FIVE

*E*lly suddenly felt awkward and unsure. She walked over to a dresser to remove the veiled pillbox hat she'd worn for her wedding.

"Well—here we are," Matt told her. "By the way, Bo said to tell you he's happy for us and wishes us good luck. He's leaving in the morning for Rock Springs. He runs messages for mine owners, sometimes rides shotgun for gold shipments—things like that." Matt removed his tie as he talked. "Sounds like the kind of job a wandering man like that would like. He travels all over these mountains."

"I appreciate how he helped us," Elly told him as she set her hat on the dresser, "but don't you be thinking about a job like that, Mister Stover. I want a husband who comes home every night." *Small talk,* she thought.

In the next moment Matt was behind her, removing the pins and combs from her hair.

"Don't get all nervous," he told her. "I just like looking at you with your hair down."

Elly stood there in doubt and feeling a bit defensive as Matt removed all the pins and ran his hands into her hair to fluff it out. He turned her then, looking her over with those incredibly blue eyes.

"There. That's better." He gently took her face in his hands. "May I at least kiss you?"

Watch his eyes, Elly told herself. Gentleness. Honesty. Sureness. And was that a hint of love she saw there? "Yes," she answered.

His eyes sparkled with sweet desire, but also with an assurance he would keep his promise to expect nothing more. Their lips met in a hot, sweet kiss, and all of Elly's good intentions of waiting melted away as she in turn melted into Matt's arms. And that quickly, she felt as wanton as the women who worked above the Whiskey Gold.

Matt picked her up and carried her to the bed. She clung to him and breathed deeply of his stirring scent, wondering what had suddenly happened to her resolve to wait. She remembered his scent from when she first woke up to him holding her, and she couldn't help thinking how thoughtful it was of him to bathe and smell so good, knowing the horror she'd suffered being with Pete and Stacy. How could she deny this man his pleasure after what he'd done for her?

Matt set her on the bed and turned to pull up a chair to sit beside her. "That kiss was all I asked for. I made you a promise about the rest."

"I know." Elly looked down, a little embarrassed. "I guess I... I'm giving you permission to break your promise." She covered her face. "I mean, you aren't really breaking it if I say it's okay." She dared to look into those blue eyes that had a way of undoing her. "Whether we're truly in love or not, I can't imagine undoing this marriage, because it would mean leaving each other. I already can't imagine you not being in my life, so why should I deny you, for any length of time, when I know we'll always be together?"

He smiled softly, reaching out to grasp her wrists and pull her hands away from her face. "You mean we should get things over with?"

"Something like that."

Matt shook his head. "No, ma'am. I don't want anything to do with taking a woman like you out of some kind of duty you feel you owe me. You're my *wife*. I'm not breaking my promise if you're going to lie in that bed stiff as a board like it's some kind of wifely chore. I meant what I said about not consummating this union if it's not what you really want."

Elly swallowed. "I just… I didn't want you to think of me as brazen or wanton if I told you I wanted you that night at Fort McPherson. I've thought about no other man but you ever after that. If you asked Betty, she'd tell you. We talked about you, and —" Her eyes teared with embarrassment, and she looked down at her lap again. "Matt, the only drawback was what I've just been through. It was so awful, but when I'm in your arms it all goes away and I want to be with you that way. I mean, it's legal now, strangers or not."

"Look at me, Elly."

She raised her eyes and was instantly a captive of his gaze.

"We aren't strangers. We've learned a lot about each other in a very short time, that's true, but we definitely are no longer strangers."

Elly nodded. "Sometimes I feel like I've known you all my life. I don't understand how this could happen so fast, but—" She reached out and hugged him around the neck as Matt stood up with her in his arms.

"Are you *sure*?"

Elly swallowed again. "Yes. I'm just scared I'll disappoint you."

Matt laughed as he kissed her cheek, her neck. "I hardly think that's possible. Maybe *I'll* disappoint *you*, Mrs. Stover.

Elly smiled nervously as Matt lowered her to the bed again and knelt in front of her to begin unbuttoning her dress from her throat downward.

"One more time, Mrs. Stover. Stop me if you don't want this," he told her. "If you let me keep going too much farther, I make no guarantees. A man can handle only so much."

Elly shivered with desire. She was Mrs. Matt Stover now. There was absolutely nothing wrong with letting this man enjoy his husbandly rights. "Just so it's *me* you want," she answered. "I know you're still grieving."

Matt sobered as he unbuttoned the lowest button and gently pulled the dress off her shoulders. He put a hand to her throat, ran it down to trace a finger into her cleavage, then ran the back of his fingers over the swell of her breasts, holding her gaze as he did so.

"We've talked about that," he told her. "It's you I want, because you understand that I *am* still grieving, and you accept that." He began unlacing her camisole. "You aren't a replacement for Lora, Elly. You are my current, living, beautiful wife, a woman sent to help me start over, just like *you* are starting over. I could be a replacement, too, you know, but I don't feel that way at all. You had a husband and you loved him." He put a hand to the side of her face. "I had a wife, and I loved *her*. But they're both gone, and now all we have is each other. This is right. And now's the time to make up your mind, because if I pull off this pink, lacy camisole you're wearing, it's done. I'm not stopping."

He leaned forward with another warm, tantalizing kiss, and touched her breasts again.

Elly answered by pulling off the camisole on her own. Matt's kiss deepened as he gently massaged her breasts. Elly answered his kiss with her own hungry passion. It had been so, so long since a man had touched her this way, so gently, almost reverently. Matt scooted her back onto the bed and straddled her, pulling off her shoes and tossing them. He pulled her dress the rest of the way down, then her slips, her underwear, her stockings.

She lay there naked as he remained over her and removed his white ruffled shirt. Elly drank in the sight of broad shoulders, hard muscles, a flat stomach with hair that led downward. He moved off the bed just long enough to unbuckle his pants and remove boots, socks, pants and long johns.

What she saw then told her she most certainly would not be disappointed by what Matt Stover had to offer. She pulled a blanket over herself and over her face as he climbed back onto the bed and gently pulled the blanket away again and leaned close. "You're beautiful, Mrs. Stover."

Elly smiled and touched his hair. "So are you, Mister Stover."

Matt moved his legs between hers. She ran her hands through his hair and down over his arms, the bandaged one reminding her what he'd risked for her. She grasped his hair again when he leaned close and tasted her breasts, gently pulling at the nipples to bring forth an incredible hunger to let him have more, an awakening of what she'd been missing for so long.

"Matt—"

He hesitated.

"I *do* love you."

He came close and kissed her passionately then kissed her cheek, her neck, her throat. "And I love you, Elly. This might all seem too soon, but I love you," he said between more kisses.

He found her mouth again, and she felt the back of his hand against her most private place as he guided himself into her. She cried out when he entered her, his hard, warm shaft reminding her what she'd been missing for too long.

The intercourse hurt at first because it had been so long since she'd taken a man, but in seconds she was arching up to him, wanting him, meeting his every thrust. She wanted this man so badly that she hadn't even needed any foreplay to stir the juices needed to fully enjoy their union. Just the newness of it, the fact that Sheriff Matt Stover was inside her, was all she needed to produce a sweet, slippery welcome for her new husband. His groans of pleasure told her she'd done the right thing by not waiting for this. And though she'd been ready to do this just for him, she took far more joy in it herself than she thought she would, feeling selfishly satisfied in return.

Matt kept up the rhythmic thrusts for several minutes, grabbing her bottom in strong hands and ramming himself deeper. Finally, she felt his life flowing into her. Maybe he would even make her pregnant. She wanted nothing more now than to give him a child to replace the one he'd lost in such a horrible, crushing way.

With one last thrust he held her fast.

"Just lie still," he told her. "That was kind of quick, but I've wanted to do this since that first night I met you. And I think I could do this again and again... maybe all night."

"Then do what you must do, Mr. Stover," she told him in a husky, suggestive whisper.

He braced himself on his elbows and grasped her hair, leaning down to smother her with more kisses. Elly felt captured and helpless, and she didn't even mind. He moved his lips farther down to relish the taste of her breasts again.

"You have beautiful breasts. You're beautiful all over," he told her. "I want to see and taste every part of you."

He moved even farther down to kiss her belly, sending almost agonizing sensations through her so that she felt no bashfulness when he worked his way even farther down to places her first husband had never tasted.

Elly grasped the brass bed rail when his tongue slicked into private areas that only minutes before she couldn't imagine she could let this man touch, let alone taste and explore. She cried out his name when in minutes her insides rippled and pulsed with a deep climax. He worked his way back up, and she could taste herself on his lips when they shared yet another hungry, pressing kiss. She felt him enter her again.

After several deep, hard thrusts, he raised up to his knees and grasped her hips, pulling her to him and ramming himself into her again. Elly drank in the sight of his broad shoulders and hard arms, the overwhelmingly tempting male body that she felt almost guilty for being allowed to enjoy—just her—just Elly Stover, the wife of Matt Stover.

Was this real? Did she deserve this? What a contrast he was to awful men like Pete Garner. She shook away the memory, wondering how long it would take to get that horror out of her mind and enjoy this man who was truly a man in every way. Brave and sure. And he'd said he loved her. He loved her!

Again, his life spilled into her. He held her hips in a firm grasp for a moment before releasing his hold. Both of them were bathed in perspiration when he lay down beside her then, breathing deeply.

"I didn't expect to be afforded such pleasure our first night," Matt told her.

Elly smiled. "Neither did I." She scooted to put her head on his shoulder. "I hope I satisfied you, dear husband."

"Same here."

"Oh, I am deeply satisfied."

Matt supported his head with his good arm and looked down at her. "So am I."

Elly grinned and put a hand over her face. "I behaved like those women over at the Whiskey Gold, didn't I? *Worse!*"

He reached over and smoothed back her damp hair. "Do you hear me complaining?"

She grasped his firm wrist. "I just decided to make sure you didn't feel a need for their services."

Matt laughed lightly. "I can't. I'm a married man now."

She met his gaze. "Yes, well, I'm sure plenty of married men go to see those women."

"Not this one. Why go looking someplace else when I have the best right here in my bed?"

Elly studied his eyes lovingly. "Did you mean it? That you love me? Or was it just in a moment of passion?"

He leaned down and kissed her softly. "I meant it. I've heard that sometimes love can happen real fast."

"I meant it, too. I think I knew I loved you that very first night I met you back on the trail."

Matt lost his smile. "Yeah, well, I'm sorry that led to so much horror for you."

Her eyes teared. "That horror led you back to me, and that's all that matters." She pressed her hand against his chest. "Life will be good for us now, Matt. We'll find my family, and you can write yours and let them know what's happened. They'll be happy for you. I can't wait to meet them some day."

"And I can't wait for them to meet *you*."

Elly traced her fingers over his lips. "I just wish—" She hesitated.

"I know. You're worried about the Liberty brothers."

A tear slipped down the side of her face. "Matt, let's just go on to California and find my family. Please don't go after those men. It's probably not just the two of them. They could ambush you and shoot you to pieces. I couldn't stand losing you now."

"I can handle them." Matt lay back down and pulled her into his arms. "I won't rest until they're dead, Elly, and I won't be able to fully let go of Lora until I've avenged what happened to her. You'll just have to understand and accept that."

Elly kissed his neck. "I'm trying. I just... I can't lose you now, Matt. I can't!"

"You won't. This was meant to be. I'm sure of it. And God wouldn't have led us together just to let us be torn apart again. You have to trust my abilities. I know those boys, and I know the kind of men with them. And I know gunplay." He moved on top of her again. "And right now, things are fine. We're safe and just married and I want to have my way with you the rest of the night and into the morning. Once more, and then we'll clean up and have the landlady order up some food. And then we'll do this again... and again."

"You'll wear me out."

"That's exactly what I intend to do."

Elly smiled. She decided she'd have to push away her fears over the Liberty boys and enjoy the here and now - enjoy the man who shared her bed - enjoy the fact that she was Mrs. Matthew Stover and she was safe and happy. Matt met her lips, and she laughed through the kiss at the thought of what Betty would have to say about this. Her sister-in-law had felt so sorry for her that she no longer enjoyed these things.

If only you knew what I was doing now, Betty.

She opened herself to her new husband once more, then let out a long, groaning sigh when he entered her. After all these years she'd forgotten what this was like. Any worries she'd had over marrying this near stranger were gone.

She heard a woman scream and laugh somewhere, heard a couple of gunshots. She knew that somewhere in South Pass City the wild, unpredictable residents were doing their own celebrating, drinking and dancing.

But here, in this room, alone with Matt Stover, there could be no better way of celebrating their marriage than getting to know each other in every intimate way possible. Here she was safe, protected, loved, and lost in a passion she'd not known for far too long.

CHAPTER THIRTY-SIX

LATE JULY...

Tex Liberty tossed five dollars into the growing pile of money on the poker table. No one but his brother, Joe, and their two remaining friends, Randy and Tim, knew he'd taken the money from their fellow gang member Fats Howard, after shooting the whale of a man in an argument. Fats had wanted to move on and quit waiting around for Matt Stover to show up.

"Five bucks is a hell of a lot of money," one of the other players complained.

"Match it or fold," Tex growled. He slugged down another shot of whiskey, even though it was only two o-clock in the afternoon. He'd been in a foul mood ever since killing Fats and leaving him somewhere in the mountains to rot. Fats had declared he was leaving their little gang, and Tex, drunk, told him if he tried to leave, he'd kill him. Fats made the fatal mistake of waving him off and mounting his horse.

"Four kings," Tex said after men either matched his five dollars or folded. He laid down his cards.

"Shit!" another man swore. He threw down his cards, took what was left of his gambling cash, and left.

Tex pulled in his winnings, chuckling. "Once we take
care of Matt Stover, we'll have a good life," he told his
brother. "From that robbery back at River's Bend and that
rancher we stole from after we left South Pass City —"

"And that traveling salesman in Atlantic City and the
store owner we held up there, and now this," Joe
interrupted. "Yeah, we have money, big brother, but when
in hell are we gonna' light someplace and enjoy it. You
said all the way out here that we'd get into ranching. Hell,
there're men out here who make money by just letting
outlaws graze their stolen cattle on their land. We
wouldn't even have to do much work."

Tex's mood darkened. "Don't tell me *you're* gonna' start
naggin' me about Matt Stover, too."

"Jesus, Tex, it's been what? Almost four months since
we rode out of River's Bend? Stover ain't showed up yet.
What if he ain't comin' at all?"

One of the other men at the table sat up a little
straighter. "Did you say Matt Stover?"

Tex eyed the man warily. "What's it to ya'?"

"Is he a lawman?"

Joe and Tex leaned closer.

"That's right," Joe answered. "Do you *know* him?"

The man studied them closely. "I might. But I have
some advice for you two. I heard what you said about
robbin' people. And I seen that fight you got into in this
saloon last night." He directed the words at Tex. "You
gotta' be more careful. The men in these places will put up
with only so much. People in Rock Springs are even talkin'
about gettin' a lawman right here in town. Settin' up more
law and order. You'd better watch what you say around
here, and you'd sure better stay out of trouble or they'll
haul you off and hang ya'. That's how it is out here. Even
the lawmen, if they do get any, are former outlaws, so they
don't care much about trials and such."

"What's that got to do with Matt Stover?" Tex asked. "And how in hell do you know the man?"

The man glanced at Tex's pile of winnings. "It'll cost you the five dollars I lost in that last hand."

Tex glared darkly at him. "That depends on the worth of what you've got to tell us. What's your name, anyway?"

"Bo Decker. I came out here to hunt for the railroaders when the U.P. was bein' built. I got no family to go back to in Oklahoma, so I stayed. Now I work for the mining companies, coal and gold both. I run messages up and down through mountain towns, so I get around. A couple weeks ago I was in South Pass City. Heard about you boys from a man who came there lookin' for you. Name was Matt Stover, and we all found out he used to be a sheriff back in Nebraska."

"I'll be goddamned!" Tex almost roared the words. People turned to stare as he grabbed five dollars and slapped the money in front of Bo. "Tell us more!"

Bo sat there quietly a moment, a cigarette hanging from his lips. He slowly took the money. "You talk too loud and too much. If you want to know more, follow me outside into the alley." He rose and walked over to the bar to pay for his drinks, then left.

Tex looked at Joe. "Go get Tim and Randy over at that whore house and send them over here. Hurry it up!"

"Hell, they might be in the middle of —"

"I don't care if they have to come runnin' half naked! Go get 'em, dammit!"

Joe quickly took his cash and shoved it into his pockets, then grabbed his hat and ran out of the saloon. Tex did the same, shoving his way past two men who were just coming inside.

"Who the hell was that?" one asked someone inside.

"I think he called himself Tex," someone answered. "Troublemaker is all he is. Came here from the East

thinkin' he could do anything he wanted and get away
with it. He don't understand the code out here."

"We'd better keep an eye on him and his brother both,"
the bar tender spoke up. "They bragged about robbin' a
store owner back at South Pass City. They ain't gonna' get
away with that here."

Most returned to their card playing, grumbling their
agreement with the bar tender. Outside Tex hurried
around the corner and down an alley between the saloon
and a tobacco store. He found Bo Decker leaning on some
barrels and lighting another cigarette. Tex took a pouch of
tobacco from his shirt pocket and scooped some into his
fingers, then pressed them into his mouth between his
right cheek and lower gums. He replaced the pouch and
approached the tall, bearded Decker. "OK. What's this all
about?"

Bo took the cigarette from his mouth. "You asked about
Matt Stover. Last I knew he was up in South Pass City.
That was two weeks ago. Had a big shootout with some
buffalo hunter who'd taken some woman Stover cared
about, stole her off a wagon train and tried to sell her into
prostitution. Me and some other men helped him get her
out of the place she'd been taken. Matt shot the buffalo
hunter, and we finished him off by hangin' him. Hanged
the bitch who'd bought her, too. Found out she takes
decent women and drugs them. Men out here don't like
treatin' women like that. Stover was gonna' marry the
woman that buffalo hunter stole, and he *did*. I left right
after the wedding. He was gonna' stay there and let the
woman rest up more before comin' south to catch the U.P.
and head to California to find her family."

Before Tex could react, Joe came running with Randy
and Tim, who were both barefoot and still pulling on
shirts.

"What the hell is this?" Tim asked. The deep scar on his

left cheek showed up even whiter in the mid-day sun. "I was still sleepin' with a damn nice-lookin' woman."

"I *told* you," Joe answered excitedly. "We found a man who knows Matt Stover! Seen him recently!" He looked at Bo. "Ain't that right?"

Bo kept his cigarette between his lips. "I'll let you explain."

Tex scratched his head. "I don't understand," he told Bo. "The Matt Stover we knew left Nebraska to come after us on account of we accidentally killed his wife in a bank robbery. Him and his wife, they were really close. Stover must still be grieving over her. That's why he's comin' after us—for revenge. But you said Stover got *married* again, to some woman from a wagon train?"

Bo nodded. "That's right."

"*What?*" Joe frowned. "I don't believe it."

"Believe it," Bo told him. "Hell, a man needs a woman, right? I expect Stover's still grieving, but he knew a good woman when he met one, and it looks like he met one on the way out here. Nothin' wrong with wantin' a woman in your bed at night, is there? Things like that happen out here pretty often. Strangers marry strangers out of loneliness or for survival. Men don't think much of them things out here."

Joe and Tex looked at each other in bewilderment, then glanced at the other two men. Randy shrugged. "Stover had a right to remarry, I expect. What difference does it make? You still want him dead, don't you, Tex?"

"I sure do," Tex grumbled. "Him bein' remarried don't mean he's not still lookin' for me and Joe on account of the first wife. New wife or not, that man is still after us." He looked at Bo. "What more can you tell us? Do you think he's left to come this way?"

Bo took a long drag on his cigarette. "I expect the new wife has had enough rest that they're on their way south right now. I can't tell you if he'll board the train with her and head to California and then here to find you boys, or if he'll put her on that train by herself while he stays here to finish what he came out here for. All I know is they've surely left South Pass by now and are on their way down here."

Tex nodded and put out his hand. "Mister, that five dollars was worth everything you just told us."

Bo looked down at Tex's hand and refused to shake it. "I just want a promise, and if you *don't* promise, I'll warn Stover about you boys, and I'll help him against you."

Tex frowned, moving a hand to his six-gun. "What the hell are you talkin' about?"

"I'm talkin' about the woman. You boys strike me as the kind of men who'd kill a woman if she's in the way of what you want. Apparently, that's what happened to Stover's wife. I don't want his new wife hurt. She gets hurt or killed, I'll find out, and I'll make sure this town hangs all four of you."

Joe removed his hat and scratched his head. "Hell, we got nothin' against the woman. We didn't have nothin' against Stover's first wife. She just got in the way and —"

"That's what I'm talkin' about," Bo interrupted. "She got in the way, so you shot her, givin' no thought to her bein' a woman and carryin' and all. It's Stover you want, so leave the woman out of it."

"We *will*, unless by accident she becomes part of it."

"No accident. No *nothing*. The woman doesn't get hurt."

Tex glowered at Bo. "She won't get hurt. That's a promise."

Bo threw down his cigarette stub and stepped it out. "She'd better not. As far as findin' Stover when he gets here, that's up to you boys. I don't want any part of what happens. But make it fair, or there are men in this town

who won't like it. Believe it or not, there's a code out here
about layin' low for a man and shootin' him in the back.
You'll face him straight on, or you'll never get out of Rock
Springs alive. Understand?"

"Why did you bother to even tell us what you know?"
Joe asked.

Bo grinned. "Because I wanted my five dollars back. I
don't give a damn about any of you or about Matt Stover. I
just wanted my money." He turned and walked off.

Tex watched after him. "I'm not sure I trust that man to
be tellin' the truth." He looked at his brother. "Maybe he's
good friends with Matt Stover and is lookin' to help him."

"Hell, his story makes sense," Joe answered. "If the guy
is tellin' the truth, all we have to do is wait around town
for Matt Stover and the woman to show up. They ain't got
no choice if they want to catch the train. And at least now
we have a pretty good idea that stayin' here is worth the
wait."

Tex sighed deeply. "I reckon' so." He looked at the
others. "But that means layin' low and stayin' out of
trouble. You heard Decker. The men in this town only put
up with so much. They might not care about our beef with
Stover, but they do care about them and their friends here
in town, so no more fights—no stealin'—and be good to
the whores. Once this is over, we can finally go our
separate ways if we choose." He looked at Joe. "I promise
we can start that ranch if that's what you want."

Joe nodded. "Fine with me."

Tex scanned the mountains around town. "First we
take care of Stover for once and for all, so's we don't have
to be always lookin' over our shoulders."

"Hell, Tex, maybe he's not even after us anymore. He
could have changed his mind. You heard that Bo Decker.
Stover took a new wife, and he's takin' her to California."

Tex glared darkly at Joe. "But he still has to come here

to catch the train. And I know Matt Stover. He's had it in for us since we was little. New wife or not, he ain't gonna' let go of losin' Lora and that baby. No, sir. You remember that, little brother. You can bet your ass he's still comin' for us." He scanned the mountains again. "And we'll be ready for him."

CHAPTER THIRTY-SEVEN

$\mathcal{E}$lly shook her head at the scene before her. "I feel like we're lost in a world of canyons and spires and arches and rock and sand and—I don't know how else to put it—nothingness."

She turned to Matt, who sat smoking quietly on the ledge of the very small cave they'd found to hole up in. It was more of a washout in the side of a massive canyon wall, and just big enough for them to fit into and sleep out of the elements. They'd camped here earlier, using the cave to get out of the sun, which seemed extra hot today… so hot that they sat in their underwear, since there was no one to see but an occasional eagle from above.

Elly felt happier and more alive than she'd felt in years. Matt had been good enough to let her rest almost two weeks back at South Pass City, a wonderful time of making love, getting to know each other better, making love, talking about their future, making love. She knew every inch of him, and he knew every inch of her, and learning about each other's bodies had been a glorious lesson. Now her ankle was healed, and Matt's arm was still tender but healing.

They'd been traveling through some of the most glorious landscape either of them had ever seen. How strange that such rugged, dangerous country was so spectacularly beautiful—God's country, Matt called it. Yet it was full of outlaws.

Matt pointed to the distance. "Look. A herd of wild horses."

Elly watched—figuring close to a hundred horses were charging through the valley, maybe a mile away. She'd quickly learned that out here, distance could be deceiving. Their own horses were hobbled farther out in the valley, where they grazed leisurely, but Rusty raised his head and whinnied when he sensed the thundering herd.

"Good thing our own horses can't take off running," Matt added. "They might get the calling."

Elly watched. "Beautiful, isn't it? I love watching horses run."

The mustangs disappeared around the curve of a butte that had probably been formed over thousands of years ago, maybe millions. Elly noticed that their own horses calmed down once the wild ones were gone.

They had four horses now. The citizens of South Pass City had given her and Matt so many going-away gifts that Matt had purchased a second pack horse, as well as a buckskin mare named Sandy for Elly to ride. She loved the horse's creamy color, contrasted with a black mane and black tail and feet. The supply horse, which could also be alternated as a saddle horse, was a gelded paint called Rocky.

"Is any of this real, Matt?" Elly glanced to the side to watch him smoke. She loved watching him do *anything*. There was such a masculine sureness about him. She felt so safe. "How on Earth did we end up married and sitting half-naked out here in a land forgotten by time?" She looked out again to watch an eagle fly over a red-rock spire in the distance.

Matt grinned. "I like that description—forgotten by time." He drew on his cigarette again. "It fits what we're looking at. Makes a man wonder if you and I and the horses are the only things alive out here. It's so damn quiet, it almost hurts your ears."

He sighed and tossed his cigarette butt into the sand below the ledge.

"You're thinking about the Liberty boys, aren't you?"

"I'm thinking about what to do with you when I go after them. I'm worried you'll be with me and they'll wage a surprise attack. You could get hurt or killed."

"I'm not staying behind somewhere, Matt Stover, left to wonder what happened to my husband. And I'm not going on to California alone. Don't even think that."

Matt ran a hand through the thick waves of his hair, which he still kept shoulder-length. "Damn it, Elly, I can't just let you ride right into trouble along with me. The hard part is, I don't know where or when that trouble might show itself. It could be out here somewhere, or in the next town. They could be in Rock Springs, or maybe all the way south to Brown's Park. Back in South Pass City they told me Brown's Park was a favorite of outlaws, especially wanted men. It's about as remote a place as a man could ask for, and they have had plenty of time to get there."

"They probably *didn't* go there because it *is* so remote. They want to make sure you find them, Matt. They're going to be bold, and they're going to blab about where they are and who they're looking for, just like they did back at South Pass City. That's why Nettie and the others already knew your name and knew you were a lawman."

Matt frowned, facing her. "Well, now, how is it you can think like an outlaw, Elly Stover?"

Elly grinned. "I'm not sure. I just think they'll be easier

to find than you think." She leaned over and kissed him.
"And if *I* was an outlaw, I'd *want* you to find me, Sheriff
Stover. Then I could try all kinds of ways of asking you for
mercy." She raised her chin and looked at him coyly. "I'll
bet I could even talk you into letting me go free."

Matt looked her over with a teasing look in his eyes.
"Oh, yeah?" He turned to face her more fully. "And just
what would you do to convince me to let you go?"

Elly shrugged, drinking in the sight of his broad
shoulders. "First, I'd kiss you like I just did, but more
deeply."

"Show me, Ma'am."

Elly leaned closer and kissed him again, this time
suggestively, enjoying the feel of his full, warm lips on her
mouth, fire moving through her at the thought of other
places those lips had been. She released the kiss, and Matt
shook his head.

"That's not enough, Ma'am. I still have to take you to
jail."

Elly frowned. "Sir, you are not being fair. What more
could you want from a decent lady?"

Matt flashed an evocative grin. "Maybe for her to be
*in*decent."

Elly feigned indignance. "You are cruel and
reprehensible!" She unhooked her camisole and tossed it
aside. "Is *this* enough?"

Matt studied her naked breasts. "Maybe. I'd have to
touch and taste those breasts to know for sure."

"And you are decadent and mean." She threw back her
head. "Very well. Do what you must." She breathed
deeply from keen desire when he leaned close and toyed
with her breasts and tasted them with tantalizing licks
and gentle sucking. He moved his lips to her throat and
set her on fire with little kisses and licks as he fondled her
breasts.

"*Now* are you satisfied?" she asked him with a soft groan.

"No, Ma'am. If I'm to let you go, you'll have to show me more and allow me any pleasure I want."

He kept an arm around her under her breasts as he got up and pulled her into the shade of the little cave. He laid her back on their make-shift bedding and stood up to remove his long johns, then stretched out beside her.

"Surely you don't expect more!" she pretended to protest.

"Oh, I expect a *lot* more." He took hold of her right hand and moved it to his privates. "I expect you to touch me here."

Elly grasped his penis gently and began stroking it. "Like this?"

He met her mouth hungrily then, moving his tongue between her lips. "For a proper lady, you have a very *im*proper way of touching a man."

"Oh, but you *told* me to do this. It's such torture for me."

"I don't really want to torture you."

Elly studied those blue eyes that always melted any resistance. "Then to relieve my torture, you'd better do something more with this instrument of love that is in my hand, Sheriff Stover."

"First you have to do one more thing if you want me to free you."

Elly ran her hand over his stomach, his chest. "*Now* what is it you want of me?"

Matt straddled her and pulled off her pantaloons. He leaned down and kissed her belly, the hairs around her love nest. He moved fingers inside her. "I want you to show me every secret place most proper women would never show a man."

"Sheriff! How *dare* you!" Elly closed her eyes and

breathed deeply with almost painful desire. "But if you insist —" She opened herself to him and moaned with acute pleasure as she allowed him to taste and touch and explore.

Matt kissed his way back over her belly and breasts, throat and ears, eyes and to her lips, where she tasted her own juices as he moved between her legs and entered her with hard thrusts that made her cry out with incredible pleasure. They'd been married two weeks, but every time he took her it felt like the first time all over again. And every time this man was inside her, she wondered how she'd been so lucky as to find him, to know this exotic mating game again, to know love again. She ran her hands over his hard-muscled chest, his arms.

It was wonderful to feel so safe, so wanted... so loved. His hands and lips stroked and tasted in what seemed sheer adoration, and she adored him in return, enjoying everything that was man about him, taking him inside herself with relish and with a prayer that his planted seeds would take hold—a son or a daughter for Matt Stover, a baby to help heal his heart from the loss of his little girl, and a part of this man she would love forever.

How many times had they done this since marrying? She'd lost count. She only knew she couldn't get enough of him, but always, always there was that dark fear that this would end. It all just seemed too good to be true. And in this wild, cruel land anything could happen, especially to a man bent on revenge.

His life spilled into her with such force she could feel it against her insides.

Matt shuddered with his release, and after a moment settled beside her, pulling her into his arms. They lay there quietly at first. Elly kissed his neck.

"You have a strange way of punishing a woman," she

told him, wanting to keep up the teasing, wanting to avoid what they really needed to talk about.

"Well, Ma'am, I've decided I can't set you free in spite of you doing everything I demanded of you."

Elly frowned and scooted back a little, meeting his gaze. "But that's not fair."

"I know, but I'm the lawman here, and I say you can't go free." He leaned close and kissed her again. "Because I want you for myself, now and forever, so I can't let you go. You are my prisoner until death."

Their gazes held on the last word, and they both sobered. "I'm going with you, Matt. Don't try to leave me behind. I'll go insane."

He closed his eyes and sighed deeply and rolled onto his back. "I'll take you to find Betty and Mark first if you want. That way you'll be with people who love you. If we go by train, we won't lose all that much time, and—"

"No! We'll be too far apart. By the time we'd get to California and find Betty's brother and then you come all the way back here—even by train you could be stranded back here for the winter. All I heard on the way out here was how early it can start snowing in the mountains, and that trains often get stranded in blizzards and snow slides." Elly sat up and pulled a blanket around herself. "I've already lost one husband, Matt. I want to be with you and make love to you as much as I possibly can, and I want to be here for you if you get hurt." She faced him as he also sat up. "Please, please don't do this."

He rubbed at his eyes. "Elly, you've married a lawman. I do what I have to do. Not only that, but you don't know what it was like—seeing my wife lying dead in that doctor's office, her swollen belly bloody from a bullet that went right through our baby girl. We'd made love just hours earlier, and there she was, the doctor cutting her open because I wanted to know about the baby, if it was a boy or a girl, if it could be saved. But of course, it couldn't." His voice wavered on the last words, and he turned away to light another cigarette. He smoked quietly for a few minutes, until Elly put a hand on his shoulder.

"Matt, I'm so sorry."

Matt inhaled deeply. "Yeah, well, maybe vengeance is something that's hard for a woman to understand." He exhaled. "Women are more forgiving than men. I wish I *could* be more forgiving myself. My parents would welcome that. But I just can't." He met her gaze. "I'm going after them, Elly. You just have to trust me to know what to do. I'm *good* at what I do. If you want us to be truly happy in this marriage, you have to let me be my own man, and that means righting the wrong that's been done."

Elly wanted to cry herself at the look of tragedy in his eyes. She reached out and touched his face. "Then promise me you'll keep me with you, no matter what. If something happens to you, I should be with you. And if the worst happens, then I don't care if I get hurt or die, Matt. I can't go through losing another man, and I can't go through the agony of waiting to find out if you're dead or alive."

He smiled through tears and reached out to pull some of her hair over her shoulder. "If that's how you want it." He moved an arm around her.

"That's how I want it."

They sat in each other's arms, gently rocking a little in shared grief, shared love, shared worry over the unknown. Elly heard the cry of the eagle she'd spotted earlier. It was closer now. One small reminder that there *was* life out here in this cruelly spectacular landscape that deceived a person by how still and peaceful it seemed. Under all of that was a wild place full of wild weather and wild landscapes, wild horses and other wild creatures, including the men who lived there.

CHAPTER THIRTY-EIGHT

*T*hey broke camp at sunrise. Elly looked at the literal hole in the wall of rock above them, where they'd made love more than once the previous day. They'd come down to camp near the horses for the night. Desolate and lonely as this part of the country seemed, Matt feared a man or men could come along while they slept and steal the horses, or wolves could attack them. He didn't want to take their "aloneness" for granted.

Elly realized it was time to face reality. They'd enjoyed two weeks of newlywed life as well as using that time to heal and rest. So far, since they'd left South Pass City, they'd ridden leisurely, taking it easy on themselves and the horses, getting to know this wild, free country, time to enjoy the incredibly quiet peace, time to drink in the awesome beauty of Outlaw Country and their own newfound love.

Now they needed to move a little quicker. Now was the time to find the Liberty brothers and settle what needed settling so they could go on with life. Elly hoped to see them hang, rather than Matt killing them outright. Who knew how men out here would react to that? Matt's grief was so deep, she worried he'd do something that could mean *he* would hang. Her other worry was the deeply-based goodness to Matt that could haunt him later and eat at his conscience if he flat-out killed the Liberty men without even giving them a chance. She reminded herself that the man she'd married and had been sharing her bed with these past two weeks was a lawman, not a murderer, but she'd also learned that life out here had a way of altering a man's thinking and turning right into wrong and wrong into right.

"How far do you think it is to Rock Springs?" She hooked a canteen over her saddle horn, then checked the cinch. "By the way, this cinch doesn't seem tight enough," she added.

"Around five to eight days to Rock Springs," Matt answered. He walked over to help her out. "That's according to Bo Decker. He left for Rock Springs the day after you and I got married. He's the one who gave me directions and told me how long it would take." He slapped a hand against her horse's belly. "Come on, Sandy, suck it in." The horse tossed its head, and Elly could see her girth twitch. Matt yanked on the cinch close to the horse's front legs to tighten it through the latigos. He moved to the cinch at the rear of the saddle, insisting on double-cinching her gear as an extra precaution so she'd have no accident from a loose saddle if something spooked her horse.

He checked the choker strap. "It could take longer than that to get there, depending on these horses. Some days we'll do twenty miles, some days forty. We have to hope none of the animals comes up lame, for whatever reason." He nodded toward the paint. "Rocky there likes to take his time. That's why I'm having you ride Sandy most of the time. Rocky is a bit of a challenge to keep moving forward. I swear he'd walk sideways the next hundred miles to

Rock Springs if you let him. If I'd known he could be so obstinate, I'd probably have picked a different horse, but he'll do for carrying supplies. I can force him to keep up. If I let you ride him instead of using him for a pack horse, you'd be forever doing a balancing act in the saddle from trying to keep him walking head-first."

He went to check the panniers slung over Rocky's back, making sure all the straps that held their supplies were secure. Elly had a feeling he was talking more than normal because he wanted to avoid the subject of *why* they were on the move again. She wondered what he'd do if they reached Rock Springs and the Union Pacific without finding the Liberty brothers. How much longer would he keep searching before heading for California?

"I'll pull Rocky so your horse doesn't have to constantly tug and fight with him to keep up the pace. Sadie's a lot easier to pull, and she doesn't seem to mind a heavy load."

Elly smiled. "Thanks to everybody back at South Pass City, we *have* this heavy load. We can practically set up house with what the pack horses are carrying."

"Yes, but it cost me a pretty penny for the extra riding saddle and extra packsaddle and all the extra strapping."

Elly frowned. "We *do* have enough money to finish this trip, don't we? I mean, to take the train through the mountains?"

He nodded. "We have enough. The parishioners at my father's church actually held a fund-raiser for me after Lora was killed and I said I was going after the Liberty brothers." He secured the straps on Rocky's other side before moving back to her. "Most of them agreed with my father that I shouldn't go, but they also knew there was no stopping me, and they wanted to help. With that and money given to us back at South Pass City when we got married, we have plenty." He leaned forward and kissed her cheek. "Just don't let any outlaws we might come across know I'm carrying decent cash. They just might try relieving me of some of it." He paused to hold a stirrup for her. "Mount up, Mrs. Stover."

Elly put her foot into the stirrup and reached up for the saddle horn. She pulled herself up, with help from Matt, who gladly gave her a boost with his hand on her rear. She settled into the blanketed saddle and adjusted her skirts.

Matt looked up at her as he took a pre-rolled cigarette from an inside pocket on his leather vest. "How's that ankle? Still doing okay?"

"It's fine. I'm more concerned about your arm, Matt. That bandage I changed this morning had some blood on it."

He paused to light his cigarette, then took a deep drag. "Buffalo guns leave deep creases. Just be glad that's all it is and that it didn't blow my upper arm all to hell." He reached into his pocket and handed her several paper bills. "Put that in the handbag tied to your gear, just in case you need some quick money and I'm not around. I have enough for general supplies in my pocket. The rest is sewn into a special lining inside my carpetbag. It's the one with a green and blue paisley design, tied to Rocky. You should know that, just in case."

Just in case what? Elly wanted to ask. *In case you die?* She watched him cross to Sadie to lead the horse to her. He tied the straps of Sadie's bridle to two latigos hooked to the rear of Elly's saddle, then proceeded to tie Rocky to his own saddle.

Elly watched him mount up, a man sure in the saddle and sure of what he intended to do, which was what she dreaded most about this trip. It should be one of joy—so much to look forward to now—excitement over finding Betty and Mark and letting them know she was all right. But first there was that dark shadow hanging over everything. *Two* shadows, actually. The Liberty brothers. And God only knew how many extra men they had with them.

Matt adjusted his hat and kicked Rusty's sides to get the horse moving. He yanked on Rocky. "Come on, you stubborn side-stepper." Rocky snorted and tossed his head, then followed, walking half sideways until Matt gave him another yank.

Elly adjusted the wide-brimmed hat Matt had bought for her. He'd insisted she keep her hair in a bun on top of her head and wear a hat to protect her face from the harsh Western sun and hide her long hair so men wouldn't so easily spot it from a distance. She urged Sandy into a gentle walk and followed her husband, pulling Sadie behind her, deciding that the best she could do for now was take each day and not worry about the tomorrows that hadn't come yet, and never really would. There was always just today, and today she was Mrs. Matt Stover and as happy and fulfilled as any woman could expect to be. She only hoped they would have years to be together, and not just days.

CHAPTER THIRTY-NINE

They followed what could be called a road. It was more of a worn-down pathway over flattened summer grass and fragile wildflowers that had no hope of surviving the onslaught of humans and horses. Elly felt almost guilty riding over them. On either side a virtual sea of grass and flowers gently waved in the wind, virgin land that she supposed one day would be inhabited, if or when the time came that people actually wanted to live in this desolation. Apparently, they did, since there were already towns out here, and these beaten pathways that ran between them, but so far, those inhabitants were nearly all made up of those avoiding the law back East.

Pathway or not, she had no doubt Matt could find his way to Rock Springs. He seemed to have an instinct for direction, and she'd learned he'd tracked and hunted a lot with a friend in his younger years, then had learned a different kind of hunting as a lawman—hunting for men instead of animals.

Occasionally a blast of air that rushed through the canyons would hit them, making the grass bend more wildly, and sending whispers and groans of wind that moved from gentle to harsh and back to gentle. She realized she was growing used to the fact that the air out here was almost never still, just like the men who lived here.

She watched Matt ahead of her, broad shoulders, sure on his horse, determined to do what he'd come out here to do no matter what the risk. Would he one day be still again? Or would he be hypnotized by the wind and the wildness out here and never again settle into a normal life? He was her husband. Whatever he decided, she would have to stay by his side and accept it. She realized that could mean living permanently in this emptiness.

Beautiful, yes, it was actually *beyond* beautiful. It was difficult to come up with adjectives to describe the magnificent mountains to their right as they headed south. In fact, the path they followed had led into deep canyons that formed fortress-like walls on both sides then opened into wide grassland again, past waterfalls and beneath the wings of eagles. They'd spotted a grizzly bear once in the foothills, causing both of them to struggle a little to keep the horses steady. Matt had the hardest time because of Rocky, who balked and tossed his head and began prancing sideways again, apparently wanting desperately to run away. She understood now why Matt had insisted on leading Rocky. She wasn't sure she could have held on to him when he fought to get away. Matt finally calmed him down, but not without shouting several unmentionable words Elly seldom heard come out of his mouth.

They moved into wide-open grassland again, where a smattering of huge boulders here and there made one wonder how on Earth they got there, since there were no rocky hillsides anywhere close. Matt drew Rusty to a halt and put up his hand, warning her to also stop.

Elly frowned, slowly moving her horse up beside Matt. She could see he was straining to listen. "What is it?"

"Men shouting and whistling. And I think cattle mooing around that butte to our left." He kicked Rusty into motion again. "Ride slowly. Out here, you can't tell what kind of men are coming. My bet is if they're herding cattle along, it's probably stolen stock."

Elly could hear them now, and a moment later they could see them, a fairly large herd. "How many men do you think are coming?"

Matt pulled down the brim of his hat against the afternoon sun. "Looks like six or eight. Let's get over to the left, beyond that pile of boulders over there." He pointed. "We need to get out of their way. Cattle spook easy, and we don't want to be in their path if for some damn reason they stampede."

Elly obeyed. They moved behind a huge boulder. Matt turned to look her over, then dismounted and rummaged through a carpetbag tied to Rocky, removing a denim jacket. He walked over and handed it up to her. "I know it's warm today, but put this on. You fill out that dress a bit too temptingly for men who've been on the trail for God knows how long."

Elly felt her cheeks flush as she took the jacket from him, suddenly self-conscious in front of her own husband. Matt had helped her replenish her wardrobe before they left South Pass City, and she'd worn the plainest dress she owned, a solid gray color without any kind of trim. She wore only one slip, long, black stockings and leather shoes that laced half-way up her legs. She wished she could put a little color on her cheeks and wear something prettier for her husband, but Matt wanted her as plain as possible when they traveled because he didn't trust what kind of men they might come across.

"Pull your hat down more so it's harder to see those beautiful green eyes," Matt told her, re-mounting.

Elly couldn't help a smile as she pulled on the jacket, which was much too big for her, but that's what Matt wanted. It covered everything that might attract a man. She yanked her hat down as Matt lit a cigarette, and now she was anxious for night to come. They would make camp and lie together in the deep grass under the stars and she could please her husband again in all the ways that brought her pleasure in return. She wanted that more than anything on this trip, because deep inside she was terrified that every time they made love it could be their last time.

Men and cattle came closer. The air began to fill louder with the moos of hundreds of cattle and the shouts and whistles of men. They slowly made their way past Matt and Elly, followed by a chuck wagon and a remuda of horses. Elly felt bad about all the wildflowers that were being trampled beneath the herd, but she was relieved to watch them keep going on by. She noticed Matt had pulled his rifle from its boot and laid it across his lap. She hoped they were in the clear, but suddenly three men pulled away from the herd and headed their way.

Matt quickly untied Rocky and handed the reins to Elly. "Hang on tight to him." He led Rusty from where they'd waited and moved toward the approaching men, rifle in hand. Once out in the open, he reined Rusty to a halt and held the rifle aimed and ready as the three men rode closer. The man in the lead held up his right hand.

"You can put that rifle away," he told Matt. "We don't mean any harm. Just checking out who's over here. There's always men prowling around out here and willing to steal cattle."

"Could be they're already stolen," Matt suggested, still not putting down his rifle.

The man who'd approached grinned. "Damn well could be, but that's nobody's business. We're headed a bit northeast to meet a friend who's building a ranch in the prettiest valley in these parts."

Matt lowered his rifle a little. "Might that friend be Sage Lightfoot?"

The leader grinned. "Might be."

"I've met him."

"Then put that rifle down," the cattleman told Matt. "Any friend of Sage is a friend of ours. Besides, there are a lot more of us than you two." He glanced Elly's way. "And I see one of the two is a woman."

"She's my wife, and I'll kill any man who treats her less than that," Matt told him, still not lowering his rifle the whole way.

"It's okay, Matt," a familiar voice drawled.

The other two men rode closer. One sat tall and lanky and had a long beard.

Matt lowered his rifle. "Bo Decker! What the hell are you doing out here?"

Elly sighed with relief. She remembered Bo Decker was one of the men who'd helped Matt the day he rescued her from Frieda's place.

"I'm on my way back up to South Pass," Bo told Matt. "Figured I'd travel a ways with these fellas. Out here there's always more safety in numbers. A man alone is a tempting target for those who'd like to have his horses and weapons."

"I sure as hell know that," Matt answered.

Elly held back as all the men introduced each other and Matt told the cattlemen to give his regards to the oddly named Sage Lightfoot. Matt had only mentioned him once and never said much about him. Once the cattlemen realized she and Matt were no threat, they turned and rejoined the herd, but Bo Decker held back.

Elly thought about all the people who'd moved into and out of her life since she'd left Kansas—people who had been friends for just a day or two, and then gone again. She only hoped Matt wouldn't be one of those. Now Bo Decker, another complete stranger who'd been a friend for a few days before he left South Pass City, was back in their lives, if only for a few minutes. He rode even closer and shook Matt's hand.

"I was hopin' you'd take the main path to Rock Springs," he told Matt in his distinctively slow drawl. He spit tobacco juice. "I've been lookin' out for you. Actually, I was hopin' you'd decided to stay up in South Pass a bit longer so's I could give you lots of warnin' and maybe you'd bring some of the men from up there with you."

Elly felt her chest tighten with alarm.

"What's going on?" Matt asked him.

Bo glanced at Elly and nodded. "Ma'am."

"Hello, Bo."

"You're lookin' mighty fine, Ma'am. Healthy, I mean. Can't tell much else under that jacket and hat."

Matt grinned. "I make her wear that jacket so from a distance she looks like a man."

Bo chuckled. "No disrespect intended, friend, but out here, a man goes long enough, he can sense a woman from a mile away, covered up or not."

Matt grinned. "I suppose so."

"Glad to know you're okay, Mrs. Stover."

"Thank you," Elly answered.

"You have a beautiful wife there, Sheriff," Bo told Matt. "Strong and brave, too. That means as much as fair looks and build."

Matt nodded. "I agree. I can already tell I made a good choice." He sobered then. "No more small talk, Bo. What's happened? Why were you looking for me?"

Bo sighed and rubbed at the back of his neck. "Well, sir,

I ran into the Liberty boys down in Rock Springs. They're waitin' there for you."

Elly put a hand to her stomach, feeling literal pain at the news. Reality had finally hit them both, full force.

CHAPTER FORTY

"Come on over here and rest your horse," Matt told Bo.

He led Rusty back to where Elly waited with the two pack horses. Seeing the look on her face tore at Matt's heart, but he also felt elation at knowing he was finally close to finding the Liberty brothers.

He reached up for Elly. "Come on down. It'll be okay." He helped her dismount and asked her to tie the horses while he lit another cigarette, then went to lean against a large boulder near Bo, who'd led his horse to a small pine tree that seemed to literally grow out of another large rock. Bo tied his horse and faced Matt.

"I'd offer you some coffee, but we have to build a fire first," Matt told him. "I'm thinking it's late enough in the day that the wife and I will just camp here for the night. It's decently private up here away from the main trail."

"Good spot," Bo answered. He paused to light a thin cigar. "Don't worry about the coffee. Once I tell you what you need to know, I'll be on my way. Got to catch up with those cowboys for a few more miles - then I'll veer off more to the north. There's a couple of mines in the mountains around South Pass that I have deliveries for, and I'm set up to ride shotgun on a gold delivery."

"You mean you won't go back with Matt and help him against the Liberty brothers?" Elly asked. "I thought maybe—"

"Elly!" Matt interrupted her. "Bo has no obligation to help. What I'm doing is personal." He turned to Bo. "I'm just grateful you even looked for us so you could warn us."

Elly quietly unloaded some firewood.

"I felt like I should do that much," Bo answered, sitting down on a nearby rock.

Matt walked over to Elly, feeling like an ass for being sharp with her. He took the wood from her arms and set it down. "Forget about a fire. It's hot out, and we might not even need one tonight. Besides, it could attract others who might come along." He took hold of her hand. "Come on over here and sit by me. There's a big log over here we can sit on." He felt twice as guilty when he saw tears in Elly's eyes. "I'm sorry I got short with you. It's going to be okay. I promise." He led her to the log and they both sat down.

"I'm sorry, Bo," Elly said softly as Matt lit another cigarette. "I can't help worrying I could lose Matt before we've even had a chance to settle somewhere."

Bo puffed on his cigar. "Well, it's normal for a woman to worry about such things, but I have a feeling your husband there is a lot more able than you realize."

Elly took a deep breath. "I don't doubt his abilities, but one man can do only so much against five, and that's how many Matt believes he'll be going up against."

"Well, now it's four."

Matt took a long drag on his cigarette. "You sure?"

Bo nodded. "Far as I know. The only extras I met were a pretty average-looking one called Randy, and a tall, lanky guy named Tim. He had a real deep scar down his left cheek, so he'd be easy to recognize. They were the only two with the Liberty boys. I reckon' you know them well enough—big braggarts, both of them, especially the one called Tex."

Matt nodded. "I know all about them. When we were younger, they were the town bullies."

"Well, from what I saw, they're *still* bullies. I warned 'em to stay out of trouble in Rock Springs, or they'd end up hanged. Rock Springs is tryin' harder than some of the other towns out here to bring some law and order. They even have a jail there, but the turnover in sheriffs there is a bit high, if you know what I mean."

Both men grinned.

"I get the picture," Matt told him.

"Them two stay around the Wild Horse Saloon mostly. And I have to tell you, I made it out like I was on their side. I gave them information about you, includin' you gettin' married and all. I told 'em all that because they were gettin' restless about you comin' for them. They talked about leavin' Rock Springs to keep lookin' for you, or maybe to just go off and start a ranch. I figured if you're after them boys, it's best to get it over with sooner than later, so's you don't have to be always lookin' over your shoulder. And so's the wife there would be safer in the future—them bein' out of the picture and all. So, I told 'em you were on your way to Rock Springs so they'd stay right there and not move on. I hope you ain't angry about it."

Matt shook his head. "I'm not. It's best this way."

"Well, I knew I was comin' back this way and that this was the most likely route you'd take, Matt, so I figured to find you before you got there. But I also figured if I didn't, you were good enough with that gun of yours to handle things, and smart enough to be careful and ask around before you walked into trouble. That bunch pretends to be brave and good with their sidearms, but I figure you're a lot braver and a lot more able, so I was hopin' for the best. I know men, and that bunch is only worth what comes out of the back-end of a horse." Bo tipped his hat to Elly. "Sorry, Ma'am."

"It's all right, Bo. I'm glad to hear your opinion. It makes me feel better."

"Well, keepin' those men in one place was the least I could do." Bo told her. "And it ain't that I wouldn't like to help your husband, but out here, men are left to deal with their own problems. Most won't go riskin' their lives for a complete stranger who's carryin' a grudge over somethin' personal that other men don't care much about. Life out here' is dangerous enough without invitin' more danger for no good reason. And I have a job to do. I have people waitin' for me up to South Pass City, so I had to get movin'."

Elly grasped Matt's right arm tightly. "I understand. At least you warned us, so Matt knows what we're riding into."

Bo turned his attention to Matt. "There's one thing in your favor. If you can catch them in the Wild Horse Saloon, the owner there has a policy. No guns inside. There's a man paid to sit outside and collect guns as men go in. They can have them back when they leave. So, if you walk into that saloon unarmed, you can confront them. Tell every man in there what they did. I guarantee some of those men will side up with you, just like what happened back at South Pass City. They'll either haul those boys off for you, or you'll at least be able to set up a fair fight someplace outside. The men there will make sure it *is* fair. That way you won't have to worry about one of them boys walkin' up later and shootin' you in the back. There's lots of killin' out here, but back shootin' ain't ever allowed. Not ever. You shoot a man in the back, and you'll be pushin' up your own daisies in no time. So, I expect if you're goin' to meet up with them boys, you couldn't ask for a better place than Rock Springs. They have the closest thing to law and order there of any other place out here."

Matt dropped his cigarette butt and stepped it out with his boot. "That's good to know. I can't thank you enough for the information."

"I'm right tempted to go back and help, but you have to understand." Bo moved his gaze to Elly. "It ain't just my job, Ma'am, but out here, men don't like those who rat on somebody else. If I go back there, no matter who wins when your husband faces them Liberty boys, others will know I warned him. Out here that means I can't be trusted with what another man tells me. Bad as them Liberty boys are, I got no right deceivin' them like this. I don't know if you can understand that kind of thinkin'. I know it's wrong in civilized places. But out here there ain't nothin' more important than a man's word." He looked at Matt again. "Which brings me to one more thing. I made them Liberty boys promise no harm would come to Miss Elly here. Even if she were to get in the way, like your wife did back there in Nebraska, they ain't to harm her. I told them if I hear she got hurt or killed, I'd tell the right people in Rock Springs and all of Outlaw Trail country. Men would be lookin' for them on account of they let an innocent woman get hurt. I made it real clear. So, no matter what happens, them men won't be goin' after your wife aimin' to hurt her in any way. And if she's around when the shootin' starts, she'd better not get shot. Either way, they're dead men if anything happens to her. I'll make sure that happens. That's a promise."

Matt nodded. "I owe you. You helped me back at South Pass, and now you're helping me again."

"I'm just doin' what a man ought to do. I ain't no angel, Stover. Not by a long shot. But like I've said, there's a code out here, and most men live by it. War does some shameful things to a man—sometimes turns him into somebody he never was before. I won't go into details, but it happened to me, so I understand your need for revenge."

Matt could see more and more that the men out here weren't the heathen murderers outsiders made them out to be. Some were just plain rotten to the core, but those were the few. Most had an innate decency that was born into them and sealed through teaching as they grew up. He thought about his father's sermons and the talks they'd had before he left to come out here. And he supposed that if and when he had his own sons, he'd be teaching them the same things.

Bo rose, adjusting his hat. "I have to get goin'." He put out his hand.

Matt rose and shook Bo's hand. "I can't thank you enough. I might never see you again, but I sure as hell won't forget you, Bo Decker."

"Nor will I." Elly stood up, reaching out and touching Bo's arm.

Bo nodded and pushed his hat back a little. "Well, Ma'am, I'll surely be hopin' for the best for both of you. I hope you find your family in California and you and the husband here can get down to normal livin'. I expect he's skilled enough that he'll be okay. And I don't doubt there'll be one or more men in Rock Springs who might end up helpin' him, so don't you fret."

"What you've told us is such a big help," Elly told him.

"I hope so." Bo turned to Matt. "I'll be on my way now." He turned and walked off, as though delivering the incredibly important message was just part of his daily routine. He mounted his horse and rode off without even looking back.

Matt turned to Elly, who fell into his arms. He hugged her close, breathing deeply of the smell of her hair as she trembled against his shoulder. He never dreamed he could love another woman this much, or this soon, but she'd already proven she made a damn good wife, and he relished her scent, her goodness, her soft voice, her patience, her devotion, and the feel of her body against his in the night. "This is good news, Elly. We have the warning we needed." He grasped her arms and pushed her slightly away, then kissed her cheek. "I have a good feeling about this. Tell me you do, too."

"I want to." Elly searched his eyes. "I love you so much. I can't lose you."

"You won't." He kissed her cheek once more, then left her to unpack their supplies and unsaddle the horses. "So," he muttered softly, "the Liberty boys are waiting for me in Rock Springs." He patted Rusty's neck. "They're in for a big surprise, aren't they boy?"

CHAPTER FORTY-ONE

*E*lly gazed at the night sky, wondering how many stars there really were if you counted the ones so far away they couldn't be seen. Billions? Trillions? What came after that? She felt small and insignificant, and she wondered what God thought about the anger and revenge that seethed in men's hearts.

God, please protect my husband. If He could create such an endless universe, such magnificent landscapes as what she'd seen out here in the mountains, surely He could make sure nothing happened to her husband. Maybe He could even find a way to rid Matt of the hatred that was causing him to go after men for personal revenge, rather than as a lawman out to arrest men for committing crimes.

They'd made camp in heavy shrubbery in the foothills just outside Rock Springs, and their fire had dwindled to red coals. Through the spaces in the branches of the shrubs and pine trees that hid them, Elly could see the dim lights from the oil lamps lighting the city's streets. Rock Springs was bigger than she'd expected, with homes and businesses scattered well beyond the main street. Because of coal mines seemingly everywhere, it had been difficult to find a private place to make camp.

Matt didn't want to ride into town this first day. He wanted to get a fresh start in the morning and first decide where she should stay before he sought out the Liberty brothers. Elly felt sick at the thought. She wanted to tell him that he must have loved Lora far more than he loved her, because otherwise he'd change his mind about this. He knew how devastated she'd be to lose another husband, but now, being this close, he seemed only to care about revenge.

After tethering the horses, Matt came over to where she lay, carrying his rifle and handgun with him. It was warm, and he wore only the bottom half of his long johns. He laid both his weapons beside their bedroll, then crawled into it with her and rested his head on his saddle. Elly moved close to him and laid her head on his shoulder.

"I'll make sure you're set up first in a nice hotel room," he told her. "A real bed after these past nearly two weeks on the trail will feel damn good. I just didn't want to go into town when it was already near dark."

Elly kissed his solid chest. "It doesn't matter where I stay."

"Yes, it does. And I'll give you my money. If things go wrong, buy a train ticket to California and hire a good guide to help you find your family."

"They won't likely be there yet. I'll have to find Betty's brother's place near Cisco and wait for them." Elly put an arm around his middle. "I don't want to have to do that alone, Matt."

He sighed deeply and kissed her hair. "I know. Just trust me."

"It's not *you* I don't trust. The Liberty boys sound like men who won't play fair. They'll gang up on you."

"I know them better than you think. Tex likes an

individual challenge. If I call him out, he'll tell the others, including his brother, to back off and let him handle it. He's a bully, and he likes to show off. He'll growl like a bear and come at me in an effort to prove his prowess to those watching. If I can bring him down, I'll have a good chance against the other three."

"You don't even know what two of them look like."

"Between Bo's descriptions I have a damn good idea what they look like. Besides, I suspect all four of them hang around together most of the time. Find one, and you find the rest of them." Matt rolled to his side and moved on top of her, kissing her neck as he ran a hand along her leg under her gown.

Elly wanted to tell him no. It was too heart-wrenching to think this could be their last time together this way. Yet if he died tomorrow, she'd regret *not* doing this. She was tempted to tell him she *might* be carrying his child. It was far too soon to tell, and it could be from all the trauma she'd been through in the last month, but she should have had her time of month about four days after they were married. So far, nothing. If not for what could happen tomorrow, she'd be overjoyed, but right now it only meant she could be left a widow with a child to raise—a child who would never know his or her father.

Ordinarily, she couldn't imagine ever saying no to Matt Stover. It angered her that he'd put her in this situation— wanting him desperately, yet afraid of the hurt that might follow. Understanding his pain over Lora and his need to avenge her death, yet angry with him for *wanting* that revenge over her need to have him alive and well.

His lips devoured her mouth in sudden desperation, a deep need to make sure they both remembered this. She opened herself to him, temporarily wanting nothing more than to feel his manliness inside her, surging, loving, stirring a greedy need to take and take, to give and give, as though branding her forever, no matter what might happen tomorrow. He pushed deep, and she arched up to him in an effort to both please and to take her own personal pleasure. She was soon panting with his almost-angry thrusts, wincing when he reached beneath her and grasped her bottom with a little too much strength. Her body jerked with his force, and sooner than normal his life spilled into her in a throbbing release.

He'd taken her suddenly, hard and fast, with no foreplay. It had felt more like an urgent necessity than making love. He remained on top of her, kissing her neck again, her ears, her eyes.

"I'm sorry, Elly."

"I wanted you just as much, and out of the same desperation."

He wilted against her, pulling himself away and lying beside her again, keeping her close. "Before morning I'll make love to you again. The right way. I don't want this to be what you remember of me."

As in—if you die? Elly couldn't bring herself to say the words. He'd told her to trust him. Told her he had a plan. Would he change his mind if he thought she was carrying? Probably not. And knowing it would distract him from what he had to do, maybe sway his concentration and cost him his life, she chose not to tell him yet.

Wolves howled up in the hills, and a strange, steady clanging sound came from an unknown place, probably one of the coal mines that operated all night long. They were too far away from Rock Springs to hear any of the noises from there, but tomorrow they would see it all for themselves. Tomorrow would bring the fulfillment Matt had come here for. It would finally be over, and they could go on with life, settle and have babies and put all this behind them.

Matt kissed her forehead. "Don't ever doubt my love

for you, Elly, but there are just some things a man has to do, right or wrong. I'm not one to do the wrong, but in this case —"

"I know," Elly interrupted. "You don't need to explain any more than you already have. I'm just going to have to pray real hard and hope my prayers are answered."

Matt kissed her again—the more familiar, gentle kiss she knew well. The kind of kiss that had seared his face into her mind from their first kiss back at Fort McPherson. Had that only been a couple of months ago? Where had the time gone? It felt as though she'd been on this trip for a year, but it was only mid-summer. She'd almost forgotten her reasons for setting out on this journey. It had all been turned upside-down, and she hardly knew herself any more.

Here was that handsome, able man who'd walked into their campsite a stranger, and now he was her husband. Now he'd made love to her. More times than she could count. She could only pray that he wouldn't be like all the other strangers in this land—here today - and gone tomorrow—not by choice, but by another man's fist or gun.

CHAPTER FORTY-TWO

*E*lly and Matt both found Rock Springs to be amazingly busy and well populated for its location. It was also perfectly named, since the landscape was nothing *but* rocks. Everywhere from the mountains all the way down through the town. She wondered if farming anything here was even possible. How did a man plow ground like this? It was no surprise that the only industry was mining, and by using dynamite to open the ground. If not for that and the railroad, Elly was sure Rock Springs wouldn't exist. Matt had mentioned that the only reason the town was bigger than others out here was because of the railroad stop.

"Seems like new towns spring up almost daily along the U. P.," he told her now from where they sat at the edge of town.

A train whistle wailed in the distant foothills, announcing progress and settlement. Smoke curled skyward in various places in the mountains, from coal-mining camps and smelters at a few straggling gold mines. Elly thought what a contrast this place was to the country they'd come through to get here. The last two days had her scared they would never find their way to civilization again, even though they'd followed the beaten path of the herd of stolen cattle they'd come across and were following Bo Decker's directions. The land was turning into a confusing maze of rocks and desert, bounded by miles and miles of buttes and mesas, all looking the same. An old prospector they'd come across reassured them they were on the right path.

"You're right lucky you ain't lost out here, bein' as how you ain't never traveled this way before," he'd told them. *"When you've traveled this country as much as I have, you come across the skeletons of humans and their horses, men who got lost and never found their way out. Once I seen a whole dang wagon train— six or eight wagons—just lying in the sun rotting away."*

Elly wrestled with the horror of the picture he'd presented.

"Outlaws know their way out here, though," he'd continued. *"A wanted man couldn't ask for more than the thousands of caves to hide in out here. Some are even lived in year-round, and some serve as saloons, if you can believe that. A man makes do when he has to. Know what I mean?"*

Matt had nodded his understanding, apparently deciding not to reveal that he was a lawman, not an outlaw. Elly wondered if something would go wrong when he met up with the Liberty boys that would brand him an outlaw and force him to live out here forever. She wasn't sure she could live that life, but then she had to wonder how many of the families here in Rock Springs had started out that way and now lived pretty normal lives. Still, railroad or not, this city and others like it were located in one of the most remote parts of America. It was strange how confined a person could feel in such incredibly huge country.

"Let's stay on the outskirts," Matt spoke up. "We'll ride around the back side of everything 'til we see a hotel or rooming house. I'll find a good place to put you up."

"It'll feel good to get out of the sun."

The country they were in was too high to be hot, yet the sun seemed relentless, as though being higher brought them too close to it.

Matt stayed in the lead as they cautiously rode into Rock Springs, the noises of a busy town growing louder as they approached. A stagecoach clattered past, stirring up a cloud of dust that reminded them that in spite of Rock Springs being a railroad town now, a lot of people couldn't afford to travel that way. Three different wagons rattled by, a farm wagon filled with hay tied into bundles, a large supply wagon full of barrels of flour and sugar. Another wagon carried farming and mining tools.

Matt had trouble keeping Rocky on the straight and narrow. The horse kept jerking his head backward and trying to dance sideways every time a wagon clattered by, its driver whistling and shouting at teams of mules. Matt led the horses to the right and behind the outskirts of town until they finally came to a two-story building that simply said ROOMING on the back side. Matt pulled his rifle from its boot and dismounted, tying Rusty to a small tree and leaving Rocky tied to his saddle.

"You stay here," he told Elly. "God knows where the Liberty boys are right now. It's early."

Elly waited, watching his solid gait and broad shoulders as he disappeared into the shadows of an alley beside the apparent rooming house. She felt alone, vulnerable, and helpless to change anything that might happen. Matt was bent on getting things over with so they could go on in peace and find her family and stop watching their backs. She couldn't imagine anything more wonderful than seeing Betty and her brother and father again, but she dreaded the fact that she might be a woman twice widowed when she found them.

She looked around nervously at a few walkers and riders in the area where she waited. Some turned and stared, curious.

"You need any help, Ma'am?" one man asked when he stopped to tip his hat.

"I'm fine. I'm just waiting for my husband to get us a room. Thank you."

The man frowned. "Why didn't he leave you on the main street?"

"He—he feared there wouldn't be room to hitch all four horses," she lied. "And the main street is so busy, he was afraid one of our pack horses would get spooked." She nodded toward Rocky. "That one's a troublemaker, and my husband didn't want any accidents on the main street. Someone could get hurt."

The man nodded and tipped his hat again. "I can understand that. I've had my share of obstinate horses."

To Elly's relief, he rode off. Matt finally re-appeared from the alley. "Untie what supplies we'll need just for today and tonight," he told her. "I paid a man who works for the rooming house to board and feed the horses. The lady who runs the place owns that barn over there behind us. She has bins by the stalls that can be closed and locked. They'll put the rest of our supplies in there, and the man in charge will rub down the horses and get them fed and watered. Once things are settled, I'll see about taking the train from here through the mountains."

Once things are settled. He'd said it as though going after the Liberty boys was just part of his daily routine. Things seemed to move too fast then. They carried their most necessary belongings inside. The rooming house was owned by a couple named Bess and John Valley. Bess led them to a surprisingly large room with clean bedding and lace curtains at the windows. It was at the back of the first floor, insulated from the noise in the streets.

They silently unpacked. Elly poured water into a bowl and remained turned away, cringing a little as she heard Matt open his repeating rifle to load it. The sound of the barrels whirling on two six-guns as he checked those also made her stomach tighten. She finally turned to see him wearing a holster fully loaded with extra cartridges, one gun in the holster, an extra one shoved into his belt at his back.

"We'll eat breakfast here," he told her. "Mrs. Valley said she cooks breakfast and supper, but not lunch."

"I'm not sure I can eat anything," Elly answered.

"I'd like you to try." Matt tied his holster to his thigh. "And we can take our time. I'm betting the Liberty boys are still snoring away somewhere, probably above the saloons with the only kind of women who'll put up with them."

They went through all the movements. Elly washed and changed while Matt went outside to peruse the street and see if he could spot the Wild Horse Saloon. He returned when breakfast was served and sat down beside Elly at a large dining table with four other roomers—three men and one older woman. All of them kept glancing at Matt because he was so heavily armed.

"You planning on going to war today?" one of the men asked.

Matt swallowed a piece of ham. "You might say that."

"I hope the battle doesn't include any of us," another commented.

Matt took a piece of home-made bread from a tray. "Of course not. And to settle some of your questions and misgivings, I'm a lawman. Sheriff from River's Bend,

Nebraska. I'm hunting a couple of men I've tracked here to
Rock Springs, and today they'll either go to jail or die.
Makes no difference to me which. They killed my first wife
and the baby she was carrying."

The female guest glanced at Elly. "Oh, my dear, you
must be frightened to death for your husband."

Elly glanced at Matt, realizing that right then he
needed her support, not her doubts.

"He's an able man," she answered. "He knows what
he's doing."

"Well then, I hope all goes well."

The woman introduced herself as Millie Teed, a widow
heading back East to be with her sister.

"Ernest Bale," the middle-aged man spoke up. "School
teacher."

"Henry Otis, traveling salesman," a younger man with
black hair slicked back at the sides told them.

"Andrew Sikes," the heavy-set third man added. He
wore a fancy silk suit and vest, with a gold watch hanging
from the vest pocket. His hair was as white as snow. "I
came out here to help establish a branch of the Western
Wyoming National Bank. I'll only be here a week, then I'm
heading back to St. Louis, Missouri."

They all sat staring at Matt and Elly with the obvious
question in their eyes. Matt drank some coffee, saying
nothing.

"Elly and Matt Stover," Elly finally told them. "Matt's
from Nebraska, as he already told you. I'm from Kansas.
How we met is a long story, but we're headed to California
to find some of my family who are already well on their
way there to settle. Matt wanted to take care of what he
really came out here for first—to find the men he told you
about."

Matt put down his coffee cup and leaned back in his
chair. "Tex and Joe Liberty. There are two other men with

them, call themselves Tim and Randy. Randy has a deep scar on his left cheek." He eyed the three men carefully. "Have any of you heard of them?"

The three men looked at each other, as though each was waiting for the other to say something.

"We have," Henry Otis spoke up. "Mister Bale here, he's only heard talk because the men you mentioned have made a lot of trouble around here. I've actually met them. They like to hang around the Wild Horse Saloon, and I've been there a couple times selling whiskey glasses. I've never talked to them, but they're the kind of men you notice and remember, if you know what I mean."

"Oh, I know what you mean, all right," Matt answered. "Any idea when they normally show up there?"

Henry leaned back and folded his arms. "Usually not long after lunch. They start drinking early and don't stop. They seem to have a huge capacity for whiskey without being stumbling drunk. And I've heard them talk about you—how they know you're headed this way and they're waiting to surprise you."

Matt grinned a rather wicked smile Elly had never seen on him before. "*They* are the ones who'll be surprised, I assure you. And I'll pay you, Mister Otis, to go over there around noon and come back when they're there and report to me. And I'll want to know if the other two are with them."

"You're going up against four men?" the banker asked.

Matt nodded. "I know the Liberty boys and how to handle them."

"The Wild Horse doesn't allow guns inside," Henry told Matt. "That'd be a good place to trap them."

"I'm not doing that. I'm calling them out into the street."

"Matt!" Elly blurted out his name in surprise and

worry. At the same time Millie Teed and Bess Valley both gasped.

Matt faced Elly, and for the first time since she'd met him she couldn't read his eyes. Cold. She'd never seen him this way, and she didn't know how to react.

"I want them out in the open, man to man," he told her. "I want the whole town to know what this is about and why I'm doing it. When all is said and done, I don't intend to be the one who gets hanged for killing a man. Or men. The Liberty boys will either be dead by my hand, strung up, or at the least, sitting in jail and waiting for extradition back to Nebraska. I'll escort them myself, if I have to."

"You're biting off a big piece of trouble," Henry warned Matt.

"The Liberty boys are the ones who bit into a big piece of trouble when they killed my first wife." Matt scooted back his chair. "Will you go to that saloon and keep an eye open for me?"

Henry nodded. "Sure, as long as I'm damn well out of there when the trouble starts."

"I appreciate it." Matt looked at Bess Valley. "That was a good breakfast, Ma'am. The wife and I thank you. We haven't had a really decent meal in days." He stood up. "Excuse me, everybody. I'm going out on the porch for a smoke." He nodded to Henry. "I'll be waiting there for you to come back early afternoon."

"I'll let my husband know what's going on," Mrs. Valley told him. "He's out back tending the guests' horses."

"Tell him not to say a word to anyone." Matt scanned the other faces. "Same with all of you. It's important the Liberty boys don't know I'm in town. They've no idea I already knew they were here waiting for me, and that's the edge I have on them, so don't any one of you tell another soul what's going on, understand? They probably think I'll go strolling into that saloon unaware."

They all nodded their agreement not to get involved.

Matt took his hat from where it hung on the corner of his chair and put it on, then took hold of his rifle, holding it in his right hand while he grasped Elly's arm with his left. "Come out on the porch with me for a minute. Then I want you to come back inside and *stay* inside."

Elly obeyed, her legs feeling weak when she stood up. Matt led her out the front door, where the morning sun was already warming the air, and people busily rode or walked up and down the streets tending to their individual shopping and visiting needs.

Matt leaned his rifle against the outside wall and looked down at Elly. "Don't expect a kiss good-bye, Elly. I can't afford an ounce of sympathy or to think about love right now. I hope you'll forgive me for making this seem more important than you and our marriage because it isn't. It's only important because it will free me to be the man I need to be for you, the father I'll need to be for our children. I feel like I can't be totally yours until this is done. I'm sorry for that."

Elly studied those blue eyes, searching for the Matthew Stover she'd married. "You don't need to be sorry. I'm just trying my best to understand the man I'm looking at right now, because he's not the man I married. I've never seen or felt this coldness about you."

Matt sighed deeply. "I can't help that. You're a damn good wife, Elly, and a woman I'll be glad to share the rest of my life with when this is over."

Elly swallowed to keep from crying. "Then you remember one thing, Matthew Stover. You're a *law*man, not an outlaw! You see things in black and white—right and wrong, plain and simple. Obey your own principles so you don't live with regrets."

A flicker of feelings sparked in Matt's eyes, then disappeared. He turned and leaned against the wall to light a cigarette. "Go on back inside now. I'm pretty sure the Liberty boys are still sleeping, but if by some odd chance they're awake and could spot me, I don't want you in the line of fire."

Henry Otis came outside then, pausing in front of both of them. "I'm heading over to the Wild Horse."

"I'll be right here—waiting," Matt told him.

Henry donned a bowler hat and left.

Elly touched Matt's arm. "I will also be waiting," she told him. "You remember that." Her heart racing with dread, she went inside and down the hallway to their room. On the way she heard Bess Valley talking to someone in the kitchen.

"He looks ready to kill somebody," Bess said. "You'd better go get the sheriff, John."

Elly rushed into the kitchen. "Don't! Please don't! If the sheriff knows, he'll go over to the Wild Horse and ruin everything. This is extremely important to Matt. Please don't interfere."

"But you husband could be killed," Bess told her.

"God is with him. I'm sure of it." She wished she truly could be sure. "I'm begging you not to get the sheriff. Matt knows what he's doing."

Bess and John Valley looked at each other. John shook his head and faced Elly. "If you're sure. But I think by the end of today you'll be a grieving widow. I've seen those Liberty boys, and they aren't anybody most men will mess with."

"Matt will. He knows them better than anyone. And he'll never rest easy if this doesn't work out. He needs to do this."

John nodded.

"I'll be here if you need me, dear," Bess told her.

"Thank you." Elly went to their room at the end of the hall. She stood there looking at their baggage, at Matt's extra clothes. She walked over and picked up one of his shirts and held it to her face, breathing in his scent.

"Dear God, protect him today," she prayed. She sat down on the edge of the bed and wept.

CHAPTER FORTY-THREE

"Thank you for the coffee and for letting me help you clean up from breakfast." Elly set down her coffee cup with slightly-shaking hands, enjoying the quiet comfort of Bess Valley's large kitchen. "I didn't even mind helping hang up the laundered bed sheets."

Bess wiped her hands on her apron. "Well, my goodness, dear, if keeping you busy means getting some free help around here, I certainly don't mind." Bess walked over and poured more coffee for Elly. "It's been three hours now. It must be hard for you not to go out onto the front porch and sit with your husband, knowing what he's waiting for. I still think you should let my husband tell the sheriff."

Elly rubbed her forehead. The stress of what could happen any time now had brought on a headache so painful that she felt ill. She'd tried to lie down, but sleep would not come. The only way she could bear this waiting was to stay busy. "I'd like nothing more than to get the sheriff involved," she answered, "but Matt is a sheriff himself, Bess, and he'd feel betrayed if I interfered with what he feels he needs to do. As difficult as it is for me, I intend to honor his desire to handle this his own way."

The little bell hanging over the front door rang then as someone came into the parlor. Elly's heart beat faster when she heard rapid footsteps. John Valley rushed into the kitchen then, looking from his wife to Elly. "Henry Otis just delivered a message to your husband, Mrs. Stover," he told her excitedly. "The Liberty brothers want to meet him in front of the Wild Horse Saloon at one o'clock. It's nearly that now, and Sheriff Stover is headed up the street!"

"Oh, dear God!" Elly rose, nearly knocking her chair backward when she did so. She grabbed a shawl from the chair and threw it around her shoulders, then hurried past John and to the front door.

"Be careful!" she heard Bess call after her.

John followed her out.

"You'd best stay out of sight," he warned, having trouble keeping up with Elly because of his old age. "If your husband sees you, he'll be distracted."

"I know. I'll be careful!" Elly called back, moving well ahead of him. She spotted Matt at the front of a crowd that had gathered as he charged toward the saloon. Apparently word of what was about to happen had traveled fast. Elly worried that the two extra men with the Liberty boys could be in that same crowd and could shoot Matt in the back.

"My God, Matt," she murmured.

She hurried along, staying behind barrels and benches and wagons and people, moving amid whispers and comments about what might be happening.

"Who is that man?"

"What's he got against the Liberty boys?"

"Them boys don't play fair. He's gonna' get himself killed!"

"Anybody get the sheriff yet?"

Elly practically shoved people out of the way to get through.

"Hey, pretty lady, where you goin'?" A man grabbed her arms and stopped her.

"Let go of me," Elly ordered. "That's my husband out there!"

"Your *husband*? What the hell's he doin'?"

"None of your business." Elly jerked away and kept walking, moving behind a freight wagon when Matt stopped and planted his feet as though ready for a fight. Elly watched four men emerge from the Wild Horse Saloon, two of them big as bears. She figured those two had to be the Liberty brothers. The third man was of medium build and ordinary looks, the fourth one tall and slim, with a deep scar on the left side of his face that showed up an ugly white against his tanned skin.

"Well, I'll be goddamned!" The biggest man spoke gruffly. He had shoulders like a guerilla and a several-inch-long beard. "If it ain't fuckin' Matt Stover, sheriff of River's Bend, Nebraska, for sure and true in the flesh!" His big belly shook as he laughed. "How in goddamn hell did you know we was in Rock Springs, Matt?"

Matt didn't flinch or show one sign of fear. "You brag too much, Tex. And men talk. You thought you'd lie in wait for me and use my back for target practice, but it's not going to be that way." He held out his rifle, never taking his eyes off of Tex. "Somebody take this for me." He didn't even look when John Valley stepped up and took his rifle, then moved to the side of the street. "You've always taken the *coward's* way," Matt told Tex. "You and your brother both. But this time you're going to face me like the man you've never been, and if you want to live, you'll tell me how sorry you are for shooting down my wife and the baby she was carrying. That's your only slight chance of me arresting you rather than *killing* you!"

Gasps moved among the crowd at Matt's remarks. People stepped farther back off the street and against buildings, leaving Matt to face the Liberty boys and the other two men alone.

"You know damn well that was an accident, Matt," the other big man spoke up.

Elly figured that man was Tex's brother, Joe. She cautiously moved closer to John Valley.

"All I know is that my wife got in your way, and one of you saved your own worthless hide by shooting her down!" Matt shouted defiantly.

"But we *are* sorry, Matt," Joe told him.

"Shut the fuck up!" Tex ordered. "Don't you be groveling in front of Matt Stover, little brother! He can't prove it was even our bullets that killed Lora." Tex spread his feet and moved a hand toward his gun. "All *five* of us was involved, and all *five* of us was shootin' off our guns."

"Where's the fifth man?" Matt asked.

"I done *killed* him," Tex answered, almost proudly. "He was gettin' on my nerves complainin' about waitin' for you. But now here you are, just like I figured would happen. And I'm gonna' shoot you down just like I shot *him* down!"

"You figured you'd find it easy to kill me*!*" Matt declared. "You didn't figure on facing me like a real *man!* This is something you *won't* find easy. You deserve to *die*, Tex Liberty, and it will be by my hand!"

"*You'll* be dead, too, Stover, by the time we're done with you, even if you shoot me first!"

"That could be, but either way, you'll go down first, so if you're willing to do this the right and honorable way, *draw*! I'll even let you have a head start!"

Tex just stood there.

"What's wrong, you bastard?" Matt goaded. "You afraid of dying, maybe? Or are you just afraid everybody'll find out you aren't worth a shit with a gun? It's *easy* to shoot down an unarmed, pregnant *woman*, isn't it? How about standing up to an *armed* man? One on one? Just you and me! Leave Joe out of it!"

Suddenly, the slim man with the scar pulled his gun with no warning or cause whatsoever. Women screamed and people ducked or ran for cover, while everything happened so fast it was difficult for Elly to determine who did what first. She only knew Matt's gun was out before the slim man even fired his handgun, and she couldn't imagine how Matt knew what was happening, since his gaze had been concentrated on Tex Liberty.

A hole opened in the slim man's chest. At the same time, Joe drew his gun and fired. Matt spun around. Elly couldn't tell at first where he'd been hit, but he didn't go down. Everything occurred in a matter of two or three seconds. Matt fired twice more, opening a hole in Joe's head and hitting the fourth man in the throat.

All the while, Tex hadn't fired his gun. It was as though he was waiting for the others to wound Matt so he could easily finish him off himself. Matt ducked and rolled as Tex finally pulled his six-gun and fired two shots, both misses. His gun jammed and Matt got to his knees, pointing his .44 straight at Tex. He cocked the gun and continued holding it steady as he got to his feet. Elly sucked in her breath at the sight of blood flowing down the right side of his face from where Joe's bullet had ripped across his cheek.

"Drop it!" Matt demanded. "You're going to prison, Tex Liberty, for the bank robbery in River's Bend, Nebraska, and for the murders of a bank teller, Lora Stover and her unborn daughter!"

Elly thought she detected a slight quiver in Matt's voice when he mentioned his baby girl. Her heart ached for him. She knew the loss of his wife and baby was finally hitting him full force. *Don't fold now, Matt. Tex Liberty is still alive. He's still dangerous!*

Tex threw his gun aside and put up his hands. "Go ahead and shoot, Stover." He grinned then. "You won't do it, on account of you're a *law*man, not a fuckin' killer!" He stepped a little closer. "Go ahead, *shoot* me! It'll be murder, on account of I'm *unarmed*. They don't like that here in Rock Springs. Sheriff or not, and whether I'm guilty or not, you'll get hanged right along with me."

Still aiming directly at Tex, Matt pulled his second gun from behind his back and tossed it to the ground in front of Tex. "Pick it up!"

Tex grinned. "Hell, no! If you're gonna' kill me, pull the trigger. That's what you want, ain't it? That's what you came all the way out here to do. I hear you even picked up a new woman on the way. It don't seem to me like you took very long to grieve for the first one, seein' as how you're already married again."

Matt continued holding his gun steady. "You rotten bastard! Pick up the gun!" he roared.

"What's going on here?" A man with a badge stepped into the street carrying a rifle.

Tex Liberty used the distraction to dive for the gun Matt had thrown in front of him.

More screams. More confusion. More gunfire. Matt shot the extra gun out of Tex's hand just as he picked it up. Tex cried out, and Matt stumbled backward, his head wound and loss of blood starting to take its toll. That gave Tex time to dive into the town sheriff. He knocked him backward, causing the sheriff's head to hit a hitching post not far from where Elly stood. He yanked the sheriff's gun from its holster and aimed it at Matt.

Elly didn't take any time to think. She grabbed Matt's rifle from John Valley, then put it to her shoulder and cocked it.

Tex fired at Matt, winging him across his left shoulder. Matt fired back, hitting Tex in the middle of his chest.

Tex stood there staring at Matt. "You sonofabitch!"

Tex raised the sheriff's gun again, and Elly fired, sending Tex sprawling sideways at the same time Matt fired his sixth shot, hitting Tex in the belly.

It was then that Joe stirred, sitting up to point his gun at Matt.

"Get him!" some man shouted.

Joe Liberty was surrounded and dragged off before he could get off another shot.

The sheriff lay by the hitching post, unconscious.

"I for one am glad this town's rid of them Liberty boys," someone exclaimed.

Several more shouted their agreement.

It was all over in roughly ten seconds, Elly guessed. A few people slowly retreated into stores and saloons, leaving others to stare at three men lying dead and bloody in the street as though it was a common event. They mingled and talked among themselves as others continued to drag Joe up the street.

"Let's hang him!" someone declared.

"Shit, don't bother!" another yelled. "The sonofabitch is already dead! That bullet finally did him in."

Such casual talk about such a violent event. Those dragging Joe dropped his body in the street and walked away.

Elly almost felt like she'd been in a trance. She ran to a bleeding Matt to help him up.

"Elly! How did you..." He looked her over in dismay. "You shot Tex!"

Elly held Matt's arm with one hand and still clung to his rifle with the other. "I hardly realized what I was doing! I only knew Tex shot at you again!"

"My God, Elly!" Matt pushed his .44 into its holster,

then held on to Elly as they both stumbled over to where Tex's dead body lay. Matt picked up his spare pistol and shoved it back into his belt. It was only then that Elly realized John Valley stood near them.

"I'll explain all of this to the sheriff," he told them, "whenever he comes around. He's sitting up now but still pretty dazed." He carefully took Matt's rifle from Elly. "And I'll take care of this here rifle for you."

Elly realized only then that she was still holding it. She blinked, just becoming aware that she'd actually aimed it at Tex Liberty and shot the man. "Just take it back to our room," she told John. She turned to Matt as John walked away. "I can hardly believe I actually shot that man."

Matt looked at her lovingly, then put a hand to the side of her face, while blood continued to run down his own face and over the front of his shirt. "You damn well did, Elly Stover." He looked her over adoringly. "And I've never loved you more."

Elly's eyes teared.

"Matt, I thought you'd die! I didn't know what else to do. There wasn't time to think."

To her surprise, Matt broke into a rather goofy smile.

"I'll be damned," he said, looking a bit dazed and confused now. "You're some woman."

Elly could see the change in his eyes. She saw a hint of tears there now. The cold, angry, vengeful Matt Stover was gone. She grasped his wrist and kissed his palm. "And you're some man."

"I'm sorry, Elly. I had to do this. Tell me you understand."

"I do."

Matt suddenly grabbed her shoulders. His body grew heavy, and Elly held on to him as best she could as he slumped to the ground. She couldn't help but go down with him. Two men from the crowd rushed over to help both of them up, and one of them ordered someone to load Matt into a nearby buckboard.

"Take us to John and Bess Valley's rooming house," Elly asked. She climbed into the wagon and sat down with Matt's head in her lap. "And please get a doctor."

"I expect he'll be okay, ma'am," someone told her, while another ran off to find whoever claimed to be the doctor in town.

Elly leaned down and talked softly into Matt's ear. "It's over," she told him. "It's finally over."

Someone drove the wagon to the rooming house. Elly wondered if she was really the same Elly who'd left Kansas for California.

How in God's name had she ended up out here in Outlaw Country with a shot-up, bloody sheriff from River's Bend, Nebraska lying in her lap—and he was her husband, no less? Crazy as it seemed, all she could think about at the moment was how Betty would react, wide-eyed and spell-bound, when Elly would relate to her sister-in-law what had happened to her since Pete Garner took her from their wagon train—a snake bite, a kidnapping, a whore house, a rescue, a wedding, a wild shootout. It was all so unreal.

Not far away locomotive engineers clanged the engine's bell. Three short whistles signaled another train was leaving Rock Springs to head west. Elly smiled at the realization that, finally, as soon as Matt was healed, they'd board the Union Pacific together and head for California, where they'd put the past behind them and start life over.

Law was coming to a lawless land, in the form of Sheriff Matt Stover, and she was going to be right by his side... day... and night.

EPILOGUE...

MARCH, 1878...

*S*heriff Matt Stover set his rifle into the wall cabinet that held six other Winchester repeating rifles. He turned then at the sound of a horse galloping to the front of the Cisco Sheriff's Office. Before he could reach the door, his brother-in-law, Mark Grace, barged inside.

"The baby's coming, Matt! And fast! The doc's on his way over to your house now, and Betty's with Elly."

Matt hurried out, yelling to one of his deputies who sat in a chair on the front boardwalk to keep an eye on things. He mounted his horse, which he'd kept saddled and ready lately in case he had to get home fast. He galloped up the street, Mark right behind him. His neat frame house was less than a mile from town, but that mile seemed like ten when a man was in a hurry, and he was damn well in a hurry. Elly was having his baby!

As they drew closer, Matt could see Doc Madison's buggy out front. Matt dismounted beside it before his horse even came to a full halt.

"Tie my horse for me!" he called to Mark as he ran inside.

He stopped short then. Betty stood at the dining table gently washing off a crying, kicking, red-faced baby, and the doctor hadn't even had time to open his bag yet.

"You stay out here, Matt," Doc Madison ordered. "I have to take care of your wife and make sure there's no problem. I just got here. As you can see, the baby came really fast. Pretty unusual for the first one. Your wife could go into shock."

He went through the bedroom door, and Matt stood dumbfounded as Mark came charging inside.

"She's good and healthy," Betty told Matt as she wrapped the baby in a blanket. With a gleaming smile, she turned to him. "Do you want to hold your daughter? I haven't had time to clean her as well as I should. So far I've mainly just managed to get the membrane out of her little mouth and nose so she can breathe, and she's breathing just fine! You should go ahead and hold her before I finish cleaning her up."

A slew of emotions rushed through Matt—thoughts of Lora and the baby girl they'd lost, and now another little girl from his seed. And in the bedroom lay another woman he loved.

"Is Elly going to be okay?" he asked Betty.

"She's seems fine. The baby came so fast, and there's the after-birth to take care of. Doc Madison will do that. He just wants to clean her up and make sure all is fine before you go see her. She was calling for you, but it all happened so quickly. It's a good thing I came extra early today." Betty held up the baby. "Go on. Take her. She won't break."

Matt cautiously took the baby into his arms, staring down at her ruddy red face and the spots of dried blood and membrane still showing. None of that mattered.

"She's beautiful," he told a grinning Betty.

He turned and showed the baby to Mark just as Elly's father came inside then with young Mark and Tommy. Everyone beamed with delight at the perfectly-formed little girl who was sucking on one of Matt's knuckles.

"Congratulations," Mark told Matt. "Does she have a name?"

"Elly said if it was a girl, she wanted to name her Destiny because she believes our finding each other out here was destined to be."

"That's a beautiful name," Betty told him.

"I can't wait for my folks to see her," Matt answered. "According to their last letter, they'll be coming out later this summer."

"Oh, that's good," John told him. "Maybe your folks will decide to stay and start a church here. Then you could all be together again."

"Maybe." Matt kissed Destiny's forehead. "But I'd like to go to River's Bend once more so Elly can see where I came from. And I have things to settle there, since I was sheriff. Plus, I have money in a bank there."

Mark nodded. "It's understandable you'd need to go back at least once. And now that you can go by train, it won't be such a bad trip, or take so long."

Matt couldn't take his eyes off of Destiny.

By train, he thought. *If only Elly's journey here had been so easy.* After all they'd been through, he could hardly believe they'd both been able to start a new life in California—that he was still a sheriff and they had a home here and a new baby girl. And he had a whole, big new family in Betty and Mark, Elly's nephews and her father. John Grace had nearly died of a broken heart when he thought he might never see Elly again. Now he was happier and healthier than he'd been in years.

"We've got to get back to the farm, Matt," Mark told

him. "After staying here a week to be ready for the baby, I have to start planting. The spring rains we've had make things perfect for putting in vegetable seeds. And I'm thinking about planting grapes. The California sunshine and soil are perfect for them. Some of the other farmers are also planting grapes—wine grapes. It's a different kind of farming for us, but we'll learn."

"No harm in giving it a try," Matt told him. "I'm just glad all of you were here for Elly."

"Betty'll stay on a few days 'til Elly's feeling good and strong." Mark shook his head. "We still can't get over how all this turned out. You showing up with Elly last fall, the two of you married and her expecting. God sure does answer prayer."

"Now you sound like my father," Matt told him.

"We'll be proud and honored to meet your folks." John put an arm on young Mark's shoulder. "Come on, Grandson. Let's get back to the farm. Come help me hitch the wagon." He glanced back at Mark. "Somebody'll have to ride to Betty's brother's place and let him know about the baby."

"I'll take care of it," Mark answered. He gave Matt a nod and a smile, then followed his sons and father out the door.

Matt turned to Betty, who was grinning so broadly that all her gums showed. The woman could be as giddy as a child sometimes, but he figured no one had a bigger heart than Betty Grace, and no one had been more thrilled to see him and Elly show up together. He leaned down and kissed her forehead. "Thanks for your help."

"I'm just so happy for both of you," Betty told him. "Sit down 'til the doctor comes out, Matt. You keep holding that baby. She should get used to your face and your voice. As soon as Elly's had a chance to hold her, I'll clean her up better."

Matt kept holding Destiny and paced, rather than sitting down. He kept looking at her blue eyes, eyes that looked right back at him. "Shouldn't she be crying? Hungry?"

"Not necessarily." Betty put another kettle of water on Elly's wood-burning stove. "She's in her daddy's arms and she knows it, Matt. She's contented. She'll cry soon enough when she realizes she wants something in her little belly."

Destiny wrapped tiny fingers around Matt's index finger when he touched her soft cheek. "I'll never let anything bad happen to this kid."

"Oh, I'm sure you won't. She couldn't have a more protective father than Sheriff Matt Stover."

After another half hour, the doctor finally came out of the bedroom. "You can go in now, Matt. Your wife is anxious to hold her baby."

"She okay?" Matt asked him.

"She's fine. I was a bit worried because the baby came so fast, but she's okay. She'll feel even better when she can hold that baby."

Matt grinned and walked past him. He heard Betty offering the doctor some coffee as he walked into the bedroom, holding the baby in one arm and closing the door with his other hand. He moved to the bed, where Elly lay propped against pillows, her deep auburn hair spread out behind her and looking damp. Her smile was as big as Betty's had been.

"What do you think, Mister Stover?"

Matt sat down in a chair beside the bed. "I think I'm the happiest man in Cisco."

Elly reached out. "Give me our daughter. She's going to want to be fed."

Matt laid the baby beside her, and Elly pulled her close. "I was in kind of a daze when she was born and Betty took her out to clean her up. Is she as perfect as I thought?"

Matt leaned close. "More than perfect. Betty needs to bathe her more, but she let me hold her first, and I didn't want to give her back."

Elly opened the blanket to examine the squirming, tiny infant now sucking on her own little fist. She counted fingers and toes, felt of the baby's limbs and touched the velvety skin of her cheeks. The baby took her fist from her mouth and made a little "o" with her lips.

Elly looked at Matt. "She's going to be beautiful, Matt, and smart and lively." She looked at the baby again. "It's hard to decide who she looks like yet, but she does have your eyes."

"Let's hope she'll look like you... beautiful and perfect."

Elly met his gaze, realizing there were tears in his eyes. "I'm glad I could give you another little girl. The next one will be a son, I'll bet."

Matt leaned closer. "And the one after that? And then the one after that?"

Elly laughed lightly. "Slow down, Sheriff Stover."

He leaned even closer and kissed her gently. "That's hard to do with a woman like you in my bed at night, especially when I love her so much."

"And it's hard for me to say no to my hero."

Matt chuckled. "I'm no damn hero. I'm just a man who was lost and lonely, and then you came along. You're *my* hero."

Elly frowned. "Can a woman be a hero?"

"Why not?"

"I've never considered such a thing."

Matt sat back and removed his boots, then stood up and removed his gun belt. He hung it over the chair and walked around to climb into the bed beside Elly. He moved an arm around her and the baby. "Thank you, Elly, for saving me from the black hole I was falling into."

She turned her face enough that she could kiss the scar on his cheek where Tex Liberty's bullet would have taken his life if it had been one more inch to the right.

"You did the same for me," she told him. "I thought I was going to end up in a loveless marriage to Glen until you came along."

"And now Glen is already married to Greta Jones."

Elly laughed again, turning back to kiss the baby. "Isn't it odd how you can meet a complete stranger and know right away you belong together? Glen and Greta got married two months after the family got to California."

Matt kissed her behind the ear. "A man gets lonely. When he sees a damn good woman, he knows he doesn't *want* to be alone any longer."

Elly kissed the baby again. "Am I a damn good woman, Mister Stover?"

"You know you are." Matt looked over her shoulder at his new daughter, and the baby smiled.

"See?" Elly said. "She even has your smile, Matt." She met his gaze. "Do you believe now? In destiny?"

Matt touched the baby's cheek again. "I believe." He leaned close and kissed Elly's cheek. "Thank you. You and this baby have helped heal the wounds inside. I didn't believe I could ever be this happy again."

"I'm sure your family has been praying for you. This is God's doing."

"Maybe so."

Elly took hold of his hand. "Your parents will be thrilled to see their new granddaughter. They'll be so happy for you."

Matt squeezed her hand. "I'm a lucky man."

"And I'm a lucky woman. I look at you and wonder how long it will take for real law and order to come to places like South Pass City and Rock Springs."

Matt grinned. "It won't come soon or easy."

The remark brought a little pang of memories to Elly's heart, bad and good. It seemed so unreal that they'd traveled that wild, lonesome, lawless country, alone but together.

Together always now.

ABOUT THE AUTHOR

I have been writing about America's wild, beautiful West for 37 years now, everything from the first pioneers through the gold rush and the Indian wars and the building of the Union Pacific. I have also written about the French & Indian wars, the Revolutionary War, the Civil War and the Mexican War, including the Alamo. My books span just about every location and every event that occurred in settling this country. For these books about Men of the Outlaw Trail, my main resource was *The Outlaw Trail* by Robert Redford, Grosset & Dunbar, 1976.

If you would like to read more about Sage Lightfoot, the man who helped Matt Stover in this story, and about the ranch Sage builds in Paradise Valley, read my book of the same name, *Paradise Valley* (Sourcebooks). And I wrote a sequel in a short story that is called "Christmas in Paradise." It's in an anthology called *Longing for a Cowboy Christmas* (Sourcebooks). Both titles are available on Amazon.com.

For more information about me and my writing, as well as the list of over 70 books I have had published over the years, please visit my web site at www.rosannebittner.com. I also have an Author Facebook page and am on Twitter, Goodreads, Instagram, Pinterest and several writing/reading Facebook groups and blogs. Nearly all my books are available through Amazon.com and through Barnes & Noble. You can also read my many blogs at www.rosannebittner.blogspot.com.

Enjoy! I love to hear from my readers!

rosannebittner17@outlook.com

Made in the USA
Middletown, DE
29 August 2020